Hair-Breadth Escapes

The Adventures of
Three Boys in South Africa

by

H. C. Adams

Hair-Breadth Escapes
The Adventures of Three Boys in South Africa
by H. C. Adams

ISBN: 978-93-62203-47-2

Published by

DOUBLE 9 BOOKS

2/13-B, Ansari Road
Daryaganj, New Delhi – 110002
info@double9books.com
www.double9books.com
Tel. 011-40042856

ABOUT THE AUTHOR

Reverend Henry Cadwallader Adams (1817-1899) changed into a distinguished English cleric, schoolmaster, and renowned author of kid's novels at some point of the nineteenth century. Born on November four, 1817, he got here from a splendid lineage because the grandson of Simon Adams from Ansty Hall in Warwickshire. Adams acquired his schooling at prestigious institutions, together with Westminster School and Winchester College. Subsequently, he continued his educational journey at Balliol College in 1835 and Magdalen College, Oxford in 1836. His academic interests culminated in becoming a fellow of Magdalen in 1843, reflecting his scholarly achievements. Notably, Adams served as a Commoner Tutor at Winchester College, wherein he contributed to the schooling of young minds. His dedication to schooling and spirituality led to his appointment as the chaplain of Bromley College in 1855. Bromley College turned into an almshouse devoted to the aid of widows of priests, wherein Adams persevered his carrier to the community and the church. In addition to his clerical obligations, Adams made a lasting effect on children's literature together with his creative and engaging novels. His existence's work remains a testament to his multifaceted contributions as an educator, cleric, and writer at some point of the Victorian technology. Henry Cadwallader Adams exceeded away on October 17, 1899, leaving behind a legacy of literary and academic accomplishments.

CONTENTS

Dedication

To the Rev. G.G. Ross, D.C.L., Principal of St. Andrew's College, Grahamstown, Cape Colony.

My dear Ross,

I dedicate this Tale to you for two reasons: first, because it is, in some sort, a souvenir of a very interesting visit to South Africa, rendered pleasant by the kind hospitality shown us by so many in Grahamstown, and by no one more than yourself. Secondly and chiefly, because it gives me the opportunity of expressing publicly to you my sympathy in the noble work you are carrying on, under the gravest difficulties—difficulties which (I am persuaded) many would help to lighten, who possess the means of doing so, were they but acquainted with them.

H.C. Adams.

Dry Sandford, *August 1876.*

Chapter One

It was the afternoon of a day late in the November of the year 1805. His Majesty's ship *Hooghly*, carrying Government despatches and stores, as well as a few civil and military officers of the East India Company's service, was running easily before the trade wind, which it had caught within two days' sail of Madeira—and was nearing the region of the tropics. The weather, which had been cold and stormy, when the passengers left England some weeks before, had been gradually growing bright and genial; until for the last three or four days all recollections of fog and chill had vanished from their minds. The sky was one vast dome of the richest blue, unbroken by a single cloud, only growing somewhat paler of hue as it approached the horizon line. The sea stretched out into the distance—to the east, an endless succession of purple wavelets, tipped here and there with white; to the west, where the sun was slowly sinking in all its tropical glory, one seething mass of molten silver.

It was indeed a glorious sight, and most of our readers will be of opinion that those who had the opportunity of beholding it, would—for the time at least—have bestowed little attention on anything else. But if they had been at sea as long as Captain Wilmore, they might perhaps have thought differently. Captain Wilmore had been forty years a sailor; and whether given, or not given, to admire brilliant skies and golden sunsets in his early youth, he had at all events long ceased to trouble himself about them. He was at the outset of this story sitting in his cabin—having just parted from his first lieutenant, Mr Grey—and was receiving with a very dubious face the report of an old quartermaster. A fine mastiff was seated by the captain's chair, apparently listening with much gravity to what passed.

"Well, Jennings, Mr Grey tells me you have something to report, which he thinks ought to be brought straight to me, in order that I may question you myself about it. What is it? Is it something about these gentlemen we have on board? Are they dissatisfied, or has Lion here offended them?"

"No, cap'en," said the old sailor; "I wish 'twas only something o' that sort. That would be easy to be disposed of, that would."

"What is it, then? Is it the men, who are grumbling—short rations, or weak grog, or what?"

"There's more rations and stronger grog than is like to be wanted, cap'en," said Jennings, evasively, for he was evidently anxious to escape communicating his intelligence, whatever it might be, as long as possible.

"What do you mean, Jennings?" exclaimed Captain Wilmore, roused by the quartermaster's manner. "More rations and stronger grog than the men want? I don't understand you."

"Well, cap'en, I'm afraid some on 'em won't eat and drink aboard this ship no more."

"What, are any of them sick, or dead—or, by heaven, have any of them deserted?"

"I'm afeared they has, cap'en. You remember the Yankee trader, as sent a boat to ask us to take some letters to Calcutta?"

"Yes, to be sure; what of him?"

"Well, I've heard since, as his crew was going about among our chaps all the time he was aboard, offering of 'em a fist half full of guineas apiece, if they'd sail with him, instead of you."

"The scoundrel!" shouted Captain Wilmore. "If I'd caught him at it, I'd have run him up to the mainyard, as sure as he's alive."

"Ay, cap'en; and I'd have lent a hand with all my heart," said the old seaman. "But you see he was too cunning to be caught. He went back to his ship, which was lying a very little way off, for there wasn't a breath of wind, if you remember. But he guessed the breeze would spring up about midnight, so he doesn't hoist his boats up, but hides 'em under his lee, until—"

"I see it all plain enough, Jennings," broke in the captain. "How many are gone?"

"Well, we couldn't make sure for a long time, Captain Wilmore," said Jennings, still afraid to reveal the whole of his evil tidings. "Some of the hands had got drunk on the rum fetched aboard at Madeira, and they might be lying about somewhere, you see—"

"Well, but you've found out now, I suppose?" interjected his questioner sharply.

"I suppose we has, cap'en. There's Will Driver, and Joel Grigg, and Lander, and Hawkins, and Job Watson—not that *he's* any great loss—and Dick Timmins, and—"

"Confound you, Jennings! how many?" roared the captain, so fiercely, that the dog sprang up, and began barking furiously. "Don't keep on pottering in that way, but tell me the worst at once. How many are gone? Keep quiet, you brute, do you hear? How many, I say?"

"About fifteen, cap'en," blurted out the quartermaster, shaking in his shoes. "Leastways there's fifteen, or it may be sixteen, as can't be found, or—"

"Fifteen or sixteen, or some other number," shouted the skipper. "Tell me the exact number, you old idiot, or I'll disrate you! Confound that dog! Turn him out."

"Sixteen's the exact number we can't find," returned Jennings, "but some of 'em may be aboard, and turn up sober by-and-by."

"Small chance of that," muttered the captain. "Well, it's no use fretting; the question is, What's to be done? We were short-handed before—so you thought, didn't you, Jennings?"

"Well, cap'en, we hadn't none too many, that's sartain; and we should have been all the better for half a dozen more."

"That comes to the same thing, doesn't it?" said the skipper, who, vexed and embarrassed as he was, could not help being a little diverted at the old man's invincible reluctance to speaking out.

"Well, I suppose it does, sir," he answered, "only you see—"

"I don't see anything, except that we are in a very awkward scrape," interposed the other. "It will be madness to attempt to make the passage with such a handful as we have at present. If there came a gale, or we fall in with a French or Spanish cruiser—" He paused, unwilling to put his thoughts into words.

"'Twouldn't be pleasant, for sartain," observed Jennings.

"But, then, if we put back to England—for I know no hands are to be had at Madeira, we should be quite as likely to encounter a storm, or a Frenchman."

"A good deal more like," assented the quartermaster.

"And there would be the loss and delay, and the blame would be safe to be laid on me," continued the captain, following out his own thoughts rather than replying to his companion's observations. "No, we must go on. But then, where are we to pick up any fresh hands?"

"We shall be off the Canaries this evening, cap'en," said Jennings. "We've been running along at a spanking rate with this wind all night. The peak's in sight even now."

"The Canaries are no good, Jennings. The Dons are at war with us, you know. And though there are no ships of war in the harbour at Santa Cruz, they'd fire upon us from the batteries if we attempted to hold communication with the shore."

"They ain't always so particular, are they, sir?" asked the sailor.

"Perhaps not, Jennings. But the Dons here have never forgiven the attack made on them seven or eight years ago, by Nelson."

"Well, sir, they might have forgiven that, seeing as they got the best of it I was in that, sir—b'longed to the *Foxy* and was one of Nelson's boat's crew, and we got nothing out of the Dons but hard knocks and no ha'pence that time."

"That's true. But you see Nelson has done them so much harm since, that the damage they did him then seems very little comfort to them. No, we mustn't attempt anything at the Canaries."

"Very good, sir. Then go on to the Cape Verdes. If this wind holds, we shall soon be there, and the Cape Verdes don't belong to the Dons."

"No; to the Portuguese. Well, I believe that will be best. I have received information that the French and Spanish fleets are off Cape Trafalgar; and our fellows are likely to have a brush with them soon, if they haven't had it already."

"Indeed, sir! Well, Admiral Nelson ain't likely to leave many of 'em to follow us to the Cape. We're pretty safe from them, anyhow."

"You're right there, I expect, Jennings," said the skipper, relaxing for the first time into a grim smile. "Well, then, shape the ship's course for the Cape Verdes, and, mind you, keep the matter of those scoundrels deserting as quiet as possible. If some of the passengers get hold of it, they'll be making a bother. Now you may go, Jennings. Stay, hand me those letters about the boys that came on board at Plymouth. I've been too busy to give any thought to them till now. But I must settle something about them before we reach the Cape, and I may as well do so now."

The quartermaster obeyed. He handed his commanding officer the bundle of papers he had indicated, and then left the cabin, willing enough to be dismissed. The captain, throwing himself with an air of weariness back on his sofa, broke the seal of the first letter, muttering to himself discontentedly the while.

"I wonder why I am to be plagued with other people's children? Because I have been too wise to have any of my own, I suppose! Well, Frank is my nephew, and blood is thicker than water, they say—and for once, and for a wonder, say true. I suppose I *am* expected to look after him. And he's a fine lad too. I can't but own that. But what have I to do with old Nat Gilbert's children, I wonder? He was my schoolfellow, and pulled me out of a pond once, when I should have been drowned if he hadn't I suppose *he* thought that was reason enough for putting off his boy upon me, as his guardian. Humph! I don't know about that. Let us see, any way, what sort of a boy this young Gilbert is. This is from old Dr Staines, the schoolmaster he has been with for the last four or five years. I wonder what he says of the boy? At present I know nothing whatever about him, except that he looks saucy enough for a midshipman, and laughs all day like a hyena!

"'Gymnasium House, Hollingsley,

"'September 29th, 1805.

"'Sir,—You are, no doubt, aware that I have had under my charge, for the last five years, Master George Gilbert, the son of the late Mr Nathaniel Gilbert, of Evertree, a most worthy and respectable man. I was informed, at the time of the parent's decease, that you had been appointed the guardian of the infant; but as Mr Nathaniel had, with his customary circumspection, lodged a sum in the Hollingsley bank, sufficient to cover the cost of his son's education for two years to come, there was no need to trouble you. You were also absent from England, and I did not know your direction.

"'The whole of the money is not yet exhausted; but I regret to say I am unable to retain Master George under my tuition any longer. I must beg you to take notice that his name is *George*, as his companions are in the habit of calling him "Nick," giving the idea that his name, or one of his names, is Nicodemus. Such, however, is not the case, George being his only Christian appellative. Why his schoolfellows should have adopted so singular a nomenclature I am unable to say. The only explanation of it, which has ever been suggested to me, is one so extremely objectionable, that I am convinced it must be a mistake.

"'But to proceed'—('A long-winded fellow this!' muttered the captain as he turned the page; 'who cares what the young scamp's called?')—'But to proceed. I cannot retain Master George any longer. His continually repeated acts of mischief render it impossible for me any longer to temper the justice due to myself and family with the mercy which it is my ordinary habit to exercise. I will not detail to you his offences against propriety'—('thank goodness for that,' again interjected Captain Wilmore, 'though I dare say some of his offences would be entertaining enough')—'I will not detail his offences—they would fill a volume. I will only mention what has occurred to-day. If there is any practice I consider more objectionable than another, it is that of using the dangerous explosives known as fireworks. Master Gilbert is aware that I strictly interdict their purchase; in consequence of which they cannot be obtained at the only shop in Hollingsley where they are sold, by any of my scholars. But what were my feelings—I ask you, sir—when I ascertained that he had obtained a large number of combustibles weeks ago, and had concealed them—actually concealed them in a chest under Mrs Staines's bed! The chest holds a quantity of linen, and under this he had hidden the explosives, thinking, I conclude, that it was seldom looked into. Seldom looked into! Why, merciful heaven, Mrs Staines is often in the habit of examining even by candlelight'—('I say, I can't read any more of this,' exclaimed the captain; 'anyhow, I'll skip a page or two.' He turned on a long way and resumed.)—'When I found out this morning that he was missing, I felt no doubt that my words had produced even a deeper effect than I had designed. Mrs Staines and myself both feared that in his remorse he had been guilty of some desperate act; and we made every effort, immediately after breakfast, to discover the place of his retreat. Being St Michael's day, it was a whole holiday, and we were thus enabled to devote the entire day to the quest. It has been extremely rainy throughout; but when we returned, two hours ago, exhausted and wet to the skin, after a fruitless search, we found him, dry and warm, awaiting us in the hall. This was some relief; but judge of our feelings when we discovered that the shameless boy had put on my camlet-cloak and overalls—they had been missing, and I had been obliged to go without them! he had taken Mrs Staines's large umbrella, and had waited for us, from breakfast time, round the corner, under the confident assurance that we should go to look for him. Sir, it has been his amusement to follow us about all day, gratifying his malevolent feelings with the spectacle of our exposure to the elements, our weariness, our ever-increasing anxiety! You will not wonder after this, sir—'"

"There, that will do," once more exclaimed the skipper, throwing aside the letter with a chuckle of amusement. "I must say I don't wonder at the doctor's refusing to keep him any more after that! Well, his father wanted him to be a sailor, and maybe he won't make a bad one. Only we must have none of his tricks on board ship. I'll have a talk with him, when I can spare the time. That's settled. And now I can see Dr Lavie about this other lad, young Warley. Hallo there, Matthews, tell the doctor I am at liberty now."

In a few minutes the person named was ushered into Captain Wilmore's presence. The new comer was a gentlemanly and well-looking young man, and bore a good character, so far as he was known, in the ship. The captain was pleased with his appearance, and felt at the moment more than usually gracious—possibly in consequence of his recent mirth over George Gilbert's exploits. He spoke with unusual kindness.

"Well, doctor, what can I do for you? You have come to speak to me about young Ernest Warley, I think?"

"Yes, Captain Wilmore, I want to ask your advice. His father was the best friend I ever had. He took me by the hand when I was left an orphan without a sixpence, and put me to school, and took care of me. When he was dying, he made me promise to do my best for his boy, as he had for me. But I'm afraid I can't do that, glad as I should be to do it, if I could—"

"But I don't understand, doctor. Old Warley—I knew a little of him—was a wealthy man, partner in Vanderbyl and Warley's house, one of the best in Cape Town. The lad can't want for money."

"Ah, he does, though. His elder brother has all the money. He was the son of the first wife, old Vanderbyl's daughter, and all the money derived from the business went to him. The second wife's fortune was settled on Ernest; but it was lost, every farthing of it, in the failure of Steinberg's bank last year."

"Won't the elder brother do anything?"

"No more than very shame may oblige him to do. He hated his father's second wife, and hates her son now."

"How old is the lad?"

"Past nineteen; very steady and quiet, but plenty of stuff in him. He wouldn't take his brother's money, if he had the chance; says he means to work for himself. He wanted to be a parson, and would have gone this autumn to the University, but for the smash of the bank. He'll do anything now that I advise him, but I don't know what to advise."

"'Nineteen!'—too old for the navy. 'Wanted to be a parson!'—wouldn't do for the army. 'Do anything you advise!' Are you sure of that? Few young fellows now-a-days will do anything but what they themselves like."

"Yes, he'll do anything I advise, because he knows I really care for him. Where he fancies he's put upon, he can be stiff-backed and defiant enough. I've seen that once or twice. Ernest hasn't your nephew Frank's temper, which is hot and hasty for the moment, but is right again the next. He doesn't come to in a minute, as Frank does, but he's a good fellow for all that."

The captain's brow was overcast as he heard his nephew's name. "Frank's spirit wants breaking, Mr Lavie," he said in an angry tone. "I shall have to teach him that there's only one will allowed aboard ship, and that's the captain's. Frank can ride and leap and shoot to a bead they tell me, but he can't command my ship, and he shan't. I won't have him asking for reasons for what I order, and if he does it again—he'll wish he hadn't. But this is nothing to the purpose, Mr Lavie," he added, recovering himself. "We were talking about young Warley. You had better try to get him a clerkship in a house at Cape Town. You mean to settle there yourself after the voyage, do you not?"

"Well, no, sir, I think not I had meant it, but my inclination now rather is to try for a medical appointment in Calcutta. You see it would be uncomfortable for Ernest at the Cape with his brother—"

"I see. Well, then, both of you had better go on to Calcutta with me. I dare say—if I am pleased with the lad—I may be able to speak to one of the merchants or bankers there. What does he know? what can he do?"

"He is a tolerable classical scholar, sir, and a good arithmetician, Dr Phelps told me—"

"That's good," interposed the captain.

"And he knows a little French, and is a fair shot with a gun, and can ride his horse, though he can't do either like Frank—"

"Never mind Frank," broke in Captain Wilmore hastily. "He'd behave himself at all events, which is more than Frank does. Well, that will do, then. You two go on with the *Hooghly* to Calcutta, and then I'll speak to you again."

Mr Lavie rose and took his leave, feeling very grateful to his commanding officer, who was not in general a popular captain. He was in reality a kind-hearted man, but extremely passionate, as well as tenacious of his authority, and apt to give offence by issuing unwelcome orders in a peremptory manner, without vouchsafing explanations, which would have smoothed away the irritation they occasioned. In particular he and his nephew, Frank Wilmore, to whom reference more than once has been made, were continually falling out Frank was a fine high-spirited lad of eighteen, for whom his uncle had obtained a military cadetship from a director, to whom he had rendered a service; and the lad was now on his way to join his regiment. Frank had always desired to be a soldier, and was greatly delighted when he heard of his good fortune. But his uncle gave him no hint that it was through him it had been obtained. Indeed, the news had been communicated in a manner so gruff and seemingly grudging, that Frank conceived an aversion to his uncle, which was not removed when they came into personal contact on board the *Hooghly*.

The three lads, however, soon fraternised, and before they had sighted Cape Finisterre were fast friends. Many an hour had already been beguiled by the recital of adventures on shore, and speculation as to the future, that lay before them. Nor was there any point on which they agreed more heartily than in denunciation of the skipper's tyranny, and their resolve not to submit to it. When Mr Lavie came on deck, after his interview in the captain's cabin, they were all three leaning over the bulwarks, with lion crouching at Frank's side, but all three, for a wonder, quite silent. Mr Lavie cast a look seaward, and saw at once the explanation of their unusual demeanour. The ship had been making good way for the last hour or two, and was now near enough to the Canaries to allow the Peak of Teneriffe to be clearly seen, like a low triangular cloud, and the rest of the island was coming gradually into clearer sight Mr Lavie joined the party, and set himself to watch what is perhaps the grandest spectacle which the bosom of the broad Atlantic has to exhibit. At first the outline of the great mountain, twelve thousand feet in height, presented a dull cloudy mass, formless and indistinct. But as the afternoon wore on, the steep cliffs scored with lava became visible, and the serrated crests of Anaga grew slowly upon the eye. Then, headland after headland revealed itself, the heavy dark grey masses separating themselves into hues of brown and red and saffron. Now appeared the terraced gardens which clothe the cultivated sides, and above them the picturesque outlines of the rocks intermingled with the foliage of the euphorbia and the myrtle, and here and there opening into wild mountain glens which the wing of the bird alone could traverse. Lastly, the iron-bound coast became visible on which the surf was breaking in foaming masses, and above the rocky shelf the long low line of spires and houses which distinguish the town of Santa Cruz. For a long time the red sunset light was strong enough to make clearly distinguishable the dazzling white frontages, the flat roofs, and unglazed windows, standing out against the perpendicular walls of basaltic rock. Then a dark mist, rising upwards from the sea, like the curtain in the ancient Greek theatre, began to hide the shipping in the port, the quays, and the batteries, till the whole town was lost in the darkness. Higher it spread, obscuring the masses of oleander, and arbutus, and poinsettia in the gardens, and the sepia tints of the rocks above. Then the white lava fissures were lost to the eye, and the Peak alone stood against the darkening sky, its masses of snow bathed in the rich rosy light of the expiring sun. A few minutes more and that too was swallowed up in darkness, and the spell which had enchained the four spectators of the scene was suddenly dissolved.

Chapter Two

Three or four days had passed, the weather appearing each day more delicious than the last. The *Hooghly* sped smoothly and rapidly before the wind, and at daybreak on the fifth morning notice was given that the Cape Verde Islands were in sight. The sky, however, grew thick and misty as they neared land; and it was late in the forenoon before they had approached near enough to obtain a clear view of it.

"I wonder why they call these islands *Verdes*?" observed Gilbert, as the vessel ran along the coast of one of the largest of the group, which was low and sandy and apparently barren; "there doesn't seem to be much *green* about them, that I can see."

"No, certainly," said Warley; "a green patch here and there is all there is to be seen, so far as the sea-coast is concerned But the interior seems a mass of mountains. There may be plenty of verdure among them, for all we know."

"No," said Mr Lavie, who was standing near them. "Their name has nothing to do with forests or grass-fields. There is a mass of weed on the other side of the group, extending for a long distance over the sea, which is something like a green meadow to look at—that's the meaning of the name. There are very few woods on any of the islands, and this one in particular produces hardly anything but salt."

"They belong to the Portuguese, don't they?" asked Frank.

"Yes; the Portuguese discovered them three centuries and a half ago, and have had possession of them ever since. Portuguese is the only language spoken there, but there are very few whites there, nevertheless."

"Why, there must be a lot of inhabitants," remarked Ernest, his eye resting on the villages with which the shores were studded.

"Yes, from forty to fifty thousand, I believe. But they are almost all of them half-breeds between the negroes and the Portuguese."

"Well, I suppose there's some fun to be had there, isn't there?" inquired Frank.

"And something to be seen?" added Warley.

"And first-chop grub?" wound up Gilbert. "There's plenty to see at Porto Prayo," returned Mr Lavie. "The town, Ribeira Grande they call it, is curious, and there are some fine mountain passes and grand views in the interior. As for grub, Master Nick" (for this sobriquet had already become young Gilbert's usual appellative), "there are pretty well all the fruits that took your fancy so much at Madeira—figs, guavas, bananas, oranges, melons, grapes, pine-apples, and mangos—and there's plenty of turtle too, though I'm not sure you'll find it made into soup. But as to fun, Frank, it depends on what you call fun, I expect—"

"Let us go ashore," interrupted Nick, "and we shall be safe to find out lots of fun for ourselves. It would be jolly fun, in itself, to be walking on hard ground again, instead of these everlasting planks. I suppose, as these islands belong to the Portuguese, and we've no quarrel with them, the skipper will go ashore, and allow the passengers to do so too?"

"He'll go ashore, no doubt," said a voice close at hand; "but he won't let you go, I'll answer for that."

The boys turned quickly round, and were not particularly pleased to see the first lieutenant, Mr Grey, who had come aft, to give some orders, and had overheard the last part of their conversation. Mr Grey was no favourite of theirs. He was not downright uncivil to the boys, but he was fond of snubbing them whenever an occasion offered itself. It was generally believed also that a good deal of the captain's harshness was due to the first lieutenant's suggestions.

"You'd better leave the captain to answer for himself," remarked Frank, his cheek flushing with anger. "I don't see how you can know what he means to do."

"Perhaps you mayn't see it, and yet I may," returned Mr Grey calmly.

"Why shouldn't he let us go ashore, as he did at Madeira?" asked Warley. "Nothing went wrong there."

"I beg your pardon," replied the lieutenant; "things did go wrong there, and he was very much displeased."

"Displeased," repeated Warley, "displeased with us? What do you mean, Mr Grey?"

"I mean that you are not to go ashore," returned the other curtly, and walking forward as he spoke.

Ernest's cheek grew almost as crimson as Frank's had done. The apparent insinuation that he had misconducted himself while on his parole of good behaviour, was one of the things he could least endure. Mr Lavie laid his hand on the boy's arm.

"Hush, Ernest!" he said, checking an angry exclamation to which he was about to give vent. "Most likely Mr Grey is not serious. Anyway, if the captain does forbid your going ashore, you may be assured he has good reasons—"

"What reasons can he have?" interposed Gilbert; "we are no more likely to get into trouble here than at Madeira, and who has a right to say we did anything wrong there?"

"The first lieutenant *didn't* say so," observed the surgeon. "I think there is some mistake. I'll make inquiries about the matter before we enter the harbour."

He moved away, and the boys resolved to retreat to their den, where they might hold an indignation meeting without molestation. This den, to which its occupants had given the classical name of "Dionysius's ear," or more briefly, "Dionysius," was an empty space on the lower deck, about six foot square, where various stores had been stowed away. By some oversight of the men a dozen chests or so had been left ashore, and a vacant place in a corner was reserved for them. When, however, they were brought aboard, they could not conveniently be lowered, and were secured on deck. Master Nick, in the course of his restless wandering, had lighted on this void space, and it occurred to him that it would make a snug place of retreat, when he wished to be alone, as he not unfrequently did, in order to escape the consequences of some piece of mischief. When his friendship with his companions had been sufficiently cemented, he had communicated the secret to them, and Frank at once appreciated its value. Advantage had been already taken of it on one or two occasions, to evade an unwelcome summons from the skipper, or smoke a pipe at interdicted hours.

To be sure it was not a very desirable retiring room, and most persons would have considered a Russian or Neapolitan dungeon greatly preferable to it. As the reader has heard, it was about six foot square. It was lighted by a dead light in the deck above, which had fortunately been inserted just in that spot. Whatever air there was, came through the barrels, or along the ship's sides. But it is needless to say it was at all times suffocatingly close, and nothing but a boy or a salamander could have long continued to breathe such an atmosphere. Entrance was obtained by pulling aside a small keg; the removal of which allowed just enough room for any one to work his way in, like an earthworm, on his stomach. Then the keg was drawn by the rope attached to it into its place again, and firmly secured to a staple in the ship's side. Whatever might be its other defects, it was certainly almost impossible of detection.

Arrived here, our three heroes lay down at their leisure on some sacks with which they had garnished their domicile, and proceeded to discuss the matter in hand, lowering their voices as much as possible, as they had discovered that conversation might be heard through the barrels by any one on the other side, which fact, indeed, was the explanation of the name bestowed on their retreat. They were not at first agreed as to the steps to be adopted. Nick was for going ashore under any circumstances—the difficulty of accomplishing his purpose, and the fact of his having been forbidden to essay it, being, in his eyes, only additional incentives. Frank was not disposed to make the attempt, if his uncle really had interdicted it; but he professed himself certain that no such order had been given by anybody but the first lieutenant, and he was not, he said, going to be under his orders. Warley for once was inclined to go beyond Frank, and declared that though he would obey the captain's order if any reasonable ground for it was assigned, he would not be debarred from what he considered his right as a passenger, by any man's mere caprice. He added, however, that he thought it would be better to hear what Lavie had found out, before coming to any resolution.

"Well, it is time we should see the doctor, if we mean to do so," remarked Frank, after an hour or so had passed in conversation. "We must be entering Porto Prayo by this time, or be near it at all events; and he must have had lots of time to find out everything."

"Very good; one of us had better see Mr Lavie at once," said Ernest. "I'll go, if you like, and come back to 'Dionysius' here, as soon as I have anything to tell."

He departed accordingly, and returned in about half an hour, looking very cool, but very much annoyed.

"Hallo, Ernest, what's up now?" exclaimed Nick, as he caught sight of his face. "What does the doctor say?"

"I haven't seen the doctor," answered Warley. "One of the crew has been taken dangerously ill, and the doctor has been with him ever since he left us."

"What have you learned, then?" asked Frank. "Are we in the harbour?"

"We're in the harbour, and the skipper's gone ashore. I saw his boat half-way to the beach. Captain Renton, Mr May, and Mr De Koech have gone with him. They are the only passengers who wanted to go."

"Well, but I suppose there are some shore boats that would take passengers to and fro."

"The captain has given orders that no shore boat is to be allowed alongside. He won't even allow the fresh provisions, or the water, to be brought aboard by any but the ship's boats. I saw the largest cutter with the empty water-casks in her, lying ready to go ashore presently."

"Who told you this?" inquired Wilmore, half incredulous.

"Old Jennings, the quartermaster. He has charge of the boat. He said the captain's resolved we shan't leave the ship."

"It's an infamous shame," said Frank. "I declare I've half a mind to swim ashore. It can't be very far."

"No," said Nick, "but it wouldn't be pleasant to land soaking wet, to say nothing of the chance of ground sharks. Even Lion had better not try that dodge. But I'll tell you what—if the boat is lying off the ship's side, with a lot of ankers in her, why shouldn't we creep in among them, and go ashore unbeknown to the first lieutenant?"

"We should be seen getting aboard," said Frank.

"No, we shouldn't. The men are at dinner just now, and we can slip in when the backs of the fellows on deck are turned."

"I forgot that," said Frank; "but we should be certain to be seen when we landed."

"Ay, no doubt. But that will be too late, won't it? Once ashore, I guess they must be pretty nimble to catch us; and besides, old Jennings is too good-natured to do anything against us, which he isn't obliged to do."

"Well, that's true, certainly," returned Wilmore. "What do you say, Warley? Are you game to make the trial?"

"Yes, I am," returned Ernest. "I think it is regular tyranny to oblige us to stay in the ship, when there is no reason for it, except the captain's caprice. But if we mean to try this, we must make haste."

The three lads hurried on deck; and a glance showed them they were just in time. There were only two or three men to be seen, and they were at the other end of the ship. They skimmed nimbly down the ladder, and found no difficulty in concealing themselves at the bow end of the boat, which was completely hidden from sight by the empty casks. They had not been in their hiding-place very long, before the old quartermaster and his men were heard coming down the side. The shore was soon reached, and the keel had no sooner grated on the sand, than the boys sprang out and ran up the beach, saluting old Jennings with a parting cheer as they went.

"Well, I never," muttered the old man. "The cap'en 'ull be in a nice taking when he hears of this! And there ain't no chance but what he *will* hear of it. We've Andy Duncan in the boat, and he carries everything to the first lieutenant, as sure as it happens. Well, I ain't bound to peach, anyhow—that's one comfort!"

Meanwhile the captain had gone on shore, his temper not improved by the report of the doctor which had been brought to him as he was leaving the vessel, that another of his best hands was rendered useless—for several weeks to come at all events—by a bad attack of fever, which might very possibly spread through the ship. He returned on board after nightfall, still more provoked and vexed. He had met with the greatest difficulty in his attempts to fill the places of his missing men. There were, as the reader has been told, very few whites on the island, and none of them were sailors. The blacks were very unwilling to engage, except upon exorbitant terms, and hardly one of those with whom he spoke appeared good for anything. He had at one time all but given up the matter in despair. But late in the afternoon he was accosted by a dark-complexioned man, lean and sinewy as a bloodhound, who informed him that the vessel in which he traded between the South African ports and the West Indian Islands, had been driven on the Cape Verdes and totally wrecked. But the crew had escaped, he said, and were willing to engage with Captain Wilmore for the voyage to Calcutta.

The captain hesitated. He had little doubt that the lost vessel had been a slaver, and he had an instinctive abhorrence of all engaged in that horrible traffic. Still there seemed no other hope of successfully prosecuting the voyage, and after all it would be a companionship of only a few months. He resolved to make one effort more to obtain less questionable help, and if that should fail, to accept the offer. Desiring the stranger to bring his men to the quay in an hour's time, he once more entered the town, and made inquiries at all the houses to which sailors were likely to resort. His success was no better than it had been before, and he was obliged to close with the proposal of the foreign captain. He liked the looks of the crew even less than those of their captain. There were eighteen of them, however, and all strong serviceable fellows, if they chose to work. He must hope for the best; but even the best did not appear very promising; and if the Yankee captain, who had been the prime cause of the mischief, had been delivered into his hands at that moment, it is to be feared he would have met with small mercy.

In this frame of mind he regained the *Hooghly*, and shortly after his arrival was informed by the first lieutenant of the escapade of the three boys, with the gratuitous addition that he had himself delivered them the captain's message—that no one was to be permitted to leave the ship, except those who had gone ashore with the captain.

The skipper's wrath fairly boiled over. He vowed he would straightway give his nephew a smart taste of the cat-o'-nine-tails, and put the other two into irons, to teach them obedience. The boatswain accordingly was summoned, and the delinquents ordered into custody, but after a delay of half an hour, during which the captain's wrath seemed to be every moment growing hotter, it was announced that the boys could not be found, and the boat's crew sent ashore with the water-casks positively declared that they did not return with them. As no other boats but theirs and the captain's had held any communication with the land, it appeared certain that the young gentlemen were still on shore, intending probably to return by a shore boat later in the evening.

"Do they?" exclaimed Captain Wilmore fiercely, when this likelihood was suggested to him by Mr Grey. "They'll find themselves mistaken, then. Up with the anchor, Crossman, and hoist the mainsail. Before their boat has left the quay, we shall be twenty miles from land. Not a word, Mr Lavie. A month or two's stay in these islands will be a lesson they'll keep by them all their lives."

No one ventured to remonstrate. The anchor was lifted, the great sails were set, and in half an hour they were moving southward at a pace which soon left the lights of Porto Prayo a mere speck in the distance.

But the boys had not been left behind, though no one but themselves and old Jennings was aware of the fact. He had kept the boat from putting off on her return to the ship, on one pretext or another, as long as he could venture to do so, in the hope that the lads would make their appearance. But he was aware that Andy Duncan's eye was upon him, and could not venture to delay longer. It happened, however, that soon after his return, Mr Lavie had found it necessary to send on shore to the hospital for some ice, of which they had none on board, and old Jennings had volunteered to go. He took the smallest boat and no one with him but his nephew, Joe Cobbes, who was completely under his orders. He landed at a different place from that at which the boat had been moored in the morning, and sent his nephew with the message to the hospital. He then made search after the boys, whom he soon discovered at the regular landing-place, waiting anxiously for some means of regaining the *Hooghly*.

"Hallo, Jennings," exclaimed Frank, as he caught sight of the old man's figure through the fast gathering darkness; "that's all right, then. I was afraid we were going to stay ashore all night?"

"I hope it is all right, sir," answered Jennings, "but if the captain finds out that you've been breaking his orders—"

"I don't believe he has given any order—" interrupted Frank. "And it would be monstrous if he had," exclaimed Ernest in the same breath.

"I don't know what you believe, Mr Frank, but it's sartain he has ordered that no one shall leave the ship; and I don't know as it's so unreasonable, Mr Warley, after the desertion of the hands at Madeira."

"We never heard of their deserting," cried Warley.

"I dare say not, sir. It was kep' snug. But that's why the cap'en would allow no boats to go ashore, except what couldn't be helped. You see, sir, if more of the men were to make off, there mightn't be enough left to work the ship, and if there came a gale—"

"Yes, yes; I understand that," again broke in Frank, "but we didn't know anything about their deserting."

"Well, sir, it was giv' out this morning as that was the reason, and every one, I thought, knew it. But anyways, sir, you'd best come and get aboard my boat, and keep out of the skipper's way. He'll be sure to find out about your doings. Andy 'ull tell the first lieutenant, and he'll tell the skipper—"

"I am sure I don't care if he does," exclaimed Warley.

"Ah, you don't know him, sir. He's not a man as it's wise to defy. Wait a bit; let him cool down and he's as pleasant a man as any one. But when he's put up, old Nick himself can't match him. I don't mind a gale of wind off the Cape, or boarding a Frenchman, or a tussle with a pirate, but I durstn't face the cap'en, when he's in one of his takings. Come along, and get into the boat."

The lads obeyed, somewhat subdued by Jennings' representations, which were evidently given in good faith. They allowed the old man to cover them with a tarpaulin, which he had brought for the purpose, and in accordance with his directions lay perfectly still.

Presently Cobbes returned with the ice, and the boat was rowed back to the ship. It was pitch dark before she came alongside, and her approach was hardly noticed. Jennings made for the gangway, and having ascertained that Captain Wilmore was still on shore, sent his nephew with the ice to the doctor's cabin. He then suffered the boat to float noiselessly to the stern, where he had purposely left one of the cabin windows open; through this the boys contrived, with his help, to scramble.

"You'd better hide somewhere in the hold, Mr Frank," he whispered, as young Wilmore, who was the last, prepared to follow his companions.

"No, on the lower deck, Jennings; we've a hiding-place there, no one will find out. When you think it's safe for us to show ourselves, come down, and whistle a bar or two of one of your tunes, and I'll creep out to you. But I hope we shan't be kept very long, or we shall run a risk of being starved, though we have got some grub in our pockets. Good night, Jennings, and thank you. You're a good fellow, any way, whatever the captain may be."

"Good night, Mr Frank; mind you keep close till I come to let you out. I won't keep you waiting no longer than I can help, you may be sure of that."

Wilmore followed his friends; and the three boys, creeping cautiously along in the darkness, gained the lower deck unperceived, and were soon safely ensconced in "Dionysius." Tired out with their day's work, they all three fell sound asleep.

Chapter Three

The boys were awakened next morning by the pitching and tossing of the ship. A storm had come on during the night, which increased in violence as the morning advanced. It was well for the *Hooghly* that the fresh hands had been taken on board, or she would have become wholly unmanageable. Frank and his friends, in their place of retreat, could hear the shouts and cries on deck, the rolling of the barrels which had broken loose from their fastenings, and the washing of the heavy seas which poured over the gunwales. They made their breakfasts on some of the fruit and sausages with which they had filled their pockets on the previous evening, and waited anxiously for old Jennings' arrival. It was late in the afternoon before he came, and when he did appear, he would not hear of their venturing to show themselves for the present.

"The cap'en wasn't altogether in a pleasant state of mind yesterday," he remarked, "but he's in a wuss to-day. He's found out that the most part of his crew ain't worth a tobacco stopper. I must say the Yankee made a good pick of it. He got away pretty nigh every smart hand we had aboard. These new chaps is the best we has now."

"New chaps?" asked Frank. "Has my uncle got any fresh hands?"

"Picked up nineteen new 'uns at Port Prayo," replied Jennings. "Stout nimble fellows they are, no doubt. But I don't greatly conceit them neither. They keep together, and hardly speak to any one aboard, except Andy Duncan and Joel White and Bob O'Hara and that lot. They're no good either, to my mind. Well, young gents, you must stay here till the gale breaks, as I guess it will to-morrow, or the next day, and then the skipper will be in good-humour again. I've brought you a heap of biscuits and some fruit and a keg of water. But I mustn't be coming down here often, or we shall be found out I've tied the dog up in the fo'castle, or he'd be sniffing about after Mr Frank here, and most likely find him out."

"Very well, Tom," said Frank, "then we'll wait here. But it's terribly dull work. Nothing to do but to sleep and smoke."

"I think the skipper would let us off, if he knew what we'd gone through during the last twenty-four hours," observed Nick, yawning. "Well, I suppose one must grin and bear it." So saying, he rolled himself into his corner and endeavoured to lose the recollection of his *désagréments* in sleep.

The evening wore on heavily enough. It was past midnight before the gale began to lull, and the lads at length fell sound asleep. But they were roused soon afterwards by a loud commotion on deck. Voices were heard shouting and cursing; one or two shots were fired, and Frank fancied he could once or twice distinguish the clash of cutlasses. But presently the tumult died away, and the ship apparently resumed her customary discipline. Daylight came at last, glimmering faintly through the crevices of their prison, and the boys lay every minute expecting the advent of the old quartermaster. But the morning passed, and the afternoon began to slip away, and still there was no sign of Jennings's approach. The matter was more than once debated whether they should issue from their hiding-place, which was now becoming intolerable to them, altogether disregarding his advice; or at any rate send out one of the party to reconnoitre. But Ernest urged strongly the wisdom of keeping to their original resolution, and Frank after awhile sided with him. It was agreed, however, that if Jennings did not appear on the following morning, Warley should betake himself to the doctor's cabin and ask his advice.

Accordingly they once more lay down to sleep, and were again awoke in the middle of the night, but this time by a voice calling to them in a subdued tone through the barrels.

Wilmore, who was the lightest sleeper, started up. "Who is that?" he asked.

"It is I—Tom Jennings," was the answer. "Don't speak again, but push out the barrel that stops the way into your crib there. I'll manage to crawl in, I dare say, though I am a bit lame."

Wilmore saw there was something wrong. He complied literally with Tom's request, and pushed the keg out in silence. Presently he heard the old man making his way, stopping every now and then as if in pain. At last there came the whisper again: "Pull the barrel back into its place, I've got a lantern under my coat which I'll bring out when you've made all fast."

Frank again obeyed his directions, having first enjoined silence on his two companions, who were by this time wide awake. Then Jennings drew out his lantern, and lighted it by the help of a flint and steel. As the light fell on his face and figure, the boys could hardly suppress a cry of alarm. His cheeks were as white as ashes, and in several places streaked with clotted blood. His leg too was rudely bandaged from the knee to the ankle, and it was only by a painful effort that he could draw it after him.

"What's the matter, Tom?" exclaimed Frank. "How have you hurt your leg in that manner?"

"Hush! Mr Frank. We mustn't speak above a whisper. There's pirates on board. They've got possession of the ship."

"Pirates!" repeated Wilmore. "What, have we been attacked, and my uncle—"

"He's safe, Mr Frank—at least I hope so. Look here. You remember them foreign chaps as he brought aboard at Porto Prayo? It was all a lie they told the cap'en, about their ship having been lost. They were part of a crew of pirates—that's my belief, any way—as had heard Captain Wilmore was short-handed, and wanted to get possession of his ship. They was no sooner aboard than they made friends with some of the worst of our hands—Andy and White and O'Hara and the rest on 'em—and I make no doubt persuaded them to join 'em. About ten o'clock last night, when the men were nearly all in their berths, worn out with their work during the gale, these foreigners crept up on deck, cut down and pitched overboard half a dozen of our chaps as were on deck, and then clapped down the hatches."

"That was what we heard, then," remarked Gilbert. "Were you on deck, Tom?"

"Yes, sir, I was, and got these two cuts over the head and leg. By good luck I fell close to the companion-ladder and was able at once to crawl to my berth, or I should have been pitched overboard. Well, as soon as it was daylight, the captain and the officers laid their heads together to contrive some means of regaining the ship; but, before they could settle anything, a vessel came in sight, and the fellows on deck hove to and let her come up—"

"The pirate ship, I suppose, hey?" cried Frank.

"Yes, sir, no other. She'd followed us beyond a doubt from Porto Prayo, and would have come up before, if it hadn't been for the gale. There wasn't nothing to be done, of course. The pirates threatened the captain, if he didn't surrender at once, that they'd fire down the hatchways and afterwards pitch every mother's son overboard. And they'd have done it too."

"Not a doubt," assented Frank. "So my uncle surrendered?"

"Yes, sir, he did, but he didn't like it. I must say, from what I've heard of these fellows, I judged that they'd have thrown us all in to the sea without mercy. But it seems White and O'Hara and the rest wouldn't allow that, and insisted on it that every one, who chose it, should be allowed to leave the ship. I did 'em injustice, I must say."

"What did they go in?" inquired Wilmore, a good deal surprised.

"In the two biggest of the ship's boats, sir. You see we've been driven a long way south by that gale, and are not more than a few hundred miles from Ascension. They'll make for that, and with this wind they've a good chance of getting there in three or four days."

"Are all the officers and passengers gone?" asked Warley.

"Well, no, sir. Mr Lavie ain't gone. The men stopped him as he was stepping into the boat, and declared he shouldn't leave the ship. But all the rest is gone—no one's left except those who've joined the mutineers, unless it's poor old Lion, who's still tied up in the fo'castle."

"Why, *you* haven't joined them, Jennings, to be sure?"

"I! no, sir; but with my leg I couldn't have gone aboard the boats; and to be sure, I hadn't the chance, for I fainted dead off as soon as I'd reached my berth, and didn't come to till after they was gone. And there's my nevvy too—he wouldn't go, but chose to stay behind and nurse me. I hadn't the heart to scold the lad for it."

"Scold him! I should think not," observed Warley.

"Well, sir, it may get him into trouble if he's caught aboard this ship, and I expect he'll get into troubles with these pirates too. But there's no use fretting about what can't be helped. I'm thinking about you young gents. You see if I'd been in my right senses when they went away, I should have told the cap'en about you, and he'd have taken you away with him. But I wasn't sensible like, and no one else then knew as you was aboard."

"No one knew it *then*?" repeated Warley. "No one knows it now, I suppose."

"Yes, sir, Mr Lavie knows it, and Joe too; I told them an hour ago, and we had a long talk about it. The doctor's resolved he won't stay in the ship, and I suppose you don't want to stay neither?"

"We stay, Tom!" replied Frank. "No, I should think not indeed, if we can help it. But how are we to get away?"

"This way, sir. These pirates have been choosing their officers to-day, and they've made O'Hara captain. They say he's the only man who's up to navigating the ship. Anyhow, they've made him captain, and one of the foreign chaps, first mate. They're to have a great supper to-morrow night in honour of 'em, and most of the crew—pretty nigh all I should say—will be drunk. Well, then, we claps a lot of things, that Mr Lavie has got together, aboard one of the boats—there are enough of us to lower her easy enough—and long before daylight you'll be out of sight."

"*You'll* be out of sight. Don't you mean to go yourself, Jennings?" asked Frank.

"My leg won't let me, Mr Frank. I couldn't get down the ship's side; and besides, I ain't in no danger. My old messmates won't let me be hurt, nor Joe Cobbes neither. I'd best stay here till my leg's right. Mr Lavie says it wants nothing but rest, and a little washing now and then. No, sir; Joe and I would rather stay on board here and take the first opportunity of leaving the ship that offers. Mr Lavie and you all 'ull bear witness how it happened."

"That we will, Tom," said Warley. "Well, then, if I understand you, we've nothing to do but to remain quiet until to-morrow night, and you and Mr Lavie will make all the preparations?"

"Yes, sir, that's right. Stay quietly here till you've notice that everything's ready."

"But I don't like you having all the risk and trouble, Tom," said Wilmore.

"You'd do as much for me, sir, and more too, I dare say, if you had the chance. Besides, I am anxious you should get away safe, because you're my witnesses that I and Joe had no hand in this. I shall get well all the sooner, when you're gone."

"All right, Jennings," said Warley. "And now I suppose you want to get out of this again?"

"Yes, sir; you must help me. Getting out will be worse than getting in, I am afraid."

The lantern was extinguished, the keg removed, and with much pain and difficulty the old man was helped out. The next twenty-four hours were passed in the utmost anxiety by the three lads, who would hardly allow themselves even to whisper to one another, for fear of being overheard by the pirates. All the morning they could hear the preparations for the feast going on. Some casks in the lower deck, which, as they knew, contained some unusually fine wine, were broken open, and the bottles carried on deck. Planks also were handed up to make tables and benches. From the conversation of the men employed in the work, they learned that the feast was to take place in the forecastle, none of the cabins being large enough to hold the entire party. Once they caught a mention of Mr Lavie's name, and learned that he had been all night in attendance on Amos Wood, the sailor who had been attacked by fever at Porto Prayo, and that the man had died that morning, and been thrown overboard. The doctor, it was said, had now turned in for a long sleep. The boys guessed that his day would be differently employed. About six o'clock in the evening, everything seemed to be in readiness. The tramp of feet above was heard as the men took their places at table, and was followed by the rattling of plates and knives and forks, and the oaths and noisy laughter of the revellers. These grew more vociferous as the evening passed on, and after an hour or two the uproar was heightened by the crash of glass, and the frequent outbreak of quarrels among the guests, which were with difficulty suppressed by their more sober comrades. Then benches were overturned, and the noise of bodies falling on the deck was heard, as man after man became stupidly intoxicated. The uproar gradually died out, until nothing was audible, but drunken snores, or the unsteady steps of some few of the sailors, who were supposed to be keeping watch.

It was about two hours after midnight when the expected summons came. Frank crept out first, followed by Nick and Ernest. They found Mr Lavie and Joe Cobbes waiting for them.

"Everything is ready, Ernest," whispered the doctor. "We've put as many provisions and arms into the jolly-boat as we can safely carry; but you had better take a brace of pistols apiece. There are some one or two of the men who are the worse for drink, but still sober enough to know what they are doing, and we may have a tussle. Put on these caps and jackets, and come as quick as you can. The jolly-boat is on the starboard side, near the stern. She's not in the water yet, but everything is ready for lowering her. Quiet's the word."

The boys obeyed. They crept cautiously on deck, pulling the caps over their foreheads, and imitating as well as they could the movements of drunken men. They soon reached the jolly-boat, where old Jennings was waiting for them. The helm had been lashed, but every ten minutes or so one of the watch came aft to see that all was right. Jennings had unfastened the lashings and taken the rudder, telling the first man who came up that he would see to it for the rest of the watch. The man willingly enough accepted his services, and this skilful manoeuvre saved them for the time from further interruption.

"Lower quickly, Mr Lavie," he whispered in the doctor's ear. "Andy Duncan has had liquor enough to make half a dozen men drunk, but he knows what he's doing for all that. He's keeping an eye on the ship, and may be down upon us any minute."

THE ESCAPE FROM THE "HOOGHLY."

He was obeyed promptly and in silence. The boat was lowered without attracting notice. Warley was the first to slip down the rope, and was safely followed by Nick. Frank was just climbing over the bulwark when a man staggered up, and accused them with a volley of drunken oaths of intending to desert.

"No, no, Andy," said Jennings quickly, "no one means to desert. There's a man overboard, and we're lowering a boat to pick him up. Make haste, my lad," he continued, addressing Wilmore, "or he'll be too far astern for us to help him."

Frank promptly took the cue, and vanished over the side. For a moment Duncan was staggered by the old quartermaster's readiness, but the next he caught a momentary glimpse of Frank's features.

"Hallo, that's young Wilmore, that's the captain's nevvy, as you said had been left behind," he shouted. "There's some devilry here! Help, my lads, there!" He drew a pistol as he spoke, and fired at Mr Lavie's head, who was attempting to seize him.

His nerves were unsteady from drink, and the bullet missed its mark; but it struck Joe Cobbes on the temple, who fell on the instant stone dead. Some of the men, startled by the pistol shot, came reeling up from the forecastle.

The doctor struck Andy a heavy blow with the butt end of his pistol, and the man dropped insensible on the deck. He then turned to Jennings. "You must go with us now, Tom," he said, "or they will certainly murder you. Go, I tell you, or I'll stay behind myself."

The old man made a great effort and rolled himself over the bulwarks, reaching the boat by the help of the rope, and the hands of the boys below, though he fainted from pain and exhaustion immediately afterwards.

Mr Lavie fired at the nearest man, who dropped with a broken leg. The others hung back alarmed and stupefied. Lavie skimmed down the rope, and disengaged her before they had recovered their senses. Just at this moment there was a heavy splash close beside them.

"Hallo!" cried Ernest, "one of the fellows has fallen overboard. We must take him in. We can't leave him to drown."

"It isn't any of the crew," said Frank. "It's old Lion. I can see his head above water. He has broken his fastenings and followed us. Haul him aboard, Nick."

The dog was soon got in, and Lavie and Warley, seizing the oars, rowed away from the ship. An attempt was made to lower a boat, and one or two shots were fired. But the crew were in no condition for work of any kind, and in a few minutes the *Hooghly* was lost sight of in the darkness. Lavie and Wilmore, who understood the management of a boat, hoisted the sail and took the rudder.

Meanwhile, Warley and Gilbert were endeavouring to restore the old quartermaster from his swoon. They threw water in his face, and poured some brandy from a flask down his throat, but for a long time without any result. At last the boat was in proper trim, and Mr Lavie set at liberty to attend to his patient. Alarmed at the low state of the pulse, and the failure of the efforts to restore consciousness, he lighted his lantern, and then discovered that the bottom of the boat was deluged with blood. The bandages had been loosened in the struggle to get on board, and the wound had broken out afresh. The surgeon saw that there was now little hope of saving the old man's life. He succeeded, however, in stanching the flow of blood, and again bound up the wound, directing that Jennings should be laid in as comfortable a position as possible on a heap of jackets in the bow.

This had not been long effected, when morning appeared. Those who have witnessed daybreak in the tropics, will be aware how strange and brilliant a contrast it presents to that of northern climates. The day does not slowly gather in the East, changing by imperceptible degrees from the depth of gloom to the fulness of light, but springs as it were with a single effort into brilliant splendour—an image of the great Creator's power when He created the earth and skies—not toiling through long ages of successive processes and formations, as some would have us believe, but starting at one bound from shapeless chaos into life and harmony.

The doctor cast an anxious look at the horizon, and was relieved to find that the *Hooghly* was nowhere visible. "Well out of that," he muttered. "If we could only bring poor Jennings round, I shouldn't so much regret what has happened. But I am afraid that can't be." He again felt the old man's pulse, and found that he was now conscious again, though very feeble.

"Is that Mr Lavie?" he said, opening his eyes. "I'm glad to see you've come off safe, sir. I hope the young gentlemen are safe too."

"All three of them, Jennings, thank you," was the answer; "not one of them has so much as a scratch on him."

"That's hearty, sir. I am afraid poor Joe—it's all over with him, isn't it?"

"I am afraid so, Tom. But he didn't suffer. The ball struck him right on the temple, and he was gone in a moment."

"Yes, sir, and he was killed doing his duty. Perhaps if he'd remained among them villains, he'd have been led astray by them. It's best as it is, sir. I only hope you may all get safe to land."

"And you too, Tom," added Frank, who with his two companions had joined them unperceived.

"No, Mr Frank, I shall never see land—never see the sun set again, I expect. But I don't know that I'm sorry for that I'm an old man, sir, and my nevvy was the last of my family, and I couldn't have lived very long any way."

"No," said Mr Lavie, "and you too have met your death in the discharge of your duty. When my time comes, I hope I may be able to say the same."

"Ah, doctor, it's little good any on us can do in this world. It's well that there's some one better able to bear the load of our sins than we are! But I want to say a word or two, sir, while I can. I advised you, you'll remember, to run straight for the nearest point of the coast, which I judge is about eight hundred miles off. But I didn't know then where them pirates meant to take the *Hooghly* to. Their officers only let it out last night over their drink.

They were to make the mouth of the Congo river, where they've one of their settlements, or whatever they call them. Now, that happens to be just the point you'd be running for, and they'd be pretty sure to overhaul you before you reached it. You'd better now try to reach the Cape, sir. It is a long way off—a good fortnight's sail, I dare say, even with this wind. But there's food and water enough to last more than that time; and besides, you may fall in with an Indiaman."

"We'll take your advice, you may be sure, Jennings."

"I'm glad to hear that, sir. It makes my mind more easy. Make for the coast, Dr Lavie, but don't try for it north of Cape Frio—that's my advice, sir; and I know these latitudes pretty well by this time."

"We'll take care, Jennings," said Warley. "And now, isn't there anything we can do for you?"

"You can say a prayer or two with me, Mr Ernest," replied the old man feebly. "You can't do anything else, that I knows of."

Warley complied, and all kneeling down, he repeated the Lord's Prayer, and one or two simple petitions for pardon and support, in which old Jennings feebly joined. Before the sun had risen high in the heavens his spirit had passed away. His body was then reverently committed to the deep, and the survivors, in silence and sorrow, sailed away from the spot.

Chapter Four

It was early morning. Lavie and Warley were sitting at the helm conversing anxiously, but in subdued tones, unwilling to break the slumbers of their two companions, who were lying asleep at their feet, with Lion curled up beside them. It was now sixteen days since they had left the ship; and so far as they could ascertain, Table Bay was still seven or eight hundred miles distant. They had been unfortunate in their weather. For the first few days indeed the wind had been favourable, and they had made rapid progress. But on the fifth morning there had come a change. The wind lulled, and for eight and forty hours there fell a dead calm. This was followed by a succession of light baffling breezes, during the prevalence of which they could hardly make any way. On the twelfth day the wind was again fair; but their provisions, and especially their supply of water, had now run so low, that there was little hope of its holding out, even if no further *contretemps* should occur. Under these circumstances, they had thought it better to steer for the nearest point of the African coast. They were now too far to the southward to run any great risk of falling in with the pirates, and at whatever point they might make the land, there would be a reasonable prospect of obtaining fresh supplies. The course of the boat had accordingly been altered, and for the last three days they had been sailing due east.

According to the doctor's calculations they were not more than sixty or seventy miles from shore, when the sun set on the previous evening; and as they had been running steadily before the wind all night, he fully expected to catch sight of it as soon as the morning dawned. But the sky was thick and cloudy, and there was a mist over the sea, rendering objects at the distance of a few hundred yards quite undistinguishable.

"We cannot be far from shore," said the doctor. "My observations, I dare say, are not very accurate; but I think I cannot be more than twenty or thirty miles wrong, and according to me we ought to have sighted land, or rather have been near enough to sight it, three or four hours ago."

"I think I can hear the noise of breakers," said Warley, "I have fancied so for the last ten minutes. But there is such a fog, that it is impossible to make out anything."

"You are right," said Mr Lavie, setting himself to listen. "That is the beating of surf; we must be close to the shore, but it will be dangerous to approach until we can see it more clearly. We must go about."

Ernest obeyed; but the alarm had been taken too late. Almost at the same moment that he turned the rudder, the boat struck upon a reef, though not with any great force. Lavie sprang out and succeeded in pushing her off into deep water again, but the blow had damaged her bottom, and the water began to come in.

"Bale her out," shouted Lavie to Frank and Nick as he sprang on board again. "I can see the land now. It's not a quarter of a mile off, and she'll keep afloat for that distance. Take the other oar, Ernest; while they bale we must row for that point yonder."

The fog had partially cleared away, and a low sandy shore became here and there visible, running out into a long projecting spit on their left hand. This was the spot which Lavie had resolved to make for. It was not more than two or three hundred yards distant, and there was no appearance of surf near it. They rowed with all their strength, the other two baling with their hats, in lieu of any more suitable vessels. But the water continued to gain on them, nevertheless, though slowly, and they had approached within thirty yards of the beach, when she struck a second time on a sunk rock, and began to fill rapidly. They all simultaneously leaped out into four-foot water, and by their united strength contrived to drag the boat on until her keel rested on the sand. Lavie then seized the longest rope, and running up the low, shelving shore, secured the end to a huge mass of drift-wood which lay just above high-water mark. Fortunately the tide was now upon the turn, so that in three-quarters of an hour or so she would be left high and dry on the beach.

The first impulse of all four was to fall on their knees and return thanks for their deliverance, even the thoughtless Nick being, for the time, deeply impressed by his narrow escape from death. Then they looked about them. The fog had now almost disappeared, and a long monotonous line of sand hills presented itself in the foreground. Behind this appeared a dreary stretch of sand, unenlivened by tree, grass, or shrub, for two or three miles at least, when it terminated in a range of hills, covered apparently with scrub. Immediately beyond the narrow strip of beach lay a lagoon, extending inland for about a mile. This was evidently connected with the sea at high-water; for a great many fish had been left stranded in the mud, where they were obliged to remain, until the return of the tide again set them at liberty. Presently a low growl from Lion startled them, and they noticed an animal creeping up round a neighbouring sand hill, which on nearer approach they perceived to be a hyena. It was followed by several others of the same kind, which forthwith began devouring the stranded fish, while the latter flapped their tails in vain attempts to escape from the approach of their enemy. Availing themselves of the hint thus offered them, the boys, who had not yet breakfasted, pulled off their shoes and stockings, and followed by Lion, waded into the mud. The hyenas skulked off as they approached, and they soon possessed themselves of several large eels and barbel Mr Lavie, whose appetite also reminded him that he had eaten nothing that morning, gathered a heap of dry weed and drift-wood, and drawing out his burning-glass, soon set them ablaze. Frank undertook to clean and broil the fish, which was soon afterwards served up, and pronounced excellent.

By the time they had finished their meal, all the water had run out of the boat, and the sand was sufficiently dry to enable them to convey their stores on shore. Having completed this, and covered them with tarpaulin to prevent damage from the broiling sun, their next task was to turn her over and examine her bottom. It took the united strength of the four to accomplish this; but it had no sooner been done, than it became evident that it would be useless to bestow further trouble upon her. The first concussion had merely loosened her timbers, but the second had broken a large hole in the bottom; which it was beyond their powers of carpentry to repair, even had they possessed all the necessary tools.

"Thank God she didn't strike on that sharp rock the first time," exclaimed Lavie, as he saw the fracture; "we should not be standing here, if she had."

"Why, we can all swim, Mr Lavie, and it was not more than a quarter of a mile from land," observed Gilbert, surprised.

The doctor made no reply, but he pointed out to sea where the black fins of more than one shark were visible above the surface.

Nick shuddered and turned pale, and all present again offered an inward thanksgiving.

"Well," resumed Frank, after a few moments' silence, "what is to be done, then? I suppose it is pretty certain that she will never float again."

"Well, not certain, Frank," suggested Warley. "There may be some fishermen—settlers, or natives—living about here, and they of course would have boats, and would therefore be able to repair ours. The best thing will be to make search in all directions, and see if we can discover anywhere a fisherman's hut."

"I am afraid there's not much chance of that, Ernest," said Wilmore. "If there were any fishermen about here, we should see their boats, or any way their nets, not to say their cottages; for they would be tolerably sure to live somewhere near the beach."

"The boats might be out to sea, and the nets on board them," suggested Gilbert, "and the huts may be anywhere—hidden behind those hillocks of sand, perhaps."

"So they may, Nick," observed Mr Lavie, "though I fear there is no very great chance of it. It is worth trying for, at all events. Look here, one of us had better go along the shore to the right, and another to the left, until they get to the end of the bay. From thence they will, in all likelihood, be able to see a long way along the coast, and if no villages or single dwellings are visible, it will be of no use making further search for them. It will take several hours to reach the end to the left there, and that to the right is probably about as far off; but it is still so hidden by the fog that, at this distance, it can't be made out."

"And what are the other two to do?" asked Frank.

"They had better stay here and make preparations for supper and passing the night," said Mr Lavie. "It is still tolerably early, but whoever goes out to explore won't be back till late in the afternoon, and will be too tired, I guess, to be willing to set out on a fresh expedition then. Besides, the night falls so rapidly in these latitudes that it wouldn't be safe. Now, I have some skill in hut making, and I think you had better leave that part of the job to me."

"By all means, Charles," said Warley; "and Frank here showed himself such a capital cook this morning, that I suppose he'll want to undertake that office again. Well, I'm quite ready. I should like to take the left side of the bay, Nick, if you've no objection."

"It's all the same to me," said Nick; "anything for a quiet life—and it seems quiet enough out there anyway. Well, then, I suppose we had better be off at once, as I don't want to have to walk very fast. I should like to have Lion, but I suppose he wouldn't follow me."

"No, he's safe to stay with Frank, but you two had better take your guns with you," said Mr Lavie. "I don't suppose you are likely to meet any wild animals on these sand flats—nothing worse than a hyena, at any rate."

"Thank you kindly, Mr Lavie, I don't particularly want to meet even a hyena," said Nick.

"Pooh, Nick, he wouldn't attack you, if he did meet you. But you may want our help for some reason or other, which we can't foresee, and we shall be sure to hear you, if you fire. Here, Nick, you shall have my rifle for the nonce. It is an old favourite of mine, and has seen many a day's sport. And here's Captain Renton's rifle for you, Ernest. By good luck he had asked me to take care of it, so it was safe in my cabin the day we got away. I've never seen it perform; but if it is only one half as good an article as he declares, you'll have no cause to complain of it."

"How was it that the captain didn't take it with him?" asked Gilbert.

"Because they wouldn't let him," said the surgeon. "He asked to be allowed to fetch it, and looked as savage as he dared to look, when they swore they'd allow no firearms to be taken."

"I don't wonder at their not permitting it," observed Wilmore.

"Nor I, Frank. The wonder to me has always been that they let the officers and passengers go at all. But it seems that such of our men as agreed to join these Congo pirates would not do so, except on the express condition that the lives of all on board were to be spared; and the pirates daren't cross them. But we mustn't dawdle here talking. There's plenty to be done by all of us, and more than we can do, too."

Warley and Nick accordingly set off in opposite directions, and Lavie and Frank began their work. They first took an axe from their stores, and choosing from among the drift-wood three of the longest spars, resolved to fix two of them in the ground, and lash the third to their upper ends. They selected for this purpose a hollow between two high sand hills, about a hundred yards above high-water mark. Then they were to cut six more poles, and lay them on either side against the ridge piece, burying the other ends in the sand. Over this frame-work the tarpaulin was to be stretched, and kept in its place by laying some heavy pieces of wood on the lower ends. Thus a small tent would be formed, at the bottom of which the boat's sail was to be spread, forming a convenient place on which to lay their stores, and make up their beds.

Plainly it would occupy a considerable time to complete these arrangements, but they had not advanced half-way, when Nick came hurrying back in a state of the greatest excitement, declaring that he had seen, at a short distance, the roofs of what was evidently a town of considerable size; and on a flat piece of ground adjoining it, a number of men—soldiers they seemed to be—in red and white uniforms, drawn out in long lines, as if on parade.

"A large town, Nick! soldiers in uniform!" repeated Wilmore in great astonishment. "You must be dreaming."

"I assure you I am not," replied Gilbert, whose demeanour showed that he was thoroughly in earnest. "I could see, quite distinctly above the fog, the towers of a church, apparently, and a long row of battlements, evidently part of a line of fortifications; and, through openings in the mist, the red caps and jackets of the soldiers were as plain as anything I ever beheld in my life."

"But it can't be, doctor, can it?" asked Frank. "I am sure I should be glad enough to think we were near any inhabited spot, let alone a large city. But you're pretty certain of our whereabouts, ain't you?"

"Yes; I don't think I can be mistaken very much, and I must be out of all reckoning wrong, if this is true. There is no town, that I know of, on this coast, between the Portuguese settlements, which are something like eight hundred miles to the north of where I suppose we now are, and Cape Town, which is almost as far to the south."

"Well, just come and look for yourself, doctor," said Nick. "It won't take you long. The place is not above two or three miles off at the outside."

"Of course I will go—we'll all go, Nick—Lion and all I am sure I hope with all my heart that you may be right. It will save us a very long and dangerous journey if you are."

He caught up a fowling-piece which had belonged to his friend the purser, and handed Frank the fourth gun, an ordinary seaman's carbine. "Now then, Nick, lead the way."

Gilbert complied, and the whole party stepped out briskly, their curiosity, as well as their interest, being strongly awakened. They toiled through the heavy sand, which was only varied by heaps of drift-wood flung up by the sea, and the rotten carcasses of mud fish, which had been carried too far inland by the tide to be able to recover their native element. The stench, under the burning sun, was almost insupportable, and the three adventurers were greatly relieved, when, after a walk of three-quarters of an hour, the desert of sand was passed, and they ascended a rocky plateau, where some crags, twelve or fifteen feet in height, afforded at least some shelter from the rapidly increasing heat. "We are getting near the place now," observed Nick, as they reached the last of a long chain of rocks, and came upon a wide and apparently level plain, but so much enveloped in mist as to be very imperfectly discerned.

"There it is, I declare," exclaimed Frank, who was the first of the party to turn the corner of the limestone shelf. "There it all is—houses, fortifications, and soldiers, just as Nick said!"

There, indeed, it was. At the distance, as it seemed, of scarcely more than three hundred feet, were seen distinctly the battlemented walls of a city of great size and strength. There were the gateways, the flanking towers, and the embrasures; while behind them rose domes and cupolas, and the sharp-peaked roofs of numberless houses, intermingled with lofty trees. Under the walls ran a broad river, the waters of which rippled brightly in the sunshine, and upon its banks long lines of infantry were drawn up, or what appeared to be infantry, all standing silent and motionless as so many statues.

The two boys gazed in the utmost bewilderment at this spectacle, while Lion bounded forward, evidently meditating a plunge into the cool and sparkling waters. The astonishment of the party was in no way diminished, when the doctor, raising his gun to his shoulder, fired directly at the nearest platoon of soldiers, one of whom was seen to fall. The next moment the whole of his companions rose with loud screams into the air, and dispersed themselves in all directions. Almost at the same moment the walls and battlements of the fortress and ridges of roof behind them wavered and shook, and finally vanished from the scene, as the smoke of a wood fire is lost in the surrounding atmosphere. In their place appeared a low serrated ridge of rock, on which a few stunted shrubs were growing, while in front and behind alike extended the interminable waste of sand.

"Here is your soldier, Nick," said the doctor, as he picked up the carcass of a large flamingo, which his shot had brought down. "Here's his red cap and jacket—his beak and wings, that is to say—and here are his white facings—his neck and chest. You are not the first by a good many that has made that mistake!"

"This is what is called a mirage, then?" said Frank. "I've often heard of it, and longed to see it; and it is a more extraordinary delusion than I could have supposed possible. Why that low line of rock there, and those dwarf shrubs looked as if they were at least sixty feet high. How in the world do you account for it, Mr Lavie? Why even Lion was taken in!"

"I am afraid I cannot give you an explanation, which you will understand very clearly, Frank. It is caused by the inequality of the temperature in the lower strata of the air; which again is the result of the reflected heat of the sun's rays on the barren, sandy plain. While the strata are unequally heated, these curious reflections, which are like those seen in broken mirrors, continue to deceive the eye. Objects appear to be raised high into the air, which in reality are to be found on the surface of the earth, often too they are immensely magnified, as indeed you saw just now; a single stone will seem the size of a house, and an insignificant shrub look as big as a forest tree. But when the sun gains sufficient power to raise all the strata to a uniform heat, the mirage melts away."

"But your shot seemed to disperse it just now."

"So it did. But my shot only disturbed the strata; and if the mirage had not been nearly on the point of vanishing, from the increasing solar heat, I doubt whether the same effect would have followed. But it is time for us to go back to our hut and finish our work. Nick, I suppose you will join us? We may see pretty plainly for ourselves that there are no fishermen's huts in this quarter."

Nick assented, and the three, after a short rest under the shade of the rocks, returned to the spot whence they had set out, and resumed their work. By two o'clock the two uprights were fixed in the sand, and in two hours afterwards the tent was complete. All the stores were then carefully conveyed inside, the keg of gunpowder being buried in the sand to prevent the possibility of accident. Then the two lads set about preparations for supper, which was to consist, like that of the morning, of fish broiled on the embers.

"And a very good supper too," observed Nick; "I don't think I ever ate a finer fish than this cod here."

"It's first-rate, there's no doubt of that," returned Frank; "but I must own I should like something besides. I suppose your flamingo there wouldn't be very good eating?"

"I expect not," replied Lavie. "The flamingo is too gross a feeder to make very good food itself. One might eat it, I dare say, if there was nothing else to be had. I have eaten lion steaks once in my life, but I have no ambition to repeat the experiment. No, I don't propose to make any further use of my flamingo than to cut off one of his beautiful red wings to make a fan of, and hand the rest of the bird over to Lion. What a splendid-looking bird he was; it really seems almost a shame to kill him!"

They all gathered round to admire him. The colours in which nature had dressed him, showed that he was one of her favourite children. The long thin legs—they were two feet and some inches in length—were of the most delicate shade of pink, and shaped with wonderful grace. The short thigh, chest, and neck were covered with down, the softest and whitest that can be imagined. But the great beauty of the creature lay in its wings, in which the brilliant scarlet and pure white hues were intermingled with wonderful delicacy and grace, both colours being bordered and thrown out by the deep black of the under feathers.

"I wish I could stuff that specimen," said the doctor, as he contemplated the dead bird. "It would be the making of a collection. It can't stand less than four foot four, or perhaps four foot six high. However, I'm afraid it's rather out of place to be thinking of collections. It will be a good job," he muttered to himself, "if we are not put into a collection ourselves by some Hottentot or Damara chief But it won't do to hint that to the boys."

He seated himself on one of the casks in the shelter of the tent, and appeared to be watching the preparations for supper, lost, in reality, in a reverie of mingled pain and pleasure. He was roused at last by the information that Warley was returning; and presently the youth himself appeared on the scene, throwing down, to Frank's great satisfaction, a brace of wild ducks which he had been fortunate enough to shoot. His report, however, was not encouraging. He had reached the extremity of the bay, and had ascended an eminence, perhaps two or three hundred feet high; but nothing was to be discerned from it but long wastes of mingled rock and sand, varied here and there by thickets of euphorbia, or monotonous scrub. In the distance indeed were lofty mountains; but it was impossible to say, in that transparent atmosphere, how distant they might be. As regards the more immediate object of his expedition—the discovery of some trace of man—it had been an entire failure.

While Warley was delivering his report to the doctor, the other two were busied in plucking and roasting the ducks. Presently it was announced that all was ready, and the four sat down to their repast with an appetite sharpened by a long day of exertion. It was no sooner over than fatigue began to assert itself in place of hunger. It was agreed that the fire should be kept up all night, and that each should watch for two hours by it. It was now nearly nine o'clock, and the last watch would thus bring them to five in the morning, when it would be desirable that all four should be awakened to the heavy day's work, which (as none of them doubted) lay before them.

Chapter Five

The whole party slept soundly, and by six o'clock were sitting under their tent over the remains of their breakfast. Frank and Nick were on the point of issuing forth to collect some more fish for the mid-day meal, when the doctor called to them to stop.

"It is time," he said, "that we hold a consultation, and come to some resolution respecting our future movements. Sit down here in the shade, and we'll talk the matter over."

The boys obeyed, and took their places; Lion, as usual, seating himself at Frank's side, and occasionally bestowing a broad lick of affection on his face and hands.

"I have made a fresh examination of the boat this morning," began Lavie, "and am quite satisfied that it is impossible for us to repair her. She is an old boat, and wouldn't anyway have lasted much longer, and now she is so much hurt, that no one but a regular boat-builder could make her float again. It is impossible therefore to carry out our original intention of going on to Cape Town by sea. Well, then, we must hit on some other plan."

"Wouldn't it be the simplest way to travel along the line of coast the whole way?" suggested Ernest. "As far as I remember my geography, there are no bays running far inland, or very wide rivers to interfere with us."

"You're right, Ernest," rejoined Lavie. "There are nothing but small bays all the way, and until we reached the mouth of the Gariep, there would be no rivers to interfere with us."

"And when we did reach the Gariep, said Frank, we should be pretty safe to fall in with some settlers or, any way, natives, who, 'for a consideration,' would help us through the rest of our journey. I think Ernest's advice very good."

"I should think it so also, Frank," said the surgeon, "if I didn't happen to know something of the line of country proposed. I have never been along it myself, but I have met people who know it well. It is one long sandy waste the entire way—no trees, no grass, scarcely even a rock; and if there are any water-springs, they are so few and scanty, that it is almost the same thing as if there were none at all. There would be no food to be obtained, no shade from the sun, and no resting-place at night, as it would be impossible to carry our tent with us. And, to wind up, we should certainly not meet with a human being from the beginning of our journey to its end."

"Well, that is pretty nearly enough, I think," observed Nick, "I have no fancy to be broiled like a fish on a gridiron, or have a leg of nothing and no turnips for dinner, like the clown in a pantomime. Let us hear what you propose."

"I advise that we should travel towards the east, until we come to the banks of one of the rivers which run southward into the Gariep. I know there are several at no very great distance from the coast: we can follow any one of these to its junction with the great river. When we have once got there, I have no doubt what Frank suggested is true enough. We shall come to the farmhouse of a Dutch boor, or a Hottentot village, or fall in with a hunting party, and so find the means of reaching Cape Town."

"That sounds feasible," said Frank. "We shall be sure of water, at all events, by going that way, and water's the first thing to be thought of."

"And there'll be plenty of game, most likely," added Lavie, "and, any way, fish."

"And shade from the heat of the sun, and resting-places at night," said Warley.

"But how about the wild beasts and the snakes?" struck in Nick. "Wouldn't it be better to make a canoe, or a raft, and sail down the river itself?"

"That is not a bad idea, Nick," said Frank. "What do you say to that, Charles?"

"That it would be a very good idea on some rivers, but not on these," answered Lavie. "Nick has never seen one of these South African rivers, or he'd never suggest it. At times, the channels here are reduced to mere threads, along which no boat that was ever made could pass; at others, they are swollen to raging torrents, which would shatter them to fragments. A boat journey to the Gariep is out of the question."

"Very well, then, we must make the journey along the banks," said Warley. "Of course we must follow your advice, Charles. You know a good deal about the country between this and Table Bay, while we know absolutely nothing. I suppose you would recommend that we should set off, as soon as possible, for the nearest river that runs southward?"

"Yes," said Lavie, "there is no kind of object in delaying here. There is neither food nor shelter to be had here, neither shade nor water; and the stench from the mud and the dead fish is very far from fragrant. I counsel that we move off with as little delay as possible."

"Hear, hear," said Frank; "I am quite of the same mind. Well, then, Charles, the next thing is, what are we to take with us? The boat would have held as much as we were likely to want; but our backs and pouches are different things."

"Quite so, Frank—that was the next thing I was going to speak about. We must, of course, leave by far the greater part of our cargo behind. In fact, we must cumber ourselves with as little baggage as possible. But some things will be absolutely necessary. There are the guns and powder-flasks and bullets. We cannot do without them."

"That is voted, *nem. con.*," said Warley; "and there is the flint and steel and tinder-box. The doctor's burning-glass will be no good when the sun doesn't shine."

"And we shall want the gridiron, and the knife and spoon and cup, and the iron pot for cooking and holding water," struck in Nick.

"Each of us ought to carry a change of linen," said Mr Lavie, "and a second pair of shoes; but no more, I think. I suppose one brush and comb must serve all four."

"I hope you'll take your lancets, Charles, and some physic, in case of any of us being taken ill," suggested Warley.

"I am not likely to forget that, Ernest," returned the surgeon. "Very well, then, that will be all. We had better each provide ourselves with the articles agreed on, make a hearty meal off some of the salt meat and biscuit, and then set off at once, leaving everything else in the boat, for the benefit of any one who may be thrown up, like ourselves, on these barren flats."

No one urging farther objection, this programme was forthwith carried out. Belts and knapsacks were adjusted, the various articles required for the general use were divided between the four, a hasty meal was eaten, and then each man took his gun, and the party bade farewell to the old boat and low sandy shore, and set forth on their travels.

They soon surmounted the rocky shelf which they had visited on the previous day, and, passing through an opening in the barren hills, entered a valley, which seemed even more dreary than the scene they had just quitted. On either side were rocks of a dull grey colour, broken into all kinds of fantastic shapes, and full of holes and winding caverns, which suggested the possible neighbourhood of venomous snakes. Nick, in particular, cast many a suspicious glance at these orifices; which seemed to his imagination the lurking-places, whence at any moment the hideous head of a cobra or python might rear itself, preparatory to a deadly spring on its victim. He was greatly relieved when, after an hour or two of walking, the valley gradually opened into a wide plain, and patches of vegetation began to show themselves. The euphorbia was the first to appear, with its tall stiff bunches of foliage, each of which bore a curious resemblance to a chandelier with its cluster of candles. Then the kameel-doorn, the dwarf acacia, and the wild pomegranate began to vary the landscape with their contrast of colours; and presently there appeared the aloe and the mimosa, the bright yellow of the last-named reminding Ernest of the gorse and broom among which his walks had so often lain.

But though there was a great improvement in respect of the scenery, its most important accessory, water, was nowhere to be found. Lavie looked anxiously on all sides for some indication of the vicinity of the river; which, if his information was correct, lay only a few miles eastward of the spot where they had landed. They could hardly have mistaken the way, for no other opening in the rocks had been visible in any direction, except that which they had pursued; and the gradual downward slope of the glen could hardly end in anything but water. But they had now been travelling since mid-day, only sitting down to rest for a few minutes, at intervals of two hours or so; and now the sunset was near at hand. He was greatly rejoiced when, on turning the corner of a dense clump of euphorbias, they came in sight of what was evidently the course of the river, though the dense bushes on either side hid the stream from view.

"Hurrah! my lads," shouted the doctor; "now for a good drink, and a cool bath too, if the water is only deep enough."

He broke into a run as he spoke, and was joined by the other three, who forgot their weariness and anxiety in the excitement of the moment Lion bounded along at Frank's side, as eager apparently as his master. They were the first to reach the fringe of shrubs, into which they plunged with headlong haste. But the next moment there came a loud cry of disappointment; the others hurried up, but only to catch sight of Frank and Lion standing over a dry bed of sand, which had evidently once been the channel of the river. There was now not the slightest trace of water to be seen. The sand was not even moist. Lavie now felt extremely anxious. There were rivers he knew lying to the eastward, and that at no very great distance, twenty or thirty miles at the outside, and probably they were not so far off as even twenty miles: and if so, the strength of the whole party might hold out until the nearest was attained. But then the lads were not used to roughing it in the desert; and they might miss the track and become too exhausted to travel further. He had fully reckoned on finding water at the spot which they had now reached, or he would have brought a supply with him from the water-cask in the boat, which had still contained several gallons. But it was too late now to think of returning that night to the seashore, and besides, such a step would naturally alarm and depress his companions. The best chance would be to proceed on their way as long as daylight lasted, and take the chance of falling in with some of the springs or pools, which are scattered about, though at rare intervals, in this inhospitable land.

"Well, that's a nuisance," he exclaimed aloud, as he gazed into the blank faces, and marked the dry parched lips of the boys. "That's a nuisance, but it can't be helped. Better luck next time. We had better step out as fast as we can while daylight lasts. We are safe to come to water, sooner or later, even in this country."

"All right, Charles," said Frank; "the sooner we reach it the better. We must step out, best pace."

The other two made no remark, but they also quickened their walk. Emerging from the bushes, Mr Lavie pursued his route due eastward, though the path he followed did not seem very likely to fulfil his hopes. It lay along a bare hillside, over which huge boulders of rock were scattered; while the vegetation growing more and more scarce every mile of the way, at last ended in a waste as barren as that which they had traversed at the outset of their journey. It was, indeed, very much the same character of scenery as before, only that they were no longer shut in by a hollow defile in the hill. On either sides there rose high shelves of stone pierced by what seemed to be caverns running far inward. Between these masses of rock, long vistas of bare stony plains presented themselves, seeming to the belated travellers the very picture of desolation.

The sun was now fast setting; there remained scarcely an hour of daylight, and for all they could see, Lavie and his party would have to continue their journey by starlight, or bivouac on the sand. Suddenly at this moment, Lion, who had been tramping along for the last hour or two, as much depressed apparently as any of the party, stood still, sniffed the air for a moment or two, and then sprang forward with a joyous bark, turning round, when he had proceeded a few yards, as if inviting Frank to follow him.

"Don't call him back, Frank," said Mr Lavie as Wilmore shouted after him. "His instinct is much keener than ours. Either there is some animal near at hand, which you may shoot for supper; or, as I earnestly hope may be the case, he scents water. Cock your gun, and go after him."

"I am afraid there is but little chance of his finding water here," said Ernest, as Wilmore hastened forward. "There is nothing to be seen anywhere but hard crag-stone and dry sand. But he may put up some game among the rocks there which he is scrambling up. Ha! and so he has," he added the moment after, as a steinbok came bounding down the cliff. "Now, then, to test Captain Renton's rifle."

He drew the trigger as he spoke, and the animal dropped on its knees, but rose the next minute and was making off, when a shot from Lavie again brought it down. They ran up and found that the steinbok was already dead. Ernest's bullet had struck it in the side, and inflicted what would probably have proved a mortal wound, though it would, for the time, have succeeded in effecting its escape. But Lavie had aimed directly at the heart, and his shot having gone true, death was instantaneous.

"Hurrah!" shouted Frank, at this moment, waving his cap on the shelf of rock above. "Three cheers for old Lion. It is all right now."

"All right as regards the meat, Frank," said Nick, "but how about the drink? A fellow in this wicked world requires to drink as well as to eat—at all events, I do."

"Meat," repeated Frank, peering over the edge of the precipice, which might perhaps be a dozen feet in height. "Have you got any meat? Did you kill anything when you fired just now?"

"To be sure we did, Frank," said Warley. "We're not given to miss in our part of the world. We've brought down as nice a young steinbok as you'd wish to eat. If you'd only find us some water to match, we should be quite set up."

"Water! why, that is just what we *have* found. Here has old Lion lighted on a well of water, the most delicious that any fellow ever drank of."

"Water! what, up there? You don't say so. Hurrah! here goes." Laying down their guns, the three thirsty travellers speedily climbed the stony heights, and stood by their companion's side, when their eyes were gratified by a very strange as well as a very welcome spectacle.

In the very middle of the plateau of rock surmounting the precipitous ascent appeared a circular hole, some three or four feet in diameter, and so deep, that its bottom could not be discerned. The cavity was evidently natural; nor indeed did either the Hottentots or the Bushmen—the only tribes by whom the spot was ever visited—possess either the tools or the patience necessary for so laborious a work. It was doubtless what is sometimes called, though most erroneously, a freak of nature—one of those beneficent provisions, more than one of which we shall have to notice in the course of this story, by which the providence of God supplies the wants of His creatures in the desolate wastes; without which help they must inevitably perish. The hole had retained the rain, with which it had been filled a week or two previously, and the water being sheltered by the surrounding rocks from the burning rays of the sun, was sweet, clear, and deliciously cool to the taste. The cup was passed round and round again, before the thirsty travellers were satisfied, and even then they were half disposed to envy Lion's simpler mode of satisfying his drought, viz., by plunging head over ears into the well, and imbibing at every pore the refreshing moisture.

At length thirst was satisfied, and gave way to hunger. Descending from the rocky platform, they set themselves to prepare their supper. Nick collected the grey leafless shrubs, which grew in abundance among the rocks; and which, though anything but picturesque in appearance, made capital firewood. Frank cut up the carcass, broiling some parts of it on the gridiron, and boiling as much more as the pot would hold. It was dark long before their preparations were completed, and they had to eat their dinner by the light of their fire, assisted by the stars, for the moon had not yet risen. But the road to the mouth is very easy to find, especially when men are hungry. They all four soon finished a most excellent meal. Then the fragments of the repast were handed over to Lion—Frank declared he ought to have been called to the chair, and his health drunk with all the honours—and arrangements were made for the night. Some of the shrubs which Nick had collected, and which had not been used for the fire, made very comfortable beds. These were spread inside one of the largest caverns, though not before Nick had carefully examined its recesses by the help of a blazing log, to make sure that they contained no venomous reptiles. Lion stretched himself out to sleep at the entrance of the cave; and it was considered that his instinct might be trusted to warn them against the approach of danger, without additional precautions. In a few minutes they were all sound asleep.

They might have slept for perhaps three hours, when Frank, whose slumbers were unusually light, was roused by a low growl close to him. Looking round, he saw Lion standing in the entrance of the cave over the remains of the steinbok, only a part of which had been eaten. Frank remembered that the carcass had been left at some little distance from their sleeping-place; and the dog, therefore, must have dragged it to its present place. Something unusual must have occurred to make him do this; and besides, the attitude of the animal, his hair bristling, his chest advanced, his muscles stretched to their full tension, and the fierce glare in his eye showed plainly enough that he beheld some formidable enemy.

"A hyena has scented the carcass, I have no doubt," thought Frank, "but I can hardly afford to throw away a shot upon him. He must be driven away, though, or we shall get no rest."

He stepped noiselessly up to the entrance, but recoiled instantly at the sight he beheld, and it was with difficulty that he stifled a cry of alarm. At a distance of about four yards, the outline of its magnificent figure clearly revealed in the bright moonlight, a lion of the largest size was crouching, evidently preparing itself to spring! Frank had never seen one of these animals, except in captivity. About a twelvemonth before, during his stay in London, Captain Wilmore had taken him to Exeter 'Change, where one or two lions were exhibited. But these were small of their kind, and enfeebled by age and long captivity. They bore no more resemblance to the glorious and terrible creature with which Frank was now confronted, than the trickling stream which glides lazily over the ledge of the rocks bears to the foaming cataract, swollen by snows and rains.

He perceived in a moment what had taken place. The lion had come to the water to drink; and the dog, scenting the approach of some beast of prey, had possessed itself of the remains of the steinbok, which would otherwise fall a prey to the marauder. The lion in its turn had discovered the vicinity of food, and had leaped down from the rock to seize it. All this passed through Frank's mind in a moment. It could hardly be called thinking, but was rather like a sudden revelation. He felt, too, the necessity of killing the monster without a moment's loss of time, or all their lives would be imperilled. He stooped noiselessly, and picked up the nearest gun, which chanced by good fortune to be Captain Renton's rifle. Frank was a steady shot, as the reader has already been told; but he had never fired at a mark like this. He recalled, on the instant, what he had heard Mr Lavie say that the only spots in a wild animal's body in which a bullet could be lodged with the certainty of causing instant death, were the ear, the eye, and immediately behind the shoulder, where there was a direct passage to the heart. It was impossible to aim at either ear or shoulder in the present instance, as the animal was standing directly facing him. The eye, therefore, which flashed large and yellow upon him in the broad glare of the moonlight—the eye must be his mark. He raised the rifle and brought it down to the level of his eye, drawing trigger the moment he had done so. It was well for him that his aim was true, and his hand steady. As the barrel dropped to its place, the metal flashed in the moonbeam, and its glitter seemed to rouse the creature from its momentary torpor. It rose into the air at the very moment at which the bullet struck it, and if the latter had not been aimed with the most perfect accuracy, there would have been an end of the mastiff, and probably of his master also. But the shot passed directly through the eyeball, and lodged in the brain, causing instantaneous death. The muscular power communicated to the limbs failed even before the leap was accomplished. A furious roar burst from the king of the forest as he felt the wound, but it died off abruptly, and the vast carcass fell, a lifeless mass, within two feet of the entrance of the cavern.

THE MIDNIGHT VISITOR.

Chapter Six

The noise of the gun, and the dying roar of the lion, roused the whole party from their slumbers; and in another minute they were standing round the fallen monster, eagerly asking for information.

"You did that well, Frank," said the surgeon, after carefully examining the wound; "just in the right place, and at the right moment. Half an inch either way, or ten seconds later, and there would have been a very different story to tell. You'll be a mighty hunter one of these days, I expect. It's very few who have made their *début* with a shot like this. But we must make sure that there are no more of them about. It's strange that I should have forgotten the likelihood of beasts coming down at night to drink, or the risk there would be of an encounter between them and Lion. Get in, you old rogue," he continued, giving the dog a playful kick in the ribs, and driving him inside the cave, where he secured him to a large fragment of rock. "You don't know what an escape you've had. You are ready enough to fight, I don't doubt, but 'cave cui incurras,' as the Latin grammar says, Master Lion; a single single blow of that brute's paw would have been enough to break a horse's back, let alone a dog's. There, stand in the entrance with your gun, Nick, and keep a sharp look out, while we go to examine the well."

The lads took their guns, and the three making a considerable *détour* to the left, cautiously ascended the rocks, until they gained a higher shelf than that in which the well was situated, and then looked over. The moon had by this time begun to set, and the steep summit of the crags behind them intercepted its light, throwing the shelf into deep shadow. A dark mass was indistinctly visible, lying immediately on the edge of the well, partly indeed protruding over it. "That's the lioness drinking," whispered Frank. "She has most likely followed her lord to the water, and has only just arrived here."

"Most likely," answered the doctor in the same cautious tone, "but don't fire. You can't see her plain enough to take a sure aim at her, and a mere wound would only enrage her. Leave her to me. As soon as she has done drinking, she'll get up, and then we shall have a clear sight of her."

They waited patiently for several minutes. It became evident that the animal was not, as they had supposed, drinking, but was either asleep or refreshing herself with the cool air, which the close proximity of the water produced. In either case it was impossible to conjecture how long she might retain her present attitude. "Let drop a stone upon her, Ernest," whispered the doctor. "That will put her up. I have my rifle all ready."

Warley looked round him. There was no stone near at hand, but he detached his shot-flask from his belt and threw it with a skilful aim, striking the lioness on the flank. She instantly sprang to her feet; but just as Ernest discharged his missile there came a dense cloud over the moon, and the figure of the animal was lost to sight. Before the cloud could quite pass away again, the lioness gave vent to a low savage roar. She had caught sight, notwithstanding the darkness, of the carcass below, and sprang down to examine it. "I wonder how Nick will get on with her?" exclaimed Frank. "He's no great shot. I think we had better go down to the rescue. Just hold my gun, Ernest, while I slip down."

Handing his rifle to his companion, he slid down the projecting face of the precipice, feet first, and then called to Warley to lower his weapon after him. Mr Lavie reached the shelf almost at the same moment, and both pressed forward with some anxiety to see what was passing below. The spectacle they beheld would have been extremely ludicrous, if it had not been still more alarming.

Forgetting or disregarding Lavie's directions, Gilbert had laid aside his gun as soon as his companions left him, and had gone to make an examination of the lion—an animal which he had never before seen. He was greatly struck by the enormous size and vast strength of creature, and stood for a few moments considering whether he might not be able to carry away some souvenir of the adventure. A lock of his shaggy mane, or one of his huge teeth, were the first mementos which suggested themselves to him. It would be difficult, however, to obtain one of the last-named articles—that is without the help of certain tools which they had not in their possession. No, it must be a lock of the gentleman's hair, which could be easily enough to procure, and equally easy to preserve, though the keepsake would be somewhat cumbrous. He picked up the knife, which Frank had left on a slab of stone near the entrance of the cave, and proceeded to choose the place whence the ringlet was to be cut. Suddenly it occurred to him that the tuft at the extremity of the tail would be extremely suitable for the purpose; or why, by the way, should he not retain the entire tail? Mr Lavie had been telling them, only that evening, of the practice adopted by the Bushmen of wearing a belt round the waist, by which the pangs of hunger were considerably mitigated. To judge by what happened yesterday, such a belt might be extremely serviceable, and the skin of the lion's tail would make a famous belt. At all events there could be no harm in cutting the tail off; and this he effected easily enough by the aid of Mr Lavie's hatchet. He was still engaged in examining his treasure by the imperfect light, when a whirling noise was heard over head, and a large object of some kind dropped within a few feet of him.

A good deal startled, Nick let fall the hatchet and grasping the upper end of the tail with both hands, whirled it, like a flail round his head. At the same moment the moon again broke out, and he perceived that his new companion was a large lioness, whose fierce growls were evidently the preliminary to a still fiercer assault. Nick gave himself up for dead; and if the attention of the animal had in the first instance been directed to him, there would indeed have been but small hope of escape for him. But the lioness had scented the dead body, and she proceeded to examine it all over, sniffing the tainted air, and uttering every now and then a low howl, like a mourning cry. Nick would have retreated to the cover of the cavern, but a feeling of fascination held him to the spot; and he continued to swing the tail right and left, apparently hardly conscious of what he was doing. Presently, the mood of the lioness seemed to change, and the notion to occur to her of taking vengeance for the ruthless slaughter of her mate. She glared fiercely at Nick, and gave vent to a low roar. She would, in fact, have instantly sprung upon him, but that the whirl of the tail immediately in front of her nose, dazed and bewildered her for the moment, and kept her at bay. This could not, however, have lasted, and Nick's career would soon have been run, if rescue had not been at hand. But at this moment the crack of the doctor's rifle was heard, and the brute, shot through the heart, rolled over in the death struggle.

"Bravo, Nick," exclaimed Lavie, as he leaped down from the rock. "Hercules himself never wielded his club more valiantly, than you did the lion's tail. I was sorry to keep you so long in suspense, but the beast persistently kept her back towards me, till just the moment when I fired. If I had only wounded her, she would have sprung on you all the same."

"All right, doctor," said Nick; "you couldn't do more than bring me off with a whole skin. And it's more than I deserve, too, for I didn't obey orders."

"Well, now I suppose we may go back to bed?" suggested Frank. "It's not much past midnight, and I feel as if I wanted plenty more sleep before morning. I don't fancy we shall have many more visitors to-night."

"No," said the doctor, "we may sleep soundly now. Animals don't often go near a fountain where they have seen lions drinking. Indeed, the shots which have been fired would probably be enough to keep them away. Let us turn in again, by all means."

His prognostications were fulfilled. There was no further disturbance that night, and when the travellers awoke on the following morning, they were in high health and spirits.

"Do you intend to take the same track which we were following up yesterday, Charles?" asked Warley, as they sat at breakfast, "or have you altered your mind about it?"

"I see no reason for changing it," replied the surgeon. "I am sure the river, which Vangelt told me of, cannot be above fifteen miles off at the outside, and when we are once there, it is all, comparatively speaking, plain sailing. I don't know how far this kind of country may last, but I feel sure it cannot be for any great distance. Notwithstanding yesterday's experience, I don't advise our taking water with us, or anything but a few slices of meat I am persuaded that we shall not suffer a second time, as we did yesterday; and carrying water always hampers travellers terribly."

All readily gave their assent to his suggestions, and before six o'clock the travellers were again in motion. They journeyed on for several miles, the bare rocks and sand still continuing the main features of the landscape: but about twelve o'clock their eyes were relieved by the appearance of wooded slopes in the distance. Presently they came to a small pool, surrounded by a grove of oomahaamas and acacias, among the branches of which they noticed a quantity of grey-crested parrots, which kept up an incessant screaming, from the moment the travellers came in sight to that of their departure.

"Here's a good place for a halt," suggested Ernest. "This shade is most refreshing, and the water seems clear and cool."

"I am quite of your mind, Ernest," said Nick, flinging himself at full length on the grass at the edge of the pool. "Exhausted nature can't go further without a respite. Now, if any one would be so good as to shoot two or three of those parrots, that are actually crying out to be shot, they would make a famous—What are you up to now, man?" he added sharply, as he felt a sudden blow on his shin. "You would do well to take care what you are doing."

"*You* would do well to take care," retorted Warley. "Do you see what was crawling up your leg?" He held up, as he spoke, a dead snake about eighteen inches long, with a curious-looking horn on either side of its head. "If I hadn't hit him on the neck the moment I saw him, he'd have bitten your hand to a certainty. He was making straight for it."

"A snake!" cried Nick, starting up in horror. "So there is, I declare. The nasty brute! I don't know whether it is venomous or not, but I'm much obliged, even if it isn't. They are not nice things up a fellow's leg!"

"Hand him over here," said Charles Lavie. "Oh ay, I know this fellow. He is called the cerastes, and is venomous, I believe, though not one of the worst kinds of poisonous snakes. You are well out of it, Nick, I can tell you, and must look more carefully about you in this country before you sit down in a place like this. Some of the reptiles are so nearly the colour of the ground, or the trees, that even an old stager may be taken in."

"Are there any large pythons in these parts?" asked Warley. "I've heard two quite different accounts. One says that they are never found so far south as this; the other, that they are to be met with thirty or forty feet long, and as thick round as a stout man. What is the truth of the matter?"

"Well, the truth is something between the two, I believe, as is generally the case," said the surgeon. "They are certainly not common in Southern Africa, since people who have lived here all their lives have never seen one. But now and then they are to be met with. I know persons who have seen serpents' skins thirty feet long in the possession of natives; and one case I heard of, in which a skin was exhibited fully ten feet longer than that."

"Are they difficult to kill?" asked Frank.

"Not if you bide your time," said Lavie. "If you come upon them when they are hungry, they—the larger ones, that is—are more than a match for even the strongest men: and unless they are approached unawares, and wounded, so as to destroy their muscular power, a struggle with them would be most dangerous. But after they have gorged their prey, they are killed as easily as so many sheep—more easily in fact, for they are quite torpid."

"What are the worst snakes found in these parts?" inquired Gilbert. "The cobra and the puff adder, I should say," returned the surgeon. "The first will spring at you as if it was discharged out of some engine, and with such force, that if it fails to strike its mark it will overshoot the spot by several feet. The natives call it the hair-serpent, and are in great terror of it. If no sufficient remedy is applied, its bite will cause death in less than an hour."

"*Is* there any sufficient remedy?" rejoined Nick. "I thought there was no cure."

"It's not so bad as that, Nick. There are remedies for most bites—the cobra's for instance. There is a root which the mangoust always eats, when it feels itself bitten by a cobra, and which is, so far as is known, a complete cure. Eau de luce and sweet milk are generally given in this country for a snake's bite, and the natives have beans and serpent stones, which, it is said, effect a cure. But the best thing to do — what I should have done in your case, Nick, if you had been bitten — is, first to fasten a ligature as tight as possible above the wounded part, and then cauterise or cut away the injured flesh. Snakes' bites are nasty things in these hot countries, and one can't be too careful. But come, it is time we move on again. We ought to reach the river banks early in the afternoon."

They recommenced their march accordingly, and had proceeded half a mile or so further, when Frank suddenly called upon them to stop.

"What can that noise be?" he said. "I have heard it two or three times in the course of the last few minutes. It doesn't sound like the cry of a bird, or beast either. And yet I suppose it must be."

"I didn't hear anything," said Gilbert. "Nor I," added Warley. "But my hearing is not nearly as good as Frank's. I've often noticed that."

"Let us stop and listen," suggested Charles.

They all stood still, intently listening. Presently a faint sound was wafted to them, apparently from a great distance — from the edge of the sandy desert, they fancied, which was still visible beyond the wooded tracts.

"No," said Charles, when the sound had been twice repeated, "that is not the cry of any animal, with which I am acquainted. It sounds more like a human voice than anything else. If it was at all likely that there was any other party of travellers in these parts, I should think they were hailing us. But nothing can be more improbable than that."

"Still it is possible," urged Warley, "and they may be in want of our help. Ought we not to go and find out the truth?"

"I think you are right, Ernest," said Frank.

"Well, I don't know," urged Gilbert, nervously. "I've heard all sorts of stories of voices being heard in the deserts, enticing people to their destruction, and it may be some ruse of the savages about here, who want to get us into their hands, to possess themselves of our guns. What do you say, doctor?"

"Why, as for the voices, Nick, I've heard the stories you speak of, which have been told chiefly by persons who had lost their way and were nearly dead from cold and hunger. Under such circumstances, when people's nerves and senses begin to fail them, they fancy all sorts of strange things. No doubt, too, there are all sorts of acoustic deceptions in these wild regions, as there are optical delusions; but I don't think we four — all of us in sound health — are likely to be so deceived —"

"But how about the savages, doctor?" interposed Nick, anxiously.

"Well, if these were the backwoods of America, and we had the Red Indians to deal with, there would be a good deal in your suggestion. But neither the Hottentots nor the Bushmen are given to stratagems of this kind. However, we'll move warily, and if any treachery is designed, we shall be pretty sure to baffle it."

They turned off in the direction whence the cry had come, keeping to the open ground, and giving a wide berth to any clump of trees or underwood which might harbour an enemy. Every now and then they paused to listen for the sound, which was regularly repeated, at intervals apparently of two or three minutes, and grew more distinct as they advanced. It was now certain that the cry was human, and sounded like that of a full-grown man.

"We are getting a good deal nearer," observed Warley, as they passed the last patch of trees, and entered once more the sandy wilderness. "I should say we must be almost close, only I don't see any place where the person who is crying out in this manner can be hidden."

"It comes from that heap of stones there," exclaimed Frank, "that heap to the left, I mean—about two hundred yards further on."

"I see the stones, Frank, plain enough," said Mr Lavie, "but a man couldn't be hidden among them. You call it a heap of stones, but there is no heap. There is not so much as one lying upon another."

"Nevertheless the cry comes from there," said Warley; "I heard it the last time quite plainly. Let us go up and see."

They cautiously approached the spot in question, where there were about thirty or forty moderate-sized stones scattered on the plain. As they advanced the mysterious call was again heard.

"I see who it is that's making it," shouted Wilmore. "It's a fellow whose head is just above ground. I took his head for a black stone, with a lot of moss growing on it. But now I can see that it is a head, though the features are turned away from us."

They hurried up, and found that Frank was right. The stones were lying round what seemed to have been a dry well. In this a man had been buried up to his neck, the chin being just above the level of the ground. It did not appear that he was conscious of their approach; for at the interval of every two or three minutes he continued to give vent to the shrill monotonous cry, which had attracted their attention.

"What in the world can this mean!" exclaimed Nick. "The fellow can't have tumbled into the well, and the stones have fallen in after him, I suppose?"

"Is it some penance, do you think, that he is undergoing?" suggested Warley.

"Or a punishment for a crime he has committed?" said Wilmore.

"It may be a punishment for some offence," said Mr Lavie, "though I never heard of the Hottentots punishing their people in that way, and the man is plainly a Hottentot. As for anything else, of course it is quite impossible that he can have got jammed up in this way by accident; and the Hottentots know nothing of penances. Such a thing has never been heard of among them. But the first thing is to get the poor fellow out and give him something to restore him; for he is half dead with thirst and exposure to the sun, and does not seem conscious of what is passing."

They fell to with a will, and had soon so far released the captive, that he was able to draw his breath freely and swallow a little brandy, which Mr Lavie poured on his tongue. He then opened his eyes for a moment, gazing with the utmost bewilderment and wonder on the dress and appearance of the figures round him; and then closed them again with a low groan.

"They meant this—the beggars that holed him in after this fashion," observed Frank. "The stones are fitted round him as carefully as though they had been building a wall. And, look! the poor wretch's arms are fastened by a thong to his sides. What brutes! Hand us the knife, Nick, and I'll cut them. How tough they are!"

It needed a strong hand and a sharp blade to sever the stout thongs, which on subsequent examination were found to consist of rhinoceros hide. But when his arms were at length free, the man made no effort to use them. It was evident that they were so benumbed by the forced restraint in which they had so long been kept, that he had lost all power over them. They were obliged to continue to remove the stones, until his feet were completely released, before he could be extricated from the hole; and when this was effected, it was only by the joint strength of the four Englishmen, the Hottentot himself being unable to render any assistance.

He was now carried to the shade of the nearest trees; Nick ran back to their recent resting-place, and returned with the iron pot full of water, while Warley and Wilmore, under the surgeon's direction, chafed his limbs. By the time of Gilbert's return their efforts had been successful. The sufferer once more opened his eyes, and making signs that the water should be handed to him, drank a long and refreshing draught. "He'll do now," observed Nick, as he witnessed this feat. "There's no more fear for his health after that. But I should like to know who he is, and how he came there. I say, blacky, what may your name happen to be, and how did you come to be boxed up after that fashion, like a chimney-sweep stuck in a narrow flue?"

To the astonishment of the whole party, Nick's question was answered.

"Omatoko my name. Tank Englishman much for pull him out. Omatoko soon die, if they not come. Bushmen bury Omatoko one, two day ago. Good men, give Omatoko food, or he die now."

Chapter Seven

Nick started back at the unexpected reply. "Who'd have thought that?" he exclaimed. "I should just as soon have expected to have heard Lion talk English."

"Well, it wasn't very good English," remarked Warley, "but it was as much to the purpose as if he had been Lindley Murray himself. I suppose the first thing is to comply with his request. I have got a biscuit in my pocket, which I brought away from the boat I dare say he can eat that."

"Not a doubt of it," said Nick; "and I guess he'll soon dispose of this slice of steinbok too. The worst of it is, that I had meant it for my own supper. But one can't let the poor wretch starve."

"We'll all contribute something," said the doctor, "and make him out a sufficient supper, I have no doubt. He mustn't eat very much at a time. But the first thing is to carry him to some sheltered place, where we can make him up a comfortable bed. He must have a long rest before he will be good for anything."

"Carry him, hey!" cried Nick doubtfully, as he contemplated the prostrate figure of the Hottentot; who, for one of his race, was unusually tall and large of frame. "How are we to do that, I wonder? He weighs twelve stone, I'll go bail for it, if he weighs an ounce, and we don't happen to have a horse and cart convenient."

"We can manage it easily enough," was the answer; "our guns and these thongs will make a very tolerable stretcher. Draw the charges first, though. It wouldn't be safe to carry the guns loaded."

Ernest complied, and then the doctor set about the construction of his litter. He first fastened a rifle and a gun together, reversing the direction of the barrels, so as to form a kind of staff out of them, about six feet long, with the stocks at the two ends. The other rifle and gun were then secured after the same manner, and thus the poles of the stretcher were formed. They were then tied together, about two feet apart from one another, by half a dozen thongs. The machine was now placed on the ground, and the Hottentot laid on the thongs. Then the stocks at one end were raised, and laid on the doctor's shoulders, who bent on one knee and stooped as near to the ground as he could. The other two ends were next placed in like fashion on the shoulders of Ernest who had put himself into the like attitude. Frank and Nick now took their stations in the middle of the litter, each placing one shoulder under the pole. Then Lavie gave the word and they all rose together.

"Capitally managed!" exclaimed the doctor approvingly. "Now step all together, and we'll have him under the shelter of the trees in less than a quarter of an hour."

They moved off, walking quickly and steadily, and in less than the time named by Lavie, approached the friendly cover of the thicket. As they came near, a steinbok which had been feeding apparently under a tree, bounded out of the covert, passing within twenty yards of them.

"Alas! alas!" exclaimed Nick, "there goes our supper that should have been! That is the worst of doing a good action! One is sure to be punished for it!"

"Well, Nick, I don't know about that," said Warley. "If we hadn't gone to look after the Hottentot, I don't think we should have seen anything of the steinbok. He wouldn't have come anywhere near us, I expect."

"No, you may be sure of that," observed the doctor, as they lowered their burden to the ground, and laid him on some soft grass under the shade of a large mimosa. "And what is more, I doubt whether our good action will not be rewarded in this instance. Look here, the steinbok was feeding on this melon, when we startled him. See the marks of his teeth, and here are the stalks of one or two others which he has eaten. I noticed these melons as I went by, but I was afraid to meddle with them, as I had never seen any exactly like them, and some melons in this country are more or less poisonous. But the steinbok wouldn't have eaten them if they hadn't been wholesome food, and so we may venture on them too. I have no doubt we shall find them very refreshing."

Frank and Nick accordingly began pulling them up, while the surgeon applied himself to the restoration of his patient, who was still lying in a half-conscious state. But the cool air and soft bed, together with the restoratives, which from time to time were applied, presently brought him round, and he was able to eat as much food as was judged good for him. After partaking of this and another draught of cold water, he fell into a sound sleep, which seemed likely to last for several hours.

"It is still early in the afternoon," remarked the doctor, as they sat down to their dinner of steinbok and melons, the latter of which proved most delicious; "it is still quite early, and I don't suppose we can have gone more than a dozen miles since breakfast. Nevertheless, I think we must remain here. This poor fellow isn't well enough to be left yet, though he may be to-morrow morning."

"No, we can't leave the poor wretch," said Warley, "particularly after what he told us about the Bushmen. They may be lurking about somewhere in the neighbourhood, and may pounce upon him again, and he wouldn't be able to escape them in his present weak state."

"Eh, what!" exclaimed Gilbert, jumping up in great alarm at this suggestion. "The Bushmen lurking about! The bloodthirsty savages! They'll be seizing us and burying us up to the chin perhaps, and then making a cockshy of our heads! Are the guns loaded again, Frank?"

"Long ago, Nick," was the answer. "Ernest loaded them, while you and I were gathering melons. I saw him doing it, and I don't think the Bushmen are very likely to trouble us. They have a most wholesome terror of European weapons, and more particularly of firearms, if all that I have heard is true. I think we had better try if we can't kill one or two of these grey parrots, as you yourself, if I don't mistake, were suggesting, just before the snake showed itself."

"I have no objection, Frank," returned Nick, somewhat reassured. "To be sure these Bushmen can't very well be as bad as the snakes; and if one makes up one's mind not to trouble one's self about the one, one need not trouble one's self about the other."

"All right, Nick," said Wilmore. "Now then, about these parrots. They're very shy chaps, and will keep out of shot, if they can; and we mustn't throw away powder by firing, unless with a pretty safe prospect of bringing one down. I think I'll creep round, and hide behind that big trunk yonder. Then you shy a stone up into the tree in which they are sitting, and they'll most probably fly out into the open, and give me a good shot."

Wilmore and Gilbert conducted their joint manoeuvres with so much skill, that before supper-time, half a dozen good-sized parrots had been bagged, and their flesh when boiled was pronounced by all to be excellent. After supper the doctor informed the party that Omatoko, as he called himself, had now quite recovered his senses, and had held a long conversation with him; the particulars of which he was ready to communicate, if they wished to hear it. "Hear it? to be sure we do," said Nick. "I've been longing to learn all about it, and if I had had any idea that he would have been able to talk, I shouldn't have gone out parrot shooting."

"You wouldn't have understood what he said," observed Lavie. "He told his story in Dutch. His knowledge of English was very small when he came to try it. He says he belonged to a tribe that formerly lived a good way to the south of this—not far from the mouth of the Gariep, I fancy, from his description. There were a good many farms belonging to Dutch owners in the neighbourhood; but Omatoko's was a powerful tribe, and they seem for a good many years to have lived unmolested by their European neighbours. But about fourteen or fifteen years ago, some Englishmen—traders probably sent by some commercial house—landed near their village, and offered them more liberal terms for their skins and ivory than the Dutch had allowed. Finding the trade profitable, the English returned in the following year, and by-and-by ran up a few huts, where they carried on what promised to be a very lucrative business. It was from them that Omatoko picked up the few words of English which he knows, and he appears to have contracted a great liking for them."

"Of course he did," said Frank, "old England against the world!"

"With all my heart, Frank," rejoined the doctor, "only the English are not always remarkable for making themselves popular. Well, the trade went on increasing, until it roused the jealousy of the Dutch. They didn't fancy not being able to buy hides and tusks at the old prices, and besides, were jealous of the English attempting to settle in the country."

"Ay, to be sure," said Warley, "the time you speak of must have been a year or two before the conquest of the colony by our troops."

"Just so, Ernest, and for some years previously to that there had been a feeling of uneasiness in the colony, that the English were meditating some attempt upon them. That is one of the things that induces me to believe the Hottentot's story. Well, the Dutch in the fourth year after the appearance of the strangers, got together what they call a commando in these parts—"

"I know what that is," interposed Wilmore. "I heard my uncle talking about it with some of the passengers. They get all the Dutchmen in the neighbourhood together, as well as some troops from the government, and make a raid on some unlucky Hottentot village—kill all the men, make slaves of the women and children, seize the cattle and goods of the natives, and burn the houses."

"That's what you call a clean sweep," observed Nick.

"Yes, no doubt. But it's shockingly cruel and wicked," exclaimed Warley. "I should think you must be overstating the matter, Frank."

"I am afraid he is not," said Lavie. "That is very much what they were wont to do at commandos, as I had good grounds for knowing while I was living at Cape Town. They had a great deal of provocation, no doubt. The boors' cattle was continually being stolen, and could very seldom be recovered. And it was next to impossible to prove the theft against any tribe in particular—"

"But that would not justify them in burning and shooting right and left, without any inquiry," rejoined Warley. "I could not have believed that any Christian people—"

"Well, Ernest, I am inclined to go a long way with you on this subject, though I differ somewhat," said the doctor, "but we have no time to discuss it now. Well, the Dutch commando attacked Omatoko's village by night and burnt it, as Frank says, to the ground. Probably all the other results of which he spoke would have ensued, if the English had not heard the firing, and come up to the rescue."

"I hope they peppered the Dutchmen properly," cried Nick.

"Well, they seem to have made a good fight of it; but the Dutchmen were ten to one, and the Hottentots very little good. The upshot was that a large part of the tribe escaped, and the rest, together with the survivors of the English, surrendered themselves at discretion. Omatoko was one of those made prisoners, and he was for eight years in the service of a boor. He was pretty well treated; for the colony was all that time in the hands of the English, and they wouldn't allow any cruelties to be exercised against the slaves. But two years ago the Cape was given back to the Dutch, and they began the old system again as soon as they were in possession. Omatoko and one or two others made their escape some twelve months ago; and he went back to his tribe, who are living, he says, at no great distance from this. The Dutch, he declares, have been trying to seize or kill him ever since—"

"Whew!" exclaimed Nick. "What, did those Dutch beggars bury him in the well after that fashion, then? Well, I always thought the Dutch to be brutes, but I never could have believed—"

"Stop that, Nick," interposed Frank. "Have you forgotten that the Hottentot himself told us that it was the Bushmen who buried him?"

"Oh, ay, to be sure, I had forgotten that," said Gilbert. "Go on, doctor. Did the Dutch send a commando after him?"

"Omatoko says that the Dutch had given up their system of commandos for several years, and could not easily organise them again, but they employed the Bushmen to seize any of the fugitives, and paid a large price for every one brought in."

"But if that is true, what made the Bushmen bury Omatoko in that way, instead of carrying him to the Dutch to claim the reward?" asked Warley. "I must say, Charles, that sounds very suspicious."

"So it did to me, Ernest," said Charles; "but the Hottentot answered me, readily enough, that the Dutch would have paid the same sum for a runaway's head, as they would if he had been brought to them alive. He declared that the Bushmen hated him, for having repeatedly escaped them, and for having several times requited their outrages in kind. He said they meant to have left him in the well, to die of cold and hunger; after which they would have cut off his head and carried it to the nearest Dutch village."

"Well, that might be true, I suppose," said Wilmore.

"Yes, I think so. The story hung well together. I could detect no flaw in it."

"Did you ask him whether he would act as our guide to Cape Town?" inquired Ernest.

"Yes, and he said he would; but we could not go the way I had proposed, along the course of the Great Fish or Koanquip rivers. He knew them both perfectly, so he affirmed; but neither route would be safe. We must go still further eastward—into the Kalahari in fact—he told me."

"What is the Kalahari?" asked Frank.

"A vast sea of sand," said Lavie, "extending for more than four hundred miles, from the borders of Namaqua-land to the country of the Bechuanas. There is not, so far as I know, a single river, lake, or even fountain, to be found in the whole region."

"What on earth are we to go there for?" cried Gilbert. "We should soon die of hunger or thirst, or heat!"

"Well no, not that," said the surgeon. "A great part of the sand is covered with dense scrub, which affords something like shade, and though there is neither river nor pool, yet if you dig down a few feet you will generally find a supply of water. Life may be sustained there; indeed, tribes of Bushmen and Bechuanas are to be found in most parts of it. But I should think it was the most miserable dwelling-place to be found on the face of the earth."

"Well, then, why are we to go there?" repeated Nick, irritably.

"Omatoko says it will not be safe, for the present at all events, to journey southward. It seems that the Dutch are expecting a new attempt of our countrymen to seize the colony, and their fear and anger are so greatly roused, that they would certainly imprison, and probably kill, any Englishman who at the present juncture fell into their hands. I really think he is likely to be right in what he says. When I left England two months ago, there was a good deal of talk about taking possession of the Cape Colony again."

"But granting that we must not venture south, why need we bury ourselves in a sandy desert?" persisted Gilbert. "Omatoko proposes to take us some distance into Kalahari, because his tribe is at present living there. When they were driven by the Dutch from their own homes, they retired some few miles into the desert and built a new village, where they have been living ever since. He promises us a friendly welcome from his tribe, and advises us to remain with them until we can learn what is the precise state of things between the English and Dutch. If no attack is made by our government, the hostile feeling will gradually subside, and we may safely pursue our way as at first proposed. If an attack *is* made, and the colony again taken possession of by the British arms, we can travel to Cape Town, though it would be wise to follow a different route. That is the substance of what Omatoko advises."

"And you are inclined to trust him, Charles?" said Warley, interrogatively.

"I am in two minds about it," replied Charles. "Part of what he says I know to be true, and everything is consistent with truth. Still his anxiety to get back to his own tribe is suspicious. He has let fall, unconsciously, some hints of his burning desire to be avenged forthwith on the enemies who had so nearly put him to a cruel death; and if he were to conduct us to Cape Town, he would have to put off the gratification of his revenge for many months at the least; and perhaps before his return, the tribe he longs to punish will have moved hundreds of miles away."

"And what do you advise that we should do?"

"I am inclined to follow his suggestions. If his tale is true, we should be running into the face of the most imminent peril by following the route I had marked out. And even if it is false, we shall probably not be delayed very long at the Hottentot village. His measures will be taken, I doubt not, promptly enough, and then he will be at liberty to attend to our affairs."

"You think, in fact, that he really means friendly by us, though he may care more for his revenge than our convenience."

"Just so, Ernest. His gratitude is, I believe, quite sincere."

"Then I agree with you that we had better do as you advise. What do you two say?"

"I am of your opinion," said Wilmore.

"And I don't see what else is to be done," added Gilbert.

"That's agreed, then," said Lavie. "And now, there is another thing. He says it won't be safe for us to sleep under these trees, even though we light a fire, and keep it up all night. It seems that the neighbourhood abounds with beast of prey. Indeed, if Omatoko is to be believed there would be a considerable risk of our being devoured by a lion or tiger—"

"Tiger!" repeated Warley. "There are no tigers in this country surely."

"Not the animal strictly called the tiger," returned the surgeon; "that is not found in South Africa at all, or indeed anywhere, I believe, except in Bengal. The beast they name the tiger here, is the leopard; but he is quite fierce and savage enough. I should observe that the leopard is not the only animal miscalled in this country. They talk of the wild horse, the camel, and the wolf, as abounding here. But none of these are to be found. What they mean are properly the zebra, the giraffe, and the hyena. But to go on, Omatoko says we must either keep watch, all of us, with our guns all night—"

"I say, bother that," broke in Nick; "a fellow can't do without sleep."

"Or else," resumed Charles; "we must climb into trees and sleep there."

"Well, we can do that," said Frank; "that is, we four can. But how about this Hottentot? He is in no case to climb a tree, I judge, much less to stick in one all night."

"And how about Lion?" added Gilbert. "He is a worse climber still, I expect."

"Omatoko advised us to cut down a lot of young pines that are growing in a thicket close by, and lay them across two of the lower branches of the largest tree we can find. There are several acacias of immense size about here. A sort of floor will thus be formed, where we can all sleep safely. The branches would probably be not more than six feet from the ground, so that both the Hottentot and Lion might easily be handed up."

"But these leopards can climb, can't they?" suggested Frank. "We should be safe from lions or rhinoceroses no doubt, but not from leopards, or bears either, if there are any about here."

"I don't think any bears are to be found hereabouts. No doubt panthers and leopards can climb trees, but remember, they could only get at us by walking along the bough on the end of which our platform rests, or by dropping down from a higher limb. Lion would be sure to rouse us before they could accomplish either feat, and they would be easy victims to our rifles."

"That's true," said Wilmore. "Well, then, do you three fall to work on the job, while I roast some parrots for to-morrow's breakfast."

They began the task accordingly. The doctor took his axe; and in half an hour had cut down a great number of stout firs about twenty feet long, and thicker round than his arm. These were brought up by Warley and laid across two of the lower branches of one of the giants of the forest, forming a tolerably flat stage some nine feet square. No fastening was required for the firs, their own weight and the shape of the branches, which bent slightly upwards at the ends, rendering them quite secure. Next, armfuls of dry grass and moss were handed up to form beds for the party; and then came the more difficult task of hoisting Omatoko to his place. This engaged the united strength of the doctor, Warley, and Wilmore below, while Nick, standing on the platform, received him from their hands. But the strength of the Hottentot was in some measure restored, and he was able to render some help himself, which greatly facilitated the job. As soon as Omatoko had been consigned to his bed, Lion was in like manner passed up; but he was by no means so conformable as his predecessor had been, and if anybody but Frank had had charge of his head and shoulders, they might have found their undertaking an unpleasant one.

However, in process of time he was got up, and secured by a thong to one of the poles in the centre of the platform. The guns came next, and lastly their owners. It was quite dark before their arrangements were completed, and before ten minutes had elapsed, the whole of the party were fast asleep.

Chapter Eight

The sun was high in the heavens before any of the party were roused from their slumbers. Then the doctor was the first to wake up, and his thoughts were at once turned to his patient. He was pleased to find him in a most satisfactory condition. His skin was cool, and his pulse, though still low, was steadily recovering its tone. As for Frank and Ernest—they had no sooner opened their eyes, than they hurried off to the pool, which lay two or three hundred yards off, to enjoy a refreshing bath. They were followed shortly afterwards by Lavie and Omatoko, the latter having contrived to descend from his bedchamber by the help of the doctor's arm, and to walk, though very slowly, as far as the waterside.

Having completed their ablutions, the lads set about preparing the breakfast; which, it was agreed, was to be eaten under the shade of the acacias.

"I think Omatoko must be mistaken about the wild animals," observed Frank. "I slept as sound as a top, and so did Lion; and if there had been any of his namesakes about, or tigers either, he would have been pretty sure to give us notice."

"You forget how tired we were, Frank; Lion as well as ourselves," said the doctor. "Unless they made a very great uproar we should probably not hear them."

"What does Omatoko say?" suggested Warley. "Does he think there were wild beasts about?"

The Hottentot nodded. "One, two lion," he said, pointing to some footprints in the short grass round the pool. "One, two lion; many tigers; one rhinoceros."

"Is that the spoor of a lion?" asked Warley with much interest, as he stooped down and examined the footprints. "How can you tell it from that of a large tiger?"

"You may always know the spoor of a lion by the marks of the toe-nails," said Lavie; "they turn in, whereas those of other feline animals project. Yes, that is a lion's spoor, sure enough, and those broad deep prints are as plainly those of a rhinoceros, and a pretty large one too. And there are plenty of others besides, which I am not sure of. Omatoko was certainly right. It was quite as well that we did not bivouac by this pool."

Breakfast was now announced, and the party gathered round the eatables, when it was for the first time noticed that Nick was not present.

"I suppose he is still asleep," said the surgeon. "I called to him to come and help me to get Omatoko down, but I got nothing but an intelligible growl at first, and then a sleepy assurance that he would be sure to be in time for breakfast."

"No, he is not the fellow to miss that," remarked Frank. "He must be very sleepy indeed, before he'll go without his victuals. Depend upon it he will be here in a minute or two."

Half an hour however passed away, and the meal was quite completed, and still no Nick made his appearance.

"Go, and look after him, Frank," said the doctor, "while I consult with Omatoko as to what ought to be done next. We can't afford to lose time, if it should be thought better for us to move."

Wilmore took up his gun accordingly, and walked off towards the tree where they had slept. The dense foliage almost entirely concealed the staging from sight: but as he drew nearer he was sensible of loud chattering and gibbering sounds, intermixed occasionally with shrill screams, which seemed to come from a great number of throats. Wondering what this could mean, he made his approach as noiselessly as possible, and climbing up to the top of one of the roots, which projected a foot or two upwards, he peered cautiously over the edge of the platform. A most extraordinary sight greeted him, and it was with the greatest difficulty that he restrained himself from bursting into a loud laugh.

Nick was seated in the middle of the stage, bareheaded and without shoes, and was gazing upward with a look of mingled alarm and annoyance, which seemed to the spectator of the scene irresistibly ludicrous. On the boughs immediately over his head, as far up as Frank could descry, a great number of baboons were to be seen, leaping from one resting-place to another, with hideous grimaces, and keeping up incessant and most discordant screams. The grotesqueness of their appearance was much increased by their having taken possession of such of Nick's property as they had been able to lay their paws on. One wore the blue cloth cap, with the leather peak and white edging, which was a souvenir of Dr Staines's establishment. Two more had possessed themselves, each of one of his shoes, which he had laid aside when he went to sleep; and were turning them over with an air of grave curiosity, as if to discover what their use might be. Another party had seized the knapsack, which had been pulled from under Nick's head before he was fully awake. The contents had been divided between several old baboons, who had turned the various articles to all sort of strange uses. One was scratching his ear with Gilbert's pipe; another had thrust its head into a stocking, and appeared to have some difficulty in getting it out again; a third was enveloped from head to foot in a cotton shirt, his head showing itself just above the collar; while a fourth was examining the contents of the flask, which it had contrived partially to open, and was making hideous faces over the taste of the gunpowder, of which it had swallowed a good spoonful. Nick had fortunately awoke in time to prevent the baboons from seizing his knife or gun. He now held the latter with a strong grip in both hands, and seemed disposed to discharge its contents at one of his assailants, if he could only make up his mind which to single out for attack.

"Don't fire, Nick," exclaimed Wilmore, as he noticed Gilbert's demeanour. "You'd enrage them greatly, if you were to wound or kill any of them. They have been known to tear a fellow to pieces, who shot one of their number. They're terribly fierce and strong, if they are provoked."

"What am I to do, then?" returned Gilbert. "They've not only carried off my knapsack and pipe, but my hat and shoes too; and I can't venture to walk a step in these parts without them."

"The best way will be to scare them away," suggested Wilmore, "if we could think of any way of doing it."

"I'll tell you," cried Nick, catching a sudden inspiration. "Do you climb up into the tree on the other side. The leaves are so thick that these brutes won't see you, and the branches are easy enough to climb. When you're well up over their heads, let fly with your gun. I'll do the same the moment afterwards, and between the two reports they'll be so scared, I expect, that they'll cut for it straightway."

"Very well," said Frank, laughing, "I've no objection. We can but try, any way." He carefully uncocked his gun, and began mounting the branches as quietly as possible, while Nick distracted the attention of the monkeys, by shaking his fist at them, and pelting them with fragments of bark. Presently there came the double explosion, which fully answered his expectations. Uttering a Babel of discordant screams, they dropped their recently acquired treasures, and made off at the top of their speed, bounding from tree to tree till they were lost in the distance. Nick set himself to collect the various articles thus restored, and had nearly repossessed himself of all of them, when Frank descended from his elevation and joined him on the platform.

"You get into scrapes, Nick, more than most," he said, "but you've a wonderful knack of getting out of them again, that's certain. Well, come along, if you've got everything. The doctor is anxious to start, if this Hottentot chap will let us, and you've still your breakfast to get."

"The Hottentot let us start this morning!" repeated Gilbert. "Not if he's to go with us himself, to be sure! To look at him last night, he wouldn't be fit to walk again this side of Christmas. Perhaps he expects us to carry him, as we did yesterday—do you really think that, Frank?" continued Gilbert, stopping short, and eyeing his companion with an expression of much dismay.

"No, I don't," returned Wilmore, again bursting into a laugh; "and if he did expect it, he'd find his expectations deceive him considerably. That's what I expect, at all events."

"Well, here we are," said Nick, a minute or two afterwards, as they reached the post. "Well, doctor, I'm sorry to be late, but Frank will tell you that I have been in the hands of the swell mob, and have only just contrived to escape them."

The doctor looked puzzled, but he had no time for explanations. "Eat your breakfast, Gilbert," he said, "while we settle what is to be done to-day. I suppose we are all agreed that it won't do for us to stop here longer than we can help. Now Omatoko is not able to travel very far, but he could walk a few miles if he went very slowly and had a rest every now and then. He thinks so himself, and wishes to start at once."

"We could give him an arm by turns, if that was all; but the question is, Charles, could we reach any good halting-place?" suggested Warley.

"That's just it, Ernest," returned Charles. "Omatoko says that about four or five miles from this there is a place where we could stay two or three days, if necessary, and find plenty of food and water. It is a ruined kraal— destroyed by the Dutch, he says, many years ago, but some of the cottages are still in sufficient repair to shelter us."

"Why shouldn't we stay here?" asked Nick, with his mouth full of parrot. "This is a jolly place enough—fresh water, lots of melons and parrots, and they're both of them capital eating. And a comfortable sleeping-place. If we must make a halt anywhere, why not here? It's a capital place, I think, except for the baboons," he muttered in a lower tone, as the recollection of his recent adventure suddenly occurred to him.

"Why shouldn't we stay here?" repeated Lavie. "Well, I'll tell you, Gilbert. It isn't so much the wild beasts—though a place which every night is full of lions, rhinoceroses, and leopards doesn't exactly suit anybody but a professed hunter—but there is the fear of the Bushmen returning to cut off Omatoko's head, whom they will expect to find dead. And if they find him alive, it is most probable that they will do both him and us some deadly mischief. And they may be looked for to-day, or to-morrow, certainly. Besides—"

"There's no need to say any more, I am sure," broke in Gilbert. "I didn't think of the Bushmen. Let us be off at once, I say. I'd rather carry the Hottentot on my shoulders than stay here to be murdered, probably, by those savages!"

"Well, I own I think the return of the Bushmen quite enough by itself," said the surgeon; "but I ought to add that Omatoko thinks the weather is going to change, and there is likely before long to be a violent storm. None of you have had much experience of what an African storm is like. But I have had quite as much as I desire, and do not wish to encounter it, without a roof of some kind over my head! Well, then, if we are all ready, let us set out at once."

The grove and pool were soon left behind. Omatoko stepped out valiantly, sometimes leaning on Lavie's or Warley's shoulder, and sitting down to rest, whenever a thicket of trees afforded a sufficient close screen to hide the party from sight. They noticed that before leaving any of these coverts, he anxiously scrutinised the horizon towards the north, and once or twice requested the boys to climb the highest tree they could find, and report whether anything was visible in the distance.

His strength and confidence alike seemed to improve as the day advanced. About twelve o'clock they made what was to be their long halt, in a patch of scrub which sprung apparently out of the barren sand, though there was neither spring nor pond anywhere to be seen, nor even any appearance of moisture. They had progressed about four miles in something less than five hours, and were now, Omatoko told them, hardly a mile from their destination. He pointed it out indeed in the distance—a rocky eminence, with a patch of trees and grass lying close to it. But the party had not been seated for ten minutes, and were still engaged in devouring the melons they had brought with them, when their guide again rose and advised their immediately resuming their journey.

"What, go on at once?" exclaimed Gilbert. "Why, what is that for? I am just beginning to get cool—that is, as cool as ever I expect to be again. If we have only a mile to go, we had surely better walk it in the cool of the evening than under this broiling sun."

"Must not wait," said Omatoko. "Storm come soon—not able go at all."

"The storm! Do you see any signs of one, doctor? I don't."

"Yes, I see signs; but I own I should not have thought it would break out for some hours. But the changes of the atmosphere are wonderfully rapid in this country, and I have no doubt the Hottentot is right. Will it be on us in another hour, Omatoko?"

"Perhaps half an hour, perhaps three-quarters," was the answer.

"Half an hour! We must be off this minute, and move as fast as we can. Here, Frank, Ernest—hoist Omatoko on to my shoulders; I can carry him for a quarter of a mile, any way, and that will be ten minutes saved."

"And I'll take him as far as I can, when you've done with him," added Warley, "and so, I doubt not, will the others. Lift him up. There, that's right. Now step out as fast as we can."

By the time that the doctor's "quarter of a mile," as it was called— though it was in reality nearly twice that distance—was completed, the signs of the approaching hurricane began to gather so fast, that even the most unobservant must have perceived them. The clouds came rapidly up, and gradually hid the rich blue of the sky. The light breeze which had stirred the foliage of the few trees which rose above the level of the scrub, gradually died away, and a dead, ominous calm succeeded. Warley, to whose back the sick man had now been transferred, hurried on with all the speed he could command, and rapid way was made. Every minute they expected the rain to burst forth. The black clouds which hid the horizon, every other minute seemed to be split open, and forked flashes of fire issued from them. Presently there came a furious rush of wind, almost icy cold— the immediate precursor of the outburst.

"We close by now," exclaimed Omatoko, as he was transferred from Ernest's shoulders to those of Frank. "Not hundred yards off. Turn round tall rock by pool there. Kraal little further on."

They all ran as fast as their exhausted limbs would allow. The corner was attained, and there, sure enough, some forty or fifty yards further, were the ruins of a number of mud cottages thatched with reed. They were, for the most part, mere ruins. The walls had been broken down, the thatch scattered to the four winds. Some one or two, which had stood in the background, immediately under the shelter of a limestone precipice, had retained their walls, and some portions of the thatch unhurt. But one hut only, which stood in a corner under a sloping shelf, presented the spectacle of a roof still firm and whole. Frank hurried along the narrow defile leading to this cottage, putting out all strength to reach it. He was only a few yards from it, when the tempest at last broke forth in all its fury. The wind swept down with a force, which on the open plain no man or horse would have been able to stand against. The hail, or rather the large lumps of ice into which the rain was frozen, rattled against the rocks like cannon balls against the walls of a besieged fortress, and the sky grew so dark, that it was with difficulty that the travellers could discern each other's features. But they had reached the friendly shelter of the cottage, and that was everything. For two hours the fury of the elements beggared all description. The rain, which after a quarter of an hour or so had succeeded the hail, seemed to descend in one great sheet of water, converting the path along which they had travelled not half an hour before, into a foaming torrent, bearing trees and stones before it. One flash of lightning succeeded another so rapidly that the light inside the cottage was almost continuous. Lavie looked several times anxiously at the thatch overhead, which could not have resisted the deluge incessantly poured upon it, if it had not been for the shelving rocks which nearly formed a second roof above it. As it was, not a drop penetrated, and when the raging of the wind and the deluge of rain at last subsided, not one of the party had sustained any injury.

The Hottentot had been laid on a heap of reeds which blocked up one corner of the hut, having been driven in there apparently at one time or another by the wind. He had been at first somewhat exhausted by the speed at which he had been carried for the last half mile or so, but he seemed quite restored before the storm had ceased. He now directed the boys to go out and gather some wild medlars, which he had noticed growing on a tree at no great distance from the rocky defile where they had turned aside from the main path, declaring them to be excellent eating. He also requested them to bring him a straight branch, about three feet long, from a particular tree which he described, and a dozen stout reeds from the edge of the pool. Out of these he intended, he said, to make a bow and arrows, by means of which he would soon provide the party with all the food they would require.

"Three feet long?" repeated Gilbert. "You mean six, I suppose."

"No, he doesn't," said the doctor, who had overheard the request. "The bows of all these tribes are not more than three feet in length. I have seen several of them. It is wonderful to see with what force and accuracy they discharge their arrows, considering the material of which they are made. I had better go with you, I think. I know exactly the tree and the size of the bough required."

Lavie, Wilmore, and Gilbert accordingly set out, leaving Warley to attend to Omatoko, and make the hut as comfortable as he could for a two days' halt there. Lion also remained behind. As soon as his companions were gone Ernest set about his task.

"There are no chairs or tables to be had in these parts," he thought. "We must sit on the ground when we do sit, and take our meals off the ground, when we take them. All that can be done is to strew the floor with rushes and grass, which will do also for beds at night I suppose everything outside is soaking wet, and won't be dry enough for our purpose until it has had a good baking sun upon it for several hours. But the stuff we found in here was quite dry, and perhaps there may be some like it in the other huts. If not, I shall have to cut some from the edge of the pool, I suppose, and lay it out to dry."

He took Lavie's hatchet, and went into the nearest hut, the roof of which had been broken in in one or two places, but was still tolerably sound. He saw, as he stepped through the doorway, that he had not been mistaken about the reeds. A large heap had been lodged in one corner by the wind, and seemed to be quite dry. He stepped forward, and laying down his hatchet, gathered up a large armful. In so doing, he trod upon what appeared to be the end of a log: but his foot had no sooner touched it, than it was drawn away from under him, and a sharp hiss warned him that he had disturbed some enemy. At the same instant he felt a strong pressure round his legs and waist, and perceived that he was enveloped in the coils of a large serpent, which was rapidly winding itself round his chest. A moment afterwards, the flat diamond-shaped head came in sight, the eyes glaring fiercely at him, and the slaver dropping from the open jaws. Ernest's arms were happily free, and he availed himself of the circumstance with the cool promptitude of his character. He glanced for a moment at the hatchet lying on the ground a few feet off; but he felt that it would be impossible for him to stoop to pick it up. It must be a struggle of muscle against muscle. Thrusting out his right hand, he grasped the snake by the neck, at the same time shouting aloud for help. The creature no sooner felt its antagonist's grasp, than it turned its head, endeavouring to bite. Finding itself unable to seize Ernest's hand, it drew in its folds, aiming at his face. The lad in an instant found that his muscular power was not nearly equal to that of his enemy. He seized hold of his right wrist with his other hand, throwing the whole power of his frame into the effort, but in vain. Slowly, inch by inch, his sinews were compelled to yield. Inch by inch the horrid fangs came nearer and nearer to his face. With the strength of despair he contrived to keep the reptile at bay for a few minutes longer; but his powers were fast failing him, and he expected every moment to feel the sharp teeth lacerating his flesh. Suddenly a shock seemed to be communicated to the monster's frame. The terrible grip of the folds relaxed, and the threatening head drooped lax and powerless. Ernest cast his eyes downwards, and perceived that the mastiff had seized the tail in his strong jaws, and had almost bitten it in two. The muscular force of the serpent was paralysed by the wound, and Ernest had no difficulty in disengaging himself from the folds, and flinging them—a helpless and writhing mass—on the ground. Then, catching up the hatchet, he struck off the head, just as Omatoko hobbled up, leaning on a stick, from the adjoining hut.

A NECK AND NECK STRUGGLE.

"Very big snake," was his comment, "bad poison too. Lucky him no bite white boy, or him dead for certain. Lucky, too, big dog near at hand. Never see bigger snake than that. Him seventeen—eighteen foot long! Big dog just come in time, and that all!"

Meanwhile Warley, who had partially recovered his senses, after bathing his face and hands in the fresh water, was returning heartfelt thanks to Heaven for his narrow and wonderful deliverance from the most dreadful death which the imagination of man can picture.

Chapter Nine

Warley was still resting, half sitting, half kneeling, on a large stone by the side of the pool, when the sound of voices was heard, and Lavie came up, accompanied by the two boys. They were all evidently in high spirits. The doctor carried over his shoulder the carcass of a goat, which was large and heavy enough to give him plenty of trouble; and Wilmore and Nick each led a young kid by an extempore halter of rushes. The pockets of all three were distended by a goodly heap of wild medlars, which, in accordance with Omatoko's suggestion, they had gathered, and which they had found extremely refreshing.

"Hallo, Omatoko!" shouted Gilbert as they approached the pool. "Just come here and take charge of this chap, will you? You are more used to this kind of thing than I am. He has done nothing but attempt to bolt the whole way home. I suppose we must eat up the old lady first, otherwise I should suggest that this fellow should be roasted for supper, if only to make sure that he won't run away again."

The Hottentot came out from the hut as he spoke. "One, two, three goat," he said, "dat good, plenty food, all time we stay here."

"Ay, ay," said Nick, "they say it is an ill wind that blows no one good; and the hurricane we had an hour or two ago, is, I suppose, a case in point. Any way, it was obliging enough to blow down a big tree, which fell upon the goat there, and finished her outright. She's a trifle old and tough, I expect; but she'll make first-rate mulligatawney soup nevertheless; and there will be her two kids, as tender as spring lamb, into the bargain. It makes one's mouth water to think of them. And, then, there's those medlars—but, hallo! I say, Ernest, what is the matter? Why, you look as pale and weak as if you were just recovering from a typhus fever. What's befallen you?"

"I have had a very narrow escape from a most terrible death, Nick," returned Warley, gravely, "and my nerves haven't got over it."

"Hallo! what?" again exclaimed Gilbert. "Escape from death, do you say? Why, what has happened?"

"Just go in there—into that hut to the right, and you'll see," was the answer.

Lavie and Wilmore had by this time learned the main outline of what had occurred, from the Hottentot, and they all went into the cottage to examine the remains of the great snake.

"A proper brute, that," observed Gilbert, as they stood by the side of the reptile, which had by this time ceased to wriggle. "That is the biggest snake I ever came across. There's his head gone, and a bit of his tail; but I don't think what remains can be less than twenty feet. Lion, old fellow," he continued, caressing the dog while Frank patted his head, "you did that well, and shall have a first-chop supper."

"We can ascertain its length exactly," said Lavie; "I have got a yard measure here; and here too is the remainder of the tail. Stretch the body straight out, Frank, and I'll soon tell you the measurement."

The serpent was accordingly measured, and was found to be some inches more than nineteen feet long.

"What kind of snake is it?" asked Frank, when this point had been determined.

"A python, or boa-constrictor, no doubt," answered the surgeon; "they give them other names in these parts, but that is the creature. No other description of serpents that I ever heard of attempts to crush up its prey by muscular pressure."

"But serpents which do that are seldom or never venomous, are they?" inquired Wilmore.

"I believe not," answered Lavie, "but that point has been disputed. Omatoko calls the reptile an 'ondara,' and insists upon it that its bite is not only poisonous, but causes certain death. It may be so. It is evident that it would have bitten Ernest if it could; and serpents that are devoid of venom do not often bite. Well, I suppose now that we have done measuring the snake, we may throw him away. The Hottentots, I believe, eat their flesh. But I conclude none of us have any great inclination to make our dinner off him."

"No, thank you, sir," said Frank, "not for me."

"Nor for me either, doctor," cried Nick. "I think I'd rather go without food for a week. Here, Ernest, old fellow—you had better go and lie down a bit. You look as if you were having it out with the python still."

Warley was too unwell to rejoin the party all that day and the next. The shock he had undergone was a very severe one; and would in all likelihood have prostrated any one of his companions for a far longer period. He lay under the shade of the trees on the soft grass the whole day, neither speaking himself nor heeding the remarks of others. Always inclined to be serious and thoughtful, this incident had had the effect of turning his mind to subjects for which his light-hearted companions had little relish, and which Lavie himself could hardly follow. Even when he resumed the old round of occupations, as he did in the course of the third day, Frank and Nick noticed a change in him, which they could not understand.

Meanwhile Omatoko's bow and arrows proceeded rapidly, and were completed on the morning of the third day. Their construction was a great puzzle to the English lads. The bow was a little less than three feet long, and perhaps three-quarters of an inch thick—neatly enough shaped, and rounded off, but looking little better than a child's toy. Omatoko had strung it with some sinew from the carcass of the goat. He had looped this over the upper end of the bow, and rolled it round the other in such a fashion that by merely twisting the string like a tourniquet, it might be strung to any degree of tension. The arrows too were wholly different from any they had ever seen. The strong reeds brought from the edge of the water had been cut off in lengths of about two feet. At one end the notch was inserted; to the other a movable head, made of bone, was attached, which stuck fast enough to the shaft during its flight through the air, but which became detached from it as soon as it was fixed in the body of any animal. These bone-heads, Omatoko told them, were always dipped in some poison, which caused even a slight puncture made by them to be fatal. The entrails of the kaa, or poison grub, were considered the most efficient for this purpose; but this was not to be met with at all times or in all places, and the juice of the euphorbia or the venom of serpents was sometimes substituted. In the present instance he meant to steep the bone-heads in the poison of the ondara, which he had carefully preserved. Omatoko assured them that when they set out for his village (as they probably would on the following day), they would soon have an opportunity of testing the efficiency of his weapons, and laughingly challenged them to a trial of skill between his bow and arrows and their guns.

On the following morning accordingly they resumed their route. Each of them carried some of the flesh of the kids, a dozen medlars, and a melon. It was found that the strength of the Hottentot was now so far restored that he could keep up with the usual pace at which the others walked, and only required a rest of half an hour or so, every two or three miles. They accomplished about a dozen miles that day; and at nightfall had reached a wide stony plain, covered here and there with patches of grass, but entirely destitute of shrub or tree. Omatoko pointed out a place where a deep projecting slab of rock, resting on two enormous stones, and bearing a rude resemblance to a giant's chimney-piece, afforded as convenient a shelter for the night as might be desired. It would effectually protect the party from rain and wind, nor was there the least fear of wild animals, as none were ever known to come within two or three miles of the spot, there being neither pasturage nor water.

"No water," repeated Frank, "that's rather a doubtful advantage, isn't it? What are we to drink, I wonder?"

The Hottentot only grinned in reply; and disengaging the knife which always hung at Nick's girdle, began grubbing in the ground among the stones. In a few minutes he dug up several round, or rather spherical roots, two or three feet in circumference. These he cut open with the knife, displaying the inside, which had a white appearance, and was soft and pulpy. The boys had no sooner applied this to their lips than they broke out into exclamations of delight. "That's your sort," exclaimed Nick; "it's like a delicious melon, only it's twice as refreshing."

"Omatoko, you're a trump," cried Frank. "You'd make a fortune, if you could only sell these in Covent Garden market. Nobody that could get them would ever drink water again."

"What are they called, Charles," asked Warley. "Are they to be met with elsewhere in South Africa, or only here?"

"The root is called the 'markwhae,' I believe," answered the doctor, "and it is to be found in almost every neighbourhood where there is a want of water. It is another of those wonderful provisions of Divine Wisdom for the wants of its creatures, with which this land abounds. In some parts, such of the wild animals as are herbivorous, are continually digging up and devouring these roots. Vangelt told me that he once came upon a tribe of Hottentots which subsisted entirely without water, the succulent plants supplying even the cattle with sufficient liquid."

"Well, that is very wonderful," said Frank. "I declare I feel more refreshed by that one root, than if I had drunk a pailful of water. Are there any more of these roots on the way to your village, Omatoko?"

"Omatoko's village, one, two days away. No roots, plenty water," returned the Hottentot. "Well, that will do as well, I suppose. But this is a thing worth knowing, if one should find one's self in a place where there is no water."

The next day at sunrise they resumed their way, and made their mid-day halt on the skirts of a dense growth of mingled aloes and underwood, which was scarcely anywhere more than five feet in height. Here they sat down by the side of a spring, which gushed forth from a limestone rock into a small natural basin, whence it spread itself in all directions, sustaining a rich emerald carpet for a few feet round, but soon disappearing in the sand.

"Plenty of visitors here at night," remarked Warley, gazing curiously round him on the numerous footmarks of all shapes and sizes, with which the borders of the spring were indented. "It must be a curious sight to witness such an *omnium gatherum*. Only I suppose the more timid animals make sure that the lions and leopards are well out of the way, before they venture here themselves."

"Of what creature is that the spoor?" asked Frank, pointing to a broad, deep mark, much larger than the rest. "That is the track of some beast which I do not recognise."

"It is not the track of a beast," said the surgeon. "Unless I am mistaken, that is the spoor of the ostrich—is it not, Omatoko?"

"Ya, ostrich—plenty 'bout here. See yonder." He pointed as he spoke to a distant part of the bush, where the heads of a troop of ostriches might be seen as they stalked easily along, browsing as they went.

"Eh, ostriches! You don't mean it," exclaimed Frank, starting up in great excitement. "I never saw an ostrich. I want to see one beyond anything! Couldn't we shoot one, Charles? Are they quite out of shot?"

"Much too far to make it worth while trying," said Lavie. "But we might bring one or two down by a stratagem, perhaps. If you four spread yourselves in all directions to the right yonder, and drive them this way, I could hide behind the rock there and bring one down as they went past. Couldn't that be managed, Omatoko?"

"One, two, three, four drive ostrich this way. Omatoko kill one, two— with bow and arrow. Omatoko no miss."

"What, do you think your bow and arrow better than Charles's rifle?" exclaimed Nick; "well, that is coming it strong, anyhow."

"I tell you what," said Warley, "this will be a famous opportunity for you to have the match out for which you were so anxious the other day. You and Charles shall both hide behind the rock there, and Frank, Nick, and myself will fetch a compass and drive the ostriches past you. Then we shall see which will take the longest and truest shot. What do you say, Charles?"

"I have no objection, I am sure," said Lavie, laughing; "only I hope the trial won't go against me. It would be most ignominious to be beaten by a bow and arrows. I should never hear the last of it, I expect!"

"Don't be afraid, Charles, there's no fear of that," returned Warley, reciprocating the laugh. "Well, now let us be off. If you'll take the right side, Nick, and you, Frank, the left, I'll take the middle, and we'll come upon them all together. Lion had better stay here."

The three lads set out accordingly, creeping noiselessly through the cover of the scrub, at a distance too far for even the quick-eared ostriches to perceive them, until they had all attained their appointed places. Then they advanced on the birds, shouting and hallooing, and waving sticks over their heads.

The ostriches instantly took to flight after their fashion, skimming along with expanded wings, and covering twelve or fourteen feet at every stride. They passed the rock behind which the two marksmen were concealed, at a speed which would have far outstripped the swiftest racehorse at Newmarket. But as they darted by, there came the crack of the doctor's rifle, and at the same moment Omatoko's arrow leaped from his bow. Both missiles hit their mark, but with a different result. Charles's bullet struck the bird he aimed at just under the wing; the shot was mortal, and the ostrich staggering forward a few paces fell dead to the ground Omatoko's arrow pierced his quarry through the neck, and the barbed point remained in the wound, rendering death equally certain, but not so speedy. Perceiving that the ostrich did not fall, Lion sprang after it, heedless of the doctor's order to him to return, and a sharp chase began. The ostrich would speedily have distanced its pursuer, if it had not been for the pain and exhaustion of the wound it had received, and the effect of the poison, which had now begun to work. The dog soon began to gain ground, and presently came up with the fugitive; which turned to bay at last in the agony of its rage and fear. Lion had never been trained for the chase of the ostrich, which can only be approached with safety from behind. As he came bounding up, the bird kicked at him, throwing its leg forward as a man does, and with such tremendous force that the mastiff fell to the ground on the instant, bleeding and stunned, if not dead. Then the wounded bird staggered away into the scrub, its strength and courage giving way more and more every moment.

The boys had no time to congratulate their friend on his victory, or even to examine the fallen ostrich. Their thoughts were wholly occupied with the disaster which had befallen Lion.

"Lion, Lion, dear old boy, how could you be so foolish?" exclaimed Frank, as he picked up the bleeding and insensible body of his favourite. "I am afraid he's killed. That kick would have finished a horse, let alone a dog. What fearful strength those creatures must have! Oh, Lion, Lion, my poor old fellow! I'd rather have broken my leg any day than lost you."

"Let me take a look at him," said Lavie, who had now come up. "All depends on where the ostrich's foot struck him. No, I don't think he's killed, Frank," he added presently, after feeling the animal all over. "There are a couple of ribs broken, and a large bruise in the side, but that seems to be the extent of the casualty. I'll set the ribs, and he must keep quiet for some days, and then I expect he'll be right again."

"Oh, I am so glad," said Wilmore. "Yes, you're right, Charles," he continued, as the dog opened its eyes again and attempted to get up, but fell back on the grass with a low moan of pain. "Never mind, Lion, we'll nurse you through it, old chap, won't we?"

"Relieve each other in alternate watches, change bandages, and apply fresh lotion every three hours," suggested Nick. "But with all possible respect for Lion, how are we to do that? Where are the bandages, and where the lotion? Nay, where is the hospital bed to which the patient is to be consigned?"

"Omatoko must put up a hut, and we must stay here until Lion can go with us," said Wilmore gruffly. "If we could wait three days for a pagan Hottentot, we may wait as many, surely, for a Christian dog!"

"I don't think you'll get Omatoko to stay here for all the dogs that ever were whelped," said Nick. "He's in too much of a hurry to put salt on the tails of those Bushmen."

"He must stay, and he shall!" returned Wilmore angrily; "I won't have the dog thrown over. We are four, and he is only one. Stay he shall, I say."

"Gently, Frank," said the doctor. "I'm against throwing Lion over as much as you are, but I don't see how we can stay here. The dog won't be fit to walk—no, not a hundred yards—for this fortnight, and it would probably kill him, if he attempted it."

"What's to be done, then?" rejoined Frank shortly.

"Do as we did with Omatoko. Make a litter and carry him to the Hottentot kraal. It is not more than seven or eight miles, and we can relieve one another. Luckily he is not such a weight as Omatoko. I suppose that will satisfy you, won't it?"

"Yes, of course, Charles," said Wilmore. "It is very kind of you. I am afraid I was rather cross, wasn't I? but you see—"

"All right, old fellow, I know you're fond of Lion; so we all are, though perhaps not *so* fond. Do you go and cut some of the osiers there, Omatoko will soon make them into a basket, large enough to hold the dog, and we'll carry it on a pole slung across our shoulders. Meanwhile I'll dress the old fellow's wounds."

Omatoko proved to be as skilful a basket-maker as Lavie had predicted; and the party were making preparations for a start, when the Hottentot, who had just returned from the osier bed with a last supply of twigs, announced that there was a herd of noble koodoos about half a mile off, feeding on a patch of sweet grass. They were rare in that part of the country, and the best of eating. "Suppose we kill two, three, four of them; my people like them much. They come fetch them."

"Two, three, or four," exclaimed Frank—"who is going to do that? Why, these koodoos, if I have been told rightly, are the shyest of all the boks, and won't let any one come near them. We might possibly get one shot, but certainly not more."

"Me do it," said the Hottentot; "no want help; white boy only sit still."

There seemed no reason for refusing his request, and the boys, laying aside the various articles with which they had loaded themselves, watched his proceedings with a good deal of interest. He first took the knife, and going to the spot where the body of the ostrich was lying, passed it round the creature's throat and under the wings, severing these parts from the rest of the carcass. He then slit open the long neck from top to bottom, removed the bones and flesh, and introduced in their place a strong stick, over which he neatly sewed up the skin again. He then cleared away in like manner the blood and the fat from the back and wings, and sewed another pad of skin under them. These preparations took a considerable time; but Omatoko assured the lookers-on that there was little fear of the koodoos leaving their present pasture for several hours to come at the least, unless they should be molested.

The Hottentot had now nearly done his work; his last act was to gather up in his hand some light-tinted earth, which was nearly of the same colour as an ostrich's legs, and dipping it in water, besmeared his own supporters with it. Then taking his bow and arrows in one hand, and the back and neck of the slain bird in the other, he crept down into the bush. Presently the boys saw the figure of an ostrich appear above the shrubs and stalk leisurely along, pecking at the herbage right and left, as it advanced.

"That can't be Omatoko, to be sure," cried Frank in amazement; "that's a real ostrich! Where can he be hiding?"

"He is waiting for the others," said Warley. "See yonder, the whole flock are returning. Omatoko will no doubt slip in among them. We shall distinguish him, if we watch narrowly."

It seemed as if Ernest was right. The ostriches came straggling back through the bush, and the one they had noticed first lingered about till they had overtaken him, when he accompanied them as they strayed on towards the koodoos.

"Do you see Omatoko?" asked Nick, as the ostriches and boks became mingled together.

"No, I don't," said Frank, "He can't have come out yet. He is biding his time, I expect."

At this moment there came a faint sound like the distant twanging of a bow, and one of the boks was seen to fall. The herd started and looked suspiciously round them; and the ostriches seemed to share their uneasiness. But there was no enemy in sight, and after a few minutes of anxious hesitation, they recommenced browsing. A second twang was succeeded by a second fall, and the boks again tossed their heads and snuffed the air, prepared for immediate flight. They still lingered, however, until the overthrow of a third of their number effectually roused them. They bounded off at their utmost speed, but not before a fourth shaft had laid one of the fugitives low. Then the lads, full of astonishment and admiration, came racing up, and Omatoko, throwing off his disguise, exclaimed exultingly—

"Two, three, four; Omatoko said 'four.' White boy believe Omatoko now!"

"He has you there, Frank," said Nick, laughing; "but I must own I could not have believed it possible, if I had not seen it."

"Live and learn," said Lavie. "I had seen it before, or I might have been of your mind. Well, Omatoko, what now? We have stayed so long that. We shan't be able to reach your village to-night, if we carry the dog."

"Omatoko go alone. He bring men to-morrow; carry koodoo, dog and all."

"Very good," said the doctor, "and we'll camp here. That will suit us all."

Chapter Ten

The sun had hardly risen on the following morning when the quarters where they had bivouacked were surrounded by a bevy of dark skins, whose curiosity to see the strangers was at least equal to that of the boys to see them. The latter were bewildered by the multitude of small copper-coloured men by whom they were environed, their thin faces, small sunken eyes wide apart from one another, thick lips, and flat noses, rendering them objects as hideous in European eyes as could well be imagined. Their conversation too—for they talked rapidly and incessantly among themselves—sounded the strangest Babel that ever was poured into civilised ears. It resembled the continued chattering of teeth, the tongue being continually struck against the jaws or palate; and for a long time the lads almost believed that the men were simply gibbering, like monkeys, at one another. Omatoko, however, who was either a personage of real authority in his tribe, or felt himself entitled to assume authority under the circumstances of the case, soon convinced them that his countrymen understood the orders which he gave them, and were, moreover, ready to obey him. At his command two of them took on their shoulders the basket, in which Lion had been carefully laid on a heap of dried grass, and trotted nimbly off with it; Frank, who had witnessed the manoeuvre, running by the side, and steadying the litter with his hand, whenever any piece of rough ground had to be traversed.

This part of the work despatched, Omatoko next went down to the place where the carcasses of the koodoos had been carefully protected from vultures and hyenas by a heap of logs laid over them. Committing each koodoo to the care of three or four, whom he chose out of the throng for the purpose, he sent them after the others. Then he himself, accompanied by his nephew, whom he introduced by the name of "Toboo," and the son of the chief, whom he addressed as "Kalambo," prepared to set out on the journey, as a guard of honour to the Englishmen.

In about two hours' time they arrived at the kraal, where the chief, Umboo, was expecting them; and the three lads, who had been on the look out for something entirely different to all that they had ever beheld before, were, for once, not disappointed.

The village was built in the shape of a perfect oval, each cottage approaching its next neighbour so nearly as only to allow room for passing to and fro; and on the outer side of the ellipse were enclosures for the cattle. The boys were somewhat surprised at this arrangement, having been prepared to find the oxen pastured in the space enclosed by the huts, where they would have been safe from attack until the men had been overpowered. But they learned afterwards that the Hottentots rather desired that the cattle should protect them, than they the cattle. In the event of an attack from an enemy, the latter would, it was reckoned, be unwilling to destroy the sheep and oxen—the latter, indeed, being in general the booty which had been the inciting cause of the attack—and thus time was gained, and the enemy taken at a disadvantage.

The houses themselves were circular, composed of wicker-work overlaid with matting; this latter being woven out of rushes, and further sewn with the fibre of the mimosa. The mats supplied a twofold want. They readily admitted the passage of air, and so secured good ventilation; and they were of a texture so porous that rain only caused them to close tighter, and so rendered them waterproof. Our travellers had already had satisfactory evidence of their efficiency in this respect during their three days' halt in the rocky defile. Like all other huts belonging to savages in these regions, they had only one opening, which served as door, window, and chimney.

The boys had only time for a very cursory survey of these particulars, when they were hurried into the dwelling of Umboo the chief of the tribe, who, they were told, was impatiently expecting them. Without waiting therefore to wash or cool themselves, or change any part of their dress, they passed into the royal hut, as it might be termed; though, on examination, it was not found to be materially different from those around it.

It was larger, certainly, and perhaps a foot higher, the ordinary huts not being more than five feet in height. The floor was strewn with karosses, on one of which the great Umboo was sitting when they entered. In the background several of his wives—he was said to have nearly a dozen—were sitting; mostly young, well-shaped women, though their figures were almost concealed from sight by numberless necklaces, girdles, armlets, and anklets, ornamented after a strange and bizarre fashion with shells, tigers' teeth, polished stones, and metal spangles of all shapes and sizes—obtained doubtless from tradings with the whites. The chief himself was attired after a fashion so extraordinary, that the boys, and particularly Nick, could with difficulty restrain a shout of laughter as their eyes lighted upon him.

He was a tall and very stout man, with features which, for one of his race, might be accounted handsome; and his dress, however anomalous in the estimation of Europeans, was doubtless regarded with respect and even awe by his own subjects. It consisted of a full-bottomed wig, which had probably once graced the head of some Dutch official, though every vestige of powder had long disappeared. The lower folds of this headdress fell over the collar of the red coat of an English grenadier—a souvenir probably of Muizenberg or Blauenberg—the rusty buttons and tarnished embroidery testifying to the hard service which the garment in question had seen. Below the coat, so far as the mid-calf, Umboo's person remained in its natural state, always excepting the red ochre and grease with which it was liberally besmeared, the odour from which, under the broiling sun, was almost unendurable. The royal costume was completed by a pair of top-boots with brass spurs attached—suggesting a curious inquiry as to the number of owners through which the articles must have passed, before they were transferred from the legs of an English squire to those of a Namaqua chief.

Umboo had noticed the demeanour of the younger portion of his visitors, but he had happily no suspicion of its true explanation, being himself rather inclined to attribute it to the awe which his presence inspired. He was, however, unacquainted not only with the English language, but with the Dutch also; and Omatoko was obliged to act as interpreter between the two parties—an office, apparently, which was greatly to his taste.

After a long interview, in which the chief manifested the greatest curiosity as to the previous history of his visitors, the circumstances which had led to their presence in the country, and the course which they now proposed to pursue, he was pleased to intimate to them that their audience was ended, but that he had assigned a hut for their special accommodation, and one of his people to attend on them and provide them with food, as long as they remained in the kraal.

Having expressed their thanks and taken leave, the four friends withdrew, and were ushered to their house by Toboo, the latter being, as they discovered, the attendant of whom the chief had spoken. Here they found Lion, lying in one corner on a heap of reeds, apparently none the worse for his journey.

"Well," said Nick, as he threw himself on a bed of dried grass covered with one or two karosses, "this is better than the desert, anyhow! I suppose his Majesty, King Umboo, keeps a pretty good table, and a decent cook. Are we to have the honour, by the bye, of dining at the royal board, or is a separate cuisine to be kept up for us? In the first instance, will it be necessary to dress for dinner; in the second, who is to give orders to the cook?"

"And if we are to be his Majesty's guests, will the Queen be present?" asked Frank; "and if she is, which of us is to have the honour of handing her in to dinner?"

"You forget, Frank, there is more than one Mrs Umboo. I believe there are as many as a dozen, if not more."

"Well, then, they won't all dine, I suppose, at least not on the same day. I dare say they'll take it in turns, so as to have the advantage of improving their manners by European polish," said Wilmore. "By the bye, were those his wives or his daughters that were sitting on the skins at the back of the tent. There was one of them who was very nearly being handsome. If it hadn't been for her hair, which strongly resembled a black scrubbing brush, I think she would have been!"

"Ay, I noticed her casting glances at you, Frank," said Nick. "If she was one of Umboo's wives, it is a good job that the royal eyes couldn't see through the back of the head to which they belonged, or his Majesty might have ordered you both to be burned, or impaled, or disposed of after some pleasant fashion of the like description. But we will hope she was a princess, not a queen."

"With all my heart," said Frank, laughing. "Perhaps she was the Princess Royal and, in default of issue male, the heiress presumptive of the crown. It would be great promotion to become Crown Prince of the Namaquas. But here is Charles waiting to speak as soon as he can thrust a word in edgewise. Well, Charles, what is it?"

"Why, if you fellows have done chaffing, there is something of importance which I have to tell you."

"Ay, indeed, and what may that be?" inquired Gilbert.

"Why, you know that I have had some conversations with Omatoko in Dutch?"

"Yes, we all know that."

"But you, perhaps, did *not* know that I understand something of the Hottentot language also."

"Certainly, none of us understood that," observed Frank. "Why, Charles, how could you ever learn it? It seems to me nothing but a series of chicks, as though they were rattling castanets with their tongues."

"I was laid up once with an accident on a shooting expedition, and was nursed by the Hottentots. I picked up enough of their lingo to understand generally what they say, though I don't think I could talk it," answered Charles.

"Why didn't you tell Omatoko so? It would have saved some trouble?" asked Warley.

"Why, you see, Ernest, I have had my suspicions of Omatoko from the first—that is, I have never been quite satisfied about his good faith, though I thought it better to follow his counsel. But I knew when we reached the village, that he would speak freely of his real intentions to his countrymen, not having any suspicion that I understood a word of what he was saying."

"That was very well thought of," said Warley, "and it was very wise also to keep your intention to yourself. I am glad I didn't know it, any way. But what did you learn to-day?"

"I learned, among other things, that the force which it was supposed the English government would send to reconquer the Cape from the Dutch, has actually sailed, if it has not landed; and, in my opinion, it is large enough to render any resistance on the part of the Dutch hopeless—that is, if its strength is correctly reported."

"You don't mean that, Charles! How could these Hottentots know anything about the matter?"

"They are much keener, and take a stronger interest in these things than you fancy. They have always bitterly regretted the restoration of the colony to Holland, and the idea of the English again assuming the government is very acceptable to them. It appears that an American frigate brought the news on Christmas Day of the approach of an English squadron with troops on board, and the news flew like wildfire through the country. The Hottentots heard of it nearly a week ago; but I must do Omatoko the justice to say, that he did not know it."

"Well, go on. That, I suppose, is one of the circumstances which has induced Umboo to treat us so civilly?"

"Well, perhaps, in some degree that may be so. But Umboo is not at all sure that the English will get the better of the Dutch, and he won't commit himself to either side, until he sees which is likely to gain the day."

"Ah, I see. If the English win, he will make a merit of sending us safe to Cape Town; and if the Dutch get the upper hand, he'll hand us over as prisoners to the Governor."

"That's very nearly it, I judge, Ernest. Well, as soon as Omatoko learned about the English fleet, he suggested that we should remain in the kraal, while a messenger was sent southward to ascertain the exact position of things in the colony; and meanwhile a hut should be assigned us, and he and his nephew would keep a careful eye on us."

"How kind of them!" said Nick.

"It's the way of the world, Nick," said Lavie; "in England, I am afraid, as much as in Namaqua-land. Well, that being settled, the matter about the Bushmen came up next. It appears Omatoko knows where they are to be found. He overheard them talking of their plans. They took no trouble indeed to disguise them, considering him to be as good as dead already."

"What are they going to do?" asked Wilmore.

"Going to attack and exterminate, if possible, the Bushmen. Spies are to be sent to make sure of their whereabouts, and then a chosen party of warriors will go against them."

"They don't expect us to accompany them, I hope," said Warley.

"Well, from what was said, I am afraid they do—that is, they mean to urge it. You see, they know the immense advantage our rifles have over their bows and arrows, and our presence·would enable them to effect their purpose with certainty."

"Well, I suppose you will refuse, Charles, won't you? You don't want us to become mercenary cutthroats for the benefit of these savages?"

"That is putting it rather strong," observed Gilbert. "These fellows have attempted murder—murder of the most cruel kind, and deserve punishment—remember that."

"They have done us no wrong, at all events," said Warley; "it cannot be our business to punish them. Besides, shooting these unhappy savages down is not the way to teach them better."

"You are right, Ernest," said Lavie. "I, for one, will have nothing to do with any attack upon them. They may oblige us to accompany them, to prevent our escape, but I will take no part in the fighting."

"Nor I," said Frank, "I am not going to kill these poor helpless wretches to please any one."

"Very good," added Nick; "I have no wish to do it, either."

"Well, then," said Lavie, "we are agreed. We will stay quietly here until the answer comes from the Cape. Five to one our fellows have thrashed these Dutchmen as soundly as they did before, and the colony is ours again by this time; in which case Umboo will be our humble servant. If the messenger doesn't return before the party set out to attack the Bushmen, we will go with them, if required, but only as spectators. Is that agreed?"

"Agreed, *nem. con.*," said Frank. "And now, here, I suppose, comes dinner. We are not to have the honour of seats at the royal table, then!"

"No, that will be reserved for us when Umboo has learned of the defeat of the Dutchmen," said Gilbert.

The food served up to them was better and more palatable than they had expected. It consisted chiefly of the flesh of one of the koodoos, and was partly broiled and partly sodden.

"Not bad this," exclaimed Gilbert, as a third slice was handed to him, which he disposed of after the same fashion which prevailed in the time of Adam and Eve, viz., by the help of his fingers and teeth. "They haven't so bad an idea of cooking after all."

"And these figs and pomegranates are not to be despised either," observed Frank. "They would go down well at a West End dinner!"

"But whatever are these?" cried Nick, digging his hands into a basket of what seemed to be burnt almonds, being a heap of oval substances, about the size of a filbert, and partially roasted. "Hum! a strange sort of taste, but rather nice, too. Have some, Charles, you'll find them rather good eating."

"Thank you, Nick," returned Lavie, gravely, "I am not fond of insects, or I would have a few."

"Insects!" repeated Gilbert, in a tone of mingled surprise and disgust. "You can't mean that, to be sure!" He dropped the handful to which he had just helped himself, and looked at the doctor with mouth and eyes wide open.

"They are locusts, if I don't mistake," said the latter. "Hand them up here, Frank, and I'll take a closer look at them. Yes, they are locusts. These Hottentots consider them a great dainty."

"The nasty wretches!" cried Nick, starting up and throwing away the viands he had been consuming. "To think I should live to sup on beetles! Hand us the bowl of milk there, Ernest. I suppose *that's* all right, isn't it? That comes from a cow, and not a crocodile, or something of the sort?"

"Yes, that's all right, Nick," said Lavie, laughing; "and, after all, there are many other people who eat locusts besides these Hottentots."

"Every one to his taste," said Gilbert, setting down the bowl after a long draught. "Mine doesn't incline to roasted insects. However, that milk has pretty well taken the taste out. And now, I suppose the next thing is to go to bed. I was up very early this morning, and have had a hard day of it. What do you say, Frank?"

"I say ditto to you," said Wilmore. "I shall just roll myself up in one of these skins to keep off the flies, and shut up for the night. Good night, Lion, old boy; I wish you a sound repose."

The two boys accordingly wrapped themselves in the deer-hides which were scattered on the floor, and lay down, each with a roll of matting for a pillow. In two or three minutes their regular breathing announced that they were fast asleep. But Ernest and Charles did not follow their example. They sat near the entrance of the hut, smoking their pipes, and conversing on subjects which had but little interest for their companions.

"These Hottentots are a strange race," observed Warley. "I suppose nothing is really known of their origin and history."

"Nothing, I believe, with any certainty," returned the doctor. "They seem to have no traditions on the subject, which is a rare circumstance in the history of any people. Their very name is uncertain. Europeans call them Hottentots, or Namaquas, but they themselves do not acknowledge either title. Neither word, in fact, exists in their language. They call some of their tribes 'Oerlams,' meaning new-comers in the land, and others 'Topnars,' or the ancient aboriginal inhabitants. But the early history of these latter is quite unknown."

"And what do you imagine to be their origin, Charles? They look very much like Chinese or Tartars. They have been supposed to be of Chinese origin, have they not?"

"I believe so; but on no intelligible grounds that I ever heard. I have a theory of my own about them; but I don't suppose many would share it."

"What is your theory?"

"Well, I connect them with that strange story in Herodotus, of the circumnavigation of Africa, nearly 2500 years ago. You know the story, I suppose?"

"I remember reading it. I think Herodotus says that Necos, or Pharaoh Necho, sent some Phoenicians to circumnavigate Africa. They set out from the Red Sea, I suppose, and sailed through the Straits of Babel-Mandeb. In the third year of their voyage, they returned through the Pillars of Hercules, along the northern coast of Africa to Memphis."

"Yes, that is right. They reported, if you remember as a circumstance accounted by Herodotus as incredible, that when they had sailed some distance along the eastern shore of Africa, they had the sun on their right hand."

"Just so. And I have always regarded that statement as an unanswerable proof that they really did make the voyage as they asserted."

"I quite agree with you. Well, their story was that in the autumn of *their* year, but the spring in South Africa, they went on shore, sowed some land with corn, and waited till the crop was gathered in, when they stored it on board, and resumed their voyage. They did this twice, but in the third year reached home."

"That was their report, exactly, I believe. But what then?"

"Why, I think the Hottentots must be the descendants of some of the Egyptians who went on that voyage; for though the ships were navigated by Phoenicians, the crews were in all likelihood Egyptian. If you divide the coast-line from the Red Sea to Gibraltar into three equal parts, the spots which make one-third and two-thirds of the distance, are the mouth of the Zambesi river, and the coast of great Namaqua-land. Now, the Phoenicians and Egyptians, who made up the expedition, must have remained several months at each place. What more likely that they would intermarry with any native women they might find there; nay, is it improbable that some one or two remained behind, and became the progenitors of the Hottentots and Bushmen?"

"It is what often happens in such expeditions, no doubt. But is there any resemblance between the old Egyptians and these Hottentots?"

"Yes, several very curious resemblances. Their personal appearance is exactly like that of the ancient Copts, who still inhabit some parts of Egypt; and there is one very remarkable peculiarity, which anatomists say is to be found only in these two races. The Coptic nearly resembles the Hottentot language, a good many roots and some words being the same in both. They have several customs in common; as for instance, they will not eat swine's flesh, and they worship a kind of beetle, which I believe no other nations do. Lastly, the Bushmen, who are believed to be a more degraded branch of the same race, ornament walls and flat slabs of rock with mural paintings, in which travellers have recognised a likeness to those of ancient Egypt."

"Well, that is curious, certainly. I should like to see those paintings. But, supposing your theory as to the Hottentots being of Coptic descent to be true, they might have made their way southwards in successive ages through Central Africa, might they not?"

"Of course, and so might the Kaffirs, who also are like the old Egyptians in many things. But if that were so, surely some traces of them would be found somewhere in Central Africa. They would hardly have passed through a vast tract of country in the slow succession of generations, and left no mark of their residence behind."

Chapter Eleven

Two or three weeks now passed during which nothing of any importance occurred. Lion continued to mend, though very slowly, and was unable to walk any distance. A messenger had been despatched southward, and his return was impatiently looked for. Spies also had gone out to track the Bushmen, but they too were still absent. Meanwhile the Englishmen were treated with all civility; Toboo every day supplying their table with Hottentot luxuries, and the chief, attended by Omatoko as interpreter, paying them continual visits. It was very amusing to the boys to watch the asides between their two visitors, which the latter supposed to be quite unintelligible to their guests, but which were always explained to them by the doctor, as soon as the Hottentots had departed.

They learned in this way that Umboo was very anxious to possess one, at least, of the guns which the travellers carried, and was disappointed that an offer to that effect had not been made to him by one of the party. They were, therefore, in no way surprised, when one day Toboo made his appearance, ushering in Omatoko and two of the principal personages of the village, who announced that they came with a message from the chief. The latter had heard of their skill with the "fire-tube," as they styled it, and was desirous of measuring his own skill as a marksman against theirs. He proposed that a mark should be set up at the distance of a hundred yards, which the doctor should endeavour to hit with a bullet from his rifle, and Umboo with his assegai. Whichever made the more successful shot was to be accounted the victor, and the weapons employed in the contest were to become his exclusive property.

"The cunning old rogue," exclaimed Nick, *sotto voce*, to his neighbour, Frank. "He is determined to get hold of Charles's rifle, if he can. But I suppose Charles can hardly decline the contest."

"No," said Frank, "and there is no reason why he should. He is tolerably sure to beat this nigger hollow. But let us hear what he says."

As soon as Omatoko had delivered the challenge, the doctor replied that he was quite ready for the trial proposed, and accepted the conditions. A day was then named, and an invitation given to all the party to dine with the chief after the settlement of the contest. All preliminaries having been arranged, the ambassadors withdrew, followed by Omatoko,—all three apparently greatly pleased at the result of the interview.

"What a flat that Umboo must be," exclaimed Nick, when they had departed, "to believe that he could throw a spear with a better aim than Charles can take with his rifle! Why, even Omatoko, with his bow and arrow, was no match for Charles and his gun; and it is much easier to hit with a bow and arrow than with a spear, or assegai, as they call it."

"Well, I don't know that Umboo is so very far wrong," said Lavie. "Some of these Hottentots can throw the assegai with wonderful skill. If Umboo is a good performer, as I suppose he is by his challenging me, he'll surprise you with his skill, I expect, though I hardly think he will outshoot me."

"Outshoot you! Well, as a fellow is said to take a *shot* with a spear, I suppose it may be called shooting, though it is shooting after a very funny sort," said Warley. "What is the day appointed for this match, Charles?"

"Wednesday—the day after to-morrow. I suppose two days are allowed for preparing the banquet with which he means to celebrate the victory he makes so sure of."

"Probably. But it really is odd that he should feel so confident. Omatoko must have told him of the affair of the ostriches, and that would hardly encourage him."

"They're up to some scheme," said Nick, "I have felt sure of that from the first. They are going to give you something that will make your hand unsteady, or play some trick with your rifle. If I were you, doctor, I'd hide my rifle away in some safe place till Wednesday."

"Well, I'll tell you what happened the night before last," said Warley. "I thought little of it at the time, but it looks different now. You were all asleep, and I was just going off too, when I fancied I saw something moving near the door. It might be a snake, I thought—I'm always fancying snakes are about now—so I lifted my head and looked. Presently a black head came in at the door, and lay motionless for two or three minutes. The eyes seemed to be taking stock of everything in the hut, but particularly of Charles's figure, and his rifle, which was lying by his side. After a little while the head disappeared as cautiously as it had come. I thought it was one of the Hottentots, whose curiosity had been roused by what he had been told, and wanted to see everything with his own eyes. But it looks now as though there was something more in it."

"You're about right, Ernest," said Nick. "There's a good deal more in it. Well, doctor, the first thing I advise is, that you and I change guns till

Wednesday. I don't imagine they know the difference between one gun and another, and if your belt is fastened to my weapon, and you carry it about, they'll think you've got your own, and any tricks they may attempt will be tried on the wrong article. And in the second place, we'd better take it in turns to keep watch at night till Wednesday, and so find out what they're up to."

"I think you're right, Nick," said Lavie. "You're such a dodger yourself, that these fellows can't hold a candle to you. Well, here's my rifle, and I'll take yours, and put it into my belt. We'd better watch from about ten o'clock to six in the morning—the same time as when we were on the journey. What time will you have, Nick?"

"Oh, between twelve and two, if you like," said Nick, "that is the time I prefer."

The others making no objection, this was agreed to. No disturbance took place that night or the night following it; but on the Wednesday morning— the morning of the match—Nick announced to his companions that the same fellow, no doubt, whom Ernest had watched a few days previously, had entered the hut last night and carried off, as he supposed, Lavie's rifle.

"You didn't let him take it away, did you?" exclaimed Frank in surprise.

"I did, though," said Nick, "and let him bring it back again half an hour afterwards. We had better overhaul it, and see what he has done to it."

"Hand it here, and I'll examine it," said the doctor.

The gun was passed to him, and he made a careful examination. At first he could not perceive that there was anything amiss; but on thrusting down the ramrod it was found that there was something about a half-crown in thickness at the bottom of the barrel. Probably some thick glutinous matter had been poured down the gun, and had hardened almost immediately. This would of course prevent the spark from reaching the powder, and so render the gun useless.

"We must take this to pieces by-and-by, and clean it," said the surgeon. "Meanwhile, let us change rifles again. How nicely they will be taken in, to be sure!"

About an hour afterwards notice was given them by Toboo, that all was prepared for the match. They stepped out of their hut, and found the whole kraal present, and in the greatest state of excitement. The large oval space inside the ring of houses had been chosen as the most suitable ground. At one end a square piece of dark-coloured wood had been fastened to a post, and in the middle of the wood, secured by a peg, was a round piece of white leather, some four inches in diameter. At the other end was a smaller post, at which the marksmen were to stand when discharging their weapons. Near this spot one or two lads were holding bundles of assegais intended for the use of Umboo, who was leaning against the wall of a cottage a short way off. He was now divested of all his finery, and looked in consequence a far more imposing figure. He was a tall and finely formed man, though somewhat too stout; and the great muscles of his arms and legs might have served a sculptor for a model. On a row of mats about ten yards distant from the mark, were seated his wives, fully a dozen in number, all clad in their most sumptuous apparel in honour of the triumph which their lord and master was about to achieve. Each of them wore half a dozen heavy necklaces round her throat, on which were strung beads and shells and studs; fish bones and birds' eggs; teeth of fishes and wild beasts; small bells and thimbles, and wooden reels on which thread had been wound, purchased of European traders and converted to these strange uses. It was not round their necks only that they wore these encumbrances; wrists and ankles and waists were similarly loaded, until it became almost impossible to distinguish any part of their persons, and they were absolutely unable to stand upright under the heavy burden of their garniture. The rest of the women and the men formed two long lines on either side of the scene of the contest, and it was evident from their looks, that they took the keenest interest in the issue of the struggle.

"Now you look here," began Omatoko as soon as the chief and the Englishmen had saluted one another; "you each take weapon you mean to use—no allowed to change it. Chief throw three assegais, white medicine-man fire three shots; whoever hit nearest middle white leather, he win. If white man win, he have three assegais. If chief win, he have white man's fire-tube. Is it good?"

"All right. I make no objection," said Lavie, with a nod of intelligence to his companions; and the chief also signifying his assent, the trial began.

Umboo was the first to step forward. He motioned to one of the attendants to bring him the bundle of assegais which he carried, and made a careful examination of them. The lads had never before had a good sight of this weapon. It was nearly seven feet in length, the iron head being some eight inches long and two broad. As the spears in question had been designed for the chief's own use, the best workmen had been employed upon them, and Lavie was really astonished at the skill and taste displayed in the manufacture, which could hardly have been outdone by the best English workman. Having chosen his missiles, Umboo now prepared to throw them. Brandishing the first of them in the air, and moving his hand to and fro, until it was exactly poised, he bent backwards and hurled it with all the force of his herculean frame. It flew straight to the mark, and buried itself in the dark wood a few inches from the white leather circle. Some applause was bestowed; but it was plain, from the faces of the bystanders, that this was not accounted one of his most skilful efforts. He hastened to mend his fortune with the second spear, but with no better result than before, the assegai being fixed in the board, nearly about the same distance from the centre as the first. With an impatient exclamation he caught up the third missile, resolved that this time he would not fail His exertions were successful. A burst of admiration broke forth as the weapon was seen sticking in the leather itself, though not within an inch and a half of the actual centre.

It was now Lavie's turn, and as he advanced to the spot which Umboo had just quitted, he was regarded with the utmost curiosity by the Hottentots, many of whom had never witnessed the discharge of firearms. The doctor's rifle was already loaded. He raised it to his shoulder, slowly lowering it again, until the bead exactly covered the centre of the leather. Then, instantly drawing the trigger, the crack of the report was heard, and the bullet passed so exactly through the middle of the mark, that the wooden pin was driven out, and the leather dropped to the ground.

The three lads vociferously applauded, and the greater part of the bystanders could not help lending their voices to swell the shout, albeit aware that they might incur the wrath of the chief by such a display of feeling. Umboo was, it was plain, equally astonished and annoyed. He threw a fierce glance at a man of slight supple figure who was standing near, and muttered something which the Englishmen did not understand. For a minute he seemed inclined to resent Lavie's victory as a personal injury; but he changed his purpose, and observing that, as the medicine-man's first shot had beaten all three of his, there was no need for him to shoot again, he withdrew to his hut, followed by the Hottentot of whom mention has been made; nor did he reappear until the feast was ready.

This did not take place for some two hours afterwards, by which time his equanimity appeared to be restored. He placed the four white visitors on his right hand, each seated on a separate mat, while on his left were two of his sons, Kalambo and Patoo, Omatoko, and the attendant of the morning, whose name they had now discovered to be Leshoo. He was an old favourite of the chief, it appeared, and was disliked and dreaded by his countrymen generally. He did not seem to bear the Englishmen any particular goodwill, frequently scowling at them as they sat at the feast, and whispering remarks into Umboo's ear, which were evidently disparaging, if not actually hostile.

"I say, Frank," whispered Nick, "that chap there, on the chief's left, is the one who tried to damage the rifle."

"Is he?" answered Frank. "What makes you think so?"

"I know him by that bald patch on the scalp. He has had a wound there, I suppose; I noticed that as he crawled out of the door of the hut into the moonlight. We'd better keep an eye on him."

The feast lasted a long time, the quantity devoured by the Hottentots being only equalled by the gross greediness with which they seized what they considered the chief delicacies; and it was a great relief to the English guests when it was announced that a dance was going to take place outside the hut in their honour.

"A dance?" repeated Nick; "does any one expect a fellow to dance after a feed like this?"

"They don't expect you to dance," said Lavie who overheard him. "You've only to sit by and see them dance."

"That's lucky, at all events," said Nick, "but I should think his Majesty here and his wives were still less in dancing trim than ourselves. Why, a boa-constrictor, after gorging an ox, would be as fit to dance a hornpipe as he."

"Hush, Nick," said Lavie, "somebody may understand you enough to report your words, and I don't consider our position here over safe as it is. If it hadn't been that we could not spare the rifle, I would have let the chief beat me to-day. But there is no need to provoke them more than can be helped."

Nick promised compliance, and followed the doctor out of the hut into an open space near the village, under the shade of some large acacias, which had been selected as the fittest place for the dance. It seemed that this was to be performed by the Hottentot girls, no men being visible among them. They were gathered in a circle divested of all ornaments, indeed of all attire, excepting a linen cincture round the waist, and a headdress of the same material. Several of them held melons in their hands, not the large water-melons, with which the party had been regaled, but a smaller size, about as big as a large cocoa-nut. The moon, which had risen about an hour before, and was nearly at the full, poured down a bright light, which rendered every object clearly distinguishable.

When all had taken their places, Umboo gave the signal, and the dance began. The spectators clapped their hands, keeping a kind of rude time, and accompanying the performance with a low monotonous chant, which swelled louder and louder, as the excitement grew greater. The girls, whirling their arms and throwing out their legs right and left, flew about, following each other in a circle, tossing the melons from one to another, under their thighs, and catching them with wonderful dexterity. As the dance went on, the rapidity of the movements increased. Their light figures and animated faces, as they flashed out into the moonlight, and back into the shade of the acacias, the dark forms seated round, the wild and somewhat melancholy refrain of the voices, combined to make up a scene, which was alike strange and striking. At length the chief threw up his hand; the girls, panting and exhausted, threw themselves on the ground to recover their breath; and soon afterwards Umboo retired to his hut, and the others followed his example.

On the following morning, our travellers were no sooner up and dressed, than they became aware that a great commotion was going on in the village. Assegais, bows, and quivers full of arrows had been brought out of the cottages, and several men were employed in rubbing the barbs with fresh poison. About ten of the stoutest men were smearing their bodies with fat, over which they spread a yellowish red powder; the two between them covering their persons as with a second skin. The stench from this ointment was scarcely bearable; but the boys, on inquiry, were told that its purpose was to render them supple and active, as well as to guard them from the stings of insects.

Lavie soon ascertained that the spies had returned, reporting that the Bushmen were encamped at a distance of not more than twenty miles, and that it was Umboo's purpose to set out almost immediately, before the heat of the day came on, intending to attack the Bushmen an hour or so before sunset. These tidings were soon afterwards confirmed by a message from the chief, conveyed through Omatoko, desiring their company in the course of another half-hour. The manner of their quondam guide, who was now fully armed and equipped for the march, had undergone considerable change. It was no longer deferential and submissive, but imperious and threatening. He seemed to expect a refusal, and to be prepared to take measures for punishing the contumacy of the Englishmen. But Lavie was too wary to permit this. He returned a civil answer, informing Umboo that they would be ready at the time named. Then, calling to the others to follow him, he went into the hut to get ready.

As soon as they were safe inside, and free from the jealous scrutiny of the Hottentots, the doctor addressed his companions.

"It won't do for us to stay any longer among these fellows," he said; "our lives won't be safe if we do. I have learned that they mean to use our help in picking off such of the Bushmen as may be able to escape them at close quarters. But as soon as we have done their work, they will strip us of our arms, and knock us on the head, if we resist I heard that scoundrel Omatoko, and the fellow they call Leshoo, talking over it. The chief is to have my rifle, and Omatoko Ernest's, while Leshoo *is* to have his choice of Frank's or Nick's."

"I'll make him a present of a bullet out of mine," cried Frank, "if I only have the chance."

"Hush, Frank!" said Ernest, "they'll hear you. But, Charles, how comes it that their manner towards us is so strangely altered all of a sudden?"

"Well, in the first place, it appears to be owing to Leshoo's secret machinations. He is afraid, it seems, of our favour with Umboo. In the next, the delay in the return, of the messenger sent southward is interpreted unfavourably to the English, at least Leshoo represents it so. He says the Dutch must have got the better, or the man would have been back before this. Umboo has now quite taken up this notion."

"Well, what do you advise, Charles?"

"That we go with them without any apparent reluctance, and accept whatever service they ask us to undertake. But as soon as the attack on the Bushmen begins, we will, all of us, make off as fast as we can southwards. There are not very many of the Hottentots going on the expedition. They will, almost certainly, be scattered in various directions, and be too busy to notice our movements; some will probably be killed or wounded. But even if that be not so, and if at the end of the fighting we have not got too far to be followed, still they will hardly dare to attack us. They are notoriously afraid of Europeans, and have seen what we can do with our guns." "And if they do attack us?" asked Nick.

"Then their blood be on their own heads. It is our lives or theirs, and they wantonly provoke the contest."

"We can't do better than follow your advice," said Frank; "I'm your man, at all events. Poor old Lion! we must leave him behind; but that can't be helped."

"No," said Warley, "men must be thought of before dogs, however much one may like them. Well, I agree, Charles, and so I can see does Nick."

"That's right, then," said Charles; "now we had better join them. Don't let us give the notion that we are hanging back."

They went out accordingly, and found the party just preparing to start. They were greeted by Umboo with feigned civility, which they returned with similar politeness, and were requested to take their places in the march next to him—Lavie and Frank on his right hand, and Warley and Nick on his left, with Omatoko walking next to Frank and Leshoo to Nick. In this order they proceeded at a rapid pace for several hours, until the heat of the sun became overpoweringly oppressive; then they halted in a place shaded by some trees, and provisions were served out, the Hottentots digging roots to supply the place of water. Umboo seated himself on the grass, and motioned to the Englishmen to do the same, their two attendants, or jailers, as they might more properly be called, taking the same positions as in the march.

They remained in their resting-place for three or four hours until the great heat of the day was past, and then resumed their route. About five o'clock a second halt was made, and Omatoko having spoken a few words apart with the chief, addressed Lavie. He informed him that Umboo intended to post them at various places of ambush, in the neighbourhood of the Bushmen's camp, and their duty would be to pick off any fugitives who might endeavour to make their escape—adding that Umboo would give a large reward for every Bushman so killed. Lavie and the others accepted the commission without the smallest hesitation—again apparently to the surprise of Omatoko, and the evident disappointment of Leshoo. But there was nothing more to be said on the subject. It only remained to conduct the four whites to their several stations. They had now arrived within a mile of their enemies; who it appeared had just succeeded in killing two buffaloes, and were about to make a feast on the carcasses.

Just as they were on the point of setting out, Lavie purposely dropped the case which contained his rifle bullets, which were scattered in all directions on the ground. His companions ran to pick them up, and as their heads met, he said in a subdued but perfectly clear tone, "The large motjeeri to the south, in a quarter of an hour from the present time."

The boys made no answer except a nod of intelligence, as each moved off with the guide assigned him. Then the rest of the Hottentots began creeping through the scrub, as stealthily as serpents, towards a large rock, under shelter of which a number of the doomed Bushmen might be seen, seated in a circle and engaged in devouring huge lumps of meat, which they had roasted at a large fire still smouldering close by.

Lavie watched their dusky figures as they disappeared among the foliage, and remained motionless at his post for the prescribed number of minutes. Then hurrying as fast as he could go towards the motjeeri, he found all three of his companions awaiting him.

"All right!" he exclaimed; "they are just on the point of making their attack, and won't have eyes or ears for anything else. We must put on best speed, and not stop till we are five or six miles away at the least."

A loud yell broke forth from the rock, as they commenced their flight, and was followed by another and another in quick succession. But they grew fainter as the boys hurried on, and soon ceased altogether.

Chapter Twelve

"Not bad that," said Nick, as he threw himself on the ground, panting and footsore, after a run of more than an hour. "We've not gone less than eight miles, I'll take my 'davy, and this gun isn't the lightest thing in the world to carry! Well, Charles, do you mean to make a halt of it here to-night, or are we to hoof it again?"

"We must rest here," said Lavie, "an hour or two to recover ourselves a little, but no longer. I don't suppose the Hottentots have done much more than discover our absence yet. They have had plenty to do for the present without thinking where we are, and then they will have to make out in which direction we have gone. They will find that out, no doubt, notwithstanding all our precautions, but it will take them some time. And my hope is, that we shall now baffle them altogether."

"How do you mean?" asked Ernest.

"I mean that we should all take off our shoes, and step into the brook here. We can walk along it, treading only on the stones till we reach that long patch of scrub there. Then I propose that we shall turn eastward, and go for a day's journey in that direction before again travelling south. I think that will throw these Hottentots completely out, and they will give up the pursuit."

"Well, I have no objection," said Nick, "and I don't suppose the others have. Anything to get out of the hands of those dingy brutes. How sold they will be! If they could only get hold of one of us, how they would pay it off on him!"

"I am afraid they will pay it off on my poor Lion," said Frank. "Whatever will become of him, poor fellow!"

"Oh, they'll use him kindly enough," said Lavie, soothingly. "He is too valuable and useful an animal for them to hurt. As soon as we get to Cape Town we'll send a fellow to ransom him. A dozen large beads or brass buttons will soon induce them to give him up."

"Well, at all events we'll hope so," said Warley. "Well, now, Charles, I am rested if the others are—enough, that is, to go on."

"All right," said the doctor. "Now, the first thing is to take off our shoes and stockings."

This was soon done, and the party stepping down into the bed of the rivulet, walked in Indian file one after another, taking particular care to leave no footprints in the soft earth. Presently they came to a place where the short scrub, with which the slopes were covered, descended to the water's edge. They stepped out upon this, and proceeded eastward for a considerable distance, taking the greatest pains to leave no trace behind. After half a mile or so of this cautious walking, Lavie considered the danger to be at an end. Again resuming the sharp trot at which they had previously proceeded, in another hour they reached some caves in a high range of limestone cliffs, where they resolved to rest for the night. They were too much wearied to keep watch. In five minutes all four were sound asleep.

The next morning they awoke tolerably refreshed, and resuming their journey, proceeded still eastward for some seven or eight miles, when they halted for their mid-day rest. There was no lack of food, for soon after setting out, they had come upon a grove of bananas, of which each of the party had gathered a large bunch. They could also perceive a small streamlet making its way through the brushwood. Doubtless it issued from a mass of limestone rock about a hundred yards distant. "We had better go and drink there," said Lavie. "We have no drinking-cup now, remember, and must use the hollows of our hands, I suppose, or a large leaf. But we shall manage it more easily at the spring head."

He moved off and the others followed, but they were still some yards from the fountain, when they were startled by a low deep growl, which came apparently from the other side of the rock.

The boys instantly unslung their rifles. "That's the growl of a lion," said Lavie. "He is couching by the spring, I expect. It won't do to approach him from the front."

"Hadn't one of us better go round to the clump of trees yonder?" said Frank. "We can get there under cover, and there will be a good sight of him from thence."

"I was just going to suggest it," said Lavie. "And another can climb to the top of the cliff here. It seems quite perpendicular by the spring, and if so it will be fifteen or twenty feet over the lion's head. I'll undertake that, if you like, and Frank can cross over to the clump. The other two had better mount this tree. If the brute springs out, there'll be a chance of a good shot at him from this place."

Lavie and Frank accordingly proceeded to put their designs into execution. Ernest and Nick watched them, until Wilmore was hidden in the wood, and Lavie half up the rock, when suddenly there came a shout of alarm and surprise. At the same moment their weapons were torn from their grasp, and they found themselves in the clutches of Omatoko and half a dozen others.

They were unable to make any resistance; the suddenness of the surprise, and the overwhelming numbers of the Hottentots rendering it impossible. They were soon bound with leather thongs, and hurried off to the fountain, where they encountered Lavie and Frank in the same plight as themselves.

"How like lion?" asked Omatoko, jeeringly. "Omatoko lion. He roar well. White boys go catch lion, get caught themselves!"

"I wish I had known it was you," muttered Nick. "I'd have put a leaden bullet through your carcass as sure as my name's Gilbert! Well, blackie, what next? Are you going to skin and eat us, now you've got us, or what?"

"White boy go back Umboo," said the Hottentot. "Umboo do as he please."

"And what pleases him won't please us, I guess," muttered Gilbert. "Well, there's no help for it. We must grin and bear it, as the saying is. You may as well untie these thongs, any way. You may see for yourself that we can't possibly escape."

"Omatoko no untie till get back to kraal—then untie quick."

He chuckled as he spoke. There was some sinister meaning in his words, which the prisoners could not fathom, but which it was not pleasant to hear. But they had little time for reflection. The thongs had no sooner been securely fastened, and the guns distributed among the leaders of the Hottentots, than they set out on their way home. It appeared that the Englishmen must have followed a very circuitous path, for less than four hours' journey brought them to the spot where the encounter with the Bushmen had taken place; and there the party rested for a couple of hours before proceeding further.

It was a horrid and revolting spectacle which met the eyes of the captives as the halt was made. The bodies of the Bushmen, as well as those of their women and children, were scattered about in all directions, the corpses having already begun to decompose in the scorching sun. Most of the men had been shot down by arrows from a distance, or pierced by assegais. But the weaker portion of the enemy (if they could be so called), had been killed by blows from clubs, or stabs delivered at close quarters; and the lads gazed with sickening disgust at the helpless and mangled figures, with which the plain for a long way round was overspread. But the slayers did not appear to feel the smallest compunction, and Lavie gathered from their conversation, that a considerable proportion of the men had effected their escape—a circumstance which had greatly provoked Umboo's anger.

Travelling early and late, the kraal was reached about nightfall on the following day; when the prisoners were consigned to the custody of Omatoko and Leshoo; who took effectual measures to prevent their escape. Their arms and legs were secured by thongs, and a belt was passed round the waist of each, to which was attached a chain riveted to a strong post Omatoko could not be induced to answer any questions, not even the eager inquiries made after Lion. But Toboo, who was of a gentler disposition than his uncle, told them that the dog had greatly improved during the two or three days of their absence, and could now walk about tolerably well.

On the following morning a debate was held in the chief's apartment, to which Lavie and the boys were, of course, not admitted; but the substance of which they learned afterwards. There was a considerable difference of opinion among the counsellors. Kalambo and some others were for requiring the white men to take an oath that they would make no attempt to recover their property, or punish those who had deprived them of it; and then to let them depart. Others, Omatoko among them, were for keeping them in close custody, until their friends at the Cape agreed to ransom them for a quantity of valuable goods, which were to be specified; while one or two were for allowing them to go altogether free, and take their guns with them; urging that the goodwill of the English was of more value to them than any number of guns.

This last argument was especially urged by Maroro, an old warrior, held in much esteem in the village; and his opinion might have prevailed with Umboo, if it had not been for Leshoo. The latter craftily urged that the white men would never forgive the injury already done them; and though they might take the oath proposed, they would disregard it, as soon as they were in safety. There was nothing to be hoped, he said, from the favour of the English, and nothing to be feared from their enmity. Even if they were again to become the owners of the Cape Colony, they would know nothing about these English travellers. As for ransom, they would never get anything better, they might rest assured, than the four guns, the watches, and clothes of the prisoners, which might be regarded as already their own, and which they must be fools indeed to give up.

His speech was well calculated to work on the pride and the avarice of Umboo, as well as on the fears of the others. It was resolved, by a large majority, that the strangers should not be set at liberty, either with, or without, conditions; but the danger that might arise from them should be averted by their immediate death. This point having been disposed of, the manner of their execution was the next considered, and Leshoo's counsel was again adopted. He proposed that the white man's presumption, in entering on a contest of skill with the chief, should be properly punished by each one of them affording, in their several persons, an evidence of the chiefs unrivalled skill in the use of arms. One of the four, he suggested, should be shot to death by an arrow, a second brained by a club, a third pierced by an assegai, while the fourth—the white medicine-man himself—should die by his own weapon; Umboo, in every instance, being the executioner.

The suggestion was too nattering to the chief's vanity, and too well adapted to efface the mortification of his recent defeat, to be rejected. All concurred in it; and it was resolved that it should be carried out that very day. The posts had not yet been removed from the places where they had been fixed on the day of the trial of skill, and it was agreed that no fitter scene could be chosen for the execution. Omatoko, accompanied by Leshoo, was sent to announce to the prisoners their approaching doom—an office which the latter, at least, undertook *con amore*.

It was a terrible shock, even to Lavie, whose forebodings had been of the darkest ever since their capture. But he had not anticipated anything so barbarous, or so sudden. The tidings were communicated to him in Dutch by Omatoko, and it was his office to break it to his younger friends.

"Lads," he said, after a few moments of inward prayer for support and counsel; "lads, I have something very grave and trying to announce to you. We have all known that our peril, ever since we left the *Hooghly*, has been imminent, and that we might be called upon at any moment to yield up our lives—"

"And we are called upon to yield them now, Charles?" said Ernest, as the doctor paused. "That is what you want to tell us, is it not?"

"I am sorry to say it is, Ernest. The Hottentots have resolved on putting us all four to death this morning—in an hour from the present time—"

"Oh, not in an hour, surely," broke in Gilbert; "they will give us more time than that. They cannot do it."

"They are heathens, Nick, and have never been taught better. We ought to forgive them on that account, even if our religion did not teach us to forgive all who wrong us."

"But can nothing be done?" urged Frank passionately. "Will they not listen to our assurances that we are not their enemies; that we mean them no harm; that we will ransom our lives by giving them a dozen rifles, if they want them; that our friends will avenge our deaths; that—oh! there's a hundred things that might be urged." He thrust aside Lion's head, which was resting caressingly on his knee. "Oh, Charles I let us at least try."

"I would, Frank, if it would be of the least use. But I learn from Omatoko, that the matter was most carefully considered, and everything we could urge has already been advanced and rejected. It would but waste the time still left us for preparation, and that is short enough. Let us pray for strength and resignation; that is all now left us to do."

All complied, and knelt on the floor of the hut, while Lion sat silent and motionless at their side, gazing from face to face with a wistful look, as though he would fain comprehend what was amiss. Then Warley, to whom all seemed instinctively to look, offered up a simple, but fervent petition, that God would be pleased to succour them, if He saw fit, in their present strait; but if it was His pleasure to take them from the world, He would pardon the sins of their past lives, strengthen them to meet their doom bravely, and receive them to Himself. He concluded with the Lord's Prayer, in which they all joined fervently, and then relapsed into silence; which was not broken until Leshoo returned to warn them that all was in readiness.

"You, boy," he said, turning to Frank, "you die first. Umboo shoot you through the heart with arrow. Then you he kill with club," addressing Warley. "You he throw assegai at," nodding to Nick. "Medicine-man, he come last. Umboo shoot him dead with own gun! Medicine-man never shoot better himself. Come now; chief ready."

The prisoners obeyed in silence. A sharper thrill shot through Frank's bosom as he heard he was to be the first to suffer, but the next instant it was succeeded by a feeling of thankfulness that he would not witness the murder of his friends.

"Good-bye, dear old Lion," he said, stooping over the dog, and stroking the smooth head which looked up with such sad wonder into his face; "I hope they'll treat you kindly. Charles," he added, "let us say good-bye to one another here. I shouldn't like to do it before all these fellows."

"Good-bye, Frank," said Lavie, throwing his arms round the lad's neck, and kissing him on the forehead. "Good-bye, and God bless you. We will pray for each other to the last."

"I will follow you now," said Wilmore, when he had taken leave in like fashion of the other two. "The sooner this is over the better."

He passed out of the hut with a firm step, looking without flinching on the cruel preparations without. Whatever sinkings of heart he might have felt when his doom was first made known to him, they had all vanished now. He was a noble English boy, reared in all manly ways, and instructed by a thousand brave examples. His life, if not faultless, had been pure; his conscience void of any deep offence; and for the rest he trusted in the God who had bade him trust in Him. The same heroism which the striplings of our race showed on the deck of the *Birkenhead*, and in the wild scenes of the Indian mutiny, which upbore young Herbert, the high-born and gently nurtured, in his dread ordeal among the Greek brigands, was now burning in Frank's bosom. Let them do what they would to him, he would endure it without flinching.

Lavie and the other two lads followed closely after him, and were placed by Omatoko on the right hand of the post, to which Wilmore was about to be fastened, at a distance of some twelve feet from it. "Do not let us see his death," said Gilbert in a low tone; "it will be too dreadful!"

"No," said Lavie, "it will do none of us good, though I know he will meet it bravely. We will kneel down here, and pray in silence till each in his turn is summoned."

He knelt as he spoke, and the others followed his example.

"It is not good," exclaimed old Maroro, as he noticed the action. "The white man is praying to the white man's God. He will be angry with us, for the white man has done no wrong."

He spoke loud enough to be heard even by the chief, who cast a wrathful look at him in reply. If his reputation for wisdom and goodness had not stood so high with his countrymen, his boldness might have entailed serious consequences upon him. As it was, he was listened to in angry and impatient silence.

Frank had now been led to his station, and Omatoko and Leshoo were busied in binding him. Three cinctures were passed round him, one securing the neck, a second the waist, and the third the legs, to the strong upright post. They had just completed their task, and were about to retire— Umboo had already fitted the arrow to the string, and was on the point of bending it—when a loud cry of mingled surprise and alarm was raised by the spectators nearest to the prisoner, and was presently echoed by nearly all present Lavie and the two boys started up, looking hurriedly round them, half expecting to see a band of armed Englishmen, who had come up at that critical moment to their rescue. But the eyes of the Hottentots were not turned in the direction they had expected, but into the air a few feet above them. A small beetle, of the size, perhaps, of a child's little finger, was hovering over their heads, its green back and speckled belly glittering bright in the beams of the sun. All present held their breath, and watched its motions with anxiety and awe. It gyrated awhile immediately above the post, as though seeking for some spot on which to settle. Suddenly it folded its wings, and, shooting downwards, alighted on Frank Wilmore's head. There was a second and still louder cry, rising, in the instance of the women, into a shriek of terror at this spectacle. "The god! the god!" they cried. "The white boy is the favourite of the god. He has come to save him. Cut the thongs, set him free! Pray him to forgive us, or we shall all die. He will send drought and murrain! He will kill our flocks and herds! He will strike us dead with his lightnings! Not one will escape!"

THE HOTTENTOT GOD.

A dozen Hottentots rushed up with their knives, and severed the bonds which held the prisoner. Then lifting him on to their shoulders they bore him in triumph through the village, the women singing and dancing round him, until the hut of the chief was reached. There Frank was placed by his supporters in the seat of honour, while all present prostrated themselves at his feet, entreating mercy.

The lad was at first too much startled and bewildered to understand what had happened. He had closed his eyes, expecting every moment to feel the fatal point, and even when he heard the shouts of the bystanders, believed it had been raised only because the arrow was on its way. But Lavie, who knew enough of Hottentot superstitions to understand what had occurred, hurried up to him, and informing him in a few words what was the true explanation of this extraordinary change, desired him to take the beetle from his forehead, where it was still resting, and retain it in his grasp, but to be extremely careful not to hurt it.

"It is the mantes, Frank," he said, "about which I was telling Ernest the other day. They believe that it is a god, that it will do them the most terrible injuries if they offend it, and whomsoever they imagine to be its favourite, he may issue any commands he pleases, and is sure to be obeyed. Of course this wonderful deliverance is of God's sending, and we will thank Him heartily for it; but at present you must go with them and take the mantes with you."

"What shall I have to do, Charles?" said Frank, who, between astonishment and joy, could hardly even now understand what was passing. "What are they going to do with me?"

"They'll want to make you chief very likely; perhaps offer sacrifices in your honour, and all sorts of extravagances of that kind. Of course you will refuse to allow any impiety of that description, and will decline to be made chief; but you had better demand that all our property should be at once restored to us, and that we should be suffered to depart without molestation."

"How am I to make them understand?"

"Omatoko will make them understand you well enough. He is as much frightened as the rest. You can also, if you like it, require that a guide be sent with us for the first part of the journey. You may be quite sure, that whatever you ask they will agree to."

"Won't you stay with me?"

"I think I had better not. Their feeling of awe and reverence is personal to yourself. They don't regard us as favourites of the god; and but for your protection of us, would be ready to put us to death this minute. We are going back to our hut. I need not tell you to offer up our thanks for this great mercy. We will wait there till you join us."

"Well, Charles, I will do as you advise. But I wish this was over. I can hardly realise to myself what has happened. It is all like a dream! I only feel as if I could think of nothing till I had joined with you in your thanksgiving for this wonderful deliverance."

Chapter Thirteen

It was the second day after the narrow escape of our travellers as related in the last chapter. The boys, attended by Lion, who seemed quite strong again, were sitting under the shade of some gum trees, in the immediate neighbourhood of what appeared to be a deserted village, only that the houses were much larger and more solidly built than those described in a previous chapter. They were awaiting the arrival of the doctor, who had loitered behind to take leave of Omatoko, and make sure that he had set off on his return to the Hottentot kraal. Frank had had very great difficulty in parrying the importunity of the Hottentots, who were fully convinced that the prosperity of the tribe would be secured for ever, if he would but consent to take upon himself the chiefship, from which they were prepared to eject Umboo without further ceremony. When they found that his determination on the subject could not be overcome, their chagrin was so great, that nothing but their superstitious fears of Frank's influence with their deity restrained them from using force to compel him to conform to their wishes. But he had, by Lavie's advice, adopted a very curt and lofty demeanour with them, refusing to listen to any argument, and peremptorily insisting that all the arms belonging to the party should be restored, on pain of his heavy displeasure. This demand was no sooner made known, through Omatoko, than it was complied with. All the Hottentots who had possessed themselves of the guns, shot-belts, powder-flasks, watches, etc, bringing them back, and laying them at his feet with the humblest expressions of contrition. Umboo was among the suppliants, his cowering figure presenting a curious contrast to the haughty and merciless aspect he had exhibited only a few hours previously. Frank raised him up, and gravely assured him of his forgiveness; but added that all the strangers would depart on the following day, with provisions for one day's journey, and Omatoko, as their guide, for the same space of time. But after that, he said, the tribe must make no further inquiry respecting them, under penalty, once more, of his displeasure! Umboo (who in his heart, perhaps, was not unwilling to be rid of Frank, notwithstanding the overwhelming advantages that would have attended his rule), answered submissively, that the pleasure of the "favoured one" should be fully executed; and accordingly, on the next day, the travellers had all left the village and journeyed northwards, towards the spot known as the Elephant's Fountain. Omatoko, who had been as much terrified as his countrymen, waited on them during the journey with abject servility. His time was now up, and he had been despatched on his return homewards—Lavie (as the reader has heard) accompanying him some way, to make sure that, after all, he did not intend to follow them.

"Well, Frank, you did it well, I must say," observed Nick, "and kept your countenance a deal better than I should have done, when you talked to them of the danger there was of your being displeased, if they failed to perform any particular of your sovereign pleasure. I wonder what they thought *would* have happened, if you had been angry with them!"

"Oh, they thought that there would come a murrain, and cut off the cattle; and a blight, and destroy the fruit; and a pestilence, and kill themselves. I had only to order, and I might pitch it into them any way I liked! Omatoko told me so."

"Did he, the rascal! Well, upon my honour, Frank, if I had been you, I'd have ordered them to give him six dozen, and Umboo nine dozen, and Leshoo twelve. It is not one bit more than they deserved, and it would have been a sight to see! The Hottentots would have laid it on, and with a will too!"

"You don't mean what you are saying, Nick, I am sure," struck in Warley. "I wonder you don't feel that this is not a thing to be made a joke of."

"You're right, Ernest," said Frank; "we ought not to take it in that way. Indeed, I am sure I am thankful enough for the mercy shown us, and should be sorry if you thought otherwise. And so does Nick, too, I'll answer for it."

"Of course I'm thankful," said Gilbert. "And I dare say I am too apt to turn things into jest. Well, we'll drop the matter now, at all events. And by the same token, here comes the doctor. Now, I suppose, we shall hear whether this place will do for our halt for the night or not. Well, doctor, is the rascal really gone?"

"Yes, I am satisfied he is. I doubted, at first, whether Omatoko really believed in the beetle. He has lived so long among the Dutch, that I thought he might have learned better. But he hasn't, I am persuaded. Yes, he has really gone back. He daren't follow us."

"That is well, at all events. Well, what do you think of this as a halting-place? It's an abandoned kraal, I suppose, only it must have belonged to some tribe of savages, who took more pains with their house-building than those Namaquas."

"Kraal, Nick? Do you suppose these houses, for such they may certainly be called; do you suppose these houses to be the handiwork of men?"

"To be sure I do," returned Nick; "who but men could have built them?"

"They are nests of white ants," said Lavie, "and if we were to stay here all night, our clothes, our knapsacks, our belts, and everything that could be devoured by them, would be gnawed to pieces!"

"Ants, doctor! You are joking, surely. What—that hut there, or whatever it is, is a good twenty feet high, and thirty, I'll go bail for it, in diameter? Ants make that! It isn't possible."

"It's true, anyhow," said Lavie. "I know they have been found more than a hundred feet in circumference. It is the enormous number of the ants that enables them to construct such huge dwellings. And, after all, their work is nothing compared with that of the coral insect of the Pacific."

"Don't they sometimes build in the trunks of trees?" asked Warley.

"Very frequently," answered the surgeon. "Their mode of going to work, when they do, is very much like their house-building. In the latter case, they heap together an immense mass of earth, which they form into innumerable galleries, all leading, inwards, to the central chamber of the structure. When they choose a tree, and they generally pitch upon one of the largest trees they can find—a baobab, perhaps, or a giant fig—they simply eat these galleries out of the wood, taking care never to disturb the outer bark. In this manner they will sometimes destroy the whole inside of a vast fruit tree so completely, that it crumbles to dust as soon as touched."

"Well, it is very wonderful," said Frank, "I wonder how it happens that we have seen nothing of them during the two hours or so that we have been here."

"That is because they work only by night. It is supposed, I believe, that they are torpid by day."

"Well, then, I suppose we must shift our quarters," remarked Nick. "It would not be pleasant to have the clothes eaten off one's back, certainly. We had better start, hadn't we, or it will be late?"

"Stop a moment," said Lavie, who had been carefully noting one particular ant-hill for some minutes. "Ay, I thought so," he added presently, "there is a bees' nest in yonder mound, and most likely a large accumulation of honey. If you are fond of honey, you may sup off it without difficulty."

"I am very particularly fond of honey," answered Nick, "but I don't know about there being no difficulty. The last time I assisted at the taking of a hive, there was a very considerable 'difficulty.' I was stung, in fact, so badly, that I vowed never to go near bees again. However, if *you* don't mind—"

"None of us need mind," said the surgeon; "these bees are different from our English bees. They never sting people. There isn't even any necessity to smoke them."

"Really!" returned Nick. "Now that I call the height of amiability. But are you sure, doctor? It seems too good to be possible."

"You'll soon see," said Lavie, walking up to the mound he had marked. "Ay, there is the hole where the bee went in. Just hand me the knife, Ernest." He cleared away the earth, avoiding, as much as possible, any injury to the work of the bees, and presently laid bare a great mass of comb, full of honey and pollen; of this he cut off several large pieces, as much as they could conveniently carry; the bees, in complete justification of his assurances, offering no kind of interference—a fact which drew forth a second eulogium from Nick, who only deplored, he said, that they couldn't be conveyed to England, to instruct their brethren there.

They now resumed their journey, resolving to camp for the night at the first spot where shade and water were to be found. But their quest was not fortunate. The afternoon was unusually scorching and dry; and though they came to several patches of trees and shrubs, they could find neither fount nor pool. At length the sun had declined so low in the horizon, that it was plain that scarcely more than an hour of daylight remained; and they would have to pass the night without having quenched their thirst, unless water should very speedily be discovered.

Under these circumstances they were greatly rejoiced to see Lion, who had been trotting along soberly by Frank's side ever since they left the ant-hills, suddenly throw up his head and snuff the air, which were his modes of indicating that there was a spring at no great distance.

"Hurrah! old fellow," shouted Frank; "off then, and find it. We'll have a race, Nick, which shall reach it first."

They started off, the other two following at a somewhat slower pace. Lion soon went ahead, directing the course of the boys towards a small kloof, visible about a mile off, containing a grove of palms and date trees, with a thick belt of underwood surrounding it. Heedless of the heat, which by this time, however, was a little tempered by the cool breeze that had sprung up at sunset, they bounded gaily along, and presently reached the kloof. It appeared to Frank—who, closely following Lion, was the first of the four to enter it—quite a little Paradise. Under the shade of the palms, surrounded by delicious verdure, was a large spring bubbling up from the ground, and stealing away in a brook, which ran babbling through the thicket, until lost to sight.

"Hurrah!" he shouted. "Now for a jolly drink! What is the matter, old boy?" he added a moment afterwards, as Lion instead of plunging into the cool water, as was his ordinary habit, stood still on the brink, looking up into Frank's face, with a perplexed and wistful look. "What's the matter, Lion, why don't you drink? I suppose, poor beast," he added, "he hasn't quite recovered even yet. Get out of the way, Lion; what are you about? If you are not thirsty, at all events I am!"

He pushed the mastiff out of the way as he spoke, and throwing himself on his hands and knees, took a long and delicious draught. "You don't know what is good, Lion," he said. "It's a rum colour, and there is an odd sort of taste about the water; but it is beautifully cool and refreshing. Come, drink, old chap; it will do you a heap of good."

The dog, however, persistently refused to touch the water; and Nick, who by this time had reached the grove, was so struck by the animal's demeanour, that he paused before stooping to the waterside, and eyed it with mingled doubt and curiosity. The next minute Lavie's voice was heard—

"Don't any of you touch the water till I come."

"I am afraid that warning comes rather late in the day for me," said Frank, laughing, though he felt, nevertheless, a little uneasy. "I've had a delicious draught already. Why isn't one to touch it, Charles?" he continued, as the doctor approached.

"I came upon a gnu, a minute or two ago, lying dead in the thicket. It had no wound, and I suspected it had been poisoned. I know it is very often the practice of the Bushmen to mix poisons of one kind or another with the wells, and so kill the animals that drink at them. But very likely the water is all right; only I had better examine it before—stay, what is this? Won't Lion drink it?"

"No, he won't," said Frank; "and, Charles, I am sorry to say, I have drunk a good deal of it before you called out I am afraid there is something wrong. I feel very queer, anyhow."

"How do you feel?" asked Lavie, taking his pulse.

"I feel a giddiness in my head, and a singing in the ears, and am very shaky on my legs. I had better lie down. I dare say it will go off presently." He sank, as he spoke, rather than lay down, on the bank.

"Put your fingers down your throat, and try if you can't bring the water off again," said the doctor. "Unluckily, I have no emetic in my knapsacks. The Hottentots emptied out all the drugs, while they had possession of our things."

Frank obeyed his directions, but with very little effect. He became presently very drowsy, and Lavie, making a bed for him under a mimosa, covered him up with all the spare garments of the rest of the party, and some heaps of long dry grass. In a few minutes Frank seemed to be asleep.

"Do you think he is very bad?" inquired Warley earnestly.

"I don't like the look of things, I must say," was the answer; "we don't know what the poison is which the Bushmen have mixed with the water, and therefore it would be difficult to apply the antidote, even if it could be found here. Generally these poisons work very slow in the instance of men, whatever they may do in animals. The best chance, I think, would be to give him large draughts of fresh wholesome water, if we could find it. It would probably dilute the poison and carry it off, and it would anyway be good for him, as his pulse shows him to be very feverish."

"We'll go and hunt for water," said Warley, "Nick and I; you stay with Frank."

They took their guns, and went off in different directions. Warley directed his steps towards another kloof, about two miles off, between two high and stony hills. Trees and grass seemed to be growing in it almost as abundantly as in that which he had just left, and if so, there was probably either a brook, or water underground, which might be obtained by digging. He hurried on as fast as he could, for the darkness was fast coming on, and was within a hundred yards of the kloof, when a fine gemsbok, with its tall upright horns, came bounding down the narrow path at its utmost speed. The creature checked itself the moment it saw Ernest. The hills on either side were too steep to be mounted, unless at a foot-pace, and the gemsbok's instinct taught it that this would place it at the mercy of an enemy. As soon therefore as it could stop itself, it turned short round and galloped back into the kloof. Warley fired after it, but his nerves were discomposed, and the light was so bad that he could hardly have hoped to hit. He could hear the bok rushing along with unabated speed, the sound of its feet dying off in the gorge of the mountain; but two minutes afterwards there came another sound, which seemed like the crack of a ride, though at a considerable distance.

If this was so, there must be some person, beside their own party, somewhere about; for the shot could not have been fired by either Lavie or Nick. At another time, Warley would have hesitated before going in search of a stranger in so wild a region as that of the Kalahari. The shot might have come from a party of Bushmen or Bechuanas; some few of whom, he knew, had possessed themselves of European firearms. In that case, himself and his whole party would run a very imminent risk of being seized and murdered for the sake of their rifles. And even if the person should prove to be a European, it was as likely as not, that he was an escaped convict from the Cape prisons, who might be even more dangerous to encounter than the savages of the desert. But Frank's situation forbade any considerations of this kind. To secure even the chance of obtaining help for him, was enough to overpower all other calculations.

He hurried on accordingly in the direction whence the sound had come as fast as possible, and after half an hour's exertion, was rewarded by seeing a long way off the figure of a man carrying a gun over his shoulder. Even at that distance, and in spite of the uncertain light, Ernest could perceive that he was a European. Somewhat assured by this, he shouted at the top of his voice, and presently saw the stranger stop, and look behind him. The sight of Ernest seemed to surprise him, for after looking fixedly at him for a few moments, he walked rapidly down the glen to meet him. As they approached nearer, Warley could distinguish that the new comer was a man advanced in life, but of a hardy frame, and his features showed traces of long exposure to the extremes of cold and heat His dress was peculiar. It consisted of a hunting-coat of some dark woollen material, with breeches and gaiters to match, and a broad leather belt, in which were stuck a variety of articles, which might be needed in crossing the desert:—a drinking-cup of horn, a flint and steel, a case containing apparently small articles of value, together with a powder-flask and shot-case. His long gun he carried slung over his shoulder; and a large broad brimmed hat, the roof of which was thick enough to resist the fiery rays of even an African sun, completed his attire. He was not a hunter, that was plain. He could hardly be a farmer or an itinerant trader, and tourists in those days were persons very rarely to be met with. Moreover, his first address showed him to be a man of superior education to any of these.

"I wish you good day, sir," he said in correct English, though with something of a foreign accent. "I did not know that there was any other traveller in this neighbourhood, or I should have sought his society. May I ask your name, and whether you are alone, or one of a party?"

"There are four of us," answered Warley, "we are Englishmen, who have been wrecked on the western coast, and are now trying to make our way to Cape Town."

"Indeed," returned the stranger, "but you are aware, I presume, that this is not the nearest way from the west coast to the town you name. You have come a long distance out of your way and chosen a very undesirable route."

"No doubt," said Ernest, "but we could not help ourselves. We fell in with a Hottentot tribe, and have had a narrow escape from their hands. But we are in a great strait now. One of our party has incautiously drunk a quantity of water at a fountain near here, which we have since discovered to be poisoned; and none of us—"

"What the spring in the kloof, about two miles back, I suppose," interrupted the stranger. "I passed it two or three hours ago. I noticed that it had been poisoned—poisoned by euphorbia juice. Your friend cannot have had much experience of the Kalahari, or he would have detected it at once. You may always know water poisoned in that manner by its clay-like appearance. How much did he drink?"

"A long draught, I am afraid," said Ernest. "I was not present, but he said so."

"How long ago?"

"I should think two hours."

"There is no time to be lost, if his life is to be saved," observed the unknown. "Happily, the antidote is easily found in these parts. When, indeed, are God's mercies ever wanting in the hour of need!"

He spoke the last sentence to himself, rather than to his companion. Drawing forth his flint and steel, he struck a light, by which he kindled a small lantern, which was one of the articles appended to his belt. By the help of these, he began searching among the herbage which grew thickly on either side of the path. Presently he lighted on the plant of which he was in quest. It was shaped something like an egg, which it also nearly resembled in size. He pulled up two or three specimens of this, and shook the dirt from the roots. Then he again addressed Warley.

"Where is your friend?" he said. "At the kloof, where he drank the water, I suppose? You had better take me to him as quickly as possible."

Warley complied in silence. Lost in wonder at the strangeness of the adventure, he led the way down the glen, up which he had mounted an hour or so before.

The elder man seemed as little inclined for conversation as himself. They proceeded in almost unbroken silence until they had arrived within a quarter of a mile of their destination. Warley stepped on a little in advance as they approached the kloof, and Charles came out to meet him.

"How is Frank?" asked Warley in a low tone.

Lavie shook his head. "Nick has found water, but we cannot get any quantity down his throat I have tried everything I can think of, but in vain."

"I have fallen in with a man who seems to understand the matter, and thinks he can save him."

"A man—what, here in the Kalahari? What do you mean?"

Warley hurriedly related what had occurred. "Of course, Charles," he said, "I can't answer for his knowledge and skill But hadn't we better let him try what he can do?"

"Yes, I suppose we had," said Lavie, after a pause. "I can do nothing for him; and though it is true that the poison is slow in its action, yet it is fatal unless its effects are checked. I'll go and speak to the man."

He stepped up to the stranger, and in a few hurried words described the condition of his patient. The newcomer nodded his head.

"Euphorbia poison," he said; "but I trust we shall be in time. Have you any means of heating water?"

"I have some water nearly boiling in the iron pot here."

"That is well. Be so good as to put some into this cup; rather more than half full, if you please."

He took one of the egg-shaped fruits, and pounded it in the hot water. When it had been reduced to a fluid state, he signed to Lavie to lift Frank's head, and then poured the mixture down the lad's throat. Then covering him up as warmly as he could, he sat down by his side, and took his hand.

He sat there, without speaking, for nearly three-quarters of an hour; then he looked up and said—

"Let us give thanks to God. The boy's life will be spared. He is beginning to sweat profusely. We have now only to keep him warmly covered up, and the effects of the poison will pass off."

Chapter Fourteen

"Have you practised your profession in this country for very long?" asked Nick of their visitor, as they sat over their supper an hour or two later in the evening.

The latter smiled. "Yes," he answered, "for nearly fifteen years. But are you sure you know what my profession is?"

"Are you not a doctor?" rejoined his questioner.

"Well, I suppose I may call myself a doctor," was the reply, "but a physician of the soul, not of the body—though, as you have seen, I have picked up a little knowledge of body-curing too, in the course of my travels."

"A missionary!" exclaimed Warley. "I am so glad. I have been so hoping that we might fall in with one. But we were told that there had never been more than a very few in Southern Africa, and even they had now left it."

"I am sorry to say you heard no more than the truth," said the stranger. "But I trust there is a better prospect now."

"I am glad to hear it," observed Lavie. "I guessed what your employment was, and was afraid you might be in trouble, if not in danger. When I left Cape Town two years ago—"

"Ah, you have resided in Cape Town. Then you will know something of what our trials and discouragements have been. But no one but the missionaries themselves can really enter into them."

"I wish you would give us your experiences," said Lavie. "As you say, in the colony there is a very confused and imperfect knowledge of your proceedings: and there is, besides, so large an amount of prejudice on the subject, that even those most favourably inclined towards you, have heard, I doubt not, a most unfair version of it."

Warley eagerly seconded this proposal, and the stranger, who seemed willing enough to comply with their wishes, began his recital.

"I should tell you first," he said, "what perhaps you have guessed—that I am, by descent, half English and half Dutch. Our family name was Blandford, and we were owners of large property in one of the southern counties; but it was forfeited in consequence of our determined adherence to the house of Stuart. After the unfortunate issue of the attempt in 1745, we were obliged to leave England, and took up our residence in Holland; where my father married the daughter of a Dutch merchant, named De Walden, whose name he thenceforth adopted.

"As the hopes of the restoration of the exiled family grew ever less and less, my father entered with more interest into his father-in-law's business. The latter carried on a brisk trade with the Cape of Good Hope, and thither I was sent, when barely twenty-one, as one of the junior partners in the house. I resided for many years at Stellenbosch, occasionally passing months together at Klyberg, a large farm in the north of the colony, not far from the Gariep, or the Orange river, as it has since been named."

"Not very far from where we are now, in fact," observed Lavie.

"It was nearer to the west coast than this," said De Walden, "by some hundreds of miles, and the country was very fertile. Both at Stellenbosch and Klyberg we employed a great number of Hottentots as slaves. Our treatment of them I shall remember with shame and grief to the last day of my life!" He paused from emotion. And Lavie said—

"You were not different, I suppose, in your treatment of them from your neighbours?"

"Unhappily, no. But that is small comfort. It seems wonderful to me now, with my present feelings, how I could have accepted without questioning, as I did, the opinions of those about me on the subject. We entertained the notion that the natives were an inferior race to ourselves, intended by Providence to be kept in a condition of servitude, as the sheep and oxen were; to be kindly treated if they were docile and industrious; to be subdued and punished if refractory."

"That is, of course, a perverted view," said the doctor, "but still no one, who has seen much of these races, can doubt their inferiority, or the necessity of their being instructed and kept in control by the whites."

"Granted," said the missionary. "The whites had, in fact, a mission of love and mercy entrusted to them. They ought to have taught the natives, and raised them gradually to a level with themselves. But we never taught or raised them. On the contrary, our persistent determination was to keep them down. We dreaded their acquiring knowledge; and looked with jealousy and dislike upon some earnest and devoted men, who had come from Europe for the purpose of enlightening them."

"Did you come across George Schmidt, sir?" inquired Warley, with an eagerness of manner which attracted De Walden's attention. "I have read about him, and have been anxious to meet some one who knew him."

"Yes," said De Walden, "to my shame, I did. One of the first things I remember, after my arrival at Klyberg, was an outburst of anger because the good and holy man you name had baptised one of his converts. You may well look surprised, but so it was. By the law of the Cape, no baptised person could be a slave; so that the baptism of a Hottentot had the effect of manumitting him. Of course the law was a mistake, and ought to have been altered. A slave, as Saint Paul has emphatically taught us, may be as true a Christian as his master. But the Dutch had no thought of altering the law, and were resolved rather to keep their slaves in heathen darkness than lose their services."

"That is much what I read," said Warley; "and Schmidt was obliged to leave the colony, was he not?"

"He was, and never returned to it, though he earnestly longed and prayed that he might. His prayer was heard after his death, and his spirit returned in the faithful band of servants, who were raised up to carry on his work. I never saw *George* Schmidt while in Africa. I had no wish to do so. His name was a by-word of reproach on my lips. But afterwards, while I was in Holland, during a three years' absence from the colony, I did encounter him."

The speaker paused for a few minutes, and then resumed. "I shall never forget our meeting. I was passing through one of the towns on the Rhine, when I saw a notice that George Schmidt would deliver a discourse about South African Missions, and endeavour to raise funds for carrying them on. I determined to go to the meeting, expose the falsehood and calumnies which I should be sure to hear, and raise such a tumult as would put a stop to him and his doings. I went and I heard him. What we read in the Bible of men forsaking all and following Christ—which had always seemed so difficult to be believed—came home to me in all its vividness. I was carried away by his simple eloquence. I was humbled, conscience-stricken, filled suddenly and for ever with a new purpose in life. I went to him as soon as the meeting was over, told him who I was, and asked his forgiveness for what I and mine had done to thwart and grieve him."

"And he welcomed you kindly, doubtless?" said Lavie.

"Yes, like himself I remained in Holland, and used every means in my power to obtain the leave to renew his mission, which he was seeking from the Government. My family remonstrated against the course I was pursuing, and finding that I was not to be moved, renounced all connection with me. I cared little for that; but the failure of my applications to the authorities distressed me much more than it did Schmidt; who closed his eyes, in extreme old age, fully assured that the prayer of his life would soon be granted."

"And it was, was it not?" asked Warley.

"Yes. In 1792 we obtained the long-desired permission. I was one of those who accompanied Marsveld and his colleagues to South Africa. I well remember the day when we visited Bavian's kloof, which had been the scene of George Schmidt's labours, broken off nearly fifty years before. There were the remains of the school he had built, and the cottage in which he had dwelt—all in ruins, but sacred in our eyes as the homes in which we had been born. There was the pear tree which he had planted, now a strong and lofty tree. Above all, there were the remains of the flock he brought into the Redeemer's fold—one or two aged servants of Christ whom he had instructed in the faith, and who had retained the memory of his lessons through fifty years of darkness!"

"The Dutch did not interfere with you any further, did they, sir?" asked Ernest.

"Not as they had done before, but they discouraged us indirectly in every possible way. They would never suffer us to build a church, in which to carry on our worship; and it was not until the English took possession of the Cape that we were able to do so."

"You were not interfered with during the time of the English occupation, I believe," said Lavie.

"No, if anything, helped and encouraged. When the colony was restored to the Dutch three years ago, another attempt was made to turn us out of the colony. But English rule had produced its effect on public opinion, and nothing open was attempted. The system pursued by the Dutch farmers was, nevertheless, so obstructive, that I thought it better to give up my mission to the Hottentots, and betake myself to a different part of the colony, where I have been living for the last two years."

"And where are you going now?" asked Warley.

"Back to the Hottentots. The English Government will protect me, doubtless, as it did before, and I shall have every reasonable hope of succeeding."

"The English Government!" repeated Nick, hastily. "Have the English retaken the colony!"

De Walden looked at him with surprise. "Do you not know," he said, "that on the 10th of January last, Cape Town was surrendered to the English? By this time, I should imagine, the whole of the Dutch troops have left the colony."

"No," said Lavie, "we did not know it, though we are not much surprised to hear it. When we left England, there was some talk of sending out an expedition to recover the Cape. But the Government kept their intentions very secret. The Hottentots, among whom we have been living for several weeks, had heard of the approach of a British fleet, but knew nothing as to the issue of the expedition. So the Dutch have lost the colony again, have they?"

"Yes," said the missionary; "and they will never regain it. The trust has been reposed in their hands for many generations, and they have betrayed it, and the colony is handed over to another people. For their own sakes, may they fulfil it better!"

"You are right," said Lavie; "as the New World was given to Spain, and when Spain abused the gift, it was taken from her; so have the Dutch received, and so have they forfeited, their South African dominions."

"You speak well," said De Walden. "The parallel you suggest is very much to the purpose. One's blood boils when one reads of the barbarities practised on the defenceless Indians by Cortez and his fellows; on the monstrous violations of justice, mercy, and good faith which Pizarro displayed in his dealings with the simple-hearted Peruvians. But neither Cortez nor Pizarro ever perpetrated more unjust or inhuman deeds, than have the Dutch boors during the century and a half of their possession."

The doctor shook his head as he heard this assertion. "That is strong language, Mr De Walden," he said. "I go along with you in nearly all that you have said, but not that. You refer, I suppose, to the commando system?"

"Mainly to that, but not entirely."

"Very well. I speak under correction, but I understand the commando system to be this. When property is continually and persistently stolen by the Hottentots and Bushmen, and no peaceable measures can secure its restoration, the whites in the neighbourhood are summoned to assist at an armed attempt at its recovery. They march into the domains of the robbers, seize the cattle or other property which has been plundered, or an equivalent, punish the robbers, according to the amount of the offence, and then return home. Is that a correct statement?"

"Theoretically, very fairly correct."

"Well, where is the injustice? Those who will recognise no law but force, must take their first lesson under that law. A savage has to learn that he must respect the rights and feelings of others. That is the foundation of all social order. Until he has learned it, you cannot civilise him."

"Granted. But the means you take are not the right ones. In the first place, who gave the Dutch settlers the right to the land or the cattle? They found the Hottentot and Bushman in possession. What equivalent did they give them for their land? They were savages, you will say, and could not appreciate its value. True, but the Dutchmen could. Did they not take advantage of the ignorance of the aboriginals to gain possession, on ridiculously cheap terms, of their property. If so, the rights of which you speak are founded on fraud and extortion, and are, in fact, no rights at all, but simply wrongs."

"Do you mean that there can be no dealings at all between civilised races and savages?"

"By no means. If the civilised trader is an honest man, he will appraise the land at its true value, and hold it in trust for the vendor."

"How hold it in trust?"

"He will remember that he cannot pay the fair purchase-money down, and therefore hold it for the seller, till he can pay it. He will remember, that the seller was supported off the land previously to its sale, and ought to be supported still by it, or its proceeds, or the bargain cannot have been a fair one. He will therefore supply the natives with food, if in need; will help them to live; will feel bound to furnish the means of instructing them; will show infinite forbearance, until they are instructed. He will be sensible that he cannot wash his hands clear of them as he might, in a civilised country, of men, who had sold him land at market price."

"And what, if such forbearance produced no other result than increased lawlessness and treachery?"

"You have, first, to show that it would produce it. And you would have some difficulty in doing that. When that mode of dealing with aboriginals has been fairly tried and has failed, then you may ask your question. But when has it ever been tried? I have striven to impress the truths of the Gospel on the Hottentots and the Bushmen, and I have failed; but why? Not because they could not understand the Gospel, or because they hated it; but because those who professed it did not themselves act up to it—did not, in fact, themselves really believe it. Look you here. A tribe of Bushmen have been in the habit of ranging over a large tract of country, and killing game, wherever they could, for their support. They regarded that as their natural right; and who shall say it was not? Well, some persons, of whom they have never heard, make some bargain with some of their neighbours or fellow-countrymen, and they find themselves suddenly deprived of the rights which they and their fathers have enjoyed from immemorial time. They traverse their old hunting-grounds and kill the first cattle they fall in with, as they have been ever wont to do; and for so doing, their villages are attacked by night, their huts burnt, their property destroyed, themselves, their wives and children, enslaved or murdered! Whatever sense of natural justice they may possess, must be outraged by such acts."

"I think I see. The natives have a right to be taught and cared for, in return for their possessions."

"Yes. And if this is not done, the settlers have no justification for possessing themselves of their land at all. By settling in the country, they make themselves the fellow-citizens of the aboriginals, and are bound to treat them as such. If they cannot fulfil the duties of citizens towards them, rather let them give up their lands and quit the country, than provoke God by high-handed violence and injustice. The policy of continually driving the heathen further and further away, is only one degree less detestable than exterminating them at once."

"And you think the natives could be converted to Christianity, if your programme were followed? I have heard men doubt it, whose reputation for wisdom stands high."

"I dare say. But what is man's opinion worth in such a matter? Has not God made mankind all of one blood? Did not Christ die for all? Are we to believe that He did not understand His own work? We must do so, if we believe that there is any nation on the face of the earth, which could not accept the Gospel But it is growing late. I will visit my patient once more before lying down to rest. He may want another dose, but I hardly think it."

They repaired accordingly to Wilmore's bed, and were glad to find him in a calm deep sleep, which they did not disturb. The fire was then replenished, and Warley having undertaken to keep watch during the first part of the night, the others lay down under the shadow of the palm trees and were soon sound asleep.

Ernest sat over the fire, with his rifle in his hand, buried in deep thought. Always of a grave turn of mind, the events of the last few weeks had made him a man before his time. His life during that time had been one of continual peril, and three times at least he had had the narrowest possible escape from a dreadful death. He felt—as all men of any strength of character always do feel under such circumstances—that his life had been preserved for some high and worthy purpose, and the conversation of the stranger missionary had impressed the same truth more forcibly upon him. He had always had an inclination for the life of a clergyman; its only objection in his eyes being the dull routine of commonplace duties; which, however worthy in themselves, did not satisfy his longing for enterprise and action But in Mr De Walden's career, all that he thirsted after seemed to be realised. He felt that if the latter would consent to take him as a helper in the work he had now in hand, he should prefer it to any other lot that life could offer him. But then there was the difficulty about money. He must have some means of living, and the life of a missionary in Africa would not supply any, not even the barest necessaries. Mr De Walden, it was evident, did possess some private income; but it might not be enough to support two; and even if it should be, he could hardly ask him, a total stranger, to bestow it on him. There was his brother, who might allow him just enough to start him in business. So at least he had intimated. But it was unlikely that he would give him a farthing if he turned missionary—a calling especially odious in the eyes of the residents at Cape Town at that time. Besides, Ernest had always felt the greatest repugnance to taking Hubert's money. No, he feared he must give it up—for the present at all events. He must take the Indian clerkship, which Lavie had told him he thought he could get for him. He might save money, and then later in life perhaps—

As he sat brooding over these thoughts with his arm resting on some pine boughs which he had gathered, he was startled by seeing a dark object crawling out of a bush at no great distance. It passed across the pathway, and was hidden in the scrub on the other side before he had time to look fixedly at it. It occurred to him at once, that it might be one of the large black snakes which infest that country, and whose bite was said to be extremely dangerous. He paused a moment in doubt. He could still distinguish the black mass in the shrub though very imperfectly. Should he fire at it and take the chance of killing or crippling it. Well, he might miss, and if so, there would be a shot thrown away; Frank would certainly be woke up, and it was most important for him to get a sound night's rest. At all events he would see the object, whatever it might be, by a clearer light before firing. He cocked his gun and rested it against his knee. Then taking a handful of dry fir leaves, he threw them on the fire which had sunk somewhat low. A bright blaze sprung up, and showed in strong relief the stems of the palms and the thickets of scrub around them. But the black mass on which his eye was fixed was hidden by the shadow of a large tree, and he could not determine with any certainty its outline, before the blaze had sank again. Presently he felt something creep stealthily past him, and Lion stirred uneasily in his sleep. He seized another and a larger heap of pine leaves; but before he could throw it on the fire, he felt his gun seized in a gentle, but firm, grasp by the muzzle, and gradually drawn away from him. Before he could recover from his surprise, the lock caught against a tuft of weed and exploded. The report was followed by a yell of rage and pain, and at the same moment Lion sprang forward. All the party, except Frank, were instantly on their legs, and De Walden, with ready presence of mind, caught up a pine bough and thrust it among the embers. It soon burst out into a flame and showed a dark-skinned savage extended on the ground, a second struggling in the grip of Lion, while several more were hurrying away in all directions.

"Those Kaffirs have tracked me, after all," he muttered. "I thought I had got rid of them, but it is next to impossible to do so. Well, let us see whether they are much hurt."

Lavie and Warley had by this time obliged Lion to relax his hold, and it was found that the man he had seized had only sustained a few slight injuries from the dog's teeth. The other was bleeding from a gun-shot wound, but that too was not dangerous.

"They are neither of them really hurt," said Lavie; "but we must question them to-morrow, and meanwhile take care they don't escape." He took some strong leathern thongs, which De Walden handed him from his wallet, and with these dexterously tied their hands and legs. Then desiring Lion to watch them, he lay down again and was soon fast asleep. Warley followed his example, but the other two kept watch till sunrise.

Chapter Fifteen

Daylight broke at last, and the two watchers were rejoiced to perceive that their prisoners, though evidently recovered from any injuries which they might have sustained, still remained in the same place, indeed in the same attitude as on the previous night. This, however, appeared to be mainly due to Lion's vigilance, the latter still keeping the most jealous watch over them, breaking out into an angry growl, and showing a formidable broadside of teeth, whenever either of them moved hand or foot. As soon as the morning meal was over, De Walden untied the thongs by which they had been secured, and taking them apart, addressed a long and seemingly an angry remonstrance to them. They replied submissively, and appeared to be entreating pardon, which he was reluctant to grant. At length the conference came to an end. With a low inflection of their bodies, they turned away, and pursued the path up the kloof, never turning their heads to look back, till they had vanished from sight.

Mr De Walden now rejoined his companions. "In what direction is it your purpose to proceed?" he inquired.

"We were about to ask your advice," said Lavie. "We have turned out of our direct way to avoid being followed by the Hottentots among whom we have been living for several weeks, and now want to make our way as quickly as we can to Cape Town."

"I will accompany you there," said the missionary, "if it be agreeable to you. Until last night it was my intention to travel into the country you have just quitted, and resume my old mission work, which I left three years ago. But, singularly enough, I am now in the same strait as yourself. I have been living for the last year or two in the Bechuana country; and the idea has latterly taken possession of one of the Kaffir chiefs, named Chuma, that I have the power of controlling the elements, and driving away disease at pleasure."

"It is not an uncommon one, is it?" asked Lavie.

"It is common enough for impostors among the Kaffirs themselves, to pretend to such power, and they gain a certain amount of credence from their countrymen," answered De Walden; "but they do not often fancy that

Europeans are so gifted. The fame of a very simple cure of a Bechuana child, which was suffering from croup, and the circumstance that a seasonable rain, after long drought fell, while I was residing in the Bechuana village, are, I believe, the only grounds for the notion. But Chuma was so possessed with it, that he has repeatedly made me the most splendid offers, if I will take up my abode in his kraal."

"I wonder you did not accept it," remarked Lavie.

"You think it would have been an opening for teaching them better things, I suppose. But that would not have been so. I could only have gone as a professed wizard or prophet—under false colours, in fact. And the moment I threw any doubt on the reality of my pretensions, they would have turned on me as an impostor, and justly too. No, I told Chuma that I would come to him as the servant of the God who sent the rain and the sunshine, if he would have me. But that He alone could command these, and I had no power over them, any more than Chuma himself had."

"And he?" pursued Lavie.

"He did not believe me, and once or twice tried to seize me, and compel me to comply with his wishes. I was very glad when the news of the reoccupation of the Cape by the British, offered an opening for my return to Namaqua-land. I thought I had managed my departure so well, that they would not discover it for many days. But I was mistaken. Chuma sent those men yesterday with peremptory orders to seize and convey me to his village."

"And you are going to change your route, in consequence?" said Lavie.

"Yes; I do not believe Chuma will abandon his purpose even now. I shall proceed to Cape Town and thence obtain a passage to Walfisch Bay. In that way I shall baffle the chief, but probably in no other. If you think Frank—that is his name, I believe—if you think him fit to travel, we had better set off for the Gariep as soon as possible. Chuma will be sure to send out a fresh company, as soon as these have returned to him."

"Frank is nearly well in my opinion," said Lavie. "The poison seems to have been driven out by the profuse perspiration. He is a little weak; but with an occasional rest, and an arm to lean on, he can go a tolerable day's journey, I have no doubt."

"Let us set off, then, as soon as possible. We have a long and very dreary tract to traverse before we reach the Gariep—three hundred miles and more, I should think. It will probably take us at least three weeks to accomplish it, even if your young friend quite recovers his strength."

"But you are well acquainted with the way?"

"Yes, indeed. I have traversed it often enough."

"We are fortunate to have fallen in with you. I will go and arrange everything for starting."

They were soon on their way, Frank stepping bravely along, and declaring that the motion and the morning air had driven out whatever megrims the euphorbia water might have left behind. They soon came into a different character of country from that which they had recently been traversing. Hitherto they had been moving to and fro on the skirts of the great Kalahari; they were now about to pass through its central solitudes. As they advanced, the groups of trees and shrubs grew scantier, and at length almost wholly disappeared. Interminable flats of sand, varied only by heaps of stone scattered about in the wildest disorder, succeeded each other as far as the eye could reach. For miles together there was no sign of animal or vegetable life—not the cry of an insect, not the track of a beast, not the pinion of a bird. The red light of daybreak, the hot and loaded vapours of noontide, the gorgeous hues of sunset, the moon and stars hanging like globes of fire in the dark purple of the sky, succeeded each other with wearying monotony. There was no difference between day and day. They depended for their subsistence almost entirely on the roots, which De Walden knew where to search for, and which relieved the parched lips and burning throat as nothing else could have done. Their resting-place at mid-day, and at night alike, was either the shadow cast by some huge stone, or a natural hollow in its side, or more rarely a patch of scrub and grass, growing round some spring, either visible or underground. The cool sunset breeze every evening restored something of vigour to their exhausted frames, and enabled them to toil onward for another, and yet another, day.

After nearly three weeks of this travel, they found the landscape begin once more to change. The kameel-doorn and the euphorbia again made their appearance, at first in a few comparatively shaded spots; then the aloe and the mimosa began to mingle with them; and in the course of a day's journey afterwards, birds chirped among the boughs, the secretary was seen stalking over the plain, and the frequent spoor of wild animals showed that they had again reached the world of living beings.

Their guide now told them that they were within two days' journey or so of the Gariep; which he proposed to pass at some point immediately below one of the great cataracts. The river at this spot ran always, he said, with a rapidity which rendered it almost impossible to ford; but at the times when it was at the lowest, after long drought, as was the case now, it might be crossed by climbing along trunks of trees which had been lodged among the rocks and left there by the subsiding waters of a flood. This required nothing of the traveller beyond a steady foot and a cool head. Where there were several to help one another, the risk was reduced almost to zero.

The party woke up gladly enough on the morning of the last day of their desert travel. The country was now thickly covered with wood. Immediately before them was a plain very curiously dotted with patches of thorns, growing at regular intervals about fifty paces apart from one another, enclosing a large tract of ground with a kind of rude fence. Nick was so struck with its singular appearance, that he stopped behind his companions to examine it more closely. While thus engaged, his attention was attracted by a grunting noise in the bush near him, and peering cautiously through the bushes, saw what he supposed to be a large black hog, unwieldy from its fat, lying in a bed of thick grass. Here was a discovery! The party had not tasted the flesh of animals for weeks past, and had not tasted pork since they left the *Hooghly*. He shouted as loud as he could, to attract the attention of Lavie and the others. Failing to do this, he discharged his gun at the hog, intending at once to kill the animal and induce his fellow-travellers to return. He waited for some minutes, but without hearing anything but a distant halloo. Resolving not to lose so valuable a booty, he took the creature, heavy as it was, on his shoulders and set out, as fast as he could walk, under the burden, in the direction which they had gone.

A NARROW ESCAPE.

He staggered along until he had cleared the thicket, and was moving on towards the thorn patches, when he heard a voice at some distance shouting to him. He looked up and saw Lavie running towards him at his utmost speed. Presently the voice came again.

"Drop that, and run for your life. There's a rhinoceros chasing you."

Nick did drop his load, as if it had been red hot iron, and glanced instinctively round. On the edge of the thicket which he had quitted, a large black rhinoceros was just breaking cover, snorting with fury, and evidently making straight for him. Nick's gun was empty, and even if it had been loaded, he would hardly have ventured to risk his life on the accuracy of his aim. He threw the gun away, and took to his heels, as he had never done since he left Dr Staines's school. He was swift of foot, and had perhaps a hundred yards start. But the rhinoceros is one of the fleetest quadrupeds in existence. Notwithstanding the lad's most desperate exertions, it continued to gain rapidly on him. Nick felt that his only chance was to get within gun-shot of his companions, when a fortunate bullet might arrest the course of his enemy. He tore blindly along, until he found himself within twenty yards of the thorn bushes, which had so excited his curiosity shortly before. The next minute he felt himself passing between two of the bushes, the rhinoceros scarcely thrice its own length behind him, its head bent down, and its long horn ready to impale him.

He gave himself over for lost, and only continued to dash along from the instinct of deadly terror. As he rushed between the bushes, he suddenly felt the earth shake and give way under him. Staggering forward a few paces, he fell flat on his face, tearing up the ground from the force of the fall. At the same moment a tremendous crash was heard behind him, followed a minute afterwards by a dull heavy shock. Nick sprung up again, notwithstanding the cuts and bruises he had received, and glanced hastily round him, expecting to see his terrible antagonist close on his flank. But, to his amazement, the creature had disappeared! There was the open space between the thorn bushes, through which he had just passed, and there was the long grass through which he had rushed, but where was the fierce pursuer, who was scarcely four yards behind him?

While he was gazing round him in a maze of alarm and wonder, he heard Lavie's voice close to him. "You may be thankful for the narrowest escape I ever remember to have witnessed!" he said.

"Where, where is the rhinoceros?" stammered Nick.

"Down at the bottom of that pit, into which you would have tumbled yourself, if you hadn't been running like a lamplighter. I'll just see if the poor brute is alive or not, and if he is, put a charge through his brain."

He peered cautiously down the hole, but all was still there. The animal had been impaled on the strong stake always placed at the bottoms of such traps, and it had probably penetrated the vitals. Satisfied on this point, he returned to Gilbert, who had now somewhat recovered his self-possession.

"Why didn't you run when we first called to you?"

"I didn't know you were calling to me. What made the brute attack me?"

"I don't know. The black rhinoceroses very often attack men without any apparent reason, though the white seldom do so. But what were you carrying on your back?"

"A black hog, which I had shot—famous eating, you know. We had better go and fetch it now. It will last us—"

"A hog!" exclaimed De Walden, who with Warley and Wilmore had now joined them. "I don't fancy there are any wild hogs about here; I never heard of any. Is this what you call a hog?" he continued, a minute or two afterwards, when they had reached the place where Nick had thrown his load down. "Why this is a young rhinoceros—about a week old, I should say! There is very little mystery now in the mother having charged after you. Well, you may indeed thank God for your escape! I would not have given a penny for your life under such circumstances. However, as we have the animal, we had better take as much of its flesh as we can carry. It is very excellent eating."

"I should like to examine the pitfall, sir, if you have no objection," said Warley. "I have never seen one, though I have often heard of them."

"I'll cut up the carcass, Mr De Walden," said Lavie, "if you like to go with the lads."

The missionary consented, and taking the three boys with him, pointed out to them the ingenious construction of the trap, which had been the means of preserving Nick's life. He showed them, that the whole enclosure which had excited Gilbert's wonder, was one network of pits. The thorn bushes were everywhere trained to grow so thick and close, that it was impossible to penetrate them; and in the centre of each of the open spaces between them a deep excavation was made, the top of which was skilfully concealed by slight boughs laid over it, and covered with tufts of long grass and reeds. At times, he said, the hunters would assemble in a large body, and drive the game in from every side, towards the enclosure. The frightened animals made for the entrances, and great numbers were thus captured in the pits. Even those which had passed safely through the openings, became easy victims to the arrows and assegais of the pursuers, being, in fact, too much alarmed to attempt to escape from their prison.

Before they had completed their examination of the ground, Lavie was ready to accompany them. Setting out without further delay, they reached an hour before sunset the banks of the Gariep. Wearied as they were with one of the longest day's journeys which they had accomplished, neither Lavie nor Warley could rest till they had taken a full view of the magnificent scene which broke upon them, when, after threading the dense thickets and tortuous watercourses which border the great river, they came at last on the main stream itself. The vast mass of water—which had been narrowed in, for a considerable distance by lofty cliffs on either side, to a channel hardly more than thirty yards in width—shot downwards over a rocky shelf in an abrupt descent of fully four hundred feet in height. On either side, the crags, partly bare and rugged, partly clothed with overhanging woods of the richest green; above, the tall mountains rising into broken peaks; and below, the boiling abyss—formed a frame, which was worthy of this splendid picture. The beams of the setting sun pouring full on the cascade, and producing a brilliant rainbow which spanned the entire width from side to side, together with the ceaseless thunder of the falling waters, seemed alike to entrance and overpower the senses of the beholder. It was not until they had stood for more than an hour gazing at this glorious spectacle, that either of the travellers could tear themselves from the spot, to seek the rest which overwearied nature demanded.

On the following morning they were awakened by De Walden at an earlier hour than usual. "We must lose no time," he said, "in crossing the river. It is not so high as I expected to find it, and at the point for which we must make, we can get over without much difficulty. But it is on one of the channels which just now are almost dry, that I fear we may encounter difficulty. The sky looked threatening last night, and if it had not been too late I should have attempted the passage. It looks worse this morning. I am half afraid there must be rain further up the country; and if such be the case, the river may suddenly rise so rapidly, that it will be next to impossible to escape it. We have not a moment to lose."

They hurried on under his directions, Lion following, and in an hour's time had reached a narrow part of the stream, which was there further diminished by an island in mid-channel. The latter was steep and narrow, having evidently been worn away by the action of successive ages, until scarcely more than ten feet of it remained. Against the craggy peaks into which it rose, several massive trees had lodged during some former flood, and had been left by the subsiding waters at a height of eight or ten feet above their present level. They formed a kind of rude bridge, which might be safely traversed by any one whose nerves were firm enough to attempt the feat.

Calling to Lavie to follow him, De Walden laid down his rifle and climbed up the mossy roots of one of the largest of these wrecks of the forest, till he had reached the first fork of the branches. Here he stopped, and waited till Lavie was within six feet or so of him, when he signed him to stop also. Warley followed, and then Frank, and lastly Nick; each taking up his station a few feet off from his nearest companion. Nick then passed along the various articles from hand to hand, until they reached De Walden, who secured them by thongs to the upper branch of the fork, and then climbed on till he had reached the island, when the same process was repeated.

In this manner, in about an hour's time, they passed safely over the central stream, and began descending the bank on the other side, passing without difficulty two or three of the narrower channels. But their progress through the tangled underwood, which in some places had to be cut with the axe before it would yield a passage, was necessarily slow, and it was past noon before they came to the edge of the last and broadest of the tributary channels—a stream too wide and deep to be forded, even if there had not been fear that the overhanging banks contained holes in which crocodiles might lurk. "We must fell a tree," said the missionary. "We shan't get across in any other way. One of the longest of these pines will answer our purpose, if it is dropped in the right place; but we must go to work without delay, for I fear before nightfall there will be rain. It seldom gives long notice of its coming in this country, and when it does fall, it falls in a perfect deluge. It is lucky we have the axe, or we must have gone back to the other bank again. Hand it to me, Ernest. I think I can contrive to drop this fir exactly into the fork of that large projecting yellow-wood there."

He took the axe as he spoke, and went to work with a will, the others relieving him at intervals, and labouring under his directions. But the edge of the instrument had unfortunately become blunt from use, and made its way but slowly into the tough wood. It was nearly three hours before the task was accomplished, and the long trunk dropped skilfully into the hollow of the tree opposite.

"Now then, we must not lose a minute," said De Walden. "We are fortunate that the rain has held off so long, but it must come soon." He mounted the trunk as he spoke and crawled along it, observing the same precautions as before. They had just reached the further end, when suddenly there came—from a considerable distance it seemed—a dull hollow roar, accompanied by a rush of chilling wind.

"Quick, quick," he cried; "the flood is close at hand. If it catches us here, we are lost. Climb the tree. It is our only hope." He sprang on the nearest branch as he spoke, and mounted up from bough to bough, until he had reached an elevation of twenty or thirty feet above the surface of the stream. The others followed his example, as well as they were able, catching at the limbs of the great yellow-wood tree which chanced to be nearest to them, and scrambling from point to point with the agility which deadly peril inspires. Nick, who was the hindmost of the party, had not mounted more than fifteen or twenty feet, before they all beheld, not a hundred yards off, a vast cataract of water rolling down the river gorge, sweeping from side to side, as it advanced, and converting the whole valley into a roaring torrent. Their temporary bridge was swept away and snapped in pieces like a reed, and for a moment De Walden feared that even the great yellow-wood in which they had found refuge, might experience a like fate. It stood firm, however, and the missionary was able to assure his companions that, as the flood was not likely to rise higher, they were in comparative safety. But they would have to pass the night, and possibly the next day, in their present position, as it would be madness to attempt breasting the flood, until its fury had spent itself. They had fortunately taken their morning meal on the further bank, and each had some remains of it in his wallet But it was a dreary prospect at best, and if the rain should again fall there would be the greatest danger lest the cold and weariness should so benumb their limbs, that they would be unable to retain their hold on the branches.

"What has become of Lion?" Nick managed to ask of Wilmore, who was niched near him, in a hollow formed by the junction of three boughs in one of the largest limbs of the yellow-wood. "I haven't seen him since we got on the tree."

"Poor old boy," returned Frank, "he was swept down the stream, when the fir was carried away. I tried to catch him by the collar, but couldn't. The last thing I saw of him was his black head in the midst of the boiling waters. I think I would sooner have been drowned myself!"

Chapter Sixteen

It was a long and terrible night. The heaven was covered with vast masses of inky clouds, which the gale drove rapidly before it; and occasionally there were sharp bursts of rain, from which even the dense foliage of the tree in which they were lodged but imperfectly screened them. The howling of the wind round them, and the roaring of the torrent below, rendered all attempts to converse with one another impossible. They could only cling to their place of refuge, and count the weary minutes as they passed, gazing anxiously on the eastern sky in the hope of seeing there the first faint streaks of dawn.

A little after midnight the fury of the elements seemed to have reached its height, and now a new danger threatened them. The huge tree rocked to and fro under the gusts of wind, as though it had been a bulrush, and every now and then a loud crack from below, intimated that one of the strong roots had yielded to its violence. At length, after one blast, more fierce than any which had preceded it, the last fibre gave way. De Walden felt the great trunk bend slowly forward, and settle down in the water; and almost immediately afterwards it was carried down the current, whirling and crashing against other trees as it went, with a force which nearly shook its occupants from their hold. Fortunately they had taken their stations on a branch which still remained above the water when the tree was uprooted; but it was nevertheless only by the most desperate exertion of the little strength which still remained to them, that they could save themselves from dropping, exhausted and benumbed, into the watery abyss beneath.

At length the dawn began to glimmer, and showed that the tree, which had become entangled with a number of others, had reached a point in the river where it could proceed no further. The vast floating *débris* had lodged against lofty rocks, which projected some distance into the stream, and thus an insuperable obstacle was offered to its farther progress. As the light grew stronger, it revealed a spectacle so extraordinary, and at the same time so frightful, that De Walden, with all his long and varied experience, could not recall the like of it. Numberless animals had taken refuge, as he and his party had done, in the boughs of trees, or had been carried against them by the torrent. The confused mass of trunks and branches was now crowded with the most strangely assorted occupants that had ever been brought together since the day of the great deluge; their natural instincts being, for the time, completely overpowered by terror. The lion and the eland crouched close beside one another; the steinbok and the ocelot clung to the same limb; the hyena and the sheep, the tiger and zebra, jostled each other, all alike apparently unaware of the presence of their neighbours.

More deadly enemies still were close at hand unheeded. Huge pythons, puff adders, cobras, ondaras, black snakes, were twisted round every projecting bough, darting their heads to and fro, and protruding their tongues in the extremity of alarm. Even the huge bulk of the rhinoceros might be discerned here and there, lodged on the bole of some giant acacia or baobab; while above, the smaller boughs were tenanted by multitudes of monkeys, for once omitting their customary scream and chatter in the presence of mortal peril.

De Walden perceived that it would be possible for the party now to make their way from tree to tree, until the right hand bank should be reached. That to the left, which was the one along which their journey now lay, being cut off from them by impassable obstacles. But they must get on shore first, and again attempt the passage of the river afterwards. He shouted to the others, and at length succeeded in rousing them from the torpor, which for some time had been creeping over them. Guided by him, they crawled stiffly and wearily from their resting-places, along one trunk after another, often almost pushing aside beasts of prey, which it would have been death to approach at other times, but which now shrank away from them in deadly fear—until at last the river's bank was attained. Here they struggled on for a short distance, through the dense underwood of thorn and reed, until they had reached a patch of long grass; when all, with one consent as it were, threw themselves on the soft couch, and were soon locked in the profoundest sleep.

How long they might have slept it is impossible to say. They were awakened about the middle of the day by finding themselves in the hands of a number of black men, who had already despoiled them of their accoutrements, and were engaged in tying their arms behind their backs with rheims of rhinoceros hide. They sat up and stared about them, hardly realising at first what had happened.

"Hallo, blacky," exclaimed Nick, when he had at length taken in the situation, "what may you happen to be about? Do you know, these legs and arms, that you are handling after that free-and-easy fashion, belong to me? Why, I declare," he continued, as he caught a clearer view of the man who was employed in tying him, "I declare that is one of the fellows whom you let off one fine morning about three weeks ago, Mr De Walden! One blacky is generally as like another as an egg is to an egg, but I think I could swear to that fellow's nose and eyebrows. Ain't I right, sir?"

"Quite right, I am sorry to say, Nick," replied De Walden. "I am more vexed than surprised at this. I knew these fellows would not return to Chuma without us if they could help it, and half feared they might be following us.

But if we had got safe across the Gariep, they would have come no further. It can't be helped, Lavie," addressing the surgeon, who seemed inclined to remonstrate. "I would ask them to let you go, and take me only with them, and it is possible, though not likely, that they would consent But they would certainly seize your guns and ammunition, and without these, and without a guide, you would hardly reach Cape Town. No, we must go to Chuma's kraal now, and try what may be done with him. I don't think he will venture to hurt us—anyhow, he won't hurt you. There is the annoyance of the detention, but that will be all."

"I have no doubt you are right," said Lavie. "They have taken us by surprise; and without arms we could do nothing against their superior numbers. The less we say or do the better, until we reach their village. Is it far off, do you suppose?"

"I can't quite tell where we are. But I should think five or six days' journey. Well, since you agree with me in the matter, I will tell them we are ready to start."

The Kaffir, who seemed the chief of the party, received this intimation with evident satisfaction. It was plain that, although he was determined, if he could, to take the missionary with him, and considered that the presence of the rest of the party would be acceptable to the chief, he was more than half afraid of the Englishmen, and would have been very unwilling to employ force. He gave orders to his companions to set out without loss of time, and in another quarter of an hour they were on their way. Kamo, as the leader was called, walked first, and carried De Walden's rifle, the prisoners, all five together, following, and the rest of the blacks, seven in number, occupying their flank and rear.

De Walden's calculations proved to be very nearly correct. On the evening of the sixth day, the travellers could perceive from the demeanour of their conductors, that they were approaching their destination. A halt was made about an hour before sunset, and two of the Kaffirs set forward, carrying the rifles and other articles taken from the English. In rather more than half an hour afterwards they returned, accompanied by a considerable number of their countrymen, carrying clubs, bows, and assegais, and evidently designed as a guard of honour. They formed themselves into a sort of procession, five Kaffirs in front with clubs and shields; then the whites in Indian file, with two blacks on either side of each one of them, and the remainder of the savages bringing up the rear.

In this order, about a quarter of an hour subsequently, they entered the Kaffir kraal; which was in some respects very like, but in others different from, that of the Hottentots. The huts were not built in the same regular order, as in the instance of the latter, and they were entirely composed of wicker-work besmeared with clay. Small too as had been the amount of cleanliness and order observable among the Hottentots, there was even less here. On the other hand, there were tokens of superior civilisation to be discerned on every side. There were large fields of Indian corn (or mealies as they were called), which were carefully fenced in, and now nearly ripe for harvest. There were gardens, too, in which pumpkins and sugar-canes grew. Before almost every door stood wicker baskets, earthenware pans, and iron or copper bowls and pails—all evidently of domestic manufacture. One of the largest huts seemed to be that of the village smith, and he and his assistant were at work, engaged in hammering an axe head.

The men were much darker, as well as of a taller and more powerful build, than the Namaquas. The weather being warm, they wore scarcely any clothing, and the stalwart muscular frames and well-formed features of many among them, might have served a sculptor as models of the Lybian Hercules. The women were not equal, either in symmetry of form or regularity of feature, to the males—the consequence, probably, of the severe and incessant toil required of them. They wore, for the most part, a skin petticoat descending half-way down the thigh, to which in colder weather they added a mantle of hide, secured by a collar round the throat. It was growing dusk when the party entered the kraal; but the chief, Chuma, came forth to greet De Walden, for whom it was plain that he entertained a strange mixture of fear, admiration, and dislike. He began by reproaching the missionary for his thanklessness in rejecting his repeated invitations. Anxious as he was to bestow all manner of honours and good gifts on the prophet of the white men, it was ungrateful of him to withhold his good offices in return. "See," he said, "the best house the kraal contains is yours, if you choose to occupy it; or if that suits you not, we will build you a house after your own fancy. As many cows and sheep as you may desire, as many fields of corn, as many fruit trees as you name, shall be given you. We will be your servants, and you may choose what wives you will. They will be sent to your house without payment. Only, in return, do not suffer our cattle to die of murrain, or our crops wither up for lack of rain. What injury have we done you, that you refuse us your aid in our necessity?"

"It is in vain that I tell you I cannot do what you ask of me," returned De Walden. "Again and again I have assured you, that I am as unable to prevent the visitations of disease and drought as you yourselves are. The God, of whom I have spoken to you, and about whom you will not hear, He, and He only, can accomplish the things you ask. If you wish to obtain the blessings of which you speak, bow down before Him, and ask Him for them."

"If I so bow down, will the prophet of the white men assure me, that I shall receive what I entreat for?"

"No," replied the missionary, "I can give you no such assurance. God hears prayer always, and is well pleased with those who offer it with a true heart; but He does not always grant what men ask for. It may not be good for them to receive it."

"What good, then, to pray, if there be no favourable answer?" rejoined the chief, a cloud gathering on his brow. "You ask me to commit folly. You trifle with me. You have brought down rain for others, and driven away the disease that slew the cattle for others. Look, you shall live here in the village, and we will kill you, if you attempt to escape. If the rain does not come in its season, you shall bring it. If the cattle die of pestilence you shall cause it to depart, or you shall yourself suffer pain and hunger and death. As for these others, are they prophets and wizards too?"

"They are simply English travellers, on their way to Cape Town," said De Walden, "and their friends are persons of importance there. You have heard of the English?"

"The English," said Chuma. "Ah, the English. Yes, I have heard of them. They came over the great salt water, years ago, and fought with the Dutch — did they not?"

"They did. They fought with the Dutch and conquered them. You know well that the Dutch are dangerous enemies to meet in battle. None of the races whose skins are dark—the Bechuanas, the Basutos, the Zulus, the Namaquas—none of them can stand before the Dutch—"

"They have the fire-tubes," interposed the chief angrily,—"the fire-tubes which strike men dead from a great distance like the lightning, and no one can avoid it. They wear iron coats, and caps, which turn aside the arrows and the assegais. They ride on horses too, which are taught to fight like themselves. It is not equal. Let them lay aside their coats and their tubes, and fight on foot like our warriors, with clubs and assegais, and see who will conquer then."

"You know they are not likely to do that," returned the missionary; "but that is nothing to the present matter. I wish to show you that if you cannot stand before the Dutch, much less would you be able to face the English, who are braver warriors, and better acquainted with war, than even the Dutch."

"Ah, but the English have gone away," rejoined Chuma. "You try to deceive me, but you cannot. The Dutch rule over the country again now.

The White Queen, who is a great magician, sent messengers to the English chief not many months ago. But they came back and told her he was gone. I know that, for Kama was in the Basuto kraal when they returned, and heard their tale. She, I say, was a great magician, and they could not have deceived her, even if they dared speak falsely."

"They did not speak falsely," said De Walden. "The English went away three or four years ago, and have stayed in their own land until now. But not many weeks ago they came back over the salt water, and have again conquered the Dutch, and are masters of the land."

"Ah, the English again masters! We will not quarrel with the English. We have seen them fight. But how do I know that they have come back? How do I know that these persons are English, or that they have great friends there?"

"You have my word," returned the other.

"Ah, but you deceive me in some matters, and may in others. I must have proof of what you tell me before I let them go. But see here. Will they give me their fire-tubes and their black powder as their ransom? Then they may depart."

"They cannot do so," said the missionary. "If you deprive them of their guide and their weapons, how can they find their way so many hundred miles, and how provide themselves with food by the way? You must let them take their guns; and, if you are resolved on compelling me to remain here, you must furnish them with a guide. By him they will send you back any ransom you may agree on."

"And when they get near the dwelling of their friends, they will send their guide away empty-handed, or it may be they will kill him, and I shall hear no more of him or them either. It is not good. No, I will not quarrel with the English. But they live far off. They will know nothing of these men where they are, or what may have become of them. If I keep them prisoners, or if I put them to death"—the eyes of the savage emitted a fierce light as he spoke—"if I put them to death," he repeated slowly, "who will tell the English of it?"

"It will certainly be discovered," said De Walden. "It is known that they have landed on the sea-coast at no great distance from here, and that they are wandering about in these regions. One of them is the son of a great sea warrior; the others are his friends and companions. The great Chief of the English will send out soldiers to search for them. He will learn from many whither they have been taken; and if harm has been done them, he will exact heavy punishment."

Chuma shook his head, but he evidently was much moved by the missionary's words. He conferred apart with some of his counsellors, and an animated debate, to all appearance, ensued. At length he turned away from them, and again addressed De Walden.

"See," he said, "this is the way of it. One of the whites, whomsoever they may choose, goes alone to the great village of the whites, and Kama goes with him as guide; but the white man leaves the fire-tube here behind him, which he will not need, for Kama finds food on the way. The others— they too stay behind here in the village till Kama returns, and tells me what he has seen and heard—does this please you?"

"I will report to them what you have said," returned De Walden, "and bring you their answer."

He stepped up to the place where the four travellers were resting themselves on a heap of skins, and reported to them Chuma's proposal. "On the whole," he added, "I should advise you to accept it. I know how suspicious these Bechuanas are. Never practising anything like truthful and fair dealing themselves, they are incapable of believing that any one else can do so. If you refuse, your refusal will be imputed to some sinister designs which you are secretly cherishing; and Chuma is fully capable of relieving himself from all immediate anxiety by putting the whole party to death."

"I quite see that," said Lavie. "The only alternative is attempting to escape, and the chances are greatly against our succeeding in that. In any case," he mentally added, "such a step would bring ruin and death on you. No," he resumed, "we must certainly close with Chuma's offer. The only question is, which of us is to be the one to go."

"You must not choose me," said Gilbert. "I should only make a mess of it."

"I would go," said Frank, "but I do not think I am strong enough yet to attempt such a journey."

"And I would rather not leave Mr De Walden," added Warley. "You had better go yourself, Charles. You are in every way better fitted to manage the business."

"I should not object," said Lavie, "but I do not like to leave you in the hands of these treacherous savages."

"You leave us under Mr De Walden's care," rejoined Warley, "and I, for one, can fully trust to that."

After some further discussion, it was so arranged. Chuma was informed that his terms were accepted; and on the following day the doctor, having taken an affectionate farewell of his young companions, set out for Cape Town with Kama and another Bechuana for his guides; while the others prepared themselves to endure, as patiently as they could, the long weeks of waiting which must inevitably ensue.

"Are these Kaffirs utterly without the idea of God, as people say they are?" asked Ernest one day of Mr De Walden, about a week after their friends, departure. "I was talking one day to a gentleman on board the *Hooghly*, who seemed to be well acquainted with them, and he declared that they had positively no religion at all. But another gentleman differed from him, and was going on, I believe, to produce some proofs to the contrary, but the conversation was broken off. I should like to know what you would say on the subject."

"They have no *religion* in the proper sense of the word," answered the elder man. "No sense of connection, that is to say, with a Being infinitely powerful and good, who made and sustains them, and to whom they are accountable. It is this that constitutes a religion, and of this they know nothing. But they are extremely *superstitious*. They believe in the existence of Evil Spirits, who have alike the power and the will to afflict and torment them. To these they attribute every disaster or suffering which may befall them."

"A creed of fear, in fact, without love," suggested Ernest.

"Precisely. They have no idea of pleasing the Unseen Powers by duty and affection, but are keenly alive to the necessity of propitiating them by continual sacrifices. They believe also, that it is possible to obtain from their Evil Spirits the power of benefiting or afflicting others; and those who are presumed to be in possession of these powers are held in as great—practically in greater—reverence than the Spirits themselves."

"These persons are, of course, impostors."

"In the main, yes. But there are some who are half impostors and half fanatics—really thinking they possess some of the gifts attributed to them, though how much, they themselves hardly know. This is the common case with false prophets. Their heaviest punishment ever is, that they partially credit their own lie."

"And this chief, Chuma, supposes you to be one of these prophets?"

"He does, and nothing I can say will disabuse his mind of the idea. It is not uncommon with these pretenders, to appear to deny the possession of supernatural powers, until they have obtained their price from the chiefs! Chuma will not be persuaded that my disclaimers have no deeper meaning than this. And I have given up the point in despair."

"Are there any of these pretended prophets among the tribe?"

"There is one—a man named Maomo. He was once in great favour with Chuma; but a long drought, some two years ago, which he failed to relieve, forfeited his prestige in the chief's eyes. He has been labouring for a long time past to regain his power; and he regards me, I know, with especial dislike, because he views me as the chief obstacle to the attainment of his wishes."

"He is not likely, I suppose, to succeed in his design. The chief seems to regard you with the deepest awe, if not affection."

"Ernest," said the missionary, "that is all delusive. His awe of me is founded on an unreal basis, which *will* some day, and *may* any day, crumble into nothing. And the moment Chuma ceases to fear me, his hate will burst out in all its deadly fury. Maomo has already (as I know quite well) so far worked upon the chief's prejudices, that he views me as an enemy, though one whom it is not safe to attack. He has persuaded him that the Spirits are angry at my attempts to draw away his people from their ancient belief, and the consequence, he has assured him, will be some heavy visitation of disease, or famine, or drought. Chuma has, in consequence, positively forbidden me to attempt to make any converts, or even offer prayers to our God, under penalty of his heaviest displeasure. This very day he has told me so."

"And you, sir?" asked Ernest, anxiously.

"I, Ernest," answered the missionary, somewhat reproachfully, "I told him, of course, that I should obey God rather than him, and strive to bring any soul among his people to the knowledge of Christ. I left him somewhat subdued, as determined language always subdues him; but the moment any trouble befalls him, I know well what what will follow."

"Let me help you," said Ernest, deeply moved.

"Give me some of your work to do. I will do it to the best of my power."

"Notwithstanding the consequences?" asked De Walden.

"Notwithstanding the consequences," answered Warley resolutely. And the two shook hands with a warmth neither had before felt towards the other.

Chapter Seventeen

Time passed on: the summer heats gradually gave way to the cooler temperature of autumn, and that too began to pass into winter, and nothing had been heard of Lavie or his guide. It had been calculated that it would take them fully two months to reach Cape Town; but there they would be able to obtain horses, which would so greatly shorten the return journey, that ten or eleven weeks might be regarded as the probable period of their entire absence. But March was exchanged for April, April for May; June succeeded May, and July, June; and still there came no tidings of the travellers. The boys grew anxious, and might have become seriously alarmed, if it had not been that they found so much to interest and employ them, that they had no time for indulging morbid fancies.

All the four whites occupied one large hut, some five and twenty feet in circumference, and provided with mats, karosses, and all the other furniture of a Kaffir dwelling-house, so as to render it a very comfortable residence. They also took all their meals together, which were provided at the cost of the whole tribe, and prepared for them by Kobo and Gaiké, the two attendants chosen for them by Chuma. But before many weeks had passed, they had separated, by common consent, into two pairs; De Walden and Ernest being almost continually together, and Frank and Nick Gilbert taking up with one another, as a matter of necessity.

Warley was deeply impressed by the character of the new friend he had found. De Walden's devoted self-surrender, his resolute and uncomplaining spirit under the most trying hardships, his cheerfulness, and even joyousness, while enduring what would have broken most men's spirits altogether, were the very ideal of which Ernest had dreamed, but never expected to realise.

"Did you make many converts among the Hottentots?" he asked one day. "I remember hearing you say your mission, as a whole, had not succeeded; but I suppose you made converts here and there?"

"I cannot say I ever made one."

"Not one! And yet you were going back to them again!"

"Certainly. Why not?"

"Rather, 'Why?' I should have been inclined to ask."

"Why? because God has commanded that the Gospel should be preached to all nations, and that command stands good, whether they will hear, or whether they forbear. It is our business to do His work, and His to look after the result."

"And you would not consider that a man's life was wasted, if he passed his whole life as a missionary, without making one convert?"

"No more wasted than if he had made ten thousand. Look here, Ernest. You have never seen a coral island, I suppose?"

"No," said Warley; "I have read about them, but I have never seen one."

"You have read about them? Then you know that the coral insects labour on, generation after generation, under the water, raising the reef always higher and higher, till it reaches the high-tide level at last."

"Yes, that is what I have read, certainly."

"For generations, then, upon generations, the work of the insect was wholly out of human sight. Ernest, was their work in vain? Did not they help to build up the island as much as those whose labours could be clearly discerned?"

"You are right," said Warley. "One soweth, and another reapeth."

"Yes, and both will rejoice hereafter together; claiming, under God, the work between them. The work of the missionary—of the early missionary—may seem to man's eyes as nothing, but it is merely out of man's sight. He is building up Christ's kingdom, as the coral insect, far down below, builds up the reef; and will, unknown though he be now, have equal honour hereafter with those whom the world now accounts its greatest benefactors."

Many such conversations as these were held between the two friends—as, notwithstanding the disparity of their years, De Walden and Ernest might be called—and every day the bond between them grew stronger. Together they visited the Kaffir huts, and held long talks with the occupants; who were never unwilling to discourse on the subject nearest to De Walden's heart, little as they might be inclined to hearken to his teaching. He was, however, not without hope that he had succeeded in making some impression. More than one man resorted secretly to him to ask explanations of difficulties, which, it was plain, had been weighing on their minds; more than one woman attended the prayers, which were daily offered to the God of the Christians in the white man's hut, in spite of Chuma's interdict Maomo heard of it, and it roused still more fiercely his jealousy and alarm. He was, as has already been intimated, partly a deceiver, and partly a dupe.

He knew that many of his pretensions were simply impostures; but he did believe in the existence of Evil Spirits, and their power to injure men. Such doctrines as those propounded by De Walden, must needs, he thought, be in the highest degree distasteful to them; and they would visit the land with the most terrible plagues, if the people fell away from the faith of their fathers.

He continually beset Chuma, therefore, with entreaties to put down the evil, before it reached any greater height. He reminded the chief that he had already forbidden De Walden, or the "White Lie-maker," as he was wont to call him, to teach the people his new and dangerous creed. His commands had been openly disobeyed, and he must now enforce severe penalties against him, or suffer the most terrible consequences himself. Chuma listened, but made evasive replies. His own mind was in a state of doubt on the subject. He was incensed by the Englishman's obstinate refusals to comply with his orders, and had begun to doubt whether he really did possess the presumed supernatural powers. If that should indeed be the case, he would make short work with him. At present, however, he was not convinced that this was the case, and he had resolved to defer any action until his mind was made up.

Meanwhile Frank and Nick went out almost every day with their guns, under the tutelage of Kobo, a middle-aged, strongly built Bechuana, into whose charge Chuma had consigned them. The missionary was jealously watched, not only by the chief's servants, but by those of Maomo also. He was never allowed to leave his hut, unless accompanied by at least one man, and never to leave the village at all, except by the chief's express permission, and under the escort of three armed men. But the boys were not so carefully looked after. Chuma contented himself with warning Kobo, that if at any time they were not forthcoming, he would have to pay the penalty with his own life. The boys knew this as well as Kobo, and promised him that they would make no attempt at escape, even if a favourable opportunity should offer; and the Bechuana, strange to say, seemed quite contented with their assurance. He went out with them into the bush, sometimes to a considerable distance, allowing them to take their firearms, and carrying no weapon himself, but a light hatchet, which would have been of no service to him at all, in event of any hostile movement on their part, nor did he ever seem to entertain a suspicion that could mean treachery towards him.

"He's a good fellow, this blacky," remarked Nick one day, as they halted under the shade of a large oomahaama, to rest an hour or two before returning home from one of their shooting excursions. "He's a good fellow, not suspicious of every word one says, or of the meaning of every act one does. He really has some notion of honesty. More's the wonder!"

"Yes," answered Frank; "I should like to ask him where he got it from, only I suppose he wouldn't understand one."

"Oh yes, Kobo would—understand very well," said Kobo, joining in the lads' conversation, in broken, but very intelligible English.

"Hallo, hey, what!" exclaimed both the boys, half starting up with surprise. "What! you understand English, Kobo?" added Frank. "How in the world did you learn it?"

"And why in the world didn't you tell us long ago that you understood it?" subjoined Gilbert.

"Kobo keep it secret—chief not know—prophet not know," answered Kobo. "Kobo tell white boys, not black man."

"Do tell us, then, Kobo," said Nick, whose interest had been keenly awakened. "You may trust us to keep whatever we may hear to ourselves, if you desire it."

Kobo assented readily enough. It was plain that he was anxious, for some reason of his own, that they should learn his history, and had been awaiting his opportunity of telling it. We shall not follow the broken English of his narrative, but relate it in our own words.

Kobo had been born and reared in the Bechuana village where he was still living; but when a lad of twelve or thirteen years old, had incurred the chief's displeasure for some boyish offence, and to escape the punishment incurred by it, fled from the kraal and took refuge in a village lying at a considerable distance from his own people. He had not been there many months, when the village in which he was living was attacked by a commando, and with the usual consequences. All the males who had reached puberty and the elder women, were shot or cut down; the girls and children carried off into bondage.

Kobo's fate had at first been very doubtful. He was just on the very verge of what was considered manhood, and the sword of more than one Dutchman was raised to cut him down. But he was, luckily for himself, rather short of stature, and it was ultimately resolved that he should be spared. He was taken to the southern part of the colony, and became the slave of a Dutch farmer residing near Oudtshoorn. Here he remained for several years, until he had quite grown to manhood. According to his own statement, which it would be reasonable to receive with some degree of caution, he was treated with the utmost injustice and cruelty by his masters—ill-fed, overworked, and kicked and cuffed without any reason, whenever his employers chanced to be out of temper.

But there was no remedy for his wrongs. It was in vain to appeal to the law, which would hardly entertain his complaint at all, and would have done nothing to protect him, even if he could have made out his case. To have offered resistance would have been the extremity of folly, as it would only have brought down increased suffering upon him; and to have attempted escape, would have been almost certain death. It was a long distance to the border of the Bechuana country; and the fierce bloodhounds kept by the whites would have overtaken and torn him to pieces, before he could have gone the twentieth part of the way. There was nothing for it but to bear it patiently.

It chanced that there was a man residing in Oudtshoorn, who was of European, but not Dutch, descent. He was believed to be an Englishman, who for some unknown reason had chosen to leave his own country. He took some notice of Kobo, whose appearance and manner pleased him; and gradually the Bechuana confided to him his history, the cruel hardships he endured, and the anxious longing which possessed him to regain his freedom. Andrews, as the Englishman was called, listened attentively to his story, and then advised him to wait patiently for a few weeks more, when an opportunity he desired might present itself. Andrews was a secret agent of the English Government, and knew that an army and fleet were soon going to be sent out to attempt the seizure of the Dutch colony. If this should prove successful, he would be able to help Kobo effectually. The Bechuana followed his advice; and one evening, towards the end of December, received an unexpected visit from his English friend, who was mounted on a strong Cape horse, and led another by the bridle.

"Mount, Kobo," he said, "and ride with me. Your master is too much frightened by the news he has just received to think about you; and even if he did try to catch you, he couldn't."

Kobo obeyed willingly enough. They rode through the whole of that night, and next morning arrived at a place where fresh horses had been provided. Continuing their ride with hardly an hour's delay, they reached Simon's Bay, where an English fleet had just come to anchor. Andrew's first step was to have Kobo regularly rated as his servant. When the campaign was ended by the cession of the colony, they returned to Oudtshoorn; where Kobo's former master was still residing, but he stood too much in awe of Andrews to claim his fugitive slave again. Kobo, who had become greatly attached to his English master, continued for several years in his service, until in 1803 the colony was handed back to the Dutch. When it became certain that the English Government would take this step, Andrews advised Kobo to leave Oudtshoorn before the departure of the English troops. Van Ryk, his former master, had always looked upon him as his lawful property, of which he had been violently despoiled, and would inevitably claim him as soon as the Dutch power was again established. Kobo's affection for Andrews would have induced him to remain and brave the hazard of this; but the Englishman pointed out that he would not have the power of protecting him against Van Ryk's claim, or against any cruel usage to which he would probably subject him, and this would be worse pain to both than their separation. Kobo accordingly was conveyed by Andrews as far as the Gariep, where they took leave of one another, the Englishman returning to Oudtshoorn, and Kobo rejoining his tribe.

The latter, however, had kept the true history of his past life a profound secret from his countrymen, passing off a plausible tale of life among the Bushmen in its place. He was afraid that Van Ryk would offer the Bechuana chief a large sum for his tradition, and he knew Chuma's avaricious spirit too well to believe that he would refuse it. When he heard from De Walden of the reoccupation of the Cape by the English, he was instantly seized with an anxious desire to return to Oudtshoorn, and would have offered himself to Lavie as his guide, if it had not been that he dared not betray his knowledge of the English language. He would, however, in all likelihood, soon have left the Bechuana village alone, if he had not conceived a liking for the English prisoners, and a desire to serve them in the danger which, as he could plainly see, was threatening them. He was well acquainted with Maomo's cruel and vindictive nature. Several persons, towards whom the wizard had conceived a hatred, had suffered the most terrible tortures and death through his machinations, and towards no one had he ever felt such bitter enmity as towards De Walden.

This feeling had been increased by the failure of his schemes, thus far, to work the missionary's ruin. He had been hoping that the drought, which often visited the country during the summer months, would give him the desired opportunity of either obliging De Walden to comply with Chuma's entreaties to bring down rain by his incantations, or of provoking the chief's wrath to the uttermost by his refusal. But the summer, to his infinite vexation, had been extraordinarily cool and genial, showers falling at short intervals of one another; and causing abundance of grass and water. What was worse, he could see that Chuma attributed this exceptional season to De Walden's residence in the village. He was farther than ever therefore from accomplishing his object.

But he was not a man to be balked of his purpose; and Kobo, who had watched him narrowly, felt certain that he had some scheme on foot which would achieve the object on which his heart was set. He had been absent for two or three days in the previous week, and when he returned there was a look of triumphant malice in his face, which he tried in vain to hide. The only well-grounded hope they could have of escaping his malicious designs lay in immediate flight. Chuma, as yet, was favourably disposed, and had taken no steps which would render flight impossible. But this would not last long; and De Walden must take time by the forelock, or it would certainly be too late.

Such was the substance of what Kobo imparted to the boys, and which they made a point of laying before Mr De Walden immediately after his return to their village.

The missionary listened attentively, and asked several questions as to Kobo's sources of information, and the details of the plan of escape he had suggested; but when these had been answered he refused to avail himself of the offer.

"I have little doubt," he said, "that Kobo in the main is right, if not in every particular, but it is my duty to remain here, and remain I must, whatever may ensue. For the first time since my arrival in Africa, I have a real, well-grounded hope of gaining a considerable body of converts to our faith. What will these think of me? What hope can I have of their remaining true to the creed they have half adopted, if I myself am wanting to it? I am in God's hands, and I trust all to Him. But you, my dear lads—it is not *your* duty to stay here, and encounter this danger. You, indeed, Ernest—"

"Do you think *I* could leave you?" interposed Warley reproachfully.

"I will not ask you to do so," answered the missionary, clasping Ernest's hands as he spoke; "but you two—"

"We too will not leave you," broke in Frank. "I know I speak for Nick as well as myself. We will all stay and endure whatever may chance together. I will tell Kobo so forthwith."

He sought out the Bechuana accordingly, and acquainted him with the resolution to which all the party had come, adding however, that they would all keep Kobo's secret most inviolably, and if any occasion should arrive when his services might be required for an attempt of the kind suggested by him, they would at once apply to him to help them.

"Meanwhile," he said, "Kobo, let us have plenty to employ our time and thoughts. It will never do for us to sit down and brood over our troubles; we should go mad, I expect. Look here, didn't you tell us that the spoor of some elephants had been seen yesterday or this morning, at a short distance from this?"

"Great many elephant in bush," said Kobo; "six, seven, big bulls, twenty cows, not three miles away. Not go away to-day, perhaps not to-morrow."

"Do you hear that, Nick?" said Wilmore. "We had better set out the first thing in the morning, hadn't we, and try to get a shot at one?"

"White boys see them to-night, if they like," said Kobo. "See here. Kobo love white boys because they English. He wait here till they ready to run away. Then he run with them. Meanwhile they shoot, hunt, fish. Chuma not suspect they mean to run."

"All right, Kobo," said Nick. "You're a brick, if you know what that means, though you have been baked pretty black in the kiln. Well, let us set off at once. Where do you propose that we should pass the night?"

"Bavian's Pool, Master Nick; three miles from here—beautiful pool, sweet water, steep rock overhang it, too steep for beasts to climb, not too steep for us. There we sleep among bushes; animals come down to drink by moonlight; buffalo, gnu, zebra, giraffe, lion, rhinoceros, all sorts of beasts—elephant come too—"

"And we can shoot at them from the rock, hey?" interposed Nick.

"No, not shoot from rock. Elephant not come near enough, and light bad; but we track them when they leave waterside, and get good shot in morning."

"All right, Kobo. How soon ought we to set out?"

"Three hours past noon, now. Get to pool at five. We start in an hour, say."

"In an hour; very good. Let us go and say good-bye to Mr De Walden and Ernest, Frank, and get the guns."

"Done with you," said Frank. "Shall we ask Ernest to come with us? We have had very little of his company for a long time past, and I think he would enjoy this. You know how anxious he always was to come upon a herd of elephants, all the time when we were travelling through the country where they are said sometimes to be found. He is a good fellow, and I don't like to lose sight of him so entirely."

"I agree with you, that he is a good fellow," said Nick,—"a deal better fellow, for the matter of that, than I am. But I am afraid there is not much chance of his making one of our party. There has been a change in him ever since that escape of his from the big snake; and since he has fallen in with Mr De Walden, he has been so taken up with him that he can think of nothing else. But we can ask him, certainly."

But on reaching the hut they perceived at once that it would be no use to make any such suggestion—for the present, at all events. The two friends were on the point of repairing to the house of one of their converts, who had sent to them a message, entreating their immediate presence. One of the calamities, which the Bechuanas dreaded beyond all others, had just befallen him. It had been known for some time past, that a disease, nearly resembling that which has visited European countries of late years, was raging among the herds belonging to neighbouring tribes, and more particularly the Basutos. It was regarded with the utmost terror by all the races inhabiting Southern Africa, whom it deprived not only of all their wealth, but of their very means of subsistence. They were wholly unacquainted with any means of dealing effectually with it; indeed, for the most part, they attributed it entirely to the agency of malignant Spirits; and its appearance generally threw them entirely into the hands of the pretended prophets. In the present instance they had felt tolerably secure that it would not visit the Bechuana village, the summer having been exceptionally healthy. But that morning, two oxen had suddenly been seized with the symptoms which were only too well-known. The owner, who had unbounded faith in the missionary's powers, had sent at once to him entreating his help; and he and Warley were just setting out to render what assistance it might be possible to give.

"Poor beggars!" exclaimed Nick. "It will be a bad job for them if they do lose their cattle, seeing that is pretty well all they have. Shall you be able to do anything for them, sir?"

"I am afraid very little," said the elder man. "I have fallen in with the disease more than once during my residence in this country, and have hardly ever known a case of cure, when it has once fairly taken hold of an animal But we will do our best. Good night, lads I hope you may have a pleasant day's sport. If it hadn't been for this, I should have liked Ernest to have gone with you. As it is, I shall want his help."

Chapter Eighteen

It took Kobo and the two lads a good hour to reach Bavian's Pool. It lay in a different direction from any which they had yet pursued, through dense bush, in which they would soon have lost themselves, if it had not been for Kobo's attendance. Occasionally they came on the spoor of the elephants, a large herd of which had evidently passed that way not many hours previously. The gigantic footprints were traced sharp and clear in the sandy soil; the young trees, that had been broken off or trodden down by their bulky frames, exhibited fresh white fractures; those which had only been bent by the weight of the animals in passing, seemed hardly yet to have regained their former positions. Kobo, who spoke under his breath in awe, as it seemed, of these forest kings, told them that the herd, in all likelihood, were reposing at the distance of not more than a quarter of a mile from the path they were now traversing. This intelligence appearing to excite the lads a good deal. He added, that they must not attempt to get a sight of them now, or they would certainly spoil their pleasure that evening, and probably prevent the elephant hunt, which was to take place the next day. The whole tribe, he said, was going out in the morning, and it was hoped that a good many animals would be killed; and as there were several very fine males among them, a large prize in the way of ivory was anticipated. But if the herd should be disturbed, and especially if it should be fired upon, they would probably retreat northwards towards the great lake, and the Bechuanas would see nothing of them but their spoor and dung.

The boys yielded to his representations; and, turning in a different direction from that followed by the elephants, they arrived in another quarter of an hour at Bavian's Pool, which lay in the very heart of the bush, with a clear space overgrown with grass and short rushes of about twenty yards all round. On the west side appeared the rocks of which Kobo had told them, and which presented a most picturesque appearance. They rose abruptly from the bank of the tarn, to the height of perhaps twenty feet, and sank down with a sharp descent to the level ground everywhere, except in one place where a series of crags, piled one on another, presented a kind of rude and very steep staircase, by which the top might be attained. Up this the party climbed, and ensconced themselves snugly under a shelf of rock from which they could see the whole of the pool and the surrounding banks.

It was still broad daylight when they reached their place of ambush, and the spot was as vacant and still as though the whole landscape had been a part of the great Kalahari itself But they had not been there a quarter of an hour, when the sun disappeared behind the belt of woodland which bounded the sight, and the night of the tropics succeeded with its startling rapidity. The green waste of thorns and shrubs grew first dusky brown, and then deep black; the bright sparkling water a dull gleamy mirror, faintly rendering back the pale opal of the sky. But presently there came a further change. The moon rose higher in the heavens, and the stars came forth in all the unimaginable glories of a southern night—not mere specks of light as seen in the more cloudy skies of the north, but hung like cressets in the glowing air, the moon itself a bright globe of liquid fire. A clear soft radiancy diffused itself over the whole scene, tipping every tree top and distant eminence with silver, and causing the surface of the tarn, as it rippled lazily under the evening breeze, to flash in circlets of light. Presently there came a pattering of feet, as a crowd of small animals came down from different points of the compass to quench their thirst—antelopes with their slender legs and liquid eyes, glancing timidly round them; elands and koodoos tossing their stately heads; gnus and buffaloes in large herds consorting together for mutual protection; hyenas, jackals, and zebras, plunging to the mid-leg in the cool dancing waters, and bounding lightly away when their drought was satisfied. It was a beautiful sight to watch them come and go, like the scenes in a magic-lantern.

By and by, as the night deepened, the larger beasts of the forest made their appearance. The tall graceful heads of giraffes were seen over the tops of the bushes; tigers made their approach, singly or in pairs, with their stealthy and noiseless step; lions stalked proudly down, as though they felt that the sovereignty of the woods belonged by natural right to them; occasionally the ponderous bulk of the rhinoceros might be discerned, as he sucked in the refreshing water with his huge misshapen snout, and retreated with a grunt of satisfaction when his appetite had been appeased. Frank and Nick looked on with ever-increasing interest, though it needed Kobo's oft-repeated remonstrances to keep them from discharging their rifles at some of the larger specimens, which came within tempting distance of their fire.

It was nearly midnight, and the shores of the pool were beset by a crowd of animals, consisting mostly of the larger beasts of prey, when a sudden sensation of alarm seemed to agitate the whole of the miscellaneous group. The giraffes lifted their stately heads, snuffed the air for a moment, and then bounded silently away; the panthers and nylghaus moved more slowly off; the lions uttered low growls, apparently of dissatisfaction, but nevertheless followed the retreat of the others. Even the sullen black rhinoceros, after bending his head awhile to listen, beat a leisurely retreat, viciously snorting as he retired. In a few minutes the shores of the pool were as still and vacant as they had been when the boys arrived, five or six hours before.

"What does this mean?" asked Nick in a whisper. "What have these brutes seen or heard, to alarm them so? Are your countrymen on their way to attack them?"

"No, it not that," answered Kobo, in the same subdued accents. "Beasts hear elephant coming down to drink. All get out of elephant's way. He king among them. Listen, you hear them."

"Do you really mean it, Kobo?" asked Nick, astonished at this information. "The lions and rhinoceroses can't really be so much afraid of the elephants as that comes to?"

"I believe it's true," said Frank; "I know I've been told so before. A lion or a rhinoceros wouldn't mind a single elephant much, I dare say; but it's the whole troop of 'em together that they're afraid of. They'd run right over a lion, or a rhinoceros either, and trample the life out of them, before they knew where they were. Yes, Kobo's right. Here they come over that low bit of hill there. What a lot! and what thundering big beasts!"

As he spoke, a dull heavy sound, like the roll of loaded waggons along a hard road was heard; and the figure of an enormous elephant emerged from the cover of the thicket, its broad flat head, huge misshapen ears, and white tusks glistening in the broad moonlight. It was followed by another, and another, each seeming to loom larger than the last, until ten of the monsters had reached the banks of the tarn, all of them males, and of the largest size.

"All bull," whispered Kobo; "bull drink first, females wait till they done."

While he was speaking, the elephants had advanced up to their mid-legs in the water, and dipping their trunks in, sucked up the cooling stream with a loud gurgling noise. Frank's fingers insensibly stole to the lock of his rifle. One of the largest of the giants was now scarcely more than four or five yards from him, its figure as plainly visible in the clear cold light, as though it had been noonday. Kobo had again to lay his hand on the boy's shoulder, and whisper in his ear, "No shoot, spoil hunt to-morrow," or he might not have been able to resist the temptation.

Presently, however, the males had satisfied their thirst, and moving off slowly in a different direction from that by which they had approached the pond, re-entered the thicket. The cow elephants now took their places, some twenty or thirty in number, many of them with calves of various ages at their sides. There was scarcely room in the tarn for the whole herd, and before they retired, the bright and sparkling waters had become a turbid and discoloured flood. At length, however, they did retire, and before the moon had set, the last of the bulky figures had disappeared among the foliage.

"Now lie down and sleep;" said Kobo, "no more animals to-night."

The boys complied, and lying down among the bushes which grew here and there between the masses of rocks, were soon buried in slumber. They were awakened by Kobo at daybreak; and having eaten their breakfast, and taken a dip in the tarn, which by this time had recovered its translucent clearness, announced to Kobo that they were ready to take the field.

They accompanied the Bechuana accordingly, as he proceeded cautiously to follow the track left by the herd on the previous evening, for half a mile or so through the bush. Then desiring them to climb two trees of some size, which stood on either side of the path in the heart of the woodland—an acacia and a motjeerie—he crept on alone through the shrubs, making his way as secretly and noiselessly as a snake, and soon vanished from their view.

Presently he reappeared, with the information that the herd were browsing at the distance of a few hundred yards only, and seemed to have no apprehension of danger. Chuma, however, and the other hunters would now soon make their appearance from the opposite side, and would doubtless attack the bull elephants with their assegais, their tusks being a valuable prize. Kobo told them that they could not do better than remain where they were. The elephants would almost certainly be driven past the tree in which they lodged, and so give them the opportunity they desired of trying their skill as marksmen. There were other trees, he said, at no great distance which were larger, and therefore safer, but the elephants might never come near them at all; whereas, in their present position, they were almost sure to see what passed.

"All right, Kobo," said Frank, "we'll stay here and take our chance. After all, it must be a jolly big elephant that would bowl this tree over."

Kobo again vanished, and the boys sat on the tiptoe of expectation for the next hour or so, but without hearing any sound at all except the song of the birds and the buzzing of the insects. Suddenly, however, there broke forth a Babel of discordant sounds. The yells of the Kaffirs—as advancing at the same time from different quarters, they assailed the elephants with their assegais and arrows—were overpowered by the trumpeting of the huge brutes, and the crash of the thorn and seringa bushes, which gave way on every side before them, offering no more serious obstacle to their career, than long grass would to that of a man. Presently the whole herd broke from the cover of the jungle, hurrying on in a transport of mingled rage and terror—the solid earth seeming to tremble under their tread. The Bechuanas followed, darting their assegais from a distance, or thrusting them into the most vulnerable parts of the animals, according as opportunities presented themselves. They had broken up into two or three parties, each of which chose out one of the largest of the male elephants as the point of attack. Some of these were already so severely wounded, that it was with difficulty that they could continue their flight. It was a strange spectacle to witness. The great bulls, pierced with a perfect grove of spears, and dripping with the blood which poured from innumerable wounds, staggered along, screaming with pain and fury; while the Kaffirs continued to overwhelm them with more darts—mingling their blows with entreaties to the huge beasts not to gore or trample on them, but to have mercy and spare their lives, at the very moment when they were inflicting torture and death on the creatures, whose forbearance they implored!

CLOSE QUARTERS.

Several huge animals passed in this manner in front of the trees, where the two lads were seated; but none of them offered the desired opportunity of a fair shot. Sometimes a tree intervened; sometimes the animal's head was hidden by a bush at the moment when they levelled their rifles; sometimes the Bechuanas engaged in the attack approached the line of their aim too nearly to render it safe for them to fire. At length, however, the opportunity did come. One of the largest of the males, fully twelve foot high, had escaped the notice of the assailants; and forcing his way through the haak-doorns and young motjikaaras as though they had been so much paper, bid fair to accomplish his escape without a wound. Both lads fired as he passed. Nick, who had levelled at the shoulder, missed his mark by several inches; and his bullet striking the creature's side, inflicted only a slight wound, which the elephant hardly heeded. But Frank's aim was more successful. The bullet struck the eye, though not precisely at the spot where it would have been instantly fatal; and the pain was so acute, as to arrest the monster in his panic-stricken flight. He stopped short and glared round him, seeking for the author of the outrage. Catching sight of the barrel of Frank's rifle as it glanced in the morning sun, he charged directly at the tree in which he was seated. It was an acacia of tolerable size, and the branch which bore him was above the reach of the animal's trunk. But so terrific was the force of his rush, that the trunk snapped like a rotten bough, and Frank, gun and all, was hurled to the ground. He sprang up, having been fortunately only bruised by the fall, and leaving his rifle to take care of itself, took to his heels as hard as he could.

"Come here, come here!" shouted Nick; "this tree will hold us both, and it's too big for him to break. Besides, I'm ready for him again now." Frank cast a rapid glance round him, and saw that Nick was right. The seringas and oomahaamas near him were thinly scattered, and afforded no cover at all; and the brute which had now recovered itself from the effect of the stunning blow it had received, was preparing to charge him again. Frank flew, rather than ran, to the tree, and springing lightly up, caught the lowest bough and swung himself on to it. From this he mounted to those above it with the agility of a squirrel. But the elephant was upon him, before he could reach the spot where his companion was seated. On it came, with its trunk stretched to the full length, and just caught Frank by the toe of the left foot, as he drew the other out of its reach. Frank thought it was all over with him. The tip of the trunk had caught firm hold of the shoe; and though it was only the tip, so that the animal could not exert its full strength, he felt himself drawn downwards with a force which he could not long resist. He had thrown both his arms and the other leg round the branch, so that the elephant had not merely the resistance of the boy's muscles to encounter, but the solid and massive limb of the great motjeerie. Nevertheless, all would speedily have given way, if Nick, leaning forward and resting his rifle on the bough beneath him, had not fired directly into the monster's eye, as it glared—not two feet below—upon him. Frank felt the deadly grip relax, as the elephant sank downwards and rolled over on its side, in its death agony, ploughing up the earth with its tusks, and presenting to the eye a vast quivering mass of dull grey hide, that gradually settled down into stillness.

Before Nick could fairly realise to himself his own success, the Bechuanas had surrounded the carcass, and were greeting the two boys with shouts of admiration and approval. They had not witnessed the manner in which the elephant had come by his death, a belt of shrubs having cut them off from the tree, in which Nick had been seated. They concluded that the animal had simply been brought down, as it was rushing by, by a successful shot from the lad's rifle; which must indeed have been fired with extraordinary skill to be so instantaneously fatal. The elephant slain was the great leader of the herd, fully twelve feet in height, and with tusks that projected at least two feet beyond the lip. It was by far the most valuable prize of the day, and its ivory would fetch a considerable sum in the market. They overwhelmed the successful sportsman with applause; and mounting Nick on their shoulders, carried him back in triumph to the village, which lay at the distance of not more than a couple of miles. Nick, who did not particularly relish the honours bestowed upon him, nor the close contiguity to the persons of the natives into which he was brought, did his best to explain the occurrence to his bearers, and request them to desist from rendering compliments which were altogether unmerited.

"I say, darky," he cried, "drop that, will you? I can walk home quite well without your help, thank you all the same. I'm not much of a shot with a rifle, and shouldn't have killed the chap, I expect, if he hadn't come and obligingly put his eye within half a yard of me! Bother it man, put me down. How their skins do stink—to be sure! Here, Kobo, Kobo"—he had just caught sight of his attendant, as he spoke—"just explain to these fellows, will you, that I prefer my own legs to their arms, if they have no objection; and the flavour of grease and red ochre isn't agreeable to everybody. I prefer a different style of perfume myself!"

"Bechuanas carry white boy, 'cause he great hunter, kill big elephant, pay him great honour," returned Kobo.

"I understand that plain enough," said Nick, "but I wish they'd honour me according to my own notions, instead of theirs."

"Take it easy, Nick," said Frank, laughing. "We shall soon enter the kraal now. I hope that brute, Maomo, will be in the way to see our entry. It will do him good."

As they ran on in this way, they approached the Bechuana kraal, where indeed, in accordance, as it seemed, with Wilmore's wish, nearly the whole population, that had remained behind from the elephant hunt, were assembled. Maomo was in the middle of them, apparently engaged in making some address of a warning or threatening character to his hearers, which had the effect of exciting and terrifying them. As the lads approached nearer, they saw that the people were gathered round some object stretched on the ground; to which the prophet continually pointed during the pauses of his speech. Presently they perceived that the object was an ox, dying in great suffering from some malady. The poor brute's limbs were swollen to a huge size, froth was issuing from its mouth and nostrils, the eyes rolled dim and bloodshot, and every now and then its whole frame was shaken by violent convulsions. As the chief, who was only a few paces behind the two boys, came on the scene, Maomo burst forth into a torrent of declamation, having reserved his energies, it appeared, for Chuma's more especial hearing.

"See you here," he exclaimed; "the pestilence has smitten the oxen, this poor beast will die, and no one can heal it; what has happened to one will happen to all. There will not be an ox left alive in the village in two or three days more. And who has caused it? The White Prophet. He prays to the wicked Spirits, and they hear him and send the pestilence! Every day, for many weeks past, he and the young prophet have been praying to the Spirits to punish the Bechuanas, because they will not worship his bad gods. Why does not Chuma forbid him? Why does he not punish him? Does not Chuma care that our cattle die? Chuma's own cattle will die also."

The Bechuana chief had halted, as he reached the spot where the ox was lying, and was now standing over it with a face of evident perplexity and dismay. There was no mistaking the symptoms of the malady, which, some years previously, had nearly caused a famine in the village, by the number of horned cattle which it had swept off. Nor was there any known remedy for the disease. Its appearance in the village might well cause the utmost alarm. It was almost impossible to account for the visitation. It had been generally attributed in former years to drought and deficient pasturage; but those causes could not be assigned now, as there had been abundance both of water and sweet grass for many weeks past. He did not suspect the truth—that Maomo had paid a secret visit to a distant tribe where the disease was raging, and brought back with him some of the virus, with which he had inoculated some two or three isolated cows. All Chuma's former suspicions of De Walden rushed back upon the chief with accumulated force.

"How do you know that the White Prophet has caused this?" he asked, taking advantage of the first pause in Maomo's oration.

"My Spirits have told me so," replied Maomo. "They have sent good rains and healthy seasons to the Bechuanas, and now the White Falsehood-man has come among them and taught them to worship false and wicked Spirits, and many of the Bechuanas are beginning to pray to them, and the wicked Spirits hear them, and answer their evil prayers."

"This is not true," exclaimed Chuma, angrily. "I have forbidden the White Prophet to offer prayers to his Spirits. I have forbidden any of my people to hearken to his words. Who is there that would dare to disobey me."

"The White Prophet treats your words as if they had been the idle winds," returned the rainmaker, "and he has persuaded many of the people to disregard them too. He thinks his Spirits are strong enough to protect him against your anger; and so they would be if it were not that my Spirits are stronger still; but he does not know that, and presumes to set you at open defiance."

"Is this true?" cried the chief, whose passion was now strongly excited. "Does this white man pray, as the rainmaker says? Do any presume to join in his prayers, if he so offers them?"

His eye was fixed sternly upon Kobo, whom he regarded in a general way as answerable for De Walden's movements.

Frank and Nick glanced anxiously at their friend, hoping that he would say something which might allay Chuma's anger; but to their surprise and dismay Kobo answered—

"It is true, chief I have not ventured to speak for fear that the White Prophet should do me some hurt; but Maomo will protect me. It is true. He prays every day in the big hut to his Spirits, and many of the Bechuanas pray with him, but not Kobo. It is not their fault. The White Prophet has bewitched them."

"Let some one fetch him hither," said Chuma. "If his prayers have done this harm, his prayers shall undo it, and that without delay, or it shall be the worse for him."

"I will go to fetch him," said Kobo. "I know where he is to be met with, and how to take him when he is off his guard. Let the rainmaker come with me, and we will bind and bring him hither."

With a smile of gratified malice the wizard accepted the invitation, and hurried off to De Walden's hut, accompanied by half a dozen stout Bechuanas. The chief stood in gloomy silence awaiting his return, while Frank and Nick looked on in an agony of doubt and apprehension.

Chapter Nineteen

Maomo and his myrmidons were not long in accomplishing their errand. De Walden and Warley had returned, about an hour previously, from their visit to the hut of old Dalili, whose oxen had been stricken with the pestilence early that morning. The missionary had from the first entertained little hope of saving any of the animals. He had several times encountered the disease during his residence in various parts of Kaffir land, and had very rarely known any treatment of it to have any effect. It was too late to try inoculation with the cattle already attacked, but he had helped the old man to apply the remedy in question, or rather the preventive in such of his oxen as were still healthy. In the others, though he had done all that was possible for their relief, he had warned him that he must not expect them to recover, and several of them had died before he left the village.

He was a good deal disturbed at the old Bechuana's demeanour. He was one of the most satisfactory of his converts, and De Walden had resolved that in a few weeks more he might be admitted to baptism. But Dalili's whole nature seemed changed. He did not, indeed, say anything to imply that a change in his religious opinions had taken place, but he seemed overwhelmed with terror, and to expect some terrible punishment to fall upon himself. The missionary and Ernest had done their best to quiet him, and had returned home to take some necessary food and rest before again seeking Dalili's hut, when Chuma's emissaries, headed by Maomo and Kobo, broke in upon them.

De Walden received them with the calmness of a man who had long carried his life in his hand, and knew that at any moment he might be required to surrender it. He quietly rose, and telling his captors there was no need to bind him, or use violence of any kind, as he was quite ready to go with them, took his hat and walked out of the hut. The others however insisted on tying his hands with strong leathern thongs, apprehensive that he might work some spell if they were left at liberty.

Escorted by Maomo on one side, and Kobo on the other, he advanced to the spot where Chuma was still standing with a large crowd of Bechuanas round him; the whole population of the village having by this time gathered together. It was a strange and striking scene. The chief, attired for the chase, carrying his weapons, occupied the central place—a large and martial figure. He was surrounded by a crowd of warriors armed and arrayed like himself, many of the party bearing in their dress and persons marks of the recent encounter with the elephants, which gave them a ghastly and bizarre appearance. The women and children filled up the background, looking with awful anticipation on what would probably ensue.

The missionary stepped calmly forward into the centre of the ring, meeting the stern glance of the Kaffir chief with a firm look, under which Chuma's eye at length was compelled to falter. This, perhaps, rendered his first words more bitter than they might otherwise have been.

"Disease hath smitten the cattle of the Bechuanas," he said; "whence comes this, and who has caused it?"

"It comes, like all visitations, from the hand of God; and the reason why He sends them is sometimes to teach mankind His power, and sometimes to punish their sins."

"What is the reason why He has sent this?"

"It is impossible for any man to say. He only knows Himself His own purposes."

"But you have yourself told me you have power with God. You have said that He always hears His servants?"

"I have, and I repeat it."

"Then ask Him to take away this disease, and if He complies, then we will be His servants. Will you do this?"

"I will pray to God that He will be pleased to remove it. Whether He will do so or not, rests with Him."

Chuma hesitated. His belief in De Walden was shaken by what had happened, but not wholly overthrown. Maomo saw his embarrassment, and hastened to interfere.

"Chief," he said, "it is not by prayers, which are but words, that the White Falsehood—man has prevailed on the Evil Spirits to send this curse upon our people. Nor will it be by prayers that he can prevail on them to take it off again. There are sacrifices that he offers to his gods. I know that he was seen to pour water on Gaiké's forehead, and utter some charm while he did so. I know that there are sacrifices which he renders, when he will suffer no one but his white companions to be present. Ask him, and he cannot deny this?"

"How is this?" said Chuma, turning again to De Walden; "you hear what the rainmaker says. Is it true?"

"It is true that we have rites at which none but believers are allowed to be present," returned De Walden.

"Will you offer these to your gods, that the plague may be removed from the cattle of the Bechuanas?"

"It is not enough that you make him promise that," interposed Maomo again, dreading that De Walden would comply with this request, and so avert, for the time at all events, the chief's anger. "He must do so in public, so that you and all our people may be sure that he really sacrifices to his god."

"You hear, white man," said Chuma, sternly; "do you consent?"

"I cannot profane holy mysteries in such a manner," was the answer. "I will pray, and offer what you call sacrifices in secret, but not before you."

"You hear him, chief," exclaimed the wizard. "He seeks to put you off with empty words. Now hear me; I will take away this woe. The cattle of the Bechuanas shall not die. But I cannot do this until the White Lie-man has been put to silence. The Spirits will not hearken to me while he lives. Choose, therefore, whether this impostor shall live to work his evil pleasure, and your cattle perish, or whether he shall receive his due punishment, and your cattle shall be saved."

His words were drowned in a cry which burst simultaneously from a hundred lips, "Slay the White Wizard; preserve our cattle."

"Once more, you hear," exclaimed Chuma; "offer sacrifice or you die; which do you choose? Will you sacrifice?"

"My honoured friend and father," said Ernest, addressing De Walden in a low voice apart, as he saw that he was about to offer a final refusal, "need this be? Wherefore not comply with their demand? Did not Elijah so challenge the priests of Baal, and God upheld him in the trial. And are you not as truly God's servant as he was; and God is the same yesterday, to-day, and for ever? Why should he not answer you, by healing their diseased oxen, even as he answered Elijah, by consuming the sacrifice?"

"It had been revealed to Elijah that he was to act as he did," returned the missionary in the same tone. "I have received no such intimations, and must not so take upon myself. Our God is indeed the same, and it may please Him to interpose and save me, or leave me to glorify Him by my death; but I must leave that in His hands." He proceeded aloud, "No, chief, I will not offer the sacrifice you require. I cannot explain my reasons now, but I refuse."

"Then you shall die, and that speedily. Take him to his hut, until the preparations are made; and be careful that he does not escape, or your own lives shall be the penalty. Take the other whites, and keep them in safe custody also. We will determine in the council what is to be done with them presently."

The four Englishmen were dragged off under Kobo's charge, the latter heaping every possible insult upon them during their conveyance to the hut, and ordering the men under his charge to bind them with rhinoceros thongs, which cut them so severely, that even the attendants seemed inclined to remonstrate at such needless severity. But Kobo silenced them by threatening to report their lukewarmness to the chief. Then desiring that the guns and everything belonging to them should be removed, and placed for security in his hut, he withdrew with a parting menace, to take his place at the council about to be held in the chief's residence.

The lads were too deeply moved at the approaching execution of their friend, and the danger impending over themselves, to feel the disgust and indignation at Kobo's double-faced treachery, which at another time it would have provoked. They listened reverently to the words addressed to them by De Walden; who warned them that their position was one of the greatest peril, and though he earnestly hoped that their lives might be spared, they would do wisely to be prepared for the worst. "God's providential care for you," he said, "has been shown so often and so signally of late, that I need not bid you to trust wholly in Him. But it would be no kindness in me not to warn you that your present peril is very great—as great perhaps as it was in the Hottentot village, though at first sight it might not seem to be so."

"Not all of us are in imminent danger, I hope," said Warley. "I know they are angry with me, almost as much as they are with you, but they have no grounds of quarrel with Frank or Gilbert."

"I thought you might suppose so," returned the missionary, "and that was the reason why I spoke. It is plain that they mean to put me to a speedy death—"

"Surely they dare not," interposed Frank. "They know that Charles will be returning, before long, with messengers from the English governor at Cape Town. He is not likely to endure the murder of a British subject without a shadow of justice or reason. And when he hears—"

"Ay, Frank, that is just it," said De Walden. "They will take care that he shall never hear it. They will probably say that I have died of some disease, or have taken my departure from their kraal of my own accord. But your evidence would disprove their story, and they will have no scruples in securing your silence by the surest of all methods—that is, by putting you to death."

"Then they would have to account for all four of us," observed Gilbert, "and some one in the kraal—Dalili or Gaiké, or Mololo perhaps—might tell Charles the truth, and then very signal punishment would probably be exacted."

"You do not know these people," said De Walden. "The influence of this pretended prophet would be greater than ever after his supposed victory over me. They will be too much terrified to venture even on a word. If Kobo had remained faithful to us indeed—"

"The treacherous wretch!" exclaimed Frank, passionately. "I feel more indignant with him than with Chuma, or even Maomo himself."

"This is no time for anger, Frank," said the elder man, gravely. "I should not speak of him at all, if it had not been necessary to explain to you your true position. If Kobo had remained faithful, I say, something might have been done. We might have sent him off from the village, and Chuma would have been afraid that he had gone to report what had happened to the English. But that hope does not exist, and there is nothing for it but for us all to prepare ourselves for the worst."

"They may do what they will," said Warley. "If they take your life, I have no wish to keep mine."

"You must not say that, Ernest. God may have a great work for you to do; and if your life is preserved, I shall feel assured it is for that purpose. But we have probably but a short time to pass together; let us make the best use of that."

They all knelt down while the missionary offered up a fervent prayer in behalf of each one of them, in which all heartily joined; and they were still engaged in their prayers, when Kobo re-entered, accompanied by his satellites, to announce to them their sentence, or rather that of De Walden.

This, he gave them to understand, with diabolical exultation, was to be the most painful form of death that imagination could conceive—one which was resorted to only in the instance of enemies captured in war, upon whom they wished to inflict the worst possible sufferings. De Walden was to be eaten alive by ants! He was to be pegged down on his back over one of the large ant-hills, some three feet in height—great numbers of which were to be found at the distance of a mile or two from the village—his neck, wrists, and ankles firmly secured by thongs of rhinoceros hide, so that it would be impossible to move even an inch to the right or left. He was to be left in this position half an hour or so after nightfall, about which time the ants, which had remained in a state of torpor all day, were wont to come out of their nests in such multitudes as to blacken the whole of the ground round one of their hills. They would be sure to fasten at once on any animal substance near them, and so great was their voracity, that in the course of three or four hours, the largest carcasses would be stripped of every particle of skin or flesh, and be left a bare and whitened skeleton.

This, Kobo informed them, was to be the form of death chosen for the missionary. Some of the councillors had suggested death by poison, or a blow from a heavy club; but Maomo, he gave them to understand—Maomo, supported by himself—had insisted that the Bad Spirits would not be appeased, unless the White Enemy died by a death of the greatest agony. As for the others, they would probably be pricked with a lance-head, steeped in the juice of the euphorbia, or the venom of the poison grub. But that would not be finally decided until the following day; only, anyhow, they were quite sure to undergo death in some painful and lingering shape.

The only drawback to these tidings, he further apprised them, was, that the execution of the missionary's sentence would necessarily be deferred to the following day. A great feast was to take place at sundown on the flesh of the elephants killed that morning, and the chief could not be induced to put that off, even to gratify the anger he had conceived against the White Prophet. Maomo had made the attempt, but in vain. Nor would he leave the execution of the sentence to the rainmaker, so that the missionary's death was to be put off till sunset on the following day: but, then, Kobo added, most probably the fate of the others would be determined, and all four would be executed together.

Having delivered himself of this outpouring of malice, and once more carefully examined the rhinoceros thongs, to make assurance doubly sure, Kobo relieved them of his presence; and soon afterwards the whole party, overcome by the intense weariness which anxiety and suffering of mind occasion, sank into a heavy and dreamless sleep.

It might have been four or five hours afterwards, when Frank was roused by a pricking feeling as though some one had stabbed him slightly with a knife. He started up. The hut was quite dark, though the stars outside were faintly glimmering. He was about to cry out when a hand was placed on his mouth, and a voice whispered in his ear.

"It me—Kobo. No make noise. I come help you get away." At the same instant he again felt the prick of the knife, and the leather thong drop from his arm. In a moment the explanation of Kobo's altered demeanour occurred to him. The man had affected the bitter hatred he had expressed, in order that they might be handed over to his custody instead of that of Maomo, as they would have been, had he been suspected of being their friend.

"All right, Kobo," he said softly; "shall I strike a light?"

"No, no. That spoil all. If you have knife, cut the fastenings of your legs. I set prophet free."

The others were roused with the same caution which Frank had received, and in a few minutes they were all at liberty. Then Kobo addressed them, still speaking under his breath.

"Chief and all much drunk. Only rainmaker sober. He suspect me. He watch me while feast go on. I see him, though he not guess it. I seem to drink twice as much as any, but throw it all away on ground. When feast half over, I tumble flat Rainmaker think Kobo drunk, but I creep away in dark. Now all follow me; creep like snake among hedge and bush; lucky no moon to-night."

Following his direction, the whole party emerged one after another from the hut, and crawled on their hands and knees among the dwarf shrubs which lay scattered over the ground, until they had reached Kobo's cottage, which was on the outskirts of the village. Here they found their guns, belts, and flasks, carefully hidden away under a heap of weeds. Having possessed themselves of these, they again hurried on, keeping within the cover of the wood, until they were at least half a mile from the Bechuana village; when the wooded covert gave place to an open plain overspread with large stones, and now and then patches of thorn.

"Get on as fast as we can," was Kobo's direction now. "Too far from kraal for Bechuanas to follow to-night."

"And to-morrow they will none of them be in a condition to undertake any long journey, I expect," observed Nick.

"Rainmaker not drunk. He keep sober," said Kobo. "Very likely he gone to hut to see all safe, and find all gone!" added the savage with a chuckle. "But he no know which way to follow in dark. Not follow till to-morrow."

"You have managed very cleverly, Kobo," said Wilmore; "but I must say I wonder this wizard, or rainmaker, or whatever you call him, consented to leave us in your charge."

"He not do that," answered Kobo, "only he could not help it. I know how plague broke out among Dalili's cows. I see rainmaker putting bad stuff into their sides with a little knife. He know that I saw him, and he 'fraid to speak against Kobo, for fear Kobo speak against him. Rainmaker bad man. Look, you see that big ant-hill there close by?"

"Yes, we see it plain enough," answered Warley, with a shudder.

"That where rainmaker fasten Patoto 'bout six months ago. Patoto strong brave man, favourite with Chuma. Maomo jealous. He pretend Patoto bewitch people. Nyzée, Chuma's young wife, very sick, Maomo say Patoto bewitched her, and Nyzée believe it and persuade Chuma. Patoto say it no true, but no one believe him. He sentenced to same death as White Prophet. Kobo saw him fastened to ant-hill. Six strong posts driven into ground. Patoto's feet tied with rheims to two; his hands to two more; broad rhinoceros straps fastened to other two over Patoto's belly. They strip him naked first, for why—no good to leave clothes on him, ants eat—"

"I understand, Kobo," exclaimed Warley, interrupting the horrible narrative, which he could not endure to hear. "But why did not you set him at liberty, as you have set us?"

"Eh! Patoto only black man—not like White Prophet," answered Kobo, coolly; "besides, chief set men to watch, for fear Patoto himself get away when ant begin to eat—"

"Be silent, for Heaven's sake," exclaimed De Walden, who had hitherto repressed his emotion, but could now bear no more. "Blessed be His holy name, who has delivered His servant from torments, which are unendurable even in thought. Let us speak no further of them. How far, and in what direction, do you propose that we should proceed to-night?"

"We fly towards Basuto country. Basutos and Bechuanas not friends, or Chuma send message for White Prophet to be given back to him."

"The Basutos! Very good. I can speak their language, and they will very likely shelter us until we are rested sufficiently to travel to Cape Town. But the Basuto country lies at some distance, does it not?"

"Yes, several days' journey. But when we have passed Koodoo's kloof, all safe."

"Koodoo's kloof? What, on the Vaal river? The river is not passable there."

"Ah, you not know. We pass all safe, so they not catch us."

The missionary said no more. Kobo evidently knew what he was about, and there was very little chance of their escaping from their pursuers except through his help. By his skilful management they had probably secured several hours' start, but that was all. The Bechuanas would be sure to be on their track on the following day, and their swiftness of foot was proverbial even among the Kaffir tribes. He resolved to attend implicitly to Kobo's instructions, and a few words from him prevailed on the lads to do the same.

They hurried on till the forenoon of the next day, and then rested only a few hours during the meridian heat, resuming their journey with a speed which taxed the boys' powers to the utmost, and against which they would have rebelled, if they had not been plainly told by their guide that their lives depended on the speed with which that and the following day's travel could be accomplished. Kobo allowed another halt shortly before midnight, and the lads were further refreshed by a bathe in a deep cavity in the rock where the rain water had collected, before setting out on the following morning. The character of the country they were traversing now became more pleasing, and seemed to promise abundant shade and plenty as they advanced. The landscape was varied by groves of palms and sycamores; and not unfrequently date trees and figs offered to the travellers their ripe and tempting fruit. The dark-foliaged moshoma was relieved by the yellow of the mimosa, and the lilac of the plumbago. Herds of antelopes, and occasionally graceful koodoos and elands, bounded by them, and little rivulets, evidently on their way to mingle with some large river, covered the ground with a carpet of verdure.

"Vaal river near now," remarked Kobo, when they paused a little before moonrise on the evening of the second day. "White boys travel fast—travel like men. Bechuanas not catch them."

"That is good hearing at all events," remarked Nick. "A fellow never knows what he can do till he's tried. I didn't believe I could have gone such a distance in three days, as I really have gone in less than two—no, not to save my life."

"Well, it has been to save your life," remarked Warley; "you forget that."

"No, I don't," retorted the other. "It's about the only thing I'm safe not to forget! Well, Kobo, when shall we get to this kloof of yours—to-night, or to-morrow morning?"

"To-morrow," said the Bechuana, "'bout ten o'clock, if all well."

They resumed their journey before daybreak, in no way abating their speed, though the stamina of the three younger travellers seemed now on the point of giving way. They struggled on, however, hour after hour, until the sun began to mount high in the heavens, and the heat to grow every moment more intolerable. Then, suddenly, Kobo pointed with his finger to a narrow ravine, richly wooded with trees of every variety of leaf, running between two lofty mountain ridges, and exclaimed—

"That Koodoo's kloof. We safe now!"

Another quarter of an hour brought them within the shelter of the noble trees, which extended their network of delicious shade overhead. Kobo led them on by a path, which gradually sloped downwards for nearly half a mile, till the sound of running water broke upon their ears, and they found themselves on the margin of a broad and rapid river.

Chapter Twenty

"Well, we are here," said Frank, an hour or so afterwards as they still lay on the grassy bank of the stream, enjoying alike the rest to their limbs, and the delicious coolness of the river breeze. "We are here, thanks to you, Kobo, for the same. But how we are to get across beats me altogether. This is not a narrow channel over which you could drop a tree; and if it had been, the cliffs opposite are two or three hundred feet high, and go down straight into the water. It is too deep to ford, and too rapid to swim, even if there was a landing-place on the other side, which there is not."

"No want to cross river," answered the Bechuana, briefly.

"Not want to cross it, Kobo?" asked Warley, "why I thought you said this was the point to which Chuma might pursue us, but he dare not go beyond it."

"So I did. See now; give me the axe."

He got up as he spoke, and began lopping off the boughs of a large willow, which grew at no great distance from the spot where they had been resting, choosing those which were about six inches in diameter. When he had collected a sufficient number of them, he reduced them all to an uniform length of some ten feet, and laid them on the ground side by side. He then tore down a number of parasitical creepers, which were almost as tough and pliant as so many cords, and began binding the logs together by their means.

"What are you making, Kobo?" inquired Nick, after contemplating his proceeding for some minutes with much interest. "Make raft, cover it with reeds, and launch it on river. It carry us to island yonder." He pointed as he spoke to a group of trees, growing apparently in the middle of the river's channel, at the distance of perhaps a mile. "There we rest, find plenty of food, fruit, and fish too. Then I go to look for Basuto people, and tell them 'bout white men."

"Cover the raft with reeds? Hadn't we better go and cut some, then?" suggested Warley; "or, rather, hadn't. Nick and Frank better go and gather them, while I help you to tie the logs."

"Very good. They two take axe, one cut reeds, other bring them in armfuls."

Mr De Walden did not awake from the sleep into which he had fallen immediately on reaching the bank, until the raft was nearly completed. He understood at once the purpose for which it was constructed. "It will bear us safely enough, no doubt," he said, "and we shall find abundance of food on the island; but will not the Bechuanas suspect the place of our retreat, and follow us?"

"Bechuanas not venture on Yellow River," said Kobo; "besides, if they make raft, we shoot them from island, as easy as so many sheep. Kobo kill them all with bow and arrow—say nothing of guns."

"That is true," said De Walden; "and besides we could use our own raft to escape to the opposite shore before they came up. Well, we had better push the raft into the stream, hadn't we? It seems to be finished; and there is no wisdom in staying here longer than can be helped."

Kobo assented, and Frank coming up at that moment with his last heap of reeds, the four, by their united exertions, launched their handiwork, which was found to float very well. The guns, with the rest of the baggage, were then put on board; some long poles selected to serve as paddles, or puntpoles, as occasion might require; and the adventurers prepared to commence their voyage as soon as Nick joined them.

This he did almost immediately afterwards, but in breathless haste and alarm.

"Get on to the raft and push off," he cried, as soon as he was able to command his voice. "The Bechuanas are after us, with that scoundrel Maomo at their head."

He was obeyed with the utmost promptitude. In two minutes they had pushed from the shore and were beginning to catch the current, when the truth of Gilbert's words was proved by a headlong rush of Bechuanas to the riverside, made in the hope of arresting the progress of the raft. They darted their assegais after the travellers, and cast long lassoes of leather; some of them even rushed into the water, trying to seize the logs with their hands.

"Stoop down!" shouted Kobo; "they shoot arrows." All five threw themselves on their faces among the reeds, just in time to allow a flight of arrows to pass over them and bespatter the surface of the river beyond.

"Ah, you catch that," cried Kobo, as he drew his bowstring in answer, and saw his arrow quivering in the neck of the rainmaker. "You no cure that, Maomo—you clever doctor, but no cure that! Him dead," he continued, complacently addressing his companions, "him dead in half an hour. Poison quite fresh and good!"

"Unhappy wretch!" exclaimed the missionary, as he watched the Bechuanas gather in dismay round their fallen prophet. "I have no doubt you speak the truth, Kobo; and the impostor drew his fate upon himself. But it is a fearful ending! When will the light of God's truth shine in this benighted land?"

"Yes, Kobo speak truth," said the guide, answering the only part of De Walden's speech which he understood. "Kobo speak truth—Maomo dead for certain—he suffer bad pain too. Ah, they carry him away. No trouble us more."

The raft was by this time in the central channel of the river, sweeping rapidly down towards the island. In about half an hour this was reached; and Kobo steering it towards a spot where several willows stretched out into the stream, contrived to lodge it securely between two of them. The party then landed, and carried all their goods on shore; after which Kobo directed them to haul the raft also on to the bank, and hide it carefully among the long grass and rushes.

"People no come that way," he said, pointing down the river; "large deep falls, and no come from that bank—rocks too steep and high. But may come from other bank, or same way as we, from further down. Sometimes Basutos hunt "potmus,' as white man call him."

"Hippopotamuses!" exclaimed Frank. "Are there any of them hereabouts?"

"Plenty 'potmus. All along that bank—wonder we not see them. All among canes there—feed at night mostly—come out by and by."

The raft was by this time hidden away, and the boys, under Kobo's guidance, proceeded to explore the island, which was perhaps two hundred feet in length, by thirty in width. It was covered with a rich growth of mossy grass, interspersed with flowers of every variety of colour, and of the rarest fragrance. Wild geraniums, jessamines, arums, lilies scarlet and blue and purple, spread like a gorgeous carpet underfoot. Overhead pear trees, pomegranates, and wild plums, figs, quinces, and bananas, were intermingled with the foliage of the cypress, the gum, the willow, and a hundred others. Kobo might well say there was plenty of food to be obtained in the island, which seemed to them to be like an enchanted garden. They were delighted with the prospect of remaining there some days to rest and refresh themselves, while Kobo went on his errand. They soon chose the spot where they meant to fix their headquarters. Just about the middle of the islet, three large fig trees and a date grew so near to one another, that their interlacing boughs formed a roof impenetrable alike to sun or storm. The undergrowth of shrubs between the boles was soon cleared away by the help of the axe, and left a sort of bower about twelve feet square, open only on one side, and tapestried, as it were, with the loveliest flowers. Here they piled together the heaps of reed from the raft, which the sun had already dried, to make their beds, and here they sat down, an hour or two after their arrival, to enjoy the luxury of an abundant repast, and a long night of unbroken rest after it.

On the following morning, Kobo, having constructed for himself a much smaller raft, consisting simply of bundles of reed laid crosswise over one another, took himself off to the opposite bank, which, as he had told them, belonged to the Basutos. Here, having drawn the reeds ashore, he waved his hand to the English travellers, and then vanished among the shrubs. Left to their own devices, De Walden and Ernest withdrew to their arbour, to continue a conversation deeply interesting to them both, which they had begun on the previous evening; while Frank and Nick, having contrived to manufacture some extempore fishing-lines, betook themselves to a point where a shelf of stone, immediately on the water's edge, offered them a pleasant seat, and began fishing.

They had better success than they had expected, considering the rudeness of their tackle, and their utter ignorance as to the proper bait to be used. Half a dozen tolerable-sized fish, mostly eels and barbel, soon lay lifeless on the turf at their side, and they were still pursuing their sport with unabated eagerness, when they were startled by a loud splashing and snorting at no great distance from them. They leaped up, for a moment apprehending that the Bechuanas were in pursuit of them, notwithstanding Kobo's assurances that there was no fear of such a *contretemps*, and hurried to the southern extremity of the islet, where the noise was audible. Several dark shapeless objects, ten or twelve feet long, were to be seen floating apparently on the water; but whether they were fragments of wood, or the carcasses of drowned oxen, or living animals, it was impossible at first to determine. Presently, however, one of the floating masses disappeared beneath the waters, and anon rose again, with a loud grunting noise which could not be mistaken.

"They are the hippopotamuses Kobo told us of," said Nick. "It is very odd, but I had forgotten all about them."

"Hush!" answered Frank, "they are coming this way, I think; and if so, we shall get a clear view of them. I want to see one above all things. I've seen a picture of one, but that gives no real idea."

"Yes, they are coming this way, certainly," remarked Gilbert, a few minutes afterwards; "but how slowly and leisurely they move. I should think we might get a shot at one presently, if we keep quite quiet. Luckily, it is plain that they have not seen us, or they wouldn't come this way."

As he spoke, Frank laid his hand on his arm, and pointed silently towards a projecting point of the river bank, about two hundred yards off. The head of a canoe, formed out of the trunk of a tree apparently, and holding two persons, had just come in sight. It was followed closely by another of the same description, a good deal larger, and at some distance by several reed rafts, nearly as big as that which had conveyed them to the island on the previous day. The boys drew instantly back into the leafy covert, again fancying that the Bechuanas were on their track. A very short examination of the new-comers, however, satisfied them that this was not the case. Not only was their dress different in several particulars from that of the Kaffirs, but the weapons with which they were armed showed plainly that they had not come out for the purpose of apprehending runaways, but of hunting some animals—no doubt, indeed, the hippopotamus; for the weapons they carried were not used in the chase of any other animal But what rendered it absolutely certain that they could not belong to their late pursuers, was the presence, in the stern of the largest canoe, of a woman— evidently a personage of rank and importance. The boys looked at her, as the boats slowly approached the islet, with great surprise and curiosity. Her costume showed that she belonged to the same nation as the others, and her whole bearing and demeanour was that of a person familiarised by long habit with the scene and employment in which she was engaged But if it had not been for these circumstances, the boys would certainly have supposed that she was not a native of South Africa at all. Her complexion, though somewhat darker than that of an Englishwoman, was many shades lighter than that of her companions; her hair and eyes were totally unlike theirs. Her movements, easy and graceful as those of savages generally are, nevertheless exhibited an indefinable refinement, which was most perplexing to the spectators.

Their attention, however, was soon directed to other matters. All unconscious of the vicinity of strangers, the occupants of the boats and rafts glided noiselessly by the island, until they had reached the hippopotamuses, which were still lazily floating in the yellow waters; for the river, it may be observed in passing, well deserved its name. The huge animals scarcely seemed to notice the presence of the voyagers, whom they allowed to come close to them, without manifesting any symptoms of alarm.

By and by the canoe, in which the female already described was seated, had reached the spot where the largest of the bulky herd—fully twelve feet in length, and the same in girth—was reclining! She rose from her seat, lifting her figure to its full height, and then dexterously darted the barbed lance she carried into the body of the monster. The instant she had done so, she resumed her seat, and the rowers nimbly plying their oars, shot off from the vortex caused by the writhings of the wounded beast, and made for the shore. The girl bounded lightly on to the bank as the canoe approached it, holding in her hand the line, which was attached to the handle of the harpoon. She was followed instantly by the rest of the crew, who, seizing the cord, held it fast with their united strength to prevent the escape of the hippopotamus.

The latter had no sooner felt the wound than he dived, and commenced swimming under water, in the hope of ridding himself in that manner of his pursuers. But the barbed point held fast, and his struggles only increased the acuteness of his sufferings. He was soon obliged to rise again to the surface for air, and his reappearance was the signal of a recommencement of the attack. Fresh harpoons were continually lodged in the quivering flesh; the yellow waters grew every moment redder with the blood, which poured from countless wounds; until, at last, even his huge strength was exhausted, and the hunters were able to draw the lifeless carcass to the shore.

All this time the remainder of the herd had continued to paddle about, or lie basking in the sun within a short distance of the spot where the chase had been going on, wholly unconcerned, to all appearance, at what was passing. The rowers now resumed their places, and the woman her seat in the stern, and the same scene was enacted again; but this time not with the same success. The harpoon was thrown with equal skill, and firmly fixed in the animal's side; but before the boat could reach the shore, which at this point of the river lay at a considerable distance, it was attacked by the infuriated beast, which seemed more inclined to revenge the wound he had received, than make his escape from further injury. He swam straight towards the canoe, which he overtook before it had gone many yards, and with a single blow from his formidable tusk, completely shattered its bottom. It sank instantly, leaving its five occupants to escape to the land as they best might. The monster glared round him as if seeking for the easiest victim, and perceiving that the female, who had been stationed in the bow, was the nearest to him, he made straight at her with his huge jaws expanded to their full width, and his deadly rows of teeth displayed. Observing his approach, she dived, reappearing at the distance of a few yards, and swam swiftly for the island, which was the nearest point of land. But the animal had been on the look out for her, and made a second rush, as soon as her head emerged from the water. She dived a second time, and rose nearer to the islet; but her strength was evidently failing her, and the weight of her clothes dragged her down. She struggled bravely, but could not get away from her pursuer. In another minute the horrid jaws would, in all likelihood, have cut her in twain, if a shot, fired opportunely at this moment from the central clump of the eyot, had not pierced the unwieldy brute behind the shoulder, and passed directly into the vitals. With a loud snort of agony he turned over on his side, vomiting a torrent of blood, which stained the dull yellow stream a still duller crimson, and then floated helplessly down the current.

JUST IN TIME.

Warley, from whose rifle this unexpected deliverance had come, now hurried down the bank to complete her rescue. His attention, and that of De Walden, had been attracted to the noise on the river some time previously, and, catching his rifle, which he had taken the precaution of loading, Ernest hurried out to learn what was passing. When he first caught sight of the scene, he was indisposed to interfere, thinking the hunters able to effect their own escape, and unwilling to betray the place where he and his friends had taken refuge; but as soon as the peril of the female voyager became evident to him, he hesitated no longer. The other two lads now came hastening up, and between them they raised the woman, who was almost exhausted, from the water, and laid her on the bank. The natives, who were astonished beyond measure at the apparition of the white men, stood motionless on the further bank, or on their rafts, not knowing what was about to happen next.

The Englishmen on their sides were scarcely less astonished. The reader has already heard the surprise with which Frank and Gilbert had noticed their female visitor; but they had only beheld her from a distance, and had had a very cursory view of her face and figure. Now, however, they had leisure to take a closer survey. She was apparently about eighteen years old, tall and beautifully formed, and with a natural dignity of demeanour which would have become a princess. Her skin was somewhat darker than that of English ladies in ordinary, but, nevertheless, a very becoming colour mantled in her cheeks. Her features were formed after the finest type of Greek beauty—the shape of the face oval, the nose straight and slightly *retroussé*, the forehead broad and low, the eyebrows beautifully arched over orbs of the darkest hazel. Her hair, to complete the picture, bore no likeness at all to that of her attendants, but was glossy, long, and of a rich brown.

Her dress was almost as great an enigma as her face. It consisted of a kind of petticoat, or rather short gown, made of antelope skin, and edged with white fur, descending from her neck almost to her knees, and covering the arms about half-way to the wrist. Her feet were protected by sandals, the thongs of which were wound crosswise up her legs, and secured by a leathern garter at the knees. Round her waist she wore a girdle set with crimson beads and glittering stones. Her head had no ornament, with the exception of some eagle's feathers fixed in the coronet of dark brown hair which surmounted her forehead. Her appearance, in fact, was neither that belonging to civilised nor to savage life, but rather that of some high-born European lady, who had assumed, for some masquerading purpose, the costume of the desert.

After resting for a few minutes on the sloping patch of turf where her rescuers had placed her, she appeared to recover her strength and self-possession, and to be anxious to bestow her thanks on the strangers who had come so opportunely to her rescue, but was at a loss how to express herself. Warley and the others felt equally embarrassed. At last, after a long pause, the former called to the missionary, who had remained behind in the arbour, too much occupied with the anxieties which were pressing on him to take heed of what was passing outside.

"Will you be so good as to come here, Mr De Walden?" he cried. "Here are some natives whom we cannot make understand us, but very likely they may understand you."

A flash of intelligence passed over the girl's face as he spoke.

"I understand you myself," she said. "You are speaking English. Are you Englishmen?"

Her accent and words were those of an English lady. Still more bewildered, Warley answered—

"We are Englishmen, madam; and I need not say rejoiced to recognise a countrywoman, as we cannot doubt you are. By what strange chance you have been conveyed hither—"

"No," she interposed, "I am not an Englishwoman. I was born in this land; but I am deeply interested in everything English. If it pleases you to accompany me to our village, which is not very far distant from this, my mother will be greatly pleased to welcome you as her guests."

The boys glanced at De Walden, who was standing by, regarding her attentively. He now addressed her with much respect. "You are the daughter, I presume," he said, "of the famous White Queen of the Basutos, of whom I have heard so much. But I thought her dwelling was considerably further to the east."

"Yes, I am the daughter of Queen Laura, or Lau-au, as our people call her. My own name is Ella. You are right as to our ordinary place of residence; but the cattle disease, which is raging in the east, has obliged us for awhile to shift our dwelling. You, I conclude, are one of the white teachers whom my mother ever holds in honour. She would gladly have received you, even if I had not owed my life to your friend. We will set out at once, if you please, as the evening is now advancing."

She summoned her attendants, who had been watching this interview with looks of much curiosity, and the party were soon conveyed to the opposite shore. Then desiring them to cut off as much of the flesh of the two slain hippopotamuses as could be conveniently carried with them, she set off, with two of her visitors walking on either hand, at a brisk pace, which an English lady would have found it difficult to maintain, but which did not appear at all to inconvenience their fair conductress.

But the day's adventures were not yet concluded. After walking for a mile or two, still along the banks of the river, Nick's restless spirit seemed to grow weary of the monotony of the journey. He began to linger by the wayside; now to pick a flower that attracted his fancy; now to gather some of the fruit, of which there was plenty to be seen—figs and bananas, and ripe dates—now to examine some brilliant insect, or to chase some gorgeous butterfly. On these occasions he allowed the party to get further and further in advance of him, until once or twice he was in danger of being left alone in the bush, to find, as best he might, the track pursued by his companions.

On one of these occasions, after he had succeeded with considerable difficulty in plucking a delicious watermelon, which grew in a deep hollow, surrounded on all sides by thorn bushes, he discovered to his chagrin and alarm, that the rest of the party were by this time fairly out of sight and hearing; and the dense mass of tangled shrubs and creepers in front of him rendered it impossible to distinguish anything at the distance of a hundred yards. He hurried on as fast as he could, in the direction which he supposed them to have taken, looking carefully round him for the marks of footsteps. But these were nowhere to be distinguished. Indeed all trace of a path seemed to have disappeared. A good deal alarmed, he stood still and shouted. Presently he heard a halloo in answer, but in a direction different from that which he had been pursuing. It evidently came from a considerable distance. Nick felt there was no time to be lost, and hurried along with all the speed he could command, though the long grass much impeded his progress. As he turned the corner of a thick mass of shrubs, he saw a figure which he recognised as that of De Walden advancing towards him, and holding up his hand, urging him, as he supposed, to rejoin the party as quickly as he could. He started accordingly at a run, but had not advanced many yards when his foot caught against some obstacle which threw him forward on his face. At the same moment there was a whirring noise, followed by a loud crash, and some heavy object struck the ground within a yard of him. Almost immediately afterwards he heard De Walden's voice.

"Another escape, Master Nick. I wonder how many more you mean to have before you rejoin your friends. If you had as many lives as a cat, you would lose them all at this rate."

Nick got up, rubbing the green mud from his elbows and knees, and staring in wonder at the object the fall of which had so astonished him. An examination of it did not tend to remove his perplexity. It was a large heavy piece of wood, shaped evidently by the axe, so as to resemble a rude arrow, but as thick as the mast of a large cutter. To the end of this was attached an iron head of a corresponding size. It had penetrated deep into the ground, and would have been sufficient to shatter Nick's skull like an icicle if it had come in contact with it. "Whatever can that be?" he exclaimed; "and how came it up there?"

"A hippopotamus trap," said the missionary; "and it is a good job that it has not proved a man trap too. You must not leave your companions in this wild country, Nick, or even your good luck won't keep you out of trouble. I noticed the trap as we passed, and then perceived a minute or two afterwards that you were not with us. It is fortunate I turned back and called you. If you hadn't been running fast it might have caught your head, or at all events your leg."

By this time they were rejoined by the rest of the party, and De Walden proceeded to explain to the boys the curious construction of the machine from which Nick had had so narrow an escape. It was common enough, he told them, in the neighbourhood of the haunts of the hippopotamus. The stem of a young tree, a foot or so in diameter, was cut off at the length of about four feet. A strong and sharp iron head was fixed at one end, and at the other an eye, to which a string was attached. This rude shaft was then hung up to the branch of a large tree immediately over the path by which the hippopotamuses were wont to go down to the river. The string was passed over the branch, round a projecting root at the bottom of the tree, and straight across the path, being ultimately secured to a peg driven into the earth. This string came into contact with the feet of the hippopotamus, which, in walking, shambles along, scarcely raising its legs from the ground. The string being in this manner broken, the heavy beam instantly falls, usually striking the hippopotamus in the back, and penetrating the vitals. The blow is almost always mortal. Even if the animal is not killed on the spot, it is so badly wounded that it dies shortly afterwards. Sometimes, to make assurance doubly sure, Mr De Walden told them, the iron is steeped in poison.

"There didn't need that," said Nick, as he contemplated the barbed point, as big as the fluke of an anchor, and sharp as an arrow. "The iron head would have finished me off very handsomely, without troubling the poison-makers. Well, I'll take care another time, as the children say, and I can't do more. Let's be off now. I want to get to our quarters for the night."

Chapter Twenty One

Nightfall was near at hand, when the party approached the Basuto kraal; and the boys looked eagerly round them to see if they could discover any marked differences between it and the other native villages which they had visited. Ella, as she had called herself, had hardly spoken a word during the whole journey. A sudden shyness apparently having seized her, which was a curious contrast to the self-possession of her demeanour when she first encountered them. To the questions addressed to her by Frank and Nick, she made very brief and seemingly reluctant replies, and they soon discontinued their inquiries. But their curiosity was only heightened by the lady's unwillingness to satisfy it. It appeared that De Walden had heard something of a white Basuto Queen; but whence she came, or how she had attained to her kingdom, was a sealed mystery. Perhaps she might be one of an English colony, which had established itself in these parts, and assumed a sovereignty over all the inhabitants round about But if so, it was strange that none of them should have heard from the Bechuanas, and especially from Kobo, anything about such a colony. Well, at all events, a very short stay in the village would suffice to explain the mystery; probably, indeed, the first sight of it would be sufficient.

But this did not prove to be the case. The kraal was not very unlike those of the Bechuanas, and other neighbouring tribes. The houses were constructed of wicker-work plaited with reed, and had the usual arched entrance, which served as door, window, and chimney. There were the baskets and pails, the assegais, and bows and arrows, which usually stood in front of a Kaffir hut, or were hung against the central pole. The population, too, which had assembled, one and all, to witness the entry of the strangers, did not materially differ from the other inhabitants of the district. The whole kraal, to be sure, had the appearance of having been constructed in haste, and only partially finished; but otherwise, our adventurers would hardly have known that they had entered the country of a new people. As soon as they had entered the enclosure, Ella called up one of the natives, to whom she gave some orders in a tone that was not audible, and then, turning to her companions with a graceful bend of the head, she vanished into one of the neighbouring houses. The Basuto to whom she had spoken, now stepped up to the Englishmen and invited them, by a gesture of the hand, to follow him.

They obeyed, and presently found themselves in a room which showed, for the first time, a real contrast to ordinary savage life. It was a *room*, not the inside of a hut—a room perhaps fourteen feet square, hastily constructed of trees squared by the axe, and planks nailed horizontally to them, but a room, nevertheless, with ceiling, unglazed windows and doors, and carpeted with Kaffir matting. There were even some rude chairs and a table in the centre. Their guide pointed to these first, and then to a door opening into another apartment of about the same size, where some skins were spread on the floor. "Eat here," he said; "sleep there."

The first part of his speech was presently made good by the arrival of two Basutos, carrying some baskets, which contained rice, Indian corn, and several varieties of fruit. These were placed in the middle of the table, and a wooden platter was assigned to each guest, who sat down to something like a regular meal for the first day for many months past. "I don't understand about this Queen," said Frank, as he pushed away his wooden plate. "I remember my uncle told me that, beyond the limits of the Cape Colony, there were nothing but savages for hundreds and thousands of miles; and that it wasn't safe for white people to venture among them. Who in the world can she be?"

"You seemed to know something about her, sir," remarked Warley, turning to De Walden. "Perhaps you can explain the mystery."

"I know nothing more," said the missionary, "than that I sometimes heard, whilst living to the north of the Basuto country, that some hundreds of miles southwards, there was a tribe under the rule of a woman, whose race and colour was different from theirs, and who was generally believed to be an enchantress. That, of course, was mere barbarous superstition, but the true facts of the case I never learned. We shall doubtless, however, soon hear them, as we were to be summoned to her presence as soon as we had partaken of food. Ay, here, I suppose, comes the messenger to give us notice that she is ready to receive us."

This conjecture proved to be correct, and in a few minutes they were ushered into the apartment, where the Queen of the Basutos sat in state to receive them. It was similar in construction to the one they had just quitted, but larger, and with more attempt at ornament. The ceiling was coloured white, relieved with green, and the walls a dark yellow; the latter exhibiting something like an attempt at panelling. At the further end was a kind of dais rising three steps, on the topmost of which stood a massive chair of ebony wood, and one smaller but of the same material by its side. The floor was spread with Kaffir mats of gay patterns, while several articles belonging only to European civilisation—books, an inkstand, a writing-desk, and the like—were arranged on a large heavy table of the same material as the chair. From the ceiling there hung a lamp, like those ordinarily used on board ships, and fed with oil, which diffused a very sufficient light throughout the apartment. Behind the royal chair, and on either side down the room, were several Basutos, wearing dresses made of the skin of the koodoo, or the leché, and carrying light assegais in their hands.

The Queen herself was a woman apparently between forty and fifty; bearing a strong resemblance to her daughter, but of a fairer complexion, her hair and eyes being also of a lighter brown. She was picturesquely, even richly, dressed, in a kind of long tunic of scarlet cloth trimmed with swan's-down, over which she wore a robe of leopard skin; slippers and buskins of the same material as her gown, but thickly set with coloured beads and spangles. A tiara, similarly ornamented and surmounted by ostrich feathers, completed her attire.

She greeted her visitors as they moved up to her chair with graceful courtesy.

"You are English, I am told?" she said, interrogatively; "if so, my countrymen, and the first I have beheld for six and twenty years. But I have not forgotten the dear old language, in which, indeed, I and my daughter always converse, and it will delight us both to hear it from other lips beside our own."

"Yes, madam," answered De Walden, "we are English—my three younger companions entirely so; while I am of English descent and English parentage on the father's side. We thank you for your kind reception of us, which, it is needless to say, is most welcome after the toils and dangers we have undergone."

"Your appearance is that of a missionary," rejoined the Queen. "May I ask if that is the case, and if so, what is your name, and where have you of late been residing?"

"I am a preacher of the Gospel," said De Walden, "and my name is Theodore De Walden. I have been for many years in different parts of South Africa, both to the north and west of this land."

"I have heard of you," said the Queen, "and have long been desirous of meeting with you, or some other of your calling. I myself am by birth a member of the English Church, and still account myself one, though so long cut off from its ministrations."

"The English Church—indeed!" exclaimed Warley. "May we presume to ask how—how—"

"How it comes that an English Churchwoman should be living in this wild country, so far from her native land, and the ruler of a barbarian tribe— that is what you would ask," said the Queen, smiling. "Well, of course I knew you would wish to learn the particulars of my strange history, and it is perhaps as agreeable to me to relate, as it is to you to hear it. Seat yourselves"—she beckoned to the attendants to bring forward chairs, as she spoke—"and I will tell you the whole tale."

"I was born in one of the midland counties of England, and am the daughter of a man of good family, though at the time of my birth reduced in means. He was a surgeon in a small country town, skilful and unwearied in his profession, but unable to realise any considerable income. My mother died when I was about twelve years old, and as my father could not afford to keep any assistant, he was obliged to rely a good deal on my help, as I grew up, in making up his medicines, and occasionally attending cases of slight illness under his directions. When I was about seventeen, my father unexpectedly obtained a valuable appointment in India, in the Company's service, and thither we accordingly proceeded in the spring of the year 1778.

"But the climate never agreed with him; and after persisting for two or three years in the vain hope of becoming habituated to it, his health altogether broke down, and he died, leaving me with a very slender provision. I resolved at once to return to England, and solicit the help of my relatives there. Some of them may still be living, and doubtless believe that I have long been dead. It would only distress them if they were to learn the real facts, and I therefore shall not disclose my true name, or those indeed of any of the party.

"I took my passage homeward by the *Grosvenor*, a fine vessel belonging to the East India Company's service. It carried a great many passengers, mostly officers returning home, and a few civilians. There were also several ladies, though none about my own age. I remember, particularly, Colonel Harrison—so I will name him—an old friend of my father's, Major Piers, Captains Gilby and Andrewes, Mr Hickson, Mr Morgan, and Mr Gregg, as well as his sister, Mrs Gilby, Mrs Wilkinson, and Miss Hordern. It is strange how well I can recall all their faces and persons at this interval of time.

"The voyage was unusually quick and agreeable until we arrived off the coast of South Africa. But there we encountered a gale so violent, that the ship soon became wholly unmanageable. Everybody concurred in saying, that it was through no fault either of the captain or of the crew that the vessel was lost. The wind drove her directly ashore, the anchors that were thrown out parted during the height of the storm, and there are no harbours anywhere along that coast for which vessels can run. The end was that she was thrown upon a reef at no great distance from shore, and entirely broken up.

"By the good management of the officers in command, the whole of the passengers, and nearly all the crew, were got into the boats and safely landed on the shore. We were at first very thankful for our escape; but if we had known the fate that awaited nearly all of us, I think we should have preferred being swallowed up by the raging sea to undergoing it. The sea-coast at that point consists of long stretches of sandy beach, overgrown at a short distance from the sea by thick scrub and underwood, while further inland are dense and almost impassable forests. Our first step was to provide ourselves with some shelter against the wind and rain which continued unabated for several days. By the help of the carpenter's chest, and the various articles which were thrown ashore from the wreck, we soon established ourselves comfortably enough. Huts were run up in which the whole of the party were lodged, hunting parties organised, and then a general meeting was summoned to determine what steps were to be taken to deliver ourselves from the embarrassing position in which we were placed.

"I remember there was great difference of opinion. Some proposed to build a barque out of the remains of the *Grosvenor*, sufficiently large to convey the whole party round to Table Bay. The distance, it was reckoned, was six or seven hundred miles. We might easily row or sail on an average forty or fifty miles a day. And even if Cape Town should be too far to be so reached, we should be safe to come to some of the villages scattered here and there along the coast, which kept up some kind of communication with the interior. Others urged our continuing in our present quarters until we succeeded in attracting the attention of some passing vessel. Others, again, proposed a plan compounded of these. One of the small boats was to be repaired sufficiently to allow two or three of the most experienced sailors to go in search of help for the whole party.

"On the whole, I believe the last-named suggestion would have had the best chance of success. Any one of the three would certainly have been preferable to the one adopted, and which had in the first instance been proposed by the Captain himself, viz., that the whole of the party should make their way overland to the nearest inhabited district. This was strongly opposed by Colonel Harrison and old Mr Hickson; the former of whom warned us, that the attempt would probably result in the destruction of all. But there were among the passengers, as well as among the junior officers of the ship, a number of hot-headed adventurous spirits, to whom such a journey, as that designed, had an irresistible charm. We all set out; but after a few days of suffering, all the women and most of the men returned to the coast, while the others went on.

"I have been told that some at least of this party succeeded after a long and hazardous journey in reaching the Dutch settlements at Cape Town.

I suppose that must be so, because I learned, some years afterwards, that all the particulars of the loss of the *Grosvenor* were known to the Dutch authorities, and I do not know how they could have learned anything on the subject except from my fellow-passengers. I have also been told that a party was sent out to search for any survivors of the ill-fated ship. If that was so, they never came near the spot where I was living.

"We saw our companions depart with very mingled feelings. The confidence of their leaders had inspired some of us with hope, while others were very despondent. This despondency was increased when, a few days after their departure, Captain Gilby and Mr Gregg, returning from a shooting expedition, reported that they had seen armed savages in the neighbourhood of the huts, prowling about, evidently with no friendly intentions towards us. It was immediately resolved to protect the building with a palisade; beyond which the ladies were never to venture without an armed escort, and to keep two of the men always on guard inside the stockade with loaded muskets. But these precautions were of little avail. Several of our small party were, from time to time, captured or wounded by the natives; and all who were thus injured expired soon afterwards in great agonies from the poison, in which the weapons of the savages had been steeped. Two or three of the women also died, partly of insufficient food, and partly of anxiety and alarm. At last the whole party was reduced to four men and five women; and we then held a consultation to decide what was to be done.

"It was impossible to defend the stockade, with our reduced numbers. It was idle to hope for rescue. It would be still more useless to surrender to the savages, who would observe no terms, even should they be induced to agree to any. The only possible hope lay in flight. If we stole out of the palisades by night, and took ourselves off in different directions through the depths of the forest, it was just possible that some of us might escape the notice of our enemies. We divided into three parties, Captain Gilby, his wife, and Mrs Wilkinson chose the path by the seashore; Captain Piers, Mr and Miss Gregg, endeavoured to follow the route taken by the party several weeks before; while Colonel Harrison took Miss Hordern and myself under his charge. The Colonel had some knowledge of the colony, and knew that the best hope of escape lay towards the north, where there were but few tribes located, and an almost endless screen of forest.

"We took leave of one another only an hour after we had come to this resolution, as the danger was growing every moment more imminent. I never heard with any certainty what became of the rest of the party; but a report once reached me that Miss Gregg (so I call her, though, as I have said before, I give none of the real names), after the murder of her brother and

Captain Piers, had to submit to something of the same fate as myself. But this was only a rumour. Of the fate of Captain Gilby and his wife, I never heard anything.

"As regards ourselves, we were fortunate enough entirely to escape pursuit, and after three days of intense anxiety and fatigue, had reached a part of the forest which lay beyond the haunts of the tribes, by which we had been attacked. We were now compelled to rest awhile, and recover our strength. But though Miss Hordern and myself, who were both of us of a hardy constitution, soon rallied from the fatigues we had undergone, the old Colonel could not. He grew daily weaker in spite of all our care of him, and at last died, to our inexpressible grief. We laid his remains in an empty pit which we had found, and filled it in as well as we could, with clods and stones. We then set off—two poor desolate women—to find our way as well as we could to some place of shelter.

"The toil we underwent, and the perils, which by a miracle we contrived to avoid, would fill a volume, if I were to relate them. But it will be enough to say that, after endless wanderings, we found ourselves at last somewhere about fifty or sixty miles from the banks of the Gariep—at no very great distance, in fact, from this present spot. We had subsisted chiefly on the fruits that grow in abundance throughout the whole of the country, and were beginning to hope that, after all, we might reach the outlying Dutch farms of which Colonel Harrison had spoken, when another calamity befell us. Miss Hordern and myself were one day suddenly surprised by a party of Basutos, who had gone out on a shooting expedition to the valley of the Vaal. We instantly took to flight, but before we had gone fifty yards, Miss Hordern was struck by an arrow, and the wound proved almost instantly fatal. I stopped as soon as I saw her fall, and took her in my arms, too much distressed by this last misfortune to heed my own danger.

"What the pursuers would have done to me, I do not know. But when I recovered from the swoon of grief into which I had fallen over the body of my dead friend, I saw a tall and noble-looking warrior bending over me, his fine eyes and manly features expressing a sympathy for my affliction, which I should have supposed a savage to be incapable of feeling. He gave some orders to his men, in a language which I did not comprehend, and I was immediately carried into a hut, and carefully waited on by several women. I was ill a long time, but every day my warrior came to visit me, and gradually I picked up enough of the Basuto language to exchange a few sentences with him. I soon perceived the light in which he viewed me, and it was not unwelcome—strange as such an idea would have appeared to me a few weeks before. But I was worn out by harsh usage, he alone having shown me kindness; and my utter helplessness made me inclined to lean on any friendly arm. He was, too, one of the noblest and most generous characters I have ever met with, and his instinctive delicacy of feeling rendered him all the more attractive in my eyes. I consented to be his wife, conditionally on his taking no others, and to this he readily agreed, for, I believe, no woman but myself ever had any charm for him.

"We were married according to the Basuto forms; but at my desire we also recited the vow of husband and wife, according to the marriage service of the English Church, and for ten years lived happily together. I should mention that I found the medical knowledge I had acquired in my girlhood of the greatest benefit to my newly adopted countrymen. Several times, when epidemic fevers, common to this country, broke out, I was successful in treating them, and my husband's authority enabled me to enforce regulations, which otherwise I could not have induced the people to observe. When my husband was killed, some fifteen years ago, by the sudden fall of a tree, the tribe insisted on making me their Queen; and nothing has ever seriously disturbed the prosperity of my reign. Ella, who was born a few years after our marriage, is our only surviving child.

"Such is my history—a strange one, no doubt. Probably most persons would regard me as an object of pity, to say the least. But I do not share the opinion. I have had, in my way, much happiness; and, if I have been deprived of privileges and blessings, which fall ordinarily to the lot of Englishwomen, have also escaped many sorrows and trials, to which in my own country I should have been exposed.

"But there are two points on which I should like to say something before I conclude. I dare say you have thought it strange that I did not communicate with my countrymen at Cape Town, when the colony fell into their hands. But news travels so slowly in these wild and distant regions, that I did not know with any certainty what had taken place till long after the occurrence. Then, my husband's death for the time drove all other thoughts from my mind; and when I had regained my composure enough to attend once more to the affairs of my kingdom, and I sent an embassy to the English Governor, I found that the colony had been given back to the Dutch.

"The other matter is a more important one. I should be sorry for you, Mr De Walden, to think that I made no effort to induce my husband to adopt Christianity as his creed. It was a subject on which we often talked, and though he was slow to accept ideas so wholly new, yet they gradually grew upon him, and before his death he was a convert to Christ.

"No Christian minister ever came into our neighbourhood during the whole of our married life, or he would doubtless have gladly welcomed him, and received baptism at his hands. As it was, I myself administered the rite to him, when I saw that he was dying.

"I have done my best to bring up Ella in our faith, and to teach what I could to others round me; but I hail your coming—the first preacher of the Gospel I have encountered in this land—with the utmost thankfulness, and trust you will remain among us as our teacher and guide, assured that all the help and countenance that I can give shall be most willingly and gladly bestowed."

She ceased, and De Walden, who had listened to her story with profound interest, hastened to make answer.

"Be assured, gracious lady, that I will most cheerfully obey your wishes. The hand of God is too plainly seen in what has occurred for me to venture to refuse, even were I so inclined; but earnestly as I have, for years past, been seeking for an opening like this, and always hitherto having failed to obtain it, I cannot be thankful enough to the merciful Providence, which has at last been pleased to hearken to my prayers."

Chapter Twenty Two

De Walden soon discovered that Queen Laura had not overstated her friendly feelings towards him and his companions. Not only was every provision made for their comfort, but a large building was set apart for the special purposes of a missionary school and chapel. Here such of the Basuto children as were allowed by their parents to receive instruction from the English teachers were instructed for two or three hours every day; while morning and evening prayers were regularly offered up by the missionary, which all were invited to attend. The Queen did not directly order the people to send their children to the school thus opened, but it was known that she approved of it, and her popularity with the tribe was so great that very few held back.

The afternoons were usually given up to the more especial education of Ella; who, though she had been taught by her mother to read and write, and had studied the few English books which had been saved from the wreck of the *Grosvenor*, was of course greatly behind English girls of her age in respect of knowledge. De Walden undertook her religious instruction, and gave her besides some general lessons in history and grammar, but was obliged, by lack of time, to hand over arithmetic and geography to Warley, who, fresh from a good English school, was well acquainted with both. Such an arrangement would have been a somewhat questionable one in an English family; but here, in the heart of the African wilderness, its awkwardness was not felt, and Ella's extreme simplicity of mind prevented any embarrassments which might otherwise have arisen.

So passed several weeks, with scarcely anything to distinguish one day from another. In the morning De Walden and Warley, assisted generally by Ella, taught the village children to read, write, and cipher; then came the mid-day meal, when the whole party dined at the Queen's table; after that there were Ella's lessons, lasting two or three hours; then some excursion on horseback (for the Queen owned a large stud of horses), or on the river, when the lads took their rifles with them, and seldom returned without a goodly supply of game of one kind or another. During these expeditions, Ella would continually ply her companions with questions respecting English life, and especially the habits of English ladies, in which she took a deep and ever-increasing interest; and Warley, at least, was never tired of satisfying her curiosity. In the evenings there was the second meal, and after that De Walden or Warley read aloud; or the Queen and the missionary would talk over the Europe, and especially the England, of their young days, of which both entertained so vivid a remembrance. It was strange to think that a life so nearly resembling that of an English home, could be carried out at a distance of more than seven thousand miles from it, and amid the depths of an uncultivated wilderness!

Meanwhile nothing could be learned respecting Kobo's movements. A messenger had been despatched to the village, in which Queen Laura usually resided, it being supposed that Kobo had repaired thither in search of her. But the Basuto had returned in four or five days, with the information that nothing had been seen or heard of the missing man. A party of white men, it was however reported, had been seen travelling somewhere in the neighbourhood of the Vaal, and it was thought that Kobo might have joined them. Further inquiries were set on foot, as soon as this information was received, as to who these white men were, and whence they had come; but it was found impossible to obtain any trustworthy tidings respecting them. If there ever had been any such persons in the vicinity of the Gariep, at all events they had long since departed, and no one knew whither.

It was now again the season of early summer, and the shrubs and flowers were in their full freshness and beauty. It was resolved to gratify Nick and Frank (who were beginning to find life in the Basuto kraal exceedingly dull and wearisome) with some sport, which they had not yet witnessed. In particular, they were anxious to see the giraffe hunted; and it having been reported that a large herd of these animals had been seen browsing in a kloof at no great distance, a party was formed for going in chase of them on the ensuing day. The Queen had desisted from the sports of the field for two or three years past, and De Walden could not afford, at the present juncture, to lose even a day with his scholars. But all the others joined the expedition, accompanied by the Princess Ella, who in the use of the bow and arrow was as skilful as any warrior of the tribe. They were all mounted on fleet steeds, especially trained to the pursuit of the giraffe; for to horses not so broken in, the scent of the camelopard is so offensive that they cannot be induced to approach it.

It was a fine fresh morning. The horsemen, eight in number, were attended by a much larger company of Basutos on foot, whose business it was to spread themselves in all directions over the woodland, and drive the gigantic animals towards the spot where the horsemen were lying in ambush. These accordingly dispersed, north, east, and west; while the riders, in groups of two or three, repaired to their appointed station.

"Were you fond of riding when in your own country, Ernest?" asked the princess, as they cantered lightly side by side over the mossy turf.

"I seldom had the opportunity," answered Warley. "Horses are costly, both to buy and to keep, in England, and I was not rich, you know."

"Not rich! How strange it seems to me, to hear you say that! It seems to me that the very poorest in England must be far richer than my mother or myself. All the things that appear to me to be really valuable are within the reach of every one there, so at least I gather from what you have told me; while we can obtain none of them, even though we gave all we had for their possession."

"Viewing things in that light, what you say is true, Ella. But you have advantages which few in England possess. You have influence and power over others—"

"Ah, I understand, and you will teach us how to use these rightly. I rejoice every day more and more that you have come among us."

"And I am not less glad, Ella, believe me."

"You!—you glad to be here, Ernest? What! far away from your home and friends, in a wild and strange land like this? You are jesting, surely."

"Indeed I am not, Ella. I would not be back in England, if a wish could place me there."

Ella would have replied, but they had now reached the spot where they had agreed to assemble, and the rest of the party joined them. It was an open glade, of perhaps an acre in extent, in the heart of a thickly wooded country. For the most part, the trees were not more than ten or twelve feet high, though here and there oomahaamas and baobabs were to be seen, the former towering to a great height against the sky—the latter of enormous girth, sixty or eighty feet at the least—their trunks resembling large columns of granite, in the grey colour and rough surface they presented. It was in the midst of a group of these that the party now assembled; the massy stems and dense foliage effectually screening them from view, though they could themselves see the whole country round them. Presently a distant sound was heard, like that of trampling hoofs, which grew louder and louder, until the elegant tapering necks of a dozen giraffes came into sight, as they raced along with the gallop which appears so graceful until the legs come into sight, and then so clumsy and confused. On they sped, balancing their lengthy bodies anew, as it appeared, every time they laid leg to the ground, and whisking their tufted tails from side to side, as though to stimulate themselves to fresh exertions.

As soon as the herd had entered the open glade, the horsemen broke cover, and galloped after them, hoping to approach them sufficiently near to be able to strike them with their spears or arrows. But the animals caught the flash of the first assegai that issued from under the baobabs, and wheeling instantly round, continued their career at more headlong speed than before. The only chance now lay in riding them down; and this might be accomplished with the trained horses ridden by the party, though only after a furious gallop of many miles. As if aware of this possibility, and anxious to avoid it as much as possible, the giraffes now no longer kept together in a single herd, but fled in different directions, only two or three remaining in company, and several galloping singly off through the forest paths. As the natural consequence of this, the pursuers also broke up in smaller bands; and by and by, Warley and Ella found themselves separated from the rest, and riding at full speed in pursuit of one of the largest giraffes, which was making for a long stretch of open down, lying beyond the woodland. They were both mounted on strong and spirited horses, and being light weights, were enabled to keep the animal in sight for the first mile, in which it usually succeeds in distancing its pursuers.

"Keep on, Ernest," said Ella, encouragingly, "we shall soon begin to gain upon him. Can you fire from the saddle? If so, you will get a shot before me. My bow will not carry nearly the distance of your rifle."

"Yes, I can fire pretty steadily from a horse's back now," returned Warley, "especially when I am on Sultan, as I call him. I have had a good deal of practice lately."

"That is well," said Ella. "The country will change in a few minutes now, and we shall be out of the bush. The giraffe is already abating his speed. We shall gain on him every minute now."

Ella's words were soon made good. As they emerged from the woody cover, the animal's strength began perceptibly to fail. They were soon within two hundred yards of him, and drawing closer with every stride of their horses. Ella now bent her bow, and took an arrow from the quiver slung behind her, while Warley disengaged his rifle and cocked it. When they had approached within fifty yards, he thought he might venture to fire. Even should he fail in mortally wounding the camelopard, he was pretty sure of hitting it somewhere, and the loss of blood would gradually diminish the creature's strength. He levelled accordingly, and drew the trigger, just as they were nearing a pile of rocks on which a quantity of bushes were growing. The moment after the report of his piece had been heard, the animal suddenly recoiled, and seemed to be on the point of falling. Ernest pushed on to finish it with a second shot, but as he rode up abreast of it, a fierce roar burst from behind an angle of rock, and a lion of the largest size sprang on the back of the giraffe. Almost immediately afterwards a second appeared, and seized the unfortunate animal in the neck and chest. Under the pressure of their weight it was unable to continue its flight. It plunged violently, making desperate, but wholly ineffectual, efforts to shake off its tormentors, and tearing up the earth with its hoofs. But in less time than it takes to tell it, the giraffe was borne to the ground, feebly gasping out its life under the merciless claws and teeth of its assailants.

Meanwhile the horses had been almost as much terrified by the sudden apparition of the monarchs of the forest, as the camelopard itself. That which carried Ella rushed frantically off at a speed, which she was at first unable to check. Warley's steed sprang on one side, with an abruptness which dislodged its rider, who had dropped the rein, preparing for a second shot. Warley was thrown to the ground, his rifle falling several yards in advance of him; and the frightened animal galloped off at its utmost speed. Ernest was left in a most dangerous position. The lions having torn their prey down, did not proceed immediately to devour it, but glared round them, as though anticipating the approach of another enemy. Warley lay at the distance of only a few yards, his figure fully exposed to the view of the angry monsters, which stood over the carcass of the giraffe, lashing their flanks with their tails, and sending up roar after roar, each seeming more savage than the last. Ernest dared not move hand or foot; his instinct, rather than his reason, told him that his only hope lay in the lions believing him to be really dead, in which case they would not probably trouble themselves about him.

He lay thus for nearly a quarter of an hour, the sun beating fiercely down on his unprotected head, for his cap had been dislodged in the fall, contemplating the huge brutes through his half-shut eyes. At the end of that time his ear caught the twang of a bow from the adjoining thicket, and the nearest lion leapt into the air with an arrow sticking in his breast, while the second lion bounded off and disappeared behind the rocks. Before Ella could discharge a second missile, the wounded beast had charged her; and her horse, which was snorting with terror, and had with the greatest difficulty been forced back to the scene of the encounter, stumbled in its blind haste over the root of a tree, rolling over its rider.

Ella was in even greater danger than Ernest had been. She lay at the distance of a few yards from her fallen steed, bruised and breathless. The lion paused for a minute, seeming uncertain as to which of his fallen enemies he meant to spring upon. That moment of indecision saved the princess's life. Ernest recovered his rifle the moment the lion's attention was withdrawn from him, and now fired his second barrel at the distance of only a few yards, into the shoulder of the monster, just a few inches from the place where Ella's arrow was sticking. It was levelled at exactly the right spot. The limbs, which were just crouching for the spring, suddenly collapsed, and the terrible enemy fell lifeless in the dust.

Warley now ran up and took the lifeless form of Ella into his arms, endeavouring, by every means he could think of, to restore its animation. He chafed her cold hands, he loosened the clasp which had confined her dress at the neck; and finding these efforts vain, carried her in his arms to a small spring, which rose hard by, and threw water into her face. This last remedy presently took effect. The princess opened her eyes with a long sigh, and looked confusedly round her.

"Where am I?" she exclaimed feebly. Then, as her glance lighted on the face of Ernest bending anxiously over her, and the figure of the dead lion, lying at the distance of a few yards, the whole occurrence seemed to come back to her memory.

"Oh, Ernest," she exclaimed, "the lion! You saved me, then. Are you not hurt yourself?"

"I have escaped with only a bruise or so," said Warley; "and it is you who have saved me, not I you. Are you sure the fall from the horse has not injured you?"

"No, that was nothing," returned Ella, colouring under the earnestness of his gaze. "I threw myself from his back as he fell, and he did not touch me. I don't think he is hurt either. If we can catch the horses, we had better rejoin the party. The skins of the giraffe and lion will be a valuable prize."

Warley soon caught Ella's horse, and then went in search of his own, which he found grazing quietly at the distance of two or three hundred yards. They mounted and galloped off in quest of Wilmore and Gilbert, encountering them and the Basutos in attendance in about half an hour, and finding them greatly vexed at their ill success. The giraffes had galloped up the side of a long slope of hill, which gave them so great an advantage, that when the horsemen reached the summit of the range, the herd were quite out of sight, and after several ineffectual attempts to regain the scent, they were obliged to abandon the pursuit. They heard of Ella's and Ernest's success with equal surprise and satisfaction, and hurrying off in the direction indicated, were soon engaged in flaying the hides off both animals, as well as in selecting the choicest morsels of the camelopard's flesh to supply the Queen's table.

Late in the evening the party returned to the kraal, where they were welcomed by the Queen and De Walden, who questioned them as to what had taken place during the hunt. But neither Ella nor Warley seemed inclined to say more than they could help on the subject. The truth was, that a feeling of mutual liking had been growing up between the two since the first day of their meeting; when the princess had owed her life to Warley's promptitude. The attachment was little to be wondered at under the circumstances. Warley was now in his one-and-twentieth year—a fine well-grown young man, with a face of rare intelligence. He was the first Englishman who had come under Ella's notice; and when contrasted with the dark-skinned and coarse-visaged Basutos, he seemed like a being from some higher sphere. On the other hand, Ella's rare grace and beauty, her exquisite simplicity and frankness, were the qualities most likely to captivate a youth of Ernest's imaginative temperament; and the wild freedom of the life, by which they were surrounded, only added to the charm. But though he was conscious of the fascination, which was daily growing stronger, Warley felt perplexed and uncomfortable. He could not turn hunter, and live all his life in these remote solitudes. But to take Ella with him, to England or elsewhere, as his wife, was wholly impracticable, so far as he could see. How could he maintain her? How induce others to receive her? What would his friends say to such an alliance? or indeed to his forming any alliance at all? The life which had been arranged for him—that of a clerk in a house at Calcutta—it seemed impossible that Ella could share that. The idea of marrying Ella was, in fact, little better than a wild dream.

On the other hand, if Ella was not to be his wife, he ought not to remain in the Basuto village. There could be no doubt that they were getting to like one another—to speak the plain truth, they were both already deeply in love Ella did not think it necessary to disguise her feelings, as an English girl would have done; and though she was modest and maidenly, showed her preference plainly enough. Every day of their mutual intercourse did but deepen the feeling. If it was to end in nothing, he ought to go away at once.

But how was he to go away? It was true that Frank and Nick had long been anxious to set out on a journey to Cape Town, and he might go with them. De Walden, of course, would remain with Queen Laura, and prosecute his missionary work. He would be sorry to lose Warley no doubt, and so probably would Queen Laura; but neither would in all likelihood interpose any serious obstacle. There were, however, what seemed insuperable objections.

In the first place, they were bound to await Lavie's return. Queen Laura had despatched a messenger to Chuma, with a friendly message soon after their arrival in her dominions, and had entreated him to send to her any tidings that might be received from the white men. A favourable answer had been brought back from the Bechuana chief. The rainmaker had been killed, and as soon as he was dead, the truth as to the origin of the cattle disease had been disclosed by the natives, who had been aware of the facts from the first, but afraid to tell them. Chuma saw how he had been deceived as to the white man's truth and honesty, and was sincerely grieved at having so misused him. He promised that as soon as Lavie, or any emissary from him should appear, the tidings should be at once forwarded to the Basutos. These might now be looked for every day. It was strange that they had not arrived long before. If, then, Warley and the others were to set out for Cape Town now, they would inevitable miss the expected messengers, and might not see their friends for months, instead of for a few days only. Then there was Kobo. It was not at all certain that he was not still on the search for them. It would be a breach of faith if they were to leave him in the lurch; and after all his exertions in their behalf, this was not to be thought of. And, lastly, if Mr Lavie should not be at Cape Town when they arrived—and the chances were very greatly against his being there—there was no one to whom he could appeal for help or maintenance, excepting his brother. And the idea of applying to him was so repulsive, that he felt he would rather do anything than resort to it. No. Departure from the Basuto village was impossible at the present crisis. He must wait patiently, for a few weeks more, at all events.

Chapter Twenty Three

Of all the party, De Walden was now the only one who was contented to remain in his present position. He was, indeed, in a more contented frame of mind than any he had enjoyed since he first entered the Cape Colony. It seemed as if his wishes, so long frustrated, had on a sudden received their full accomplishment—as though the seed he had been vainly sowing for so many years, had sprung up to ripeness in an hour. Not only had he his band of regular worshippers, who every Sunday publicly attended his ministrations; not only had he his school filled with boys and girls, learning, with an intelligence which would hardly have been found among European children of the same age, the rudiments of Christianity—but there were several adult converts, who were so far advanced that they were almost ready to receive baptism; and many more, though they had not openly given in their adhesion to the new doctrines, were gravely and seriously considering the matter. If things should continue to go on as favourably as at present, such an impression would be made in the course of a few months on the whole tribe, as could hardly fail to end in their open profession of Christianity. De Walden had seen much of life—much in particular of missionary life; and felt inwardly assured that he would not be permitted to accomplish so great a work, without strong and determined opposition. He marvelled at his success from day to day; but meanwhile it was his duty to go on in faith, thankful for the mercy shown so far, and prepared to face the reverse, as soon as it should appear.

Ernest Warley, we have seen, felt perplexed and embarrassed by his position as regarded Ella; but the Basuto village had, nevertheless, an attraction for him, which would have made it full of delightful and absorbing interest, if his conscience had not every day pricked him more keenly as to the mischief he was unwillingly doing. But Wilmore and Gilbert, who had not the same sources of interest as either De Walden or Warley, began at last find their sojourn so intolerably wearisome, that they to could no longer endure it. "I tell you what it is, Frank," said Gilbert one day, when they had lain down to rest, under the shade of a large oomahaama overshadowing their hut, after an hour's practice at throwing the assegai, with which sport they had endeavoured to relieve the tedium of an idle morning—"I tell you what it is; if I stay here much longer, I shall go downright melancholy mad.

They can't put me into an asylum, because, I suppose, there are no articles of that kind to be met with hereabouts. But they'll have to appoint keepers, and extemporise a straight waistcoat of rhinoceros hide, and shave my head, and all the rest of it."

"I am pretty nearly as bad as you are, Nick," returned Wilmore. "There's De Walden for ever teaching those niggers, and there's Ernest for ever dangling about Ella; and very pleasant I dare say, they find it. But you and I don't particularly fancy young darkies, and haven't any girls to talk to, seeing Miss Ella has no ears for any one but Ernest. I am tired of trying to learn Basuto, or to throw an assegai, or shoot with one of their bows and arrows, which are about big enough for a child of ten years old. If we could only go out with our guns every day—"

"We are not to go out again," interrupted Nick. "The powder's running so very short, that there are not above a dozen charges left. So we must learn assegai throwing and archery, if we mean to have any sport in future."

"I shall never make a hand at either," said Frank. "A fellow must be born to it, to knock things over as these Basutos do. Well, I agree with you, I don't think I can stand this much longer, without going stark crazy."

"Suppose we *don't* stand it, Frank," suggested Gilbert. "It quite rests with ourselves. No one can compel us."

"I don't quite understand you," said Wilmore. "How can we help ourselves?"

"By taking ourselves off," answered the other.

"Look here. They say we ought to remain until the messengers return that were sent to Cape Town, and that it would be hard upon Lavie, if he were to come here and find us gone. Very good. But De Walden and Warley both mean to remain with Queen Laura; so that whenever he may come (if he *does* come) he will find them, and that will answer every purpose. But you and I may go our way, and leave them to go theirs."

"What! you propose that we two should set off for Cape Town alone, hey? Could we find our way, think you?"

"I don't see why we shouldn't. We know the exact position of Cape Town, and the pocket compass, which Lavie gave me, will enable us to go at all events in the right direction. It will take a long time, no doubt—"

"Three or four months, at least," said Wilmore.

"About that, I judge," rejoined Gilbert. "But then we shall be tolerably sure to fall in with some Dutch village or farm before we have got half-way;

and the Dutch are hospitable, though not civil to the English. They couldn't turn us out into the wilderness, anyhow."

"No, I suppose not," said Frank, "particularly as we have got money to pay for what we want. But then, Nick, how are we to subsist till we reach one of these villages or farms. The nearest, I believe, are fully two hundred miles off, if we went ever so straight. With only six charges in our guns—"

"We must reserve our fire for great emergencies," interrupted Nick. "I have my knife, any way, and we have learned something by this time, remember, and know where to find the roots and fruits these fellows eat. Besides, it's the season for birds' eggs now, and there'll be heaps of them."

"Yes, and we can take a lot of mealeys with us," added Wilmore. "They will go into a small compass and last a long time. Well, Nick, I don't mind, if I go in for this with you. So far as I can see, we may wait here, day after day, for the next twelvemonth; and I'd rather take my chance of being devoured alive by the wild beasts, or knocked on the head by the savages, than have to go through that. When do you propose that we should make a start?"

"Well, we must first of all lay in a store of mealeys—I always meant to take them: and I should like to get out of De Walden the nearest way to the banks of the Gariep. I've an idea that if we could reach that, we might make another raft like that on which we made our voyage to the island, and float on it till we came to the place where we were carried away by the flood. We should both know that again."

"That's not a bad idea, Nick. We should find plenty to eat as we went along. We could store up a lot of figs, or dates or bananas on the raft—enough to last us a week, I dare say; and the current runs pretty swift, I expect. Only how about the falls at different parts of the river? I've heard there are several places where there are rapids, or actual cascades."

"I don't think there are between this and the place I was speaking of. Anyhow we must be on the look out, and if we see any reason to think we are getting near one, we must run ashore. Of course there must be some risk, you know."

"Of course. Well, I am game to go, and I think we had better make a start as soon as possible. Suppose we look up the mealeys to-morrow and the next day—Tuesday, that is, and Wednesday, and set out on Thursday."

"We had better set out on Wednesday night. There is a full moon then, which will light us as well as broad day would. And it would give us a start of ten hours or so before we were missed."

"Very good. I have no objection. It is the pleasantest time for travelling during the warm weather."

On the Wednesday evening, accordingly, the two boys set out on their expedition. Nick had managed skilfully to extract the information he desired from the missionary, without exciting his suspicions; and they had had no difficulty in gathering a heap of ripe mealeys, as large as they could carry in their knapsacks, unobserved by any one. They were careful to take no more than the exact amount of powder, which they considered to be their share of the remaining stock. Frank also wrote a few lines, addressed to Warley, in which he told him, that they had found their life of late so unendurable that they had resolved to brave every toil and danger, rather than continue to undergo it. He begged that no attempt might be made at pursuit; because in event of their being overtaken, they were resolved positively to refuse to return to the Basuto village. Lastly, he assured Ernest, that if they succeeded in reaching Cape Town, they would take care that steps were immediately taken for securing his safe journey thither.

Having left this letter on the table, where it would be sure to be found on the following morning, the two lads set forth under the bright moonlight, and travelled in safety some fifteen or sixteen miles through the night and into the next day, when the burning heat warned them that it was time to rest. They started again an hour or two after sunset, and again pursued their way through almost unbroken solitude, tracking their way partly by the aid of Gilbert's compass, partly by their recollection of Mr De Walden's information. So many days passed on, until the whole of their store of provisions was exhausted, and they were fain to supply themselves with anything eatable, which the desert or forest could furnish.

But here they found, for the first time, their calculations fail them. The plains they traversed were either wastes of arid sand, or ranges of forest producing haak-doorns and kamel doorns and mimosas in abundance, and occasionally sycamores and acacias, but none of the fruit trees they had reckoned on finding. At the end of the second day, they were obliged to expend some of their dearly cherished ammunition in firing at a gemsbok, which came full upon them in one of the turnings of the forest, and which they were fortunate enough to wound with the first shot they fired, and kill with a second.

Collecting a heap of dry grass and wood, they succeeded, by the help of Lavie's burning-glass, which had been the doctor's parting gift to Frank, in lighting a fire, at which they roasted a considerable part of the gemsbok's flesh, and having made a hearty meal upon it, stored the remains in their knapsacks. A considerable supply of meat was thus obtained, and for two or three days they fared well enough, especially as there was a fall of rain, which gave them plenty of water.

But the line of country through which they passed continued as barren of the means of supporting existence as ever, and they were presently reduced to the same straits as before. They began, indeed, now to be somewhat alarmed at their situation. They had reckoned that it would be a fortnight's journey to the banks of the Gariep; but they had been ten days on their route, and had not, so far as they could calculate, accomplished half the distance. Each of them had only two charges of powder left, and it was evident that their guns alone could be reckoned on, as furnishing them with food in the country where they were now travelling. Their condition was rendered worse by two unsuccessful attempts which they made to shoot a buffalo on the day after the last batch of gemsbok meat had been consumed. They had come on the track of a herd of buffaloes, which they had resolved to follow, and after many hours of careful stalking, they had got so near to the herd at sunset as to venture a shot. But, just as in the former instance, though the animal was hit, and it might be severely wounded, it did not fall, but was able to make off with the rest of the herd.

"Oh, Frank, what will become of us?" exclaimed Nick, as he witnessed this mishap. "If we don't get food somewhere to-night, I feel as if I should perish of hunger."

"Never say die, Nick," said Frank, cheerily. "Look here! This brute is hit hard, I'm sure of that; and I'm pretty sure, too, that he won't hold out very long. Just look what lots of blood he has left behind him. They'll be quite enough to enable us to track him, even by this light. We'll follow up the blood-marks until we find him. Even if another shot should be necessary, we shall still have a charge apiece left, if we should be attacked. If we kill the buffalo it will supply us with food for a long time to come, and it is very unlikely that the country will continue as bare of all fruit, as it has been since we left the village."

"All right, Frank," returned Nick; "that is the best way of viewing it at all events. I'll just take a hole up in my belt to stop the importunities of my stomach, and then we'll be off after the buffalo. We may as well go that way as any other, at all events."

They set out accordingly, following without difficulty, by the help of the moon, the course taken by the herd across the open plain and the intervening patches of scrub for two or three hours. The marks of blood were plainly enough visible all the way, sometimes in large patches, as though the wounded animal had stopped behind the rest through momentary weakness; and then again only a drop here and there, as if it had again exerted its remaining strength to overtake the herd. At last they came to a spot where a larger puddle than any before stained the adjacent grass and sand, and then the marks no longer followed the general track, but turned aside into a deep thicket, through which the two boys had considerable difficulty in following its course.

They had advanced some distance, when Nick suddenly laid his hand on his companion's arm.

"Did you hear that?" he said.

"Hear what?" returned Wilmore.

"I fancied I heard a shot fired," said Gilbert, "but I suppose I must have been mistaken."

"A shot! Who could there be in these parts to fire one? It was the fall of a large stone from the cliffs, most likely. They are often dislodged by the wind, and make a noise like the report of a gun. Come along, we shall not have much further to go, I expect."

"Hist!" exclaimed Nick, again stopping. "I am quite sure I hear something now, though in a different quarter from that in which I fancied the gun was fired."

"What do you hear?" asked Wilmore, stopping and listening with all his ears.

"A kind of low growling, or groaning," answered Nick; "or perhaps grinding of teeth. It is very indistinct; but I am certain that I hear it."

"It is the poor brute in his dying agony," said Frank. "Push on. We must be close to him now."

By this time the dawn had begun to break, and the daylight diffused itself rapidly over the scene. The beams of the rising sun showed that they were, as Frank said, close on the buffalo's trail. The grass was trampled down, as if by heavy footsteps, and blood, evidently only recently shed, stained the bushes and long grass in profusion. And now the sound heard by Nick became plainly audible to Frank also.

"Cock your gun, Nick!" he said. "He may have life enough left in him to give us some trouble yet."

As he spoke he turned the corner of a large mass of prickly pear, which had been partly forced aside and partly torn away by the passage of some heavy body, and came upon a sight which was as alarming as it was unexpected.

The carcass of the buffalo lay on the ground, already partially devoured. Standing over it were a male and female panther (or tiger, as the natives of South Africa are wont to call them), engaged in tearing the flesh from the ribs with their long white shining teeth. The animals were as big as an ordinary English mastiff, and the glare of their large yellow eyes showed that the ferocity of their nature was fully awakened. Frank fell back, as soon as his eye lighted on them, conscious that his best hope of escape lay in instantly withdrawing from the spot; but Nick, who had already raised his gun before he had come in sight of the enemy he was about to encounter, drew his trigger, scarcely aware of what he was doing, wounding the male panther severely, but not mortally, in the chest. With a fierce howl of agony and rage combined, the tiger sprang straight upon him; and if he had not been extraordinarily light of limb and quick of eye, the next moment would have been his last. But the moment the charge left the barrel, he perceived the imminence of the danger threatening him, and, dropping his gun, he sprang lightly on one side. The brute's claws and teeth just missed their aim, but the body, in passing, struck him with sufficient force to prostrate him insensible on the ground. The wounded panther had no sooner recovered from its spring, than it turned back to fasten on its fallen enemy; but Frank, stepping instantly up, with ready presence of mind, applied the muzzle of his rifle to its ear, as it was on the very point of bending its neck, and it fell lifeless on the ground.

But the boys were now left quite helpless. The last charge had been fired, and the remaining panther, which had stood motionless since the discharge of the gun, watching as it were the issue of the struggle, now gave evident signs that it was about to avenge its mate. Erecting its tail, it uttered a low growl, which swelled gradually into a savage roar. Another minute and his teeth would have been fastened in the lad's throat; but before the animal could make its leap, the sound of pattering feet was heard, and a large dog, bounding through the bushes, sprang on the tiger and caught it by the throat. The brute turned savagely on its new assailant, and a furious combat commenced; the tiger tearing the ribs of the mastiff with its claws, but unable to shake off the hold it had fastened on its throat Frank gazed with blank amazement at the appearance of this unexpected champion, which seemed to have fallen from the skies for his deliverance; and his astonishment was increased when he perceived, as he presently did, that the dog was no other than his long-lost, faithful Lion! How he could be still living, and still more, what could have brought him there, he could not conceive. But it was no moment for speculation. His favourite was matched against an antagonist which, if it did not prove victor in the struggle, might at all events inflict the most deadly wounds before it could be overcome. Frank stooped, and drew the strong clasped knife which Nick always carried in his belt. Opening this, he stepped forward to the spot, where the two animals, now covered with dust and blood, were savagely rending one another; he waited for the moment when the panther's breast became exposed, and plunged the knife into it up to the hilt. The stab was mortal. Unfastening the grip of its teeth on Lion's side, the brute endeavoured to seize this new enemy; but it could not disengage itself from Lion's hold. Its jaws collapsed, its savage eyes grew filmy and dim, and in another minute the mastiff was tearing and shaking the inanimate carcass of its adversary.

"Lion! Lion! dear old boy!—are you much hurt," exclaimed Frank, running up, and throwing his arms round his favourite's neck; "however did you come here? and where have you been all these weeks and months? I can hardly believe, even now, that it is really you."

"Yes, it really him—it Lion for sure. Kobo and he make friends—know each other ever so long," said a tall Bechuana, who had now joined the party, and stood with a grin on his black face. "But, Master Nick—he not hurt, is he?"

"What, Kobo, you too here!" exclaimed Frank. "But we'll talk about that presently. We must see to Nick here. I declare I almost forgot him in the surprise and joy at seeing old Lion again. But men before dogs. I am pretty sure, though, Gilbert isn't hurt. He's only stunned by the weight of the leopard's body, when he sprang on him."

They raised the lad between them, and soon had the satisfaction of seeing him open his eyes, and draw in a long breath; and then, after once or twice stretching himself, and feeling his chest and ribs, declare that he wasn't a pin the worse, and would be ready for his dinner, as soon as ever Kobo could supply him with any!

Chapter Twenty Four

It was not until quite late on the morning after the departure of the boys, that the fact became known to De Walden and Ernest. It chanced to be the day appointed by the missionary for the baptism of two of his adult converts, for whom Ernest and Ella were to act as sponsors. In the interest of the occasion, the absence of the two boys was not noticed; and it was not until after the conclusion of the rite, that Ernest, happening to enter Frank's sleeping room, to ask some casual question of him, saw the note left on the table. As soon as he had read it, he repaired to his friend's apartment, and the two held an anxious consultation as to the course which, under the circumstances, it would be most expedient for them to pursue. De Walden knew—what none of the three lads could surmise—how great was the danger incurred by the truants, and how slender the hope of their succeeding in carrying out their projected scheme. They must be pursued, and overtaken, and warned of their peril, whatever might be the risk or fatigue incurred by so doing. If, after such warning, they persisted in their rash enterprise, they could not, of course, be prevented from pursuing it; but the blame would then rest wholly with themselves.

They were still engaged in arranging their plans for immediate pursuit, when Ella entered the room where they were seated, with tidings which were even more unexpected than those they had that morning received.

"My father," she said—so she always addressed De Walden—"the visitors you and Ernest have been so long expecting, have arrived, and are now with my mother. Will you come and see them?"

"The visitors, Ella!" exclaimed Warley, starting up. "Whom can you mean?—not Lavie surely—"

"Yes, he is one," returned Ella, "and there is a captain, an English captain. He is Frank's father or uncle—"

"Captain Wilmore!" cried Warley. "Has he fallen in with Frank?"

"No, we have told him that he and Gilbert have gone off by themselves, and that they cannot be very far off, and he means to go in search of them, I believe. But he wants to see you first."

De Walden and Ernest hastened to the Queen's apartment, and were soon exchanging a cordial grasp of the hand with the new-comers.

"God be praised for this!" said the missionary. "You cannot think how anxious I have been about you, Charles, though I did not tell the lads so. Unwilling as I was to leave this place, I had fully resolved that if the present month should pass without tidings of you, I would set off with them for Cape Town. I wish now I had told them of my intention; it would no doubt have prevented this foolish escapade of theirs. I knew I could trust Ernest to remain quiet, and I thought I could trust the others."

"You must not blame them, sir," said Warley. "I have no doubt they had the same idea which I have entertained myself, though I thought it best to say nothing about it, that treacherous orders had been given to your guide to prevent your ever reaching Cape Town."

"I cannot wonder that either you or they thought that," said De Walden, "after Chuma's treatment of us."

"But," resumed Warley, "if I was doubtful about Charles's safety, I was much more despondent about Captain Wilmore. I had little hope, I confess, of ever seeing him again."

"And you would have had less hope still, my lad," said Captain Wilmore, "if you had known what befell us when we left the *Hooghly*."

"You must hear the whole history from his own lips," said Lavie; "but not just now. We have a good deal to do this morning that must be attended to."

"I dare say the captain will relate it after supper," said De Walden. "Now come and hear the report of the scouts."

That evening, accordingly, when the repast in the Queen's apartments was concluded, Captain Wilmore was called upon for the particulars of his adventures, which he was no way unwilling to relate.

"You two will remember," he began, "the gale soon after we left the Cape de Verdes. The foreigners I had taken on board showed themselves much smarter hands than I had expected, and worked double tides all the afternoon. I didn't suspect their motive for showing so much zeal, which was no doubt to remove any suspicions I might have entertained, and make me relax my watch over them. It quite succeeded. I turned in about sundown thoroughly knocked up, but well satisfied with the behaviour of the ship's company, and intending to have a long sleep. A very long sleep it was nearly being—"

"Did they intend to murder you, sir, do you think?" asked Warley.

"I do not think about it," returned the captain. "I am sure of it. Half a dozen of them, with their knives drawn, and accompanied by those villains Duncan and O'Hara, were stealing down the companion to my cabin when they were challenged by old Jennings, who gave the alarm, and the pirates were obliged to make the attack openly. They cut the poor old man down, but he saved all our lives nevertheless. I have heard what became of him from Lavie, and it grieves me much to think that I shall never have an opportunity in this world of thanking the good old man for his bravery and self-devotion; but he will not miss his reward."

The captain's voice was husky, and no one spoke for a minute or two; then Warley broke the silence.

"Well, I should quite have believed that they intended to do it from all I heard from Jennings and others about Duncan and O'Hara, as well as from the well-known character of these pirates. But then, if that was their intention, why did they allow you to leave the ship unhurt?"

"Ah, why indeed," repeated the captain. "I can't blame you for entertaining that notion, my lad; for I, old hand as I am, did not suspect their infernal treachery and cunning. You see, when the pirate ship came up, we were just preparing to blow up the hatches and rush on deck. No doubt they would have got the better of us, and killed us to a man; but before they had managed that they would have suffered considerably themselves. That wily villain, Andy Duncan—I have been told since it was he, and I have no doubt it was—devised a scheme by which they would be enabled to get rid of us quite as easily as if they had blown out all our brains, but without incurring any risks themselves. We discovered, when we had been an hour or two on board the boats, that some trick had been played with them, and they were very slowly but surely filling."

"The merciless wretches!" exclaimed Ernest; "and you were some hundreds of miles from shore?"

"Yes, quite five hundred from Ascension, which was the nearest land."

"How did you escape, sir?" exclaimed De Walden.

"Only by God's mercy. The discovery was first made in the launch which Grey commanded. The night, you will remember, was very dark, or it probably would have been made before; but they did not find it out till it was too late to keep it afloat even for a time. They shouted to us for help, but she had sunk before we could reach them, and there was a strong current just where she went down, which swept them all away—except one of the mates, who managed to keep afloat until we picked him up. On hearing his story, we contrived to strike a light, and examined our own boat. There was a leak in her too, but providentially only just below the waterline. I suppose whoever did the job, thought the boat floated deeper than she did; but by lightening her as much as possible, and throwing all the weight that remained on the other side, we raised the damaged part out of water, and then baled her out. When day broke we were enabled to examine her more carefully. The injury was beyond our power to repair effectually. All we could do was just to keep her afloat, and if the sea had not been exceptionally calm we could not have done even that. Moreover, we had been obliged to throw overboard nearly all our provisions and water. In short, we should not only have never reached Ascension, but must have perished of hunger and thirst very speedily, if on the morning of the third day, shortly after dawn, a vessel had not appeared on our lee beam, apparently running before the light breeze which rippled the sea.

"We tried to attract her attention, but without effect. She was so near to us that we thought she must have seen us; but she did not alter her course, or in any way acknowledge our signals. Finding that she took no heed, we resolved, as a last chance, to reach her by rowing, though this obliged us to right our boat, and the water poured in so fast that incessant baling would not keep it down. At last, when we had got quite close to the ship, the boat was so water-logged that she could not have been kept afloat ten minutes more. We hailed again and again, but there was no answer, nor was any one to be seen on deck. We came to the conclusion that she had been deserted by her crew for some reason, or that they had all died on board, and that she was drifting aimlessly over the deep. Fortunately there was a rope hanging over her bows, up which one of the sailors climbed, and was followed by the others in succession. The last of us was hardly out of the cutter when she went down."

"Had she been deserted?" inquired Ernest. "Well, yes, by the survivors of her crew, that is. She was evidently a Portuguese trader running, I apprehend, between the West India Islands and Lisbon, and had probably twenty or twenty-five men on board. She must have been attacked by one of the terrible fevers prevalent in the hot climates, the action of which is sometimes so rapid that all attempts to stay it are useless. Several, I suppose, must have died, and the rest were so terrified by the fear of infection, that they had left her. Any way, there were no human remains on board, and all the ship's boats were gone."

"I should think the danger into which you ran was worse than the one from which you had escaped," observed Queen Laura.

"We were of the same opinion, madam," observed Captain Wilmore. "If we could have repaired our own boat, or if a single one of the ship's boats had been left, we should have preferred continuing our own voyage in it. But as that was impossible, we were obliged to remain in the vessel. But after consulting with Captain Renton, I resolved to run, not for Ascension, but for the Cape de Verdes, though they were considerably further off. I don't know whether any of you have ever been at Ascension?"

"We sighted it once, sir," said Lavie; "but I never went ashore there."

"There is not much to see if you do land," said the sailor. "It is little better than a great heap of cinders, except just in the interior, where there is some land capable of cultivation. It was for a long time believed that there wasn't a drop of fresh water to be found on it. That is a mistake. There are a few springs—enough to support life, and there are some goats, and plenty of turtle. But there are no inhabitants, and I reckoned that if the fever should break out on board we should find no doctors there, or any means of nursing the sick. We shaped our course for the Cape de Verdes, therefore. We took all possible precautions, sleeping on deck throughout the voyage, and never going below unless it was absolutely necessary to bring up food and water. Whether it was that these precautions were successful, or whether it was that I was mistaken in my conjecture as to the reason why the barque had been deserted, I cannot say. But we certainly escaped without any sickness, and reached the Cape de Verdes without the loss of a man.

"I need not tell you how welcome was the sight of Porto Prayo to us all. But I had an especial reason for rejoicing at it. You will remember, Ernest, the circumstances under which we left Porto Prayo?"

"Yes, sir," said Warley, colouring, "I remember we had behaved very ill. I have often wished to ask your pardon for it."

"Well, my lad, it was six of one and half a dozen of the other, I expect," said the captain. "We may share the blame between us. I had often reproached myself for the haste with which I acted; though, at the same time, I could not help being glad that you were safe, as I imagined, at Porto Prayo, instead of being exposed to the sufferings and dangers which had befallen us. I had no sooner landed than I made inquiries concerning you; but to my surprise and disappointment I could learn nothing. I instituted a most careful search, and offered a large reward. But it was all in vain. Nobody knew anything about you, except that three foreign-looking lads had been seen about the streets of the town one day several weeks before. But no one had fallen in with them, or had heard anything about them since that date. I was still prosecuting my inquiries, when the British fleet, under Sir Home Popham, on its way, as I learned, to make an attack on the Dutch at the Cape of Good Hope, sailed into the harbour.

"Fortunately for me, I was an old messmate of the Admiral's, and he was interested in my story. Moreover, I knew the Cape well, as was the case, I found, with very few of the officers of the squadron. Sir Home offered me the command of the *Celaeno*, a fine frigate, the captain of which had died suddenly. I, of course, gladly accepted it, and was enabled to render some service."

"Ah, you were present at the taking of the Cape," said Mr De Walden. "Did the Dutch offer a determined resistance?"

"No," said Captain Wilmore. "I suppose the experience of the last campaign disheartened them. But certainly it was a very hollow affair. Governor Jansens seemed to me to have given it up as a bad job from the first. There was hardly enough resistance to make it any fight at all. But something did happen to me, nevertheless, in Simon's Bay which was exciting enough."

"What was that, sir?" asked Ernest. "You did not encounter the *Hooghly*, I suppose?"

"Ah, but I did though," said Captain Wilmore, "the *Hooghly* herself, as large as life. The scoundrels had knocked away her figure-head, and painted her, name and all, anew; but I knew her in a moment, as well as I know my own face. We hailed her, and the moment they saw me on the quarter-deck, they cut their cable, and tried to run for it. But we were just entering the harbour, prepared for action, and sent such a broadside into her as knocked all the mischief out of her in a jiffey. O'Hara was killed, and White mortally wounded, and as for Andy Duncan, he was run up to the yardarm and hanged the next morning. The others were put into irons, and received various sentences. Some had seven dozen. Others were simply dismissed and sent home."

"Did you learn on board the *Hooghly* what had befallen us?" asked Warley.

"Yes, my lad, to my great satisfaction I did. One of the sailors came to me on the morning of Duncan's execution, and told me all that had happened, so far that is, as he knew it. But he could tell me nothing, of course, as to what had become of you after your escape from the ship. All he knew was that you had appeared suddenly on deck two days after we had left, and it was conjectured by the crew that you had been concealed somewhere by old Jennings. Mr Lavie, it also appeared, had gone off with you, and none of the party appeared to have been hurt. That comforted me a little, but still I was very anxious and uneasy—the more so because all inquiries at the Cape for a long time were wholly fruitless."

"Ah, I was afraid you would be at fault there," said Warley. "I suppose you simply heard nothing at all?"

"Very nearly that," said the captain. "Some of the messengers whom I sent out did come back with a story that some white men with guns had been seen in the neighbourhood of Elephant's kloof; but the Hottentots living near about there denied, one and all, the truth of the rumour."

"The rascals!" exclaimed Ernest. "When you heard the truth of the matter, sir, you must have been amused at their denial."

"Yes, afterwards," said Captain Wilmore; "but not at the time. I was, in fact, almost in despair when Lavie here arrived all of a moment one day, looking like a ghost returned from the grave."

"Ay, I am afraid you must have had a trying time of it, Charles," said De Walden. "I have sometimes reproached myself for allowing you to go, considering what the danger and exhaustion must needs be."

"You have no need to do so," said Lavie. "Whatever I may have undergone has been more than compensated by our meeting to-day, not to speak of the appointment which my kind friend has obtained for me. In fact, if I had not undertaken the journey, we must have remained in hopeless captivity."

"Did your Bechuana guide play false?" asked the missionary.

"No, I have no right to say so. Whether he would have been as faithful as he was, had matters fallen out differently, may be a matter of doubt. I half fancy he had received some private instructions from Chuma, which he did not carry out, for what may seem a very strange reason. He was frightened out of his senses by our dog, Lion!"

"Lion!" exclaimed Warley. "Why, he has been dead for weeks and months, hasn't he?"

"Not he! He is as much alive as you or I. He is at one of the huts along with Kama and Kobo at this moment."

"I thought I saw him swept away by the flood during that night on the Gariep."

"So you did, I dare say; but he must have contrived to swim ashore. Anyhow, we met him two days' journey from the Bechuana village, tracking us, I fancy, by his instinct, and he would have joined us there before long, if I had not fallen in with him; but he would not leave me, when we had once met, and I thought the best thing under the circumstances would be to take him with me to Cape Town. But Kama, who had never seen an animal like him, and who had heard of his having been swept away by the torrent, believed, I am convinced, that he was a sort of tutelary spirit, who would be sure to detect any knavery and avenge any false dealing on his part. It amused me, I must say, a good deal; but any way, from the day Lion joined our company to that on which we reached Cape Town, he never attempted any tricks."

"And then you and Captain Wilmore resolved to go in quest of us," said De Walden. "I understand that But how did you find out where we were? Did you go to the Bechuanas, and hear it from Chuma?"

"No; we were making our way to the village, when we fell in with a man who was known to Kama, and who, it seemed, knew me too, though I had quite forgotten him."

"What! Kobo, I suppose?" exclaimed Warley.

"Yes, that, I believe, is his name. He told us that you all had escaped in his company from Chuma, who had quarrelled with you, or with Mr De Walden. He said he had left you on an island on the Yellow River awaiting his return, and we had better accompany him to the place. So we did, but there was no trace of you to be found."

"No," said Warley. "We didn't stay twenty-four hours on the island after Kobo's departure. We have been playing at cross purposes with him. How did you find out at last where we were?"

"We met your messenger returning from his errand to the Bechuanas, and learned that the quarrel had been made up. Nevertheless, all things considered, it is quite as well that we didn't go there."

"All's well that ends well," said the Queen, who had sat listening to the discourse of her English guests with the deepest interest, recalling, as it did, so many varied associations.

"I trust it will end well, madam," observed Captain Wilmore. "But until I find my nephew, and young Gilbert, and bring them back safely, I cannot consider that there is an end to my anxieties."

"We will set off in quest of them to-morrow morning, as soon as you have had a good rest," said De Walden. "I have already set some of the best hunters to follow their track, so as to save us time to-morrow. I feel sure that in two or three days, at furthest, we shall come up with them."

So they probably would have done, had it not been for the length of the journeys made by the lads on the first two days, and the rains which had fallen on the third and fourth, which had almost entirely obliterated all traces of them. If De Walden had not remembered the questions put to him by Nick, as to the direction in which the Gariep lay, they would have been more than once completely at fault. But this served as a clue, when everything else failed, and every now and then they came upon the white embers of a fire, or heaps of dry grass, which had evidently served for beds, showing that, however slowly they might be progressing, it was in the right direction.

It was on the afternoon of the ninth day, when Kobo, who, it should be mentioned, had formed a warm friendship with Lion since leaving the Basuto village—it was just in the late afternoon, when Kobo, who had been a little in advance of the rest of the party, came hurrying back with the news, that there were both hoof marks and large stains of blood to be seen in the grass and bushes about a hundred yards ahead, as though some large animal—a gnu, or an eland, or perhaps a buffalo—had been severely wounded. If such was the case, most probably they were in the neighbourhood of the English lads, as there were neither Bechuanas or Basutos to be found thereabouts. He added, that it was with the greatest difficulty that he could restrain Lion, who wanted to rush off, at the top of his speed, in the direction of the footmarks.

"You had better let him go, Kobo," said De Walden, "and follow him up as closely as you can. He'll find Frank, if he is to be found, I'll answer for it."

"And we'll all come after you," added Lavie. "Meanwhile, I'll fire my gun. They'll hear it if they are anywhere hereabouts."

Lion was accordingly let loose, and immediately galloped off, arriving, as the reader has heard, just in time to rescue Frank and Nick from their imminent peril.

It was a joyful meeting, when the whole party assembled on the spot where the carcasses of the two leopards, and an ugly rent in Lion's side, bore evidence to how narrow had been the escape of the two boys from death. The tears stood in Captain Wilmore's eyes, as he grasped his nephew warmly by the hand, noticing, even at that moment, how his figure had improved in strength and manly bearing, and the thoughtful expression which had taken the place of mere boyish recklessness, on Gilbert's face.

"My lads," he said, "I was hasty with you. But for me, you would not have had to undergo this wandering and danger. But I have paid the penalty—"

"Oh, uncle," broke in Frank, "you mustn't say that. It was all our fault, mine particularly. And it hasn't been such bad fun, after all. I am sure we have most need to ask your forgiveness."

"You mustn't regret what has happened, captain," said De Walden. "Under God's good providence, it has been the making of them both. But now, I suppose, we must be setting out on our return to the Basuto village."

"I am afraid I cannot go there," said Captain Wilmore. "I have been away a good deal longer than I had expected, as it is: and I know my presence is urgently needed at Cape Town. I and my guides must set out homewards without loss of time—as soon, that is, as the lads are prepared to accompany me."

"I am ready to go this moment," said Frank.

"And so am I," added Gilbert. "That's well," said the captain. "Frank, I haven't told you that I have got a commission for you in a line regiment now at the Cape. Sir David Baird signed it the day I came away. That's good news, isn't it?"

"The best there could be, thank you, uncle," returned Frank, joyously.

"And you, Nick, what do you say? Will you be put on the quarter-deck of the *Atlantic*—that's my new ship;—and rated as a midshipman?"

"I should like nothing better, sir," answered Gilbert, almost as much pleased as Frank. "Thank you very much for your kindness!"

"That's well," again said the captain. "And you too," he continued, turning to Lavie and Warley. "Do you mean to return with me to Cape Town, or with Mr De Walden to the Basutos? You will not be wanted, you know, Lavie, for two months yet; so you can stay behind awhile, if you choose."

"Thank you, captain, I should like to have a good talk with Warley about his prospects; he does not, as yet, know the change that has taken place in them. And besides, I haven't stood the journey as well as you have. I think I shall remain a week or two with Mr De Walden before following you."

They shook hands accordingly, and went their several ways. De Walden, accompanied by Lavie and Warley, returned to the village; where, after a few days of rest, they were enabled to arrange their plans for the future.

"Ernest," said Lavie one morning, after they had just returned in company with De Walden from an inspection of the native school, "I am glad I delayed telling you what has happened at Cape Town. I think the effect it will have on you may be different from what I had expected."

"What has happened?" asked Warley with interest. "You have lost your brother," answered Lavie. "I know he was never really a brother to you, but you will be sorry for his sudden death, nevertheless. When the rumour of the approach of the British fleet was circulated in Cape Town, some of the English tried to organise a British force to help their countrymen. The Dutch governor heard of it, and sent soldiers to arrest the ringleaders. Your brother offered an armed resistance, and was killed on the spot. The Dutch authorities declared all your brother's property to be forfeited by his rebellion; but the new governor, Sir David Baird, at once rescinded that. As your brother had made no will, all his money has become yours."

Warley turned very white, and leaned forward on the table, covering his face with his hands.

"I have told you, perhaps, too abruptly," said Lavie, "but you must remember that you have nothing to reproach yourself with, so far as your brother is concerned. Is it not so, Mr De Walden?"

"So far as I know," said the missionary affectionately, "nothing at all."

"I hope not," said Ernest, in a low tone; "but this is very awful."

"Sudden deaths are always awful. But you have now to consider what you will do. I thought, when I first heard it, that you would return to England and go to one of the Universities. But I perceive that there is an attraction that may keep you here."

"Yes, Charles, I cannot but view this strange and unexpected event as a solution of the difficulty that has been burdening my mind for many weeks past. But I should like to have Mr De Walden's advice. He must have seen, I think, the attachment between myself and Ella—"

"Yes, Ernest, and I have seen in it the working of God's merciful providence for the enlightenment of the heathen in this land of darkness and superstition."

"You think, then, that I ought to stay here and take up your work when you leave for Namaqua-land, as I know you mean to do some day?"

"Even so. I mean that you should remain here, and become the husband of this dear girl, who is worthy to be the bride of a king. The wilderness has indeed blossomed as the rose for you. But I do not advise that your marriage should take place at once. Return to England, and prepare yourself for your office by two or three years of study, such as you can pursue only there. Meanwhile, I will remain here till your return, and complete the education of your future wife. Then, seek ordination, which also, unhappily, you cannot obtain in Southern Africa. Some day, God will set up His Church in this land, and it will grow like the mustard seed, and the people will rest under its shadow. But that time is still far off. Let it be your work, as it has been mine, to prepare the furrows for the seed that will then be cast in. Will you do this?"

"God being my helper," answered Ernest, "I will."

Appendix

The Hottentot God

The worship of the beetle by the Hottentots has been disputed. No doubt it has not been their practice during the last fifty years. But that it existed in more ancient times, is (I think) abundantly proved by the evidence of trustworthy writers. Kolben, for example, has the following explicit statement, made from his own experience.

"The Hottentots adore as a benignant Deity, a certain insect, peculiar (it is said) to the Hottentot countries. This animal is of the dimensions of a child's little finger; the back green, the belly speckled white and red. It is provided with two wings and two horns. To this little winged Deity, whenever they set eyes on it, they render the highest tokens of veneration. If it honours their kraal with a visit, the inhabitants assemble round it with transports of devotion, as if the Lord of the Universe was come among them. If the insect happens to alight on a Hottentot, he is looked upon as a man without guilt, and distinguished and reverenced as a saint and the delight of the Deity ever after. They declared to me that if this deified insect had been killed, all their cattle would certainly have been destroyed by wild beasts, and they themselves, every man, woman, and child of them, brought to a miserable end." — *Kolben*, volume one, page 99.

Kaffir Prophets

The scriptural curse of the "false prophet" has never been more strikingly fulfilled, than in the instance of the Kaffir nation in the year 1856. A false prophet, named Umhlahara, professed to have received a revelation from heaven through the visions of a girl, commanding the Kaffirs to kill the whole of their cattle, and promising that, in the event of their obedience, all their forefathers, together with their cattle, should rise to life again, that they should regain their ascendancy in the land, and live in plenty and prosperity for evermore. The object of this audacious imposture was to reduce the whole nation on a sudden to such a state of suffering that, in their desperation, they would burst in upon the settlements of the white men, and everywhere exterminate them. It is strange that in a country where the flocks and herds constitute the sole wealth of the people, such an attempt should have succeeded. But it did so to a considerable extent, at all events. Those who had contrived it, however, had made one fatal omission. They ought to have concentrated the whole people on the English border, and they forgot that men enfeebled by famine would be unfitted for warfare, or indeed for any lengthened travel. An attempt was made to remedy the blunder by postponing the day of the resurrection of the chiefs and cattle, but it failed. The people had discovered the imposture, though not until they were reduced to the most frightful condition of starvation. The English colonists did all that lay in their power to relieve them, but they were wholly unable to remedy the mischief. Vast numbers died everywhere by the most terrible of all deaths, and the strength of the nation was so completely broken by the disaster, that they were rendered wholly incapable of continuing the warfare, for which in former days they had been so renowned.

Wreck of the Grosvenor

All the particulars of the wreck of this ill-fated vessel have been given in the narrative. The whole of the crew and passengers, except seventeen, escaped safe to land, to the number of one hundred and fifty. In accordance with the proposal of the captain, they endeavoured to make their way overland to Cape Town; but after a few days' travel, during which they were harassed by the Kaffirs with repeated attacks, a fresh consultation took place. Forty-three able-bodied men persevered in the attempt. Of these, some three or four, after terrible perils and hardships, succeeded in reaching Cape Town. What became of those who were left has never been certainly known. Rumours, which are mentioned by Le Vaillant and others, declare that some women at all events survived, and were compelled to become the wives of native chiefs. An expedition was even sent out to search for these, but failed, more apparently from want of capacity in those conducting it than from anything else. Under these circumstances the fate of those who remained behind may, not unfairly, be made the subject of fiction.